BETWEEN SINNERS AND SAINTS

Marie Sexton

Praise for Marie Sexton's
Between Sinners and Saints

Winner of the 2012 Colorado Romance Writers Award of Excellence

"Needless to say, the road Levi and Jaime follow is not an easy one, and more than once, one or the other has a setback. Yet, this only makes the story more compelling and, by the time it ends, the reader will be more than satisfied."
–Literary Nymphs Reviews

"I didn't think that Marie Sexton could top One More Soldier, a book I love and have re-read many times, but *Between Sinners and Saints* showed me a different side of her writing and proved once again what an incredible author she is. …I absolutely loved this book and highly recommend it."
–Reviews by Jessewave

"*Between Sinners and Saints* is, simply put, a brilliant and beautiful story of recovery and redemption. It's a story that explores the eternal conflict between spiritual beliefs and the temptations and trials of the secular world, without ever crossing the line into sermonizing."
–Top 2 Bottom Reviews

"…I loved it, it had a great combination of angst and lightness, I cried a lot but I also laughed…"
–Romance Around the Corner

"Very enjoyable and well done"
–Between the Covers

"The message this story promoted was one of tolerance that we all could learn from. Jamie and Levi's love and their path to happiness was worth the read and I will revisit them again in the future."
–Prism Book Alliance

"This was an emotional book about trust, love and true devotion. The love scenes were sweet and sensuous and I couldn't get enough of them."
–Dark Diva Reviews

"Throughout the book, the author weaves in themes of family, acceptance, faith, and overcoming our past. And we also see surfing and massage therapy used throughout, I think, as symbols of release, and renewal. *Between Sinners and Saints* is beautifully written. I thoroughly enjoyed this one. If you haven't read it, you should definitely check it out!!"
–The Novel Approach

"This is a stellar novel with believable leads in a complicated and emotionally fulfilling romance."
–The Book Vixen

Between Sinners and Saints

Cover art by L.C. Chase

http://mariesexton.net

Published in the United States of America by
Marie Sexton, April 2016

Originally published 2011, by Amber Allure

Print ISBN: 978-0-9961741-3-8
eBook ISBN: 978-0-9961741-4-5

In addition to the usual suspects (you know who you are), I would like to thank my surfing guru, Carter, and my own slightly sadistic massage therapist, Kendra, without whom this book could not have been written.

CHAPTER 1

"Levi! I could use some help out here!" Pounding on the door to the storage room followed the words.

Although Levi heard them, he didn't answer. His fellow bartender knew what was going on. In another hour or two, it'd be his turn in the storage room while Levi handled the bar. So Levi ignored him. He leaned back against the wall, the fingers of both hands tangled in the hair of the man on his knees in front of him, and lost himself to the pleasure the kid was giving him. The wall at his back vibrated with the deep bass of the beat from the dance floor, and the kid at his feet seemed to move in time with it. Levi thought to himself, not for the first time, how very much he loved his job.

The man on his knees was named Joe. Or John. Or maybe it was Josh. Levi couldn't quite remember and didn't care. And he probably wasn't even twenty-one yet. Levi didn't care about that either. Whatever his name was, the kid had the sweetest mouth Levi had encountered in a very long time. And he'd encountered a great many in his years at the club.

"Levi!" Max yelled again, pounding on the door.

"I'm coming!" Levi yelled.

John—or Josh, or whatever the hell his name was—actually laughed, even with Levi's cock filling his mouth, and

Levi pushed himself deeper as he proved he hadn't been lying.

Once Levi let go of his head, the kid stood up. His own pants were still done up, and he ground himself against Levi's thigh as he smiled at him. "You better get back out there before your friend breaks the door down." The best thing about him, next to his warm mouth, of course, was the fact he never wanted anything in return. Not this early in the night, at any rate. He was just working himself up, which was fine with Levi.

"Another hour or two, he'll have somebody bent over that table," Levi said as he pulled away and buttoned his pants. "So I'm pretty sure he wants the door intact. Thanks, man. Drinks are on me tonight."

"I'm counting on it."

A few free drinks for a blow job. He found the men who were willing to make the trade pathetic, but it sure didn't stop him from taking advantage of what they offered. It'd kept Levi up to his eyeballs in willing men for nearly ten years. The Zone may not have been the biggest gay club in Miami, but it still saw plenty of business, and Levi was one of the hottest bartenders around, even if he was over thirty now. It made for a good combo, and a great many rendezvous in the storage room. Tight young asses and warm, willing mouths. And it wasn't as if the owners didn't know. The rumor was, Zeke and Owen had started the tradition themselves. There were boxes of condoms on the shelf, and a tube of lubricant, and a jar of Vaseline, which Max preferred, when he could find somebody willing to go bareback. The regulars knew for an extra twenty bucks they could make use of the room as well, as long as they didn't take too long and they cleaned up whatever mess they made. It was a hell of a deal all around.

"You want to go surfin' tomorrow?" Jon/Joe/Josh asked as Levi headed for the door. "I can meet you down there."

This was the part Levi hated. Yeah, they'd originally met while surfing. They'd had a few hook-ups since then, once in the kid's van and twice at the club. But now he wanted to plan something together? That was a recipe for disaster.

Levi pushed his overgrown brown hair out of his face while he debated how to answer. "I have plans tomorrow," he lied. "Maybe another time." He left the room and went back to the bar. The truth was, Levi probably *would* go surfing tomorrow. He'd just go to a different beach for a while.

"Took you long enough," Max said when Levi made it back to the bar. "You're getting slow in your old age."

Levi flipped him the bird and then it was back to work.

All in all, it was a night like any other at The Zone. The club attracted a young crowd, and Levi was the oldest of the bartenders. Tonight, he felt every bit of his thirty years and then some. He was struggling with a pain that had been slowly getting worse over the last few weeks. It always started in his lower back, but as the night wore on, it progressed down through his left ass cheek, and by morning, it would spread even farther. The next place it hit, and the worst place by far, was high on his inner left thigh. By the time three A.M. rolled around, he was having a hard time not limping.

"You still having that pain, old man?" Max asked during a lull at the bar. Max was big and black. He was only twenty-two and liked to deck himself out in leather. In another ten or fifteen years, he'd probably be a bear, but he had some filling out to do first. Still, he wasn't a small guy by any means. "A pain in your ass." He laughed. "And here I thought you were a top guy."

Levi put his hand on the back of Max's neck and pushed him forward, bending him over the bar he could ram into him from behind. "I am. And you could use a little pain in *your* ass, Max."

"Is it little?" Max teased.

"You want to find out?"

"You keep threatening, but you never follow through."

The fact was, Max was even more of a top-only guy than Levi, and given Max's fondness for going bareback, Levi had no desire to fuck him or be fucked by him. He was pretty sure Max felt the same. This was just a game they played. Levi let Max go and tried to massage his aching thigh through his jeans.

"You should see a doctor or something, man," Max said.

Levi was starting to think that was true. The problem was, he had no insurance. And what would a doctor tell him anyway? To quit surfing? To get a desk job so he didn't have to stand on his feet for hours at a time?

No, Levi wasn't going to any doctor.

When his shift ended, he went home. He took four ibuprofen tablets, rubbed some Icy-Hot on his back and thigh, then lay in bed with his ass on a heating pad. He had to admit to himself as he drifted off to sleep, it really was hell getting old.

His phone rang at eight-thirty the next morning. It was his landline, not his cell phone, which meant it probably wasn't anybody he wanted to talk to. He dragged himself out of bed, groggy and grumpy, and checked the caller ID.

Abraham Binder.

Levi groaned. Abraham Binder was his father. Of course, it wouldn't be his father calling. It would be his mother, Nancy. He didn't want to talk to her either. It was just like his mother to call early on a Sunday morning. She knew he worked until five A.M. on weekends, and even though she'd be happy and cheery and practically overflowing with good will, he knew she'd intentionally woken him.

He knew she'd say, "Oh honey, I'm so sorry! Were you still sleeping?" in a mock-innocent tone that drove him nuts. Then, one of two things would happen. Either Levi could say no, he was already awake, in which case his mother would ask hopefully if he'd finally found a "real" job, or Levi would admit he'd been asleep, at which point his mother would launch into a lecture on why his current life choices were unhealthy and self-destructive. And every single word of it would be because she *loved* him.

No fucking way was he ready to deal with her.

But now that he was awake, he figured he may as well get to the beach early. He changed into his swim trunks and grabbed his board from the coat closet.

Levi owned two vehicles: a bright red Yamaha VStar 950 motorcycle, which he loved more than anything, and an old beat-up shit-brown Toyota pick-up from the eighties, which he owned only because his surfboard fit in the back. The truck didn't have A/C, and Levi had to crank both windows down as he drove to the beach. Not that it did much good in the Florida heat and humidity. It was only June and even at nine o'clock in the morning, it was obvious the day was going to be scorching hot.

The beach he picked wasn't known for its huge swells, but Levi didn't mind. He liked it because it wasn't too crowded. He paddled out into the surf. He went much farther than he needed to, far past the swells, before straddling his board. The tide was on its way in, so Levi decided to let it carry him. He lay back on his board and let himself drift. The sun beat down on him. The water rocked him gently. He may even have dozed a bit. He could never be sure. Even running on three hours of sleep, he couldn't deny how good it felt to be out on the water, alone. He felt free.

He roused himself again when the gentle rolling of the sea became more pronounced. Now it was time to surf. He fell into a rhythm, riding the swells, waiting for one that felt just right, paddling into it, and then jumping to his feet as it grabbed his board and carried him forward. Then he'd paddle back out into the surf and do it again. It was a pattern he found exhilarating and relaxing, all at the same time. Of course, riding the wave was the exciting part, but Levi enjoyed the whole experience. It was all about understanding the ocean, knowing the beach and the waves and his own body. He lost himself in the water. There was no time to think about his mother and what she wanted him to be. There was no time to think about the club and what he'd let himself become. There was only Levi and his board, the sun and the breeze, the water and the waves.

Levi had no idea how long he was out, but when the surf around him started to fill with splashing tourists, he knew it was time to go home.

It was two o'clock when he walked back into his apartment. He was tired and ravenously hungry. His ass hurt, as well as his thigh. The surfing aggravated it, he knew, but he loved the sport so much, he did it anyway. Now he'd be paying for it for days.

He made himself a giant sub sandwich, grabbed a beer out of the fridge, and settled in front of the TV to eat while watching an insanely bad martial arts movie that looked like it'd been made on a budget of about fifty bucks. Less than halfway through the sandwich, his phone rang again. This time, it was his cell phone. And this time, it wasn't his mother calling. It was his sister, Ruth.

"Hey, Leviticus," she said cheerfully. She knew he hated being reminded of his full name. As if it wasn't bad enough his parents had given them all biblical names, they had also managed, by some strange twist of fate, to saddle him with one sure to remind him each and every time he heard it that his "lifestyle" was an abomination – at least in the eyes of his family and their God. "You avoiding Mom's call again?"

Despite her propensity to call him by his full name, Ruth was the sibling he got along with the best. "Maybe I wouldn't if she'd wait until after ten to call."

"That's what I told her. She's worried, though, Levi. Nobody's heard from you in a while." Of course they hadn't. What was he supposed to do? Check in weekly with the family who hated him? Like she was reading his mind, Ruth said, "They all love you, you know."

It always came down to this. They loved him, yes, but not his choices. Hate the sin; love the sinner. They knew he wasn't gay by choice. They accepted that he had been born this way. His mother had told him many times that she'd always known he was different—and she had four sons, so it was possible she was telling the truth. Yet, even knowing it was something he couldn't change, they still believed it was a sin. It was a test God had given him, and he was failing, because the only way to pass the test, according to them, was to deny his feelings. To spend his life refusing to give in to his needs. To "reject the homosexual lifestyle."

In short, to live his life alone and in the closet.

"Ruth, do we have to talk about this again?"

"No. But let me at least hit the major points so I can give Mom an accurate report. Still working at the bar?"

"Yes."

"Still gay?" This was said as a joke more than anything, and Levi smiled.

"Yes."

"How's the surfing?"

"It's…" He was going to say it was fine. Maybe great. Then he thought about the pain burning in his thigh and in his left ass cheek. "Ruth, I have a question for you. Or, for Jackson, actually."

Jackson was Ruth's husband and he was an orthopedic surgeon. Jackson had started out a Methodist, but had converted to Mormonism when he married Ruth, although Levi suspected his "conversion" didn't go much deeper than lip service. Levi liked him, sometimes more than he liked his own brothers, mostly because Jackson was the one person in his "family" who supported his choice to live his life his own way.

"I'm having this pain. It starts in my lower back and goes through my…gluteus." Ruth was still LDS, after all, and he did his best to not offend her, especially since she was the only member of his family who ever bothered with more than a lousy Christmas card. "And the front of my left thigh. Surfing seems to make it worse."

"Okay. Hang on." He could hear her talking to Jackson, although she'd obviously put her hand over the mouthpiece because she sounded more like the teacher from the old *Peanuts* cartoons than like his sister. And then she was back. "He says it's probably your sciatica."

"*What?* That's what happens to old people, right? I'm only thirty!"

She didn't hear him, though. "He says it could also be lumbar related." She was still listening to Jackson and relaying the information to Levi, pausing in between sentences to wait for the next bit of wisdom. "Or the psoas muscle." Pause. "He says you could see a doctor—"

"I don't want a doctor."

"But your best bet is probably a therapeutic massage."

"Really?"

"He says, not a fluff and buff."

"A *what?*"

"He says, find a massage therapist who knows about neuromuscular rehabilitation. He says they'll have 'NMR' after their name."

"So just get a massage and it'll be all better?" Levi asked skeptically.

"It's a massage, Leviticus. How bad can it be?"

"Good point."

"Okay, back to the survey for Mom. Do you have a boyfriend?"

"Yeah, I have new one almost every week."

"You know that's not what I mean. Are you dating anyone?"

"Define 'date.'"

She sighed in exasperation. "I don't know what you're trying to prove, Levi. I mean, this is exactly what Mom and Dad are always talking about—"

"Don't start, Ruth."

"It's not just being gay. It's indul—"

"'Indulging in the homosexual lifestyle.' I *know*."

"So you're just going to prove them right?"

"They've already made up their minds."

"If you were to settle down with someone and show them it's not only about sex—"

"Enough, Ruth! If I wanted to hear this lecture, I'd have answered the phone when Mom called."

She sighed again. "So this is it, Levi? You're going to work at the bar and surf and have sex with strangers for the rest of your life?"

"For as long as I can, yeah. You got a fucking problem with it?" She hated it when he swore, but now she was intentionally pushing his buttons, he'd do the same to her.

"It was one thing when you were twenty-two, but you're thirty now. Don't you think it's time to settle down and—"

"It was nice hearing from you, Ruth. Tell Jackson thanks."

"Levi, wait!"

"I don't want to talk about this anymore. You know who I am. You can deal with it or you can pretend I don't exist, just like Mom and Dad. It's your choice."

"They don't pretend you don't exist, Levi. Didn't Mom try to call you a few hours ago?"

He didn't respond. He didn't want to admit she was right. It wasn't that they ignored him. It was only that their love came with a fuck-load of expectations.

"They love you."

"They love me so much they want me to spend the rest of my life alone. Is that it?"

"You *are* alone, Levi," she said. The combative tone was gone from her voice. She just sounded sad. "And you can't blame Mom and Dad for that."

CHAPTER 2

Levi discovered relatively few of the Licensed Massage Therapists in Miami had NMR after their names. He checked the addresses on the ones who did and found the one closest to his house.

Jaime Marshall. The listing said he was an LMT, NMR, and BMT. Whatever the hell that meant. His address was a few miles away, and Levi was surprised to see it was in a residential neighborhood. It didn't occur to him until after he'd dialed the number that it was a Sunday and he probably wouldn't get an answer.

He was wrong. Not only did somebody answer, but he did so on the very first ring. "This is Jaime."

"Jaime Marshall?"

"Yes. How can I help you?" His voice was soft and quiet, and Levi pictured a perfect Boy Scout on the other end of the line. The type of man his parents would have been proud to call their son.

"I need to make an appointment. I'm having some pain in my back and thigh. My brother-in-law says it might be my sciatica."

"What's your name?"

"Levi Binder." He spelled his last name, then said it again. BIN-der. Not bine-der. People always wanted to say it the way it looked, with a long I, but his family pronounced it with a short I, like "winter." Or "sinner."

"Well, Levi, I can see you at eleven o'clock tomorrow."

"Really? That's great!"

"Since it's your first visit, I'll have a bit of paperwork for you, so come a few minutes early. Come around to the back door."

"You got it."

Jaime Marshall lived in and apparently worked out of a small, two-story brick home in a slightly older but well-maintained neighborhood. Levi followed a sidewalk around the side to the back of the house and was met at the door by a man he assumed was the Boy Scout from the phone.

"Are you Levi?" he asked through the screen door. He sounded suspicious, which seemed odd, given Levi had made an appointment.

"Yes."

The Boy Scout unlocked the door and opened it for him. "I'm Jaime. Come on in."

The room was small. It looked like it had once been a back porch, but had been enclosed. There was a cabinet in one corner and a chair in another. Most of the space was taken up by a massage table with a little wheeled stool tucked under one end.

"Can you fill this out for me, please?" Jaime handed him a clipboard with a few papers on it and a pen. He waved Levi toward the chair. "I need to put a clean sheet on the table and then we can discuss the problems you're having and get started."

The paperwork was pretty basic. Did he have any injuries? Any major diseases? Where did it hurt? There was a rough sketch of a human body, both back and front, and Levi marked the places he had pain. As he filled it out, he stole glances at Jaime putting clean sheets on the massage table.

Jaime looked young—Levi would have guessed early twenties. He had strawberry-blonde curls. He was close to Levi's height, but thin and wiry. And he had a nice ass. It was a bit rounder than some, especially given how thin he was. It was the kind of ass you could really grab hold of, and Levi could picture exactly what it would look like naked. The idea of a massage was suddenly extremely appealing.

And the best part was, Jaime was gay. Levi could tell just by watching him. He wasn't flamboyant or swishy. Levi couldn't even have said exactly what it was. Just a certain softness in his movements that gave it away.

"Are you finished?" Jaime asked, turning back to Levi.

"Yes."

Jaime took the clipboard and sat on the massage table. He pulled a pair of reading glasses out of his pocket and put them on, completing the perfect Boy Scout image. "You said on the phone somebody diagnosed this as a sciatica problem?" he asked as he looked at the papers.

"My brother-in-law. He's an orthopedic surgeon. But it was over the phone. He didn't examine me or anything. Why? Do you think he's wrong?"

"Not necessarily. The lumbar, the psoas, the sciatica, the hamstring—they're all connected. If one of them gets strained or tight, it can throw everything out of whack." He took his glasses off and looked up at Levi. He had eyes the color of the sky. "What do you do for a living?"

"I'm a bartender."

"So you're on your feet a lot?"

"Thirty hours a week." The Zone was only open Thursday through Saturday, but Levi made enough in tips on those three nights he didn't need to put in a full forty anyway.

"That can certainly aggravate it," Jaime said. "Stand up for me."

Levi obeyed. He stood there, waiting for Jaime to say something else, but Jaime just looked him up and down. It wasn't the way Levi was used to being looked at. Jaime seemed to have no interest in Levi himself. His gaze was completely analytical.

"Turn around."

Levi did, although he was starting to get annoyed. Jaime was examining him like he was some kind of specimen.

"Okay, good. Now, put both of your feet together and stand with your weight evenly distributed."

Levi hadn't even realized he was standing with most of his weight on one foot. He adjusted his stance, putting both feet together as instructed. His back was still to Jaime, and Jaime said, "Turn around again please."

Levi obeyed.

"Stand with your feet together." He hadn't realized he'd gone back to standing with most of his weight on his right foot again. It annoyed him. He felt like he was being chastised. But he did as he was told. Jaime continued to look him up and down.

"You're a surfer?" he asked.

Levi was surprised. "How'd you know?"

"It was either that, snowboarding, or skateboarding. Since we're in Florida, and you're over the age of twenty, I figured surfing was the better bet."

"You can tell by the way I stand?"

"That's part of it. Also the way you turn out your left foot."

Levi glanced down at his feet and saw his left foot did, indeed, point out to the side more than his right.

"And your propensity for standing with your weight on your right foot. And the problems you're having are fairly typical. It's probably your psoas muscle."

"My what?"

"The psoas is one of the largest and thickest muscles in the body. It starts here, at your twelfth thoracic vertebrae." Jaime stood up and turned to indicate a spot on his lower back. "It attaches to the lumbar and then runs down across the pelvis." He turned toward Levi again, using his hand to demonstrate the path of the muscle over the top of his hipbone. "It ends here, on your lesser trochanter." He pointed to a spot high on the inside of his thigh—the same place Levi'd been having pain. "It flexes your hip and spinal column." He smiled, looking almost apologetic. "There's more to it, but that's about as much as people usually want to hear."

"Can you fix it?"

"I think I can. We can go ahead and get started if you like."

"Of course."

"I'm going to step out for a minute. Go ahead and undress all the way—"

"What?"

"And lie down on the table. We'll start face-up today. You can cover yourself with the sheet."

"I'm going to be naked?"

"You can keep your underwear on if you want."

Levi felt a bit stupid for not having thought of that. Not that he was shy about his body, but it hadn't occurred to him he'd be lying naked, while the Boy Scout touched him. And Levi wasn't supposed to touch back.

This was definitely going to be interesting.

Jaime left the room, and Levi couldn't help but watch him go. He really did have a nice ass. Then Levi undressed and lay on the table as directed.

Jaime came back in a minute later. Levi was used to having people appreciate his body. After all, he worked out. He surfed. He was well-built and tanned. He fully expected Jaime's eyes to linger on his pecs or on his flat stomach, but Jaime didn't seem to notice. He walked to the head of the table. He sat down on the stool and put his hands under Levi's neck. He grabbed the back of Levi's head and pulled gently. Levi couldn't help but imagine his head popping off. He suspected Jaime wouldn't even bat an eye.

Jaime put his fingers into the back of Levi's neck, lifting his head a bit. "Let's start with three deep breaths."

"Why?"

"To help you relax. And to increase the flow of oxygen to the muscles."

"This is ridiculous."

"Humor me. Just close your eyes and take three deep breaths."

It still seemed absurd, but there was nothing to be gained by arguing. Levi closed his eyes and started to breathe. With each breath, Jaime's fingers moved a bit closer to Levi's spine, allowing his head to hang back farther.

"Good," Jaime said. It was about the same tone somebody might use when they said "Good boy," to a dog, and it annoyed him. Jaime began rubbing Levi's scalp and his temples. "I don't want to give you any false ideas. These things can't be fixed in one appointment, but we should be able to get a better idea of the exact problem spots today. The good news is, this type of problem usually responds well to massage therapy."

"Why are you rubbing my head if the problem's in my ass and thigh?" Levi asked, although the truth was, it felt fabulous.

"Everything's connected. We'll concentrate on the problem spots, but it doesn't hurt to give the rest of the body some attention."

Levi didn't argue. The massage on his head felt too good. He relaxed as Jaime rubbed his neck. Jaime eventually moved to Levi's arms and even massaged his hands. "Wow," Levi said. "That's awesome."

Jaime smiled, but didn't look up. "Some people don't like it."

Afterward, he moved to Levi's psoas—not that Levi would have known it was his psoas if Jaime hadn't told him. It was then Levi learned this wasn't going to be a relaxing massage. Jaime made him do "movements." First, he used the heel of his hand to apply pressure to the muscle on the inside edge of Levi's hipbone. His arm was stretched across Levi's body, his wrist practically brushing Levi's package as he pushed on the tender spot. Then he had Levi contract his abdominal muscles, tilting his pelvis up. It was the same movement he might have used during sex to thrust up into somebody. Jaime had him hold there while he used his other hand to stroke up the length of the muscle, along Levi's belly.

The entire thing would have been unbelievably arousing if it hadn't hurt so damn much, and Levi was relieved when it was over.

When Jaime was finished with the psoas, he moved to Levi's leg. He uncovered Levi's left foot, then his lower leg. He hooked his hand behind Levi's knee and lifted it, pulling the sheet at the same time so Levi's leg was revealed. He wrapped the sheet up and over Levi's hip, tucking the end underneath his side. It was a strange magic trick that left his entire leg exposed, but caused the sheet to be tucked tight around his upper thigh and hip so nothing inappropriate was exposed in any way.

Jaime's hands were incredibly soft. He didn't rub hard at first. He seemed to be exploring the muscle high on Levi's thigh with his fingers, watching Levi's reaction.

"Does it hurt here?"

"Not as much."

"And here?"

"Yes, more there."

"And is it focalized or does it radiate out to other places?"

"It's only there."

"That's good." His hand slid toward the inside of Levi's thigh, and Levi tensed. "Just relax, Mr. Binder." At least he pronounced it right.

"Please don't call me that."

"You prefer Levi?"

"Yes."

"Okay, Levi. Try to relax."

But Levi was finding it very difficult to relax. Jaime's soft hand was moving slowly up the inside of his thigh, stopping every inch or two to press into the muscle before moving on, and Levi's body was reacting in a way he feared was wholly inappropriate, given the circumstances.

"Relax," Jaime said again.

"I can't!" Levi snapped.

"Don't worry about it." Jaime's tone was clinical. Professional. Detached. "It's a common physical reaction. You don't need to be embarrassed."

"Easy for you to say."

"It's a natural response to physical stimulation—"

"No shit!" The stupid thing was, now they were talking about it, it was only getting worse. He was pretty much flying full mast now, and the thin sheet covering him certainly wasn't hiding it. "Are you almost done?"

Suddenly Jaime pushed harder on his tender thigh. It hurt so much Levi almost jumped off the table. "*Ow!* What the hell? Did you do that on purpose?"

"Took your mind off your other problem, didn't it?" Jaime didn't even crack a smile.

"You're a little bit sadistic, aren't you?"

"You're not the first person to think so." He pushed again on Levi's thigh, and Levi winced. "This is really a symptom of the problem with your psoas, so we'll do a few movements and then I'll try to loosen it up and release some of the lactic acid."

Those words sounded harmless, but Levi soon learned this was going to be the worst part of the whole deal. It felt like there was broken glass inside his thigh when Jaime started to work on it.

"Fuck, it hurts!"

"I know. I'm sorry."

"You don't *sound* sorry!"

"It's important for you to keep breathing—"

"That's your best advice? *Keep breathing?*"

"Are you from Florida?"

The sudden topic change flustered him. "What?"

"Some people find talking distracts them from the pain. So…are you from around here?"

Levi found the entire situation aggravating, but he gritted his teeth and answered, "My family lives in Georgetown, South Carolina."

"When did you move here?" Jaime wasn't looking at him. Not at his face, at any rate. His eyes were on Levi's thigh as his hands continued to work. His expression was distant and analytical. He didn't seem to care about the answer, but Levi gave it anyway.

"When I was twenty-one." That was the point when he'd given up on trying to pretend he could be what his parents wanted him to be. He'd dropped out of BYU and intentionally picked the one place in the country his parents associated with sin and excess. Even Vegas offended them less than Miami.

"You've been a surfer your whole life?"

"Yes."

"It looks like fun. I've always wanted to try it."

"It is fun," Levi said, relaxing now he was talking about something he loved. "I'll be happy when I can do it again without paying for it for days afterward."

"And you're a bartender?"

"Yes."

"Where at?"

"The Zone." Jaime's hands stopped moving for a fraction of a second, before resuming their assault on Levi's tender thigh. Just enough for Levi to know Jaime recognized the name. "I don't think I've ever seen you there," Levi said.

Jaime shook his head. "I don't get out much."

"But you're gay, right?"

"Does it hurt less now?"

It did hurt less. Talking *was* helping. But Levi wasn't put off so easily. "You should come by sometime. Drinks on me."

"I appreciate the offer—"

"The offer usually comes after the drinks," Levi said, and he was happy to see Jaime blush. It was the first break in his professional demeanor.

"I assure you, Mr. Binder—"

"It's *Levi.*"

"I have no interest in being one of your conquests."

"'Conquests'? You think that's the kind of guy I am?"

"Isn't it?" His eyes met Levi's as he asked the question. There was no laughter in his voice, but no accusation either.

Levi was surprised at his forthrightness and he laughed. "What gave me away?"

"I know I look like a farm boy from Kansas—you probably think the tornado missed Oz and dropped me in Miami by mistake—but I assure you that isn't the case."

"What's that supposed to mean?"

"It means I've met guys like you before."

Levi was trying to decide if he should be offended by the comment.

"Anyway, The Zone has…" Jaime hesitated and his blush deepened. It made him look even younger. "It has a reputation."

"Really?"

"There's a rumor about a storage room?"

"All true. I'd be happy to show you some time," he said, just to watch Jaime blush more. "I'll give you a *personal* tour."

"I'll pass, Mr. Binder."

"It's Levi."

"It's Levi when you're cooperating. It's Mr. Binder when you're trying to hit on me."

Levi laughed. "Fine. I'll stop." *For now, at least.*

Jaime moved on to his other leg, which was quick and painless, and then he had Levi turn over. His lower back and left butt cheek prompted more of the strange techniques. They were painful, and yet, he could tell already they were helping.

When he was done, Jaime left the room while Levi got dressed.

"How's your leg?" he asked as he came back in.

Levi flexed it, testing his weight on it. It did feel better. Not *good.* But better than it had felt in a while. "I think you might be a miracle worker."

"Not really. It will tighten back up if you let it. I'm going to give you some stretches to do. Make sure you drink a lot of water tonight, to help flush the toxins out of your system."

He spent the next few minutes explaining the stretches he wanted Levi to do. Levi doubted he'd do them, but he wasn't going to tell Jaime that. He made an appointment to come back on Thursday.

"It was nice meeting you," Jaime said at the end of the appointment.

"You too. Thanks for your help."

"You're welcome, Levi."

Levi started to open the door, but stopped and turned to look at Jaime. He really was cute, in a Boy Scout kind of way. "My drink offer still stands you know."

"Have a nice afternoon, Mr. Binder."

CHAPTER 3

Jaime Marshall finished his last massage at five-fifteen P.M., as he always did. Once his client was gone, he stripped the sheets off the massage table. He put a load of them in the washer and put fresh sheets on the table so it would be ready for his first client the next morning.

His dog Dolly was waiting for him when he came out, wagging and wiggling and panting in joy. She knew the massage room was the one room in the house she wasn't allowed in, but she also knew once he came out of the massage room, turned off the light, and closed and locked the door behind him, he was done for the day.

"Hey, Dolly, did you miss me?" Jaime got down on his knees to pet her, rubbing under her collar, and was rewarded with a wet nose against his ear. She wasn't much of a licker. Instead, she used a playful sort of head bump, as if she wanted to lick him, but forgot to stick her tongue out. He'd adopted her from the shelter when she was only two years old. She was part golden retriever and part something else—maybe chow. She was completely worthless as a guard dog, but as a companion she was the best.

The door from his back yard into the massage room had only a flimsy lock on it, but the one leading from the massage room into his house had three—one on the handle, the standard deadbolt, and another deadbolt at about eye level. Jaime made sure they were all securely latched. He'd read an article once that said the safest thing was to have two more, one at the very top of the door and one at the bottom, but he didn't have the tools he would need to install the locks himself and he didn't want anybody coming to his house to do it for him. They'd think it was weird. They'd think he was afraid of something.

Of course, they'd be right.

Jaime had also read the locks didn't matter anyway because the hinges were the weak point on the door. He'd read yet another article claiming intruders almost always entered through a sliding door or a window. In the end, he did his best not to think about those things. There was really only so much you could do. Especially when the worst monsters were in your head. Fear was strange like that—sometimes you had to fight it, but Jaime had also learned over the years that sometimes you just had to bolt the door and try to keep breathing until morning. Sometimes fighting only made it worse.

Setting up an office in his own home had been terrifying at first, but he was used to it now. The locks on the door helped. Once that semblance of security was in place, he went to the kitchen with Dolly at his heels. First, he fed her. Then he made dinner—a salad with blue cheese crumbles and ranch dressing, and a chicken patty sandwich with only lettuce and mustard. He ate the same thing almost every night. Years ago, back when he still went to a therapist, he'd learned obsessive-compulsiveness was a common aftereffect of what he'd endured. For a while, he'd thought maybe that meant he should fight it—he should force himself to try new things. To live "outside the box." He still did that sometimes, but not for something as inconsequential as dinner. Routine helped him feel in control.

As he chopped the lettuce for his salad, he found his mind drifting to Levi. Levi was *hot.* There was just no other way to put it. Dark hair grown a bit too long, and deeply suntanned skin. Hazel eyes, and a body that was fit and beautiful. He'd had dark stubble on his cheeks and he smelled like the ocean and the sun and everything that was free. He was rugged. Even his name was rugged. Levi. And his voice—it was low and sexy, and somehow he managed to make everything he said sound like a come-on. Jaime shook his head.

He didn't want to think about Levi.

Levi was one of *them*. One of those men who knew how attractive he was and used it. The type who lived his life the way he wanted to, without any thought or doubts. He probably never questioned his sexuality. He probably had sex with different men every week—maybe every night—and never bothered to feel guilty. He was one of those men who other men were happy to be noticed by, and happy to be used by. Jaime wanted to hate him, but he couldn't.

He envied him, though. He envied him a great deal.

After eating dinner, Jaime sat on the couch watching a low-budget monster movie until he couldn't keep his eyes open any longer. It was better that way—better than lying in bed, with his brain still running. He had bad dreams all the time, but he hadn't had the really bad dreams, the ones he considered true nightmares, in close to a year. He wanted to keep it that way. He dragged himself into his room, with Dolly right behind. He locked the bedroom door. He had a deadbolt on it as well and he didn't care that the man who'd installed it had looked at him funny.

He got into bed, and Dolly jumped up on the other side. She turned in exactly six circles before throwing herself down next to him with a giant sigh. He draped his arm over her and buried his face in her thick doggy fur. She was a stinky dog, yes, but he loved her more than anything else in the world. The locks on the doors helped keep his fears at bay, but it was Dolly who helped him feel normal.

Levi had his second massage on Thursday. It started much as the one before. After the three initial deep breaths and the attempt to pull his head off his body, Jaime massaged his cheeks and chin, although Levi felt in this case the term "massaged" was relative. Jaime was squeezing and pushing on different parts of his face, contorting it into expressions that were undoubtedly humorous.

"What are you doing?" Levi asked.

"There's a pressure point here somewhere. If I find it, I can make your face freeze like this, just like your mother always said."

It took a second for Levi to digest that and to realize the Boy Scout was actually making a joke. "You're full of shit."

"You think so?" Jaime stared down at him without cracking a smile, although Levi could see the mischief in his blue eyes. "All urban legends start with a kernel of truth."

Levi laughed, and Jaime moved to his side to work on his left arm. "Do most people talk or just lie here?"

"Either one is fine."

"You won't actually let me fall asleep, though, will you?"

Jaime smiled, although he didn't look up from Levi's hand as he rubbed between his fingers. "Once we get to your psoas, we'll do some movements. Probably on your lumbar as well."

"And by 'do some movements,' you mean you're going to be sadistic and hurt me, don't you?"

Jaime just smiled.

"Okay then, we might as well talk."

"Fine," Jaime said as he moved to the other side. "What would you like to talk about?"

"Sex?" Levi asked, just so he could watch Jaime blush.

"No."

"I have to work tonight. Why don't you come by and see me?"

"Don't start that again, Mr. Binder."

Levi laughed. "You're no fun at all." He meant it as a joke, but he was surprised to see Jaime wince a bit. He'd actually struck home with his barb, although he hadn't meant to.

"Tell me about your family," Jaime said, before Levi could decide whether or not to apologize. "You said you're from South Carolina?"

"Yes. Georgetown."

"Are you an only child?"

Levi laughed. "Not even close. I have three brothers and two sisters."

"Are you out with them?"

"Yes." But he couldn't keep the sadness from his voice when he said it, and he knew by the way Jaime glanced up at him that he'd heard it.

"And?" he prodded.

Levi sighed. "It's complicated."

"It always is when it comes to family."

"Are you out with your family?"

Jaime frowned. "I guess not technically."

"What do you mean?"

"Let's go ahead and work on your psoas now, shall we?"

And so Levi spent the next few minutes working through exercises, while Jaime pushed on his abdomen and then on his hip. It still hurt, although not quite as much as before. Then Jaime rubbed his thigh, which was incredibly painful. "Are you the oldest?" Jaime asked him, as he worked.

He knew Jaime was just trying to distract him from the pain, but he decided to let him. "No. I'm the fifth, actually."

"Tell me about them."

Levi sighed. He wasn't sure he wanted to talk about his family, but it did help keep his mind off his discomfort. It also helped keep his mind away from how close Jaime's hands were to his groin. "My oldest brother Isaac is a real estate agent. I guess he must be about thirty-seven now. Then there's Jacob. He manages the tire department at a Sears. Then my sister Ruth. She has a bachelor's degree in psychology, but she's a stay-at-home mom. She's married to an orthopedic surgeon."

"The one who told you to get a massage?"

"Yes."

"I like him already."

Levi laughed. "Me too. After Ruth is my brother Caleb. He's only two years older than me. He works at Ultimate Electronics. Then there's me. And then after me is my sister Rachel."

"That's a pretty big family."

"You have no idea. Between them all, my parents have nineteen grandchildren."

The number shocked Jaime enough that his hands stopped moving. "*Nineteen?*" He shook his head. "Are you Catholic?"

"Mormon."

"No way. *You're* Mormon?"

Levi sighed. People always reacted the same way. He hated this conversation. "My family is," he said, unable to hide his bitterness. "I'm not." Not anymore. It wasn't that he had ever technically left the church. His name still appeared in the rosters, and home teachers still called him occasionally to see if they could visit, but any comfort Levi had ever found in his religion had been stolen from him by their view of homosexuality.

Jaime watched him with a puzzled look on his face. Then he smiled, and Levi saw a mischievous glint in his eye. "So," he said, "how many mothers do you have?"

Levi rolled his eyes. "*One.* Polygamy was banned more than a hundred years ago."

"What about those sects out in Utah?"

"They're not recognized by the church."

"Uh-huh."

Levi tried not to be annoyed at Jaime's snide tone.

"And what about the strange magic underwear everybody talks about?"

"They're not 'magic underwear,'" Levi snapped. "They're called garments."

"Magic garments, then?"

"Stop!"

"Do they protect you from evil?"

"Of course not."

"Do they make you invincible?"

"Give me a break."

"Then what?"

Levi sighed. Catholics burned candles and tossed holy water around and ate funny little crackers and prayed with beaded necklaces to saints, and yet he doubted any of them ever had to answer ridiculous questions like these. "They're a symbol, that's all. A symbol of the covenant we make with God."

"And the stories claiming they can never be removed?"

"Are complete bullshit. People always mock what they don't understand."

"Ah," Jaime said with a teasing smile. "And why aren't you wearing yours?"

"Not all Mormons wear them, you know. Only those who choose to go through the temple ceremony. And you can't even do *that* until you've proven yourself worthy."

"I see."

He could tell Jaime was laughing at him, and it annoyed him. "What?"

"I knew you only had one mother, and I didn't expect you to believe the garments were magic."

"You were just trying to get a rise out of me?"

"You claim you're no longer a member and yet you're so quick to defend them. I find it interesting."

It was true. Levi felt shunned because of his sexuality, but he had never been able to think of himself as *not* Mormon. "People make fun of us for having strange practices, but they never look at the good things we do."

"Like what?"

"Like stressing family is the most important thing we have. And taking care of each other. When I was a kid, my dad lost his job. For almost six months, he couldn't find a new one. With six kids, it wasn't easy. Christmas was sort of bleak that year and on Christmas Eve night, while we were all sitting around playing Yahtzee, the doorbell rang. When we answered it, nobody was there, but there was a box full of packages—one present for each of us kids—and there was a big basket of groceries. And there was an envelope with gift certificates for the grocery store my mom used. I remember my mom just sat there and cried."

"And it was from your church?"

"It had to be. I mean, nobody ever said anything. There wasn't a card, but that's the kind of thing they do."

"But they don't approve of homosexuality." It wasn't even a question.

"They believe it may not be a choice, but they still believe it's a sin to indulge in the 'homosexual lifestyle.' My parents and my siblings all say they love me, but…"

"But what?"

"I disgust them."

Jaime was quiet for a minute, then said gently, "I'm sorry, Levi."

"Forget it." He tried to shake off the depression that always gripped him when he thought about his family. He loved them. He had loved growing up surrounded by his brothers and his sisters. He loved playing games on Monday nights for Family Home Evening, and he loved the dances his church held when he was young. Hell, he'd even kind of liked getting up early for seminary in high school. He'd been part of something warm and wonderful back then. He missed his siblings. Sometimes it broke his heart knowing he wasn't one of them anymore. Jaime was still watching him, looking more than a little bit sad. "What about you? Tell me about your family."

He thought changing the subject to Jaime's family would cheer them both up, but his question didn't make Jaime look any less sad. Not at all.

"Why don't you turn over now," he said. "Let's work on your back."

"Yes, master," Levi joked. But he obeyed.

CHAPTER 4

Levi saw Jaime again twice the next week. There was no doubt the massages helped. His ass and his leg still hurt. They still slowed him down, but there was a small, yet noticeable improvement as well. Unfortunately, it wasn't the only effect the massages had.

Levi was becoming obsessed with Jaime.

He didn't understand it. Jaime was young and naive. He was boyishly cute, but he wasn't the type Levi usually went for. He was pale and skinny and uptight. But the evening after his fourth massage, as Levi fucked some nameless man bent over the table in the storage room, he found his mind wandering to Jaime. He could picture all too clearly what Jaime must look like naked—the pale skin and the soft, round globes of his ass. He could imagine how Jaime's ass would feel in his hands.

On Monday, the morning he was scheduled to have his fifth massage, he woke from an erotic dream of Jaime massaging his erect cock. He let his mind wander. He let the fantasy grow as he stroked himself to climax, imaging Jaime spread eagle and waiting on the massage table in front of him.

By the time he arrived at Jaime's for his appointment that afternoon, he knew what he was going to do. He was going to seduce Jaime Marshall. He knew from experience that was all he needed—one good fuck with the kid and he'd be over it—and he figured seducing the Boy Scout would be unbelievably easy.

Jaime started him on his stomach, and Levi waited until he was on his back to make his move. He needed to be able to see Jaime's face.

"What are you doing tonight?" he asked as Jaime rubbed his right arm.

"Nothing," Jaime said. "Why?"

"You want to go out?"

"Out where?"

"Wherever. Dinner? A club?"

Jaime's eyes met his, his expression guarded. "You're asking me out?"

"Christ, isn't that what I just said?"

"As in *a date?*"

"What else?"

"No thanks, Mr. Binder."

"Don't start that again. It's *Levi.*"

"I've told you before—"

"We can stay in, if you want."

"No—"

"My place or yours?"

"Neither."

Jaime started to move down to Levi's leg, and Levi reached out and grabbed his hand. "Come on, Jaime. Don't be like that."

Jaime jerked his hand away as if he'd been scalded. "Please, don't touch me."

It was hardly the reaction Levi had expected. "Why not?"

"I don't like being touched."

"Then you sure picked the wrong profession."

Jaime pinned him with a withering stare. "Levi, there is nothing about your treatment which requires *you* to touch *me*."

"Okay, okay," Levi held up his hands in surrender. He found the whole thing amusing—a massage therapist who didn't like to be touched. Levi didn't believe it for a minute. Jaime did his magic trick of unwrapping Levi's leg and started to rub his thigh. It still hurt more than Levi cared to admit. "So when are you coming by the club?"

"I'm not."

"I've been waiting to show you the back room."

Jaime's jaw clenched and the intensity of the "therapy" on Levi's leg became considerably more painful. He may have looked small and weak, but he had strong hands.

Levi did his best not to wince. "Maybe you've already seen it?"

"I told you, I've never been there."

"To the club or to the back room?"

"Either one."

"If you've never been there, how do you know about it?"

"I worked with a guy at Borders a few years ago who told me about it."

"So *he'd* been there?"

"Yes."

"He'd actually used the room?"

"He said one of the bartenders took him there." Jaime cleared his throat awkwardly. "Was it you?"

Levi couldn't help but smile. "Could've been."

"His name was Clay."

"I don't bother with their names."

"Not ever?"

"Sometimes they tell me, but I tend to forget."

"So you only care about getting laid?"

The topic was obviously irritating Jaime, which amused Levi immensely. He liked seeing Jaime flustered for once. "Pretty much, yeah."

"And what if you're dating someone? Do you still have sex with people at the bar?"

"Good question. If I ever bother dating anyone, I'll let you know."

"And you wondered why I said no to your 'date' a few minutes ago."

Damn. Jaime had him there. Levi felt like he'd walked into a trap and wished for a second he'd kept his mouth shut.

"So you have sex with them once and that's it?"

There didn't seem to be any point in sugarcoating it now. "Once. Twice. As many times as they come back. After two or three times, I start to lose interest. Probably never more than four or five times with the same guy. Why? Does that bother you?"

"Of course not," Jaime said, although the deep blush of his cheeks and the slight waver in his voice suggested otherwise. "It's none of my business."

"It could be."

Jaime looked up, meeting Levi's eyes for the first time rather than watching what he was doing. His hands actually stopped moving. But he didn't look intrigued or flattered. He looked annoyed. "I have made my position perfectly clear—I'm not interested in being one of your conquests."

"I'm not sure I believe you."

Jaime's gaze returned to his work, and the massage resumed. "You can believe whatever you want, but I won't be visiting The Zone at all, let alone the back room."

"Come on, Jaime," Levi said. He dropped his joking tone. He chose to be suggestive instead. "Aren't you a bit curious? Don't you want to know what all the fuss is about?"

"No."

"Are you seriously telling me you *haven't* thought about it these last few weeks?"

"That's what I'm—"

"Because I have. I've thought about it a lot. About you. I think we could have a great time." Now he was thinking about it again, his body was reacting in a predictable way. He didn't fight it, though. He was having way too much fun to be embarrassed.

"You should spend less time thinking about things that aren't ever going to happen and more time stretching your leg."

"Do you have a boyfriend? Is that the problem?" Jaime didn't answer, but Levi could tell he was getting more agitated. His jaw clenched again, and he dug his fingers into Levi's thigh in a way obviously designed to make Levi squirm—and not in a good way. "No answer? Very interesting."

Jaime sighed in exasperation. "It's none of your business."

"No, then. No boyfriend. So what's the problem?"

"How does me telling you to mind your own business mean I don't have a boyfriend?"

"If you had a boyfriend and wanted me to quit hitting on you, you'd just say 'yes.' If you had a boyfriend and *didn't* want me to quit hitting on you…well, there're all kinds of ways you could handle it. But telling me to mind my own business isn't one of them."

"And if I didn't have a boyfriend and *wanted* you to keep making advances, I would have just said 'no.' Therefore, by your own logic, Mr. Binder, me telling you to mind your own business means no, I don't have a boyfriend, but I am *not* interested in sleeping with you. As I told you before."

"It's Mr. Binder again now, is it?" Again, Jaime didn't answer, and Levi's smile grew. "I think there's another option. I think you *don't* want me to stop hitting on you. I think if you *did*, you'd have lied and said 'yes' when I asked about a boyfriend."

Jaime stopped massaging his leg all together and glared at him. "Not all of us lie to get what we want. Besides which, I'm skeptical that me having a boyfriend would have deterred you much anyway."

Well, he had a point there. Levi'd seduced plenty of "taken" men in his time. "I don't see what the problem is, Jaime. You're single. I'm single. Why not have a little fun?"

"I'm not interested—" Levi reached again for Jaime's hand, and Jaime's eyes widened with fear. "Don't touch me!" He jerked his hand away, backing up in a near-panic, although there was only room to go a couple of steps before his back hit the wall.

Levi sat up on the massage table, pulling the sheet off as he did. He let Jaime get a good look at him, completely naked, his cock half erect. He knew how he looked. He knew how men usually reacted. He pushed his dark hair out of his eyes so he could meet Jaime's eyes. "I don't want to play games anymore, Jaime," he said. "I want you."

"No, you don't."

"I *do*."

"You want to add another name to your list—if you bothered to take names, that is."

"Is it because I'm a client? Because I'll switch to another therapist if it'll change your mind."

"That's not it."

"You're gay, right?"

Jaime blinked. "Yes."

"Are you attracted to me?"

"That's not the point."

"Is it a religious thing? You think it's a sin? Or you only fuck guys you're in a relationship with? What?"

"I *can't*."

"Are you HIV positive?"

"No! It's nothing like that."

"Then what's the problem?"

Jaime was visibly shaken eyes fearful, cheeks pale, his trembling hands trying to grip the wall behind him. He looked terrified. Levi didn't understand how being hit on could be frightening.

"Levi," he said, his voice quiet and shaky, "I can't. I'm not saying I don't *want* to. I'm saying I *can't*."

"You're not making any sense at all. You know that, right?"

Jaime closed his eyes for a moment and took a deep breath. And then another. When his blue eyes opened again, some of the fear was gone. But what Levi saw there instead surprised him. Jaime looked sad and beaten.

"I'm going to have to ask you to leave, Mr. Binder."

"Come on, Jaime! Don't be like that. I don't see why we shouldn't have a bit of fun together. That's all."

"I need you to leave *now*."

"Wait! Jaime, I'm sorry—"

Now that Levi was back-pedaling, what remained of Jaime's fear seemed to be turning quickly into anger. "I won't charge you for this visit, which I think is rather generous of me."

"Please don't do this. I'll stop—"

"I'll go out of the room so you can get dressed—"

"What about the therapy for my leg? And my back?" Because the truth was, the massages helped. He didn't want to stop the treatment now.

But he could tell Jaime wasn't about to be swayed. "If you're serious about treatment, I suggest you find a new therapist. Otherwise, I'm sure The Zone will provide you with all the therapy you need."

"Jaime, I'm sorry, okay? Give me another chance!"

But Jaime didn't even listen. He turned and went through the door leading into his house, closing it firmly behind him. Levi could have sworn he heard more than one lock clicking into place. As if he'd try to bust the damn thing down.

He sighed. The next nearest therapist on his list had been more than ten miles away. He could have kicked himself for fucking things up so royally with the Boy Scout, all because he wanted to get laid. Jaime was right—he could do that any time. It had been selfish of him to bring his desire here.

Still, there didn't seem to be anything he could do about it now. Jaime wasn't interested in his apologies. Levi did the only other thing he could think of to do. He got dressed, and he left.

That night, Jaime lay in his bed, debating. There was an ache deep in his abdomen and he'd been half hard all evening. Levi's advances had stirred something in him he'd always done his best to squash—desire. A normal man would have done something about it. A normal man wouldn't have been ashamed. But he was far from normal.

Jaime knew some people would have said what happened to him had caused his homosexuality. He also knew some people would argue the very idea was a load of shit. Jaime wished he knew for sure. He liked men. He knew that much. But he also knew sometimes it was hard for him to believe his attraction wasn't connected to what he'd endured, which made him want to avoid it. In his teenage years, he'd wanted very badly be attracted to women instead. He'd *tried* to want them. But he'd failed. And for every day that went by when he was sure his homosexuality was something he was born with, there would be another day when he couldn't quite make himself believe it.

He tried to tell himself it didn't matter. He told himself embracing his sexuality was the best way to leave it all behind—not to let his past ruin his present. But it was easier said than done.

It had started when Jaime was young. He couldn't even have said how young. Maybe three. Maybe four. His mother worked nights, and would often leave him with his aunt and uncle. Back then, it had been subtle. He remembered his uncle watching him as he played on the floor with his toys. He remembered how sometimes, as he watched, his uncle breathed hard and grunted. Jaime would try not to look at him.

Later, when Jaime was a couple of years older, his uncle would have him sit in his lap. He remembered the strange sensation of something hard against his leg. Soon afterward it turned into a game. His uncle would say, "Put your hand here." His big hand would close over Jaime's little one as his uncle grunted and groaned. Sometimes he squeezed so hard it hurt Jaime's hand. "It's our secret game," his uncle would say, after Jaime's hand was sticky and wet.

Jaime thought he was probably eight or nine the first time his uncle came for him in the night. He had put his hand over Jaime's mouth and said in his ear, "Don't you make a sound." Jaime had been so scared, he'd peed the bed, but his uncle didn't care. Jaime didn't know how many times it happened. Maybe twice. Maybe four times. What he did remember was the way his uncle's reeking breath smelled as he grunted away on top of him, like beer and stale cigarettes. He remembered the weight against his back, so heavy he felt like he couldn't breathe. And more than anything, Jaime remembered the pain. The pain didn't end when his uncle finally stood up and left the room, either. The pain went on for days.

He remembered the shame of his aunt finding the wet sheet. He was too old to have accidents, she'd told him.

It wasn't until years later he thought to wonder about the blood. Certainly she'd seen that, too.

He remembered having nightmares once he was back at home. The bedwetting continued. He remembered how, finally, he'd locked himself in the bathroom rather than be taken to his uncle's house, and when his mother had used a toothpick to open it, he'd sobbed and sobbed, begging her not to make him go back. He'd kicked and screamed and bitten her, pulling her hair, and finally, she'd spanked him and thrown him into his room. He hadn't cared about being punished. He only knew he was relieved. He wasn't going back.

Afterward, there were hushed phone calls. Jaime never knew what happened. He never knew how much his mother learned. He only knew he never spent a night at his uncle's house again. When his mother worked nights, she'd send him to the neighbor's or to his grandmother's instead. When he saw his aunt and uncle on holidays, they'd both pretend he didn't exist at all. It had been a relief. And yet, his mother still talked to them both. His mother still smiled at her sister. She still spoke to her sister's spouse.

Eventually, he got his bladder back under control. The pain faded. But some things never went away—the fear, and the nightmares.

And the shame.

That was the worst part of it: the shame. Even now, nearly twenty years later, it was there. Jaime'd been to counseling as an adult. He'd read books and articles on the subject. He knew it was a common aftereffect. He knew it wasn't rational.

That didn't change it, though.

It also didn't change the fact that, regardless of who was involved, he could not stand to be touched.

That was why he'd said no to Levi. Not because he didn't find Levi attractive—God knew he did. Not because he thought sex was wrong. Not because he believed it had to be about love. But because he couldn't stand to be touched. He knew, in theory, this didn't mean he couldn't have some kind of sex life. Certainly there were plenty of ways to get off. But they would require trust. They would require him to not be ashamed.

In theory, it was possible. In reality, there was no way.

Masturbation wasn't something he allowed himself to do very often. He knew most men did it. He also knew most men didn't have his hang-ups. Sometimes, he felt as if giving in to his sexual desires made him no better than his uncle. If gratifying himself was normal, then it seemed to mean what was done to him was normal as well. He knew it made no sense, rationally. He'd learned, however, to accept that when it came to sex and his past, logic held no sway.

Masturbation was further complicated by the fact he didn't like the feel of his own shaft in his hand as he stroked himself. It was too similar to something he remembered from long ago. Sometimes he'd spread a towel on the bed and hump himself against it. Very rarely, he'd fill a plastic bag with Vaseline and slide it between the mattresses of his bed. He'd kneel next to his bed and thrust into the bag. On rare occasions, he could induce orgasms simply by tapping his fingers against his frenulum. But the truth was, sometimes it just seemed like too much effort.

Tonight, though, he knew he needed it. No amount of telling himself no was going to change the terrible tightness in his groin. His erection was almost painful. He debated for a long time, but in the end, he stripped naked. He got an old pillow out of the closet—one that had been washed so many times it was worn and buttery soft. He lay on his stomach and put the pillow under his pelvis. And he thought about Levi.

He thought about Levi's body and his tan skin. He thought about the dark hair hanging in his hazel eyes, and the heat he'd seen in those eyes today. He thought about the suggestive timbre of Levi's voice. He thought of the bulge under the sheet, between Levi's legs, and his thrusts against the pillow became stronger. He thought of moving the sheet aside. He thought of Levi's cock. He thought of licking it. He imagined sucking it, and his thrusts became frantic. He thought of Levi's lips. He thought of kissing him. Toward the very end, as his climax was bearing down upon him and he both longed for and dreaded the release it would bring, he even thought of how it would feel to let Levi touch him.

Not once did he think of letting Levi fuck him.

CHAPTER 5

Levi spent the entire week contemplating Jaime's reaction to his advances, but he couldn't come up with an explanation. He was completely baffled. It wasn't the fact that Jaime had refused him. It was the fear he'd seen in his eyes that gave him pause. His overtures were not just unwelcome. They were, for some reason he did not understand, genuinely distressing.

"I have a puzzle for you, Max." It was ten o'clock on Friday night, and The Zone was busy, but not overly so. The customers tended to come in waves, and at the moment, they were in a lull.

"Riddle away, Batman," Max said, leaning against the bar.

"A gay twenty-something-year-old man who won't have sex. Not, he says, because he doesn't want to, but because he *can't*. What the fuck's up with that?"

"He's got a boyfriend and actually believes monogamy's a legitimate lifestyle choice?"

"That's not it."

"We talking about somebody you know?"

"Not really."

Max grinned knowingly at him. "You met a guy whose pants you couldn't get into and you can't figure out why."

"No," Levi said.

"You're a horrible liar. Must be your good Mormon upbringing."

"Fine," Levi admitted. "I just don't get the whole 'I want to but I can't' thing. That's all."

More customers came up then and the conversation dropped for a few minutes as they poured drinks and collected cash.

Once they were alone again, Max said, "I knew a guy once—well, *I* didn't know him, but he was my roommate's uncle, so I *heard* about him. Anyway, this guy was HIV positive *and* had a latex allergy."

Levi whistled. "Brutal."

"No shit. Talk about getting shafted. And not in the way he liked."

Levi shook his head. "He says it's not HIV."

"Hepatitis?"

"I don't know."

"Who is this guy, anyway?" Max asked, looking around the bar as if Jaime might be there wearing a sign that read, I won't fuck Levi Binder. "I want to meet him."

"He's not here."

"Who is he?"

"None of your goddamn business."

Max laughed. "Wow, he's got you good, doesn't he? Never had anybody say no before?"

Not very damn often, but Levi was saved from answering by another rush of thirsty patrons.

"So what're you gonna do?" Max asked the next time they had a break between customers. "You gonna chalk this guy up as a nut job 'cause he actually *can* resist your dubious charms, or you gonna obsess on it 'til you can nail him?"

"I guess that's what I'm trying to figure out."

"Hey, Zeke!" Max said, and Levi turned to see one of the owners enter the narrow space behind the bar he and Max occupied. "Levi's got a puzzle to solve."

Zeke was fifty, give or take a few years. He owned The Zone with his long-time partner Owen. Owen mostly handled the books and was rarely seen around the bar when it was open, but Zeke was usually around until two or three in the morning and had even been known to cover for some of the bartenders while they took quick breaks in the back room with willing guests. He was quiet and didn't have much of a sense of humor, but he was damn easy to work for.

"What's the puzzle?" he asked.

"Levi met some guy who refuses to be swayed by his charming advances and he can't figure out why."

Zeke turned to Levi with one eyebrow up and a knowing smile on his face, and Levi felt himself blush. "Must be losing your mojo," Zeke said, and Max laughed. Zeke pulled out a bottle of Jaegermeister and poured three shots. "Is this really the first time in your life anyone's ever said no?" he asked as he handed one to Levi.

"It's not because he said no," Levi said defensively as he looked down at the shot in his hand. He hated Jaegermeister, but when the boss handed you a drink, it seemed wise to drink it. He swallowed the alcohol, wincing at the licorice taste, and put the empty glass in the sink. "What confuses me is that he got all weird about it. He freaked out a little bit, like he was scared. And he said it wasn't because he doesn't want to, but because he *can't*."

Zeke seemed to ponder that. One of Max's regulars came up then, a doe-eyed man who may as well have had "dominate me" tattooed across his forehead. They put their heads together to talk. Zeke watched them, and when Max glanced his way, Zeke shrugged. That was the green light, so they headed for the back room.

"You know, Levi," Zeke said when they were gone, "Owen dated a guy once, back before we met. This guy freaked out if Owen tried to go down on him. Turned out when he was twelve, he had a foster mother who liked to go down on him, too."

"Oh God," Levi said in disgust.

"Exactly." Zeke didn't look at him. He stared into his still-full shot glass as if it was a Magic Eight-ball and was about to reveal the answer. "The thing is, sometimes he wanted it. Sometimes he wanted it so much, Owen said it was all he could think about it. So they'd try, and one of two things would happen: either he'd freak out halfway through and end up in tears, or he'd get off on it. Owen said him getting off was worse because then he'd feel guilty and ashamed, and he'd be depressed for a week. Sometimes more."

"Jesus Christ," Levi said, shaking his head. "What happened?"

Zeke shrugged. "They split up—not because of that, but because they were young and stupid and couldn't keep their dicks in their pants. But fifteen years later, Owen found out the guy had taken a bottle of Valium with a giant vodka chaser."

"He killed himself?"

Zeke finally threw back his shot. "Can you blame him?" he asked as he handed Levi his empty glass.

More customers came up, and Zeke and Levi went back to work. As Levi poured shots and mixed drinks, he contemplated what Zeke had said.

He'd considered HIV, but it had never occurred to him Jaime's problem might be an emotional issue. It changed everything. If Jaime had merely been playing hard to get, or if he was just shy, or even if it was because he had a boyfriend, Levi would have persisted. He would have looked at it as a game. But if it was something like Zeke had described, it was definitely *not* a game. And the more Levi thought about the fear and the near-panic he'd seen on Jaime's face, the more he thought Zeke might be on the right track.

He wasn't going to mess with that. After all, he liked finding guys to fuck, but he wanted them to be willing, and he didn't want to have to tiptoe through an emotional minefield to do it. He knew he was sometimes an asshole, but he wasn't so far gone he'd intentionally fuck with somebody who was troubled like that. It was one thing to be selfish. It was another altogether to be malicious.

Max elbowed him in the ribs, interrupting his thoughts. He nodded toward the end of the bar where a man was standing. He was watching Levi, a question in his eyes. Levi'd been with him before, although he couldn't remember if it had been last weekend or the one before. Or both. "I got the bar," Max said. "You go have fun."

Which was exactly what Levi did. He didn't think about Jaime again for the rest of the night.

He didn't think about him again until the following day, when Ruth called.

"Hey, Leviticus!" she said with her customary cheer. "How's life?"

"Good." But he was hesitant. He could tell by the tone of her voice she was calling to ask him for something.

"Dad turns sixty this year." Their father's birthday was early in September, but Levi hadn't thought about his exact age. "It falls on the Friday before Labor Day, and we've decided to throw him a party." Levi tried not to moan as he began to anticipate where the conversation was headed. "Can you get the weekend off?"

"I don't know, Ruth." Part of him knew he should go, but visits to his family never ended well.

"Everybody else will be there. And I know he and Mom would love to see you."

"So they can lecture me, pray for me, and tell me how wrong my life is?"

"Levi, they love you."

"Fine. They love me, but they never hear a word I say. They're so goddamn sure they know what's right, they don't care whether it's what I want or not."

She sighed with obvious frustration. "Will you think about it, at least? Is it *really* too much to ask?"

He didn't want to argue with her, and so, in the spirit of contrition, he said, "I'll consider it."

"Good." She was obviously annoyed, though, and they fell into an awkward silence.

Now it was Levi's turn to sigh. The truth was, sometimes he missed his family, but he missed the family he'd had years ago before his sexual orientation had come between them. He missed the parents who'd loved him and raised him. He missed the brothers who teased him, and Ruth, who babied him, and even Rachel, who sometimes drove him nuts.

The family he found when he visited now was a completely different story.

"How's the pain?" Ruth asked, interrupting his thoughts. "Did you find a massage therapist?"

"I did. And Jackson was right: it helped."

"Why do I hear a 'but' coming?"

"I kind of got kicked out."

"Leviticus Walton Binder, what did you do?"

Leave it to Ruth to pull out the full-name thing, as his mother had always done.

"I was flirting with my therapist." Even as he said it, though, he realized it wasn't exactly the truth. "More than flirting. I came on pretty strong."

"And he kicked you out?"

"Well, first he said no…" His sentence died unfinished, as he thought about how to finish.

"And?"

"I suppose you could say I was overly persistent."

"Why?"

"I guess I thought he was playing hard-to-get. I thought I could change his mind."

She was silent for a second and then she said with obvious relish, "In other words, you thought you knew what was right, whether it was what he wanted or not. Hmmm… Why does that sound familiar?"

Of course, she was correct. Disregarding Jaime's words and assuming he didn't know his own desires was exactly the type of thing Levi's parents did to him, and it infuriated him. It had never occurred to him how manipulative his attempts at seduction sometimes were. It made him feel small and pathetic. Especially in light of his suspicions about sexual abuse, his advances had been borderline harassment. Of course, he hadn't known about the abuse at the time, and even now it was nothing more than speculation, but that didn't excuse his actions. And since he could easily get laid almost any night of the week at the club, his insistence on seducing Jaime had been downright selfish. He was ashamed of what an asshole he'd been. "Ruth, I really hate it when you're right."

"I'm your big sister," she said. "It's all part of the job."

CHAPTER 6

It was Sunday when Levi called him. Jaime saw the name on caller ID and didn't answer. He was relieved when Levi didn't leave a message. But an hour later, his phone rang again. Once again he ignored it, but he wasn't surprised when Levi called a third time, later that night. This time, he answered, albeit reluctantly.

"Hello?"

"It's Levi."

"I know. What do you want?"

"Jaime, I'm sorry."

"Now that you've spent the weekend working and surfing and your psoas is acting up, I'm sure you are. Goodbye."

"Wait, Jaime! That's not what I meant."

"I don't believe you."

Levi sighed. "I never meant to upset you. I really didn't. I mean, yes, I meant to hit on you, but I didn't mean to scare you. And I *never* wanted to hurt you."

Now that Jaime was listening, he realized with some surprise that Levi sounded sincere. "The problem wasn't just you hitting on me. It was that I asked you to stop—more than once—and you didn't."

"I know. And I should have. I mean, I should never have started. It's just I wanted to seduce you. Maybe it was wrong. It was definitely selfish. But it wasn't malicious. I didn't realize how upsetting it would be for you. And I'm sorry."

Jaime hadn't expected such a heartfelt apology. It took him a moment to answer. Of course, it hadn't been malicious. He knew that. However, he was surprised Levi had apparently thought about the incident enough to recognize the real root of the problem. "Apology accepted," he said. "Goodnight, Mr. Binder."

"Jaime, wait!"

"What?" Jaime asked, although he was pretty sure he knew what was coming.

"I'd really like to come back. Please."

"I don't think it's a good idea."

"I promise, I won't hit on you. I won't touch you. I promise to be a perfect gentleman."

Could he believe him? That was the question. On one hand, Levi sounded sincere, and Jaime hated to lose a client. On the other hand, Levi scared him. Not all the time. Not even most of the time. But when he made advances, Jaime felt all of his old fears circling him in the darkness, snapping at his heels, waiting for him to trip and fall so they could pounce on him and swallow him whole. "I'm not sure I want to take that chance," he said. He could sense Levi's disappointment, even over the phone, but he refused to be swayed by it. "Goodbye, Levi."

He told himself over and over again he'd made the right decision. He was better off without Levi.

He saw all of his usual clients that week. There was Bill, the accountant. Bill weighed nearly three hundred pounds, but complained constantly how his desk job was too hard on his knees. There was Molly, the over-worked mother of four. She never said a word. She lay on the table, blubbery and white, silent and limp. She reminded Jaime of a dead fish in more ways than one. There was Jen, the stripper, aka Sable. She had back trouble from dancing in five-inch heels. She talked incessantly of the clients who professed their undying love as they tucked their overdue child support payments into her sequined brassiere. There was Tammy, who had hairy legs and dirty feet, and Roger, who smelled like stale beer. There was Carol, the waitress, and Cal, the CEO.

He knew them all, and even liked a few of them, but he did their massages on autopilot. He stifled his yawns, telling himself he was just tired. But the truth was, he missed Levi. He hadn't realized until he was gone how much he'd enjoyed doing Levi's massages. Except for that one terrible day, Levi had always been nice. He was funny. He answered Jaime's questions and laughed at his jokes. He was at times frustrating and infuriating and argumentative. He was bright and vibrant and fun. He was like a ray of sunshine in Jaime's small, dimly lit massage room. The fact of the matter was, Jaime never found himself on autopilot with Levi. He liked that.

For three days, he debated whether he could count on Levi's promise to behave. On Wednesday afternoon, as he locked the door behind Sheila, who was the pampered trophy wife of a rich octogenarian and brought her dog in a purse to every massage, he made up his mind. And he called Levi.

"Hello?" Even over the phone, Levi's voice had a sultry edge, making everything sound like a come-on. It unnerved Jaime a bit, but it was too late to turn back now.

"It's Jaime Marshall."

"Jaime," Levi said. "Hey. Hi. Ummm…" He was stammering, obviously surprised, but he sounded pleased. "How's it going?"

"Did you find another therapist?"

"No. Well, yes. Not really." Of course, the answer made no sense, and Jaime waited for Levi to elaborate. "What I mean is, I looked in the phone book, but I haven't called anyone yet."

"Why not?"

"I don't know. One's too far away, the next one's even farther, and the other has one of those stupid little Jesus-fish on her Yellow Pages ad, which kind of bugs me. I'm afraid she'll get all 'family values' on me."

Jaime couldn't help but smile. "Those don't seem like very good reasons."

"They're not," Levi admitted.

"How's your back?"

"It hurts. And so does my ass. And my thigh is fucking killing me." He sighed. "I know I should call somebody else, Jaime, but I don't want anybody else. I want *you*." He stopped short and then swore. "Shit! I didn't mean that the way it probably sounded."

Jaime smiled at Levi's blunder. Levi had often teased him by calling him sadistic, and right then, Jaime felt it might be true because he was definitely finding some pleasure in Levi's discomfort. For the moment at least, he believed Levi's desire to return was based on his need for a massage and not on any ulterior sexual motive. "Do you still want to come back?"

"More than anything."

"Can I trust you?"

"Absolutely. I swear I'll be good."

Jaime was fairly sure by now he was going to agree, but it was nice to have Levi on the defensive. "I don't know, Levi. Maybe you should call the lady with the fish in her ad."

"Jaime, wait! *Please* let me come back. I swear not to hit on you ever again."

"I'm not sure I believe you."

"I'll respect your boundaries."

"That'd be nice."

"I'll do everything you say. Even the stretches."

"That'd be a change."

"I'll keep my hands to myself."

"I suppose it's a start."

"I'll let you tie them down."

"I don't think that's legal."

"I'll let you duct-tape my mouth so I can't say a word."

"Now you're just getting kinky."

"I'll…I'll…" Jaime grinned as Levi struggled with something else he could offer. "I'll pay double!"

"Deal," Jaime said.

This was met by a stunned silence, and Jaime fought not to laugh. He could picture Levi on the other end of the line, realizing exactly what he'd just agreed to.

"Really?" Levi asked again. He sounded hopeful, but hesitant. "Ummm…do I have to pay double from here on out? Or only for the next one?"

"I haven't decided," Jaime said.

"I know I offered, but…ummm." He fell silent again for a second. "Wow."

Jaime couldn't hold it in anymore. He laughed out loud.

"You sadistic bastard," Levi said, and there was a note of appreciation in his voice. "You're totally fucking with me, aren't you?"

"You *did* offer."

"Can I really come back?"

Jaime sighed, hoping against hope he was making the right decision. "I still have you in my book for tomorrow anyway."

"Thank you!"

"Consider yourself on probation."

"Understood."

"I'll see you at four."

"I promise you won't regret it."

I hope not. "Good night, Levi."

"Jaime, wait!"

"Yes?" he asked, trying again not to laugh. He definitely knew what was coming this time.

"Do I really have to pay double?"

"I'll decide *that* based on your behavior."

It was all easy enough to say on the phone, but by the next morning, Jaime already regretted his decision. He had several clients before Levi, and as he worked, his anxiety grew. Why had he agreed to let Levi come back?

By the time Levi arrived, Jaime was scared to death. What if Levi had lied? What if it was all a trick to get back in the door? What if Levi really just wanted to torment him more?

He knew he was being irrational. Levi had nothing to gain by doing anything so childish. But as with most things related to his fear, being rational had no effect. The simple truth was, he was afraid to face Levi. He halfway considered not answering the door, even though he knew it was ridiculous. For better or worse, he had agreed to treat Levi again. He couldn't back out now.

He barely looked at Levi as he let him in. He quickly told him to undress and get on the table, and went to wait in the kitchen. His heart raced and his mouth was dry. Dolly, sensing something was wrong, nudged his knee. He crouched down to pet her. She rested her head on his shoulder and sighed as he rubbed under her collar. He found himself relaxing as he scratched her. She always made him feel better. She helped him feel calm. He wished he could take her into the massage room with him.

He stood up to go back in, but stopped short before opening the door. Why couldn't he take her in? It was his house, after all.

"Come on, girl," he said, as he opened the door. "Come meet Levi."

Dolly was thrilled to be let into the forbidden room. She made the rounds, sniffing around the table and thoroughly inspecting Levi's shoes.

"Do you mind if she's here?" Jaime asked. "You're not allergic to dogs, are you?"

"I don't mind." Levi was on his stomach with his head in the face cradle, and he put his hand down to let Dolly sniff him. "What's her name?"

"Dolly."

Levi looked up at him with a smile. "As in Parton?"

"I didn't choose it. They named her at the shelter."

"She's cute."

Somehow, Levi's acceptance of his dog made him feel better about everything. Suddenly, he knew this was going to be fine. "Let's get started, Levi. Why don't we start with three deep breaths?"

"Jaime, wait."

Jaime was surprised to hear Levi sound so unsure.

"I want to apologize—"

"Forget it," Jaime said, and he was even more surprised to realize he meant it. "You're forgiven. Now for once in your life, cooperate, will you? Let's start with three deep breaths."

And Levi obeyed.

CHAPTER 7

Although Levi's first trip back had started out awkwardly, it didn't take them long to get past it. By his second trip back, the tension was gone. Levi was glad the unfortunate incident seemed to be forgotten. They continued to talk through Levi's massages, and Levi was surprised at how he sometimes enjoyed Jaime's company as much as he enjoyed the massage.

Three weeks later was Levi's thirty-first birthday. It fell on a Thursday. He took the night off, not because he had any special plans, but because it seemed pathetic that he had nothing better to do than work. He lay in bed for a while after he woke, debating how to celebrate. Surfing was the obvious answer, but it would only fill his morning. He had a massage with Jaime in the afternoon. And after that? He wasn't sure. He could always do the easy thing and go out and get laid, but he did that so often it didn't feel like anything special. Maybe a movie? Maybe he'd rent something and sit at home. Not exactly an exciting birthday.

His phone rang, interrupting his thoughts. It was his landline, which meant dragging himself out of bed to get it. And, of course, it was his mother. He debated not answering, but a twinge of guilt changed his mind.

"Hello?"

"Happy birthday, honey! How does it feel to be thirty-one?"

"About the same as it felt being thirty."

"What are you doing today? Any plans?"

"I'll probably go surfing. After that, I don't know."

"Do you work tonight?"

"I took it off."

"From the club?"

Levi bit back a groan. Less than a minute on the phone and the lecture was starting already. "Yes, from the club."

"Honey, when are you going to find a different job? A *real* job?"

"Don't start."

"Oh, honey! I hate to see you wasting your life there—"

"Don't start, Mom!"

"I just want you to be happy."

Yes, as long as he was happy on their terms and not his own. Levi bit his tongue and refrained from answering. His apparent yielding of the field on the matter caused her to try a new approach.

"Do you remember Jody Carlton? She was in our ward."

"Of course." Not only had Levi gone to the same church as Jody, they'd also attended the same high school. "She graduated a year behind me."

"I spoke to her mother the other day. It turns out Jody lives in Tampa now." She paused for effect, and Levi braced himself for what he knew was coming. "She's divorced, you know."

"I doubt she'd appreciate being set up with a gay man whose main memory of her was the day she got her period during PE while wearing white shorts."

"Levi! That must've been mortifying for her!"

"I'm sure it was. All the more reason I'm sure she'd rather not see me again."

"Honey, just call her, won't you? You could meet her for dinner—"

"And then what, Mom? Date her, even though she'd be nothing more than a friend? Marry her, whether I love her or not? Spend the rest of my life telling her I can't fuck her because I have a headache, which will last until the day I die?" He regretted it as soon as he'd said it, but there was no way to un-say the word now.

"*Levi!* I don't appreciate the vulgarity."

"I'm sorry." He took a deep breath and attempted to calm himself down. "I'm sorry I said that."

"How about if I give you her number?"

He had to end this now, before it got any worse. "'Bye, Mom. Thanks for calling," he said, fighting to keep the edge in his voice so he would sound angry instead of depressed. "Nice talking to you."

"Levi, wait!"

He debated pretending he hadn't heard her and hanging up anyway. But he debated a second too long.

"Levi, are you still there?"

"I'm here."

"Will you come for your father's birthday?"

"I don't know. I don't think it's a good idea."

"It would mean so much to him."

"You say that now, but by the time it's over, we'll both wish I hadn't come."

"That's not true. We love you, Levi. We want you to come home and be part of our family again."

I want that, too. But it was never going to happen.

"What can I do to convince you?"

"Promise me there'll be no lectures. No blessings. No prayers. No discussions of—"

"I can't promise any of those things, and you know it. I could promise for myself, but I can't speak for your father or your brothers."

"Then I'm not coming."

"Oh, Levi." She was crying now, and he felt guilty, despite himself. "We miss you so much."

Did she think he didn't miss it, too? Did she think he wouldn't have given anything to go back to those years when his family had felt like home, before they started to look at him with pity and disgust? He fought the lump the formed in his own throat. "The Levi you miss doesn't exist. And neither does the home he came from."

The phone call had been a depressingly horrible start to his day. Several hours of surfing had driven away the worst of the depression, but left him feeling empty and tired. As he showered that afternoon, he realized how glad he was to be going to Jaime's. This was his birthday, after all, and he was determined to enjoy the rest of it. A massage was exactly what he needed. He left his melancholy on the sun-soaked step of Jaime's door. Just stepping into the dim back room of Jaime's house made him feel better. The spicy oils he used lingered in the air and soft music played. Dolly came to greet him, despite Jaime's good-natured scolding. And Jaime's bright smile eased something deep inside his heart.

Jaime started the massage the way he often did, by putting his hands under the back of Levi's neck and pulling gently, and Levi couldn't help but laugh. "I think one of these days my head's going to pop off while you're doing that."

"I hope not," Jaime said. "It's such a pain in the ass when that happens. I'm running out of places to hide the bodies."

It was easy to forget Jaime really did have a slightly dark sense of humor under his Boy Scout facade, and it made Levi laugh again. "Exactly how many times has it happened?"

"I've lost count to tell you the truth. But you'll notice my garden gets a little bigger every year."

"That's not funny."

"No, it's not. On the bright side, my tomatoes love it. My neighbor keeps asking for my secret."

Levi twisted his head back so he could up look up into Jaime's laughing blue eyes. "You really are sort of twisted and sadistic, aren't you?"

Jaime smiled, but didn't say a word.

"Can I ask you a question?"

"You asking that instead of simply asking the question makes me inclined to say no."

"Why do you hate to be touched so much?" He had his suspicions, but he wondered what Jaime would say.

Jaime didn't meet his eyes, but Levi could see the wariness in them. "I don't want to talk about it."

"Okay," Levi said, feeling that was an answer in and of itself. "I'm not trying to be an asshole. I'm just wondering why you picked massage therapy as a career. It seems pretty counterintuitive to me."

Jaime hesitated for a moment, and Levi thought he was going to dodge the question, but he sighed and said, "I'd probably be a hermit, if I allowed it. I'd sit in my house and do some kind of job on the computer and I'd never talk to anybody at all. But I know it wouldn't be healthy."

"So you picked a career that would force you to deal with people?"

"Exactly."

"But you could have worked at the DMV, if that was all you wanted. Why something involving physical contact?"

"It's not really like that," Jaime said. "I'm not touching people. I'm just seeing flesh and muscle and bone. The body's like a machine and sometimes it's broken. And sometimes, I can fix it. That's all."

It was a sad statement. Jaime's job was the only thing allowing him contact with people, and even then, he kept himself at a distance. Suddenly Levi knew exactly what he wanted to do. "Do you have any more clients after me?"

"No, you're the last one of the day. Why?"

"You want to go out?"

Jaime shook his head. "Levi," he scolded, "you've been so good lately. Don't fall off the wagon now."

"I don't mean a *date.* I just mean, you know, two guys hanging out."

Jaime moved around to his left side and started massaging his arm. He looked skeptical. "Why?"

"Because it's my birthday."

"It is not."

"It is. You can check my license."

Jaime moved down to his hand, rubbing the area between his fingers and then working his way down each one. It was one of Levi's favorite parts of the whole massage, and he would have closed his eyes if he hadn't been waiting for Jaime's answer. Jaime's gaze was intent on his work. "It's Thursday. Don't you have to work tonight anyway?"

"I took the night off."

"Why?"

"Because *it's my birthday.*"

Jaime looked amused, but shook his head. "I don't know."

"Fine," Levi said with exaggerated disappointment. "I'll got out for dinner alone. All by myself. Maybe if I tell the waitress it's my birthday she'll take pity on me and let me drink for free. Alone. On my *birthday.*"

Jaime dropped his hand and rolled his eyes as he moved around to the other side. "You're going to guilt me into going with you?"

"Will it work?"

Jaime didn't look at him, but he smiled a bit. "It might."

CHAPTER 8

They took Jaime's car because the horror on his face when he saw Levi's motorcycle was unmistakable. Levi directed him to a local sports bar. He was surprised at how tense Jaime was. His eyes darted nervously around the restaurant and he fidgeted in his seat like a kid.

"Are you worried about being seen with me?" Levi asked.

Jaime looked at him surprise. "What do you mean?"

"Are you in the closet?"

"No, not really."

"Then why are you so nervous?"

Jaime's cheeks started to turn red. "I don't get out much."

It didn't seem like much of an answer, but the conversation was interrupted by the arrival of their waitress. "Can I get you something to drink while you look over the menu?"

"We're ready to order," Levi told her. "We'd like two dozen buffalo wings and an order of onion rings. And some chicken nachos." He looked over at Jaime. "Anything else?"

"A salad with ranch dressing."

"Are you serious?"

"Yeah. Why not?"

Levi managed to avoid rolling his eyes. "What do you want to drink?"

"A Sprite."

Levi turned to the waitress and said, "Two Absoluts on the rocks, with lime."

Jaime didn't contradict him, but once the waitress was gone, he said quietly, "I don't drink."

"You don't drink, as in you're a recovering alcoholic, or you're morally opposed to it?" Levi asked. "Or you don't drink meaning you don't do it often?"

"The latter."

"Good. Then tonight you can make an exception."

Jaime didn't look very confident about it, but he sighed. "I guess one can't hurt."

"Exactly."

It wasn't until the waitress brought the drink and Jaime took a giant swig of it that Levi realized Absolut straight probably wasn't the best drink for him. He seemed to be having a hard time swallowing. Levi half expected him to spit it back out, but he finally choked it down. His cheeks were red, his eyes were watering, and he started to cough.

"You better bring him something with training wheels," Levi said to the waitress, as he took the drink from Jaime.

The waitress returned a few minutes later with a giant piña colada. Jaime took a sip and his eyes went wide. "This is good."

"Be careful," Levi said as Jaime took another drink. "It has rum in it. That shit's evil."

But Jaime didn't heed his warning. He'd had two of them by the time they finished their food, and he was significantly more relaxed. "Now what?" he asked Levi.

"How about a movie?"

"Sure."

"What kind of movies do you like?" Levi fully expected Jaime to go for some type of sentimental girly movie, but Jaime surprised him.

"Nothing heavy," he said. "Nothing sappy or sad."

"A comedy then, or an action flick?"

"Something with explosions!"

Levi couldn't help but smile at his enthusiasm. "You got it."

The movie theatre was in the same shopping center as the restaurant, so they walked. There was a liquor store in between, and Levi ran in and bought a couple of airline bottles, which he emptied into their fountain drinks once they were seated in the theatre. Jaime was giggling like a kid at the previews.

"I think you're drunk," Levi said.

Jaime shook his head. "No. I don't drink." It was the kind of logic only a drunk person could subscribe to, but it was good to see him relaxing and having fun. He drank his spiked soda, and as the movie wound down, he went from giggling to sitting quietly with his head back and his eyes closed.

"You okay?" Levi asked.

"Mm-hmm," Jaime said, without opening his eyes.

"You're not gonna be sick are you?"

"Should I be?"

"No."

"Good. I want French fries."

Levi laughed. "We'll hit McDonald's on the way home. You one of those people who has to sit through the credits?"

"Yeah," Jaime said. "Except I want French fries."

"Come on, then," Levi said, nudging him with his elbow. "Let's go. Give me your keys."

"I can drive," Jaime said. "I'm not drunk." Then he stood up. He swayed on his feet and sat back down quickly. He looked up at Levi in surprise. "I think I'm drunk."

"No kidding," Levi said, holding his hand out. "Keys."

It was harder than he expected to get Jaime back to the car. He seemed to think it was a good night for wandering through the parking lot. Two different times, Levi thought Jaime was behind him, only to turn around and find him gone. After that, he made sure Jaime was ahead of him. It would have been easier to direct him to the car if he wasn't so adamant about not being touched, or if he showed any propensity for going where he was told.

"Do you want French fries or not?" Levi finally asked in exasperation.

"No. I want one of those chocolate things from Wendy's."

"Either way, we need to get in the damn car."

In the end, they got both fries and smoothies, and ate them on the way back to Levi's. Levi half expected to have to argue with him about going to his apartment, but Jaime followed him in without protest and flopped down on the couch. He picked up Levi's remote. "You have the same satellite service as me," he commented as he punched in a number. The TV changed to the Syfy channel, where a group of teenagers were about to be eaten by a giant crocodile. "Ooh," he said with satisfaction. "This is a good one."

"You watch this shit?" Levi asked.

"I love crappy monster movies. Syfy's are the best."

"But they're so…" The only word he could come up with was "bad" and that didn't seem nearly strong enough.

Jaime turned to him with a smile. "So stupid they're funny?"

"You say that like it's a good thing."

"You probably don't like pro-wrestling either, do you?"

"Definitely not."

Jaime laughed and turned back to the TV. "I'm ordering the next pay-per-view. I'll convert you."

Pro-wrestling and campy made-for-TV movies weren't the way Levi had pictured Jaime spending his free time. He shook his head in amusement as he went into the kitchen to get a beer. He debated grabbing one for Jaime too, but decided he'd had enough to drink. He took him a glass of water instead. Jaime was laughing as one of the teenagers died an over-acted and under-budget death.

"Here," Levi said, handing the water to Jaime as he sat down on the opposite end of the couch. "Drink this."

"Am I going to feel like shit in the morning?" Jaime asked.

"It's quite possible, but the water will help."

Jaime dutifully started chugging the glass of water.

"You've never been drunk before?"

"Never."

"That's pretty remarkable," Levi said. "My parents would be proud of you."

Jaime put his glass down on the end table. He leaned back on the couch and sighed. "There's a lot of things I've never done."

"Like what?"

"Never been drunk. Never been high. Never been in a relationship."

"And you've never been surfing."

"Right."

"But you want to?"

Jaime shrugged. "It looks like fun."

"So why haven't you ever tried it?"

"I guess…" He seemed to debate what to say as he watched a bikini-clad girl make her escape from a toothy death. "I guess because I'm scared."

"Of getting hurt?"

"No." He shook his head. "Not that."

"Then what?"

Jaime sighed. He leaned his head back on the couch and closed his eyes. "God, Levi, you have no idea what it's like, do you? You have no idea what it's like to have fear rule your life."

Fear? Of *surfing*? "I guess not."

"It's…" Jaime floundered, struggling for a word, and finally chose, "Exhausting."

"What are you afraid of?"

"Everything."

It seemed like such a melodramatic thing to say. As overly dramatic as the lousy movie on TV. And yet, there was no mistaking the defeat Levi heard in his voice. "Are you afraid now?"

"Yes."

Levi was surprised at how sad he felt hearing it. "You're afraid of me?"

"Yes," Jaime said. "And no. I'm afraid of being here. Of talking to you. Of trying to have a friend. Of being alone. I'm afraid all the time. Every single day. It never goes away. I'm afraid when I go to sleep at night. I'm afraid when I wake up in the morning and I have to face another day. I'm afraid every time I leave my house. I'm afraid of people. I can't look at them. I can't let them touch me. I'm afraid they'll look at me, and they'll know."

"Know what?"

"That I'm damaged."

"What do you mean? You're not damaged. You're smart, and you have a great job—"

"It's all lies, Levi. It's all pretend. They'll look at me and know. They'll know I'm afraid. They'll know I'm weak." He stopped talking and shook his head. "*You'll* know I'm weak."

"Jaime—"

"And I can't let people know, because once they do, they can do anything. Once people know you're weak, there's nothing to stop them from hurting you." He looked over at Levi, and the pain in his eyes was evident. "I won't be able to stop them."

"Then I'll stop them for you," Levi said. He didn't examine why he felt the need to protect Jaime. He only knew if Jaime was scared, it was his job to fix it. He watched as his words sank in. He knew Jaime *wanted* to believe, but he didn't. He saw the doubt in his eyes.

Jaime turned away from him and looked around the room, as if surprised to find himself there. His eyes went wide. "I can't be here," he said, and tried to stand up.

"You're too drunk to drive."

"I have to go home." He swayed alarmingly, and Levi jumped up from the couch and caught him as he fell. "Please don't touch me," Jaime said, although there was no force behind it.

"I think you're going to need to relax your rule this one time." He put one arm around Jaime's shoulders and the other behind his knees and picked him up like a child. He was so light.

"I don't drink," Jaime said as Levi carried him toward the hall.

"No kidding."

"Please put me down. I don't want you to touch me."

"Come on, kid. I'm asking you to trust me."

"I'm not a kid, you know. I'm only four years younger than you."

That surprised Levi. He had assumed Jaime was younger. He *seemed* so much younger. "Today's my birthday," he said. "So you're five years younger now." Levi reached the door to his room and maneuvered them through it, but when Jaime saw the bed, he panicked.

"*No!* No, no, no!" He was suddenly struggling to break free, and it was all Levi could do to get him to the bed before he dropped him. Jaime scrambled backward on the bed until he was against the wall, his eyes wide with fear.

Levi backed up too, holding up his hands. "I'm not going to touch you, okay? I'll sleep on the couch."

Jaime looked skeptical. And yet, there was a hint of hope in his eyes as well. He wanted to believe. He just didn't know how.

"I won't hurt you," Levi said. "I promise. You can even lock the bedroom door if you want." God knew he'd never had a man in his bed begging him *not* to touch him. It annoyed him just a little, but it also made him sad.

His comment about the door seemed to penetrate the haze of alcohol clouding Jaime's brain. And the fear. He saw Jaime start to relax a bit. "Okay," Jaime said with obvious reluctance.

"I'm going to go out of the room while you get undressed and get under the blanket, then I'll be back." It was funny to be saying those words to Jaime. It was usually the other way around.

He left the room, closing the door behind him. He hoped Jaime wouldn't fight him anymore. He certainly wasn't in any state to drive himself home. He went to the kitchen and refilled Jaime's glass of water and stopped in the bathroom to raid the medicine cabinet. When he got to the bedroom, he knocked softly and got no response. For a moment, he worried Jaime had somehow slipped past him and left the apartment, but when he opened the door, he saw he'd done what Levi said. His clothes were folded in a neat pile on the chair, and he was in the bed with the covers pulled up to his chin.

Levi put the glass of water and the things from the bathroom on the bedside table. "I brought you water, some ibuprofen, and an Alka-Seltzer."

"I don't want them."

"You will in the morning."

"Levi," Jaime said. His voice was soft, and Levi could tell he was already half asleep. His eyes had already drifted closed. "You can't protect me."

Levi resisted the urge to reach out and touch those soft strawberry-blonde curls. He didn't answer, but what he thought was, *Just watch me.* "Goodnight, kid." He started to leave, but turned in the door. "Do you want me to lock it?"

It took Jaime a moment to answer. "No," he said at last, sounding as if his own answer confused him.

"Okay. If you're gonna be sick, try to make it to the bathroom, okay?"

"Yeah." Jaime sighed, his eyes still closed. "I think I like your bed."

The feelings those words stirred in Levi were unlike anything he'd ever felt. Arousal, yes. And curiosity. He wanted to know what it would feel like to be in under the covers with Jaime. To feel his thin body curled up against him. But there was also a fondness—a protectiveness and a gentleness—that was new.

"I just wish…" Jaime started, but then let his words trail away.

Levi half hoped Jaime would say he wished he would sleep in the bed with him, but he knew it was unlikely. "You wish what?" he asked quietly.

"Levi," Jaime said, "I wish you didn't smell so damn good."

CHAPTER 9

There were no bad dreams that night. Although Jaime's dreams were jumpy and frantic and confusing, at least there was nobody trying to hurt him. Somehow, he felt…not *safe*. That wasn't quite it. He barely even knew what the word meant. But he was a little less scared. For once.

He woke at two in the morning and managed to make it into the bathroom before being violently ill. The next two-and-a-half hours were spent sitting on the bathroom floor with his head on the toilet seat, swearing to God and the universe and whoever else might be listening that he would never drink again. Finally, with an empty stomach and a head that pounded with every heartbeat, he went back to bed. He saw the water, Alka-Seltzer, and ibuprofen Levi had brought to him. He'd completely forgotten about them. He took them all, then settled back into bed.

Levi's bed.

It was a queen-size bed, the same size he had at home, but it was taller, and somehow, deeper. It must have had one of those pillow-tops because Jaime felt like he could sink into it forever. The sheets were worn and soft and comfortable, the pillows were fluffy, and the comforter was thick and heavy. And everything—*everything* about it—smelled like Levi.

It made him feel at ease, more than he had for a long time. He felt he might be able to take Levi's strength, his bearing and his confidence, and wrap them around himself like a shield. He could hide in them forever. Nobody would ever know he was there at all.

He fell into a deep, dreamless slumber.

When he woke again, he was pleased to find he felt almost human. He was afraid to open his eyes, in case the light caused his head to pound again, but he stretched. He loved Levi's bed. He had never imagined he might feel at ease in another man's bed, but he did. It was more than just being comfortable. Somehow, it soothed him. Of course, it didn't hurt that it smelled so damn good. He wanted to roll over and bury himself down into it again. He almost wanted to strip off his boxers and push his naked groin into Levi's soft mattress. He thought about how good it would feel. Somehow the idea of letting Levi's scent touch him there was unbelievably arousing. It would allow him to have a bit of Levi, without ever having to let Levi touch him. Without ever letting Levi hurt him.

"Hey, kid," Levi's sultry voice cut into his thoughts. "Hope I didn't wake you."

Jaime risked opening his eyes. Levi was standing at his closet wearing only a pair of shorts while looking for a shirt. His over-grown hair was wet from the shower and sticking to the back of his tan neck. He looked absolutely amazing.

"How do you feel?" Levi asked.

"Not bad. What time is it?"

"Almost eight. Your first client is at nine-thirty?"

"Yes. I need to get home."

"Come on. I'll drive you."

"You don't have to do that."

Levi smiled at him. "I do, actually. My bike's at your house."

He waited until Levi left the room before he got out of bed and got dressed. Then he followed Levi out of his apartment and into Jaime's car. He wasn't even surprised when Levi got in the driver's seat. It was strange, riding in the passenger seat of his own car. He'd never done that before. Except last night.

Last night!

For the first time, he thought about the night before.

He didn't remember much. He remembered dinner and about half of the movie. After that, there were only random, disconnected images. He remembered Levi taking his keys. He remembered the drive-through at Wendy's. He remembered talking on the couch. He remembered Levi carrying him into the bedroom. The memory made his heart race with panic, but then he remembered very clearly Levi saying, "I won't hurt you." And he remembered cuddling down into Levi's fabulous bed.

"What happened last night?" he asked.

Levi laughed. "You don't remember?"

"Not much. I don't usually drink."

"I can tell."

"We were on your couch?"

"For a while, yeah. We were talking. Then you decided you needed to go home, but you were way too drunk to drive, so I put you to bed."

"Did I say anything really stupid?"

To his surprise, Levi blushed. "No," he said, and it didn't sound like a lie. "You're a pretty mellow drunk."

They reached his house and got out of the car. Jaime held his hand out to Levi for his keys, but Levi didn't hand them over. Instead, he stood looking at Jaime as if debating something.

"Do you work tomorrow?" Levi finally asked.

The question surprised him. "No. I don't see clients on Saturdays."

"You have any plans?"

"No." Jaime never had plans. "Why?"

Levi smiled at him. "Perfect," he said as he placed Jaime's keys in his hand. "I'll pick you up at ten. Wear your swimsuit."

"We're going swimming?" Jaime asked in surprise.

"No." Levi smiled. "We're going surfing."

Jaime was both elated and terrified at the idea of learning to surf. He felt as if he barely paid attention to his clients all day. All he could think about was being in the water the next day.

With Levi.

He wasn't sure what had prompted Levi to offer to teach him, but he wasn't complaining. He'd wished many times he knew how, but he'd never taken lessons because he was afraid there would be physical contact involved. He also wasn't sure where to go to avoid running into some type of surfer gang. He'd seen the original version of *Point Break* and while he suspected it was nothing but Hollywood bullshit, he didn't exactly want to find out the hard way he was wrong.

Levi picked him up right on time and drove them to the beach. "The waves are kind of small here," Levi told him as he parked. "Which is good for us since you're just learning, and it means there won't be any knuckleheads in our way."

They carried the boards out onto the beach, and Levi laid them both on the sand. "We won't get in the water yet. First, you're going to lie down on the board and practice jumping up."

Jaime felt a little ridiculous, but he didn't argue. He lay on his stomach on the board, then jumped to his feet.

"You have to go faster than that."

Jaime tried again.

"You have your left foot back. Try jumping up with your right foot back."

Jaime did, but found it more awkward. "Will my weight be on my back or front foot?"

"Slightly more on the back foot, but not too much. Maybe sixty-forty. Try again."

Jaime did, but it still felt awkward.

"You're pushing on the board under your chest like a push-up. Some people think that's awkward. You can try using the rails instead."

Jaime looked down at the flat board in confusion. "What rails?"

"The sides of the board."

Using the rails did make it a little easier, and a couple of tries later, he felt like he'd managed to stand up faster than before.

"You're left foot is back again," Levi said in amusement.

"Is that wrong?"

"Not necessarily." He shook his head. "Leave it to you to be a goofy-foot. Are you left-handed?"

"Yes."

"Not all southpaws put their left foot back, but some do. Go ahead and try again."

"With my left foot back or my right?"

"Whichever feels best."

It definitely felt more natural with his left foot back, and after a few more tries, Levi declared Jaime ready to try it in the water. He grabbed his own board and led Jaime out into the surf. The beach had a slow slope, and they paddled out to the point where most of the waves were crashing.

"We'll start on the whitewater first," Levi told him. "It's easier than the swells. The trick is to be in the wave right as it breaks. You'll paddle, but as soon as you feel the water grab you, stop paddling and jump up. Let the force of the water do the work."

Of course, the first few tries were miserable failures. He could feel what Levi was telling him about the water. He knew when to paddle and when to stand. The problem was staying on his feet. The first couple of times, he came up too close to one side of the board or the other. Even once he got his balance centered between the rails, he kept tipping forward into the water.

"It seems like you want to put more of your weight on your front foot," Levi said after his fourth face-first fall into the surf.

"Is that wrong?"

"Not necessarily, but you'll have to compensate for it by moving back on the board a bit."

Jaime was sitting astride his board and he scooted backward a couple of inches, while Levi scanned the waves behind him. "There's one coming now. You ready?"

"Of course not." Although Jaime couldn't keep himself from smiling like a fool as he moved to his stomach on the board.

"Here it comes," Levi said. "Paddle, paddle, paddle!"

If Levi said anything else after that, Jaime couldn't hear him. He was already paddling toward the shore. The sun beat down on his back and his eyes burned from the salt water. He felt the board lift a little and then cool water splashed over his legs as the wave broke. The force of the white water caught his board, pushing it on. Jaime quit paddling. He grabbed the rails and jumped to his feet, a bit farther back than he'd been before. He wobbled a little, but found his balance. And then…

He was surfing!

It wasn't graceful, and he thought he probably looked more awkward on his board than anything, but it felt great. He could hear Levi whooping in triumph behind him. He made it halfway to shore feeling triumphant before the force of the wave died away and his momentum slowed.

Dismounting was even less graceful than the ride had been. He tried simply stepping off the board, which threw his balance off and he landed on his back in the shallow water. Before he could get up, Levi was there. He grabbed Jaime's arms and pulled him to his feet, laughing and pounding him on the back.

"Did you see that?" Jaime asked. "I did it!"

"You did."

"Oh my God, that was great! I want to do it again!" He looked around for his board and realized it had washed farther into shore, along with Levi's.

"You're a natural," Levi said, although he only sounded half-serious.

"Yeah, right." Jaime laughed, turning to look back at him.

Levi was smiling at him. His wet hair was pushed backward off his tan face. His eyes were happy and bright. He was so at ease and so unbelievably gorgeous, Jaime found himself staring. Of course, Levi always looked great, but there was something about seeing him here, in his element, that was different. He seemed so much more real. So much happier.

Levi's hand moved on his arm, and Jaime looked down in surprise at where Levi was still hanging onto him after pulling him out of the surf. He hadn't quite realized how close he'd let Levi get, and it troubled him. He pulled away instinctively, and Levi let him go.

"Come on," Levi said, as he headed toward their boards, which were now stranded on shore. "A few more like that and we can try some real waves."

They surfed all day. They stopped once long enough to walk up the shore to a beachside restaurant where Levi ordered Coronas and the Captain's Special, which turned out to be a basket full of unidentifiable deep-fried objects, and then it was back into the water. Levi led him farther out this time and tried to show him how to ride down the face of the wave as it was cresting, before it crashed. It was harder, but Jaime thought he'd be able to do it, with a bit more practice.

By the time Levi dropped him off in front of his house, he was exhausted and extremely sunburned.

"Thanks for taking me," he said to Levi.

"You're welcome."

"I'll see you Monday for your massage?"

"I'll be there."

Jaime closed the door to the truck and was turning toward his house when Levi called out, "Hey, Jaime?"

"Yeah?" he asked, turning back to peer through the open truck window at Levi.

"You want to go again tomorrow?"

Jaime couldn't stop a giant smile from spreading across his face, even though he knew he probably looked like a fool. "I'd love to."

"Good," Levi said. "I'll pick you up at ten."

CHAPTER 10

A weekend of surfing with Jaime erased Levi's argument with his mother from his mind, but only until the following Monday when Ruth called again.

"Are you trying to break Mom's heart, Leviticus?" she demanded. "Are you *trying* to be a selfish jerk?"

"She started it." Levi knew as soon as he said it how childish he sounded.

Ruth's silence was thick with sullen disapproval. It seemed to stretch on and on. He could picture her on the other end of the line, her jaw clenched and her fist on her hip. He could see her sorting through her ammunition as she seethed. As he waited for her to choose her line of attack, he felt himself shrinking, becoming as low and horrific as a rat in a five-star restaurant.

"Leviticus," she finally said, her voice low and tight with anger, "Dad will only turn sixty once. We have no way of knowing how much longer we'll have with him with us."

"Ruth, give me a break—"

But she kept speaking, ignoring his interruption. "If we're lucky, he'll be around another twenty or thirty years, Levi. If we're lucky. But *his* father died at the age of sixty-five. And his brother died at sixty-six."

Levi closed his eyes and tried to blot out the image of himself at his father's funeral. It couldn't happen so soon. His father was a giant. A force of nature. He was invincible. It *couldn't* happen. Not yet.

Except of course, it could.

But it didn't change the fact he'd be walking into the proverbial lion's den.

"Goddamn it, Ruth. You don't know what you're asking."

"You don't think so?" she asked, her voice like ice. "Well, you're wrong. Get over yourself! So you put up with them praying over you. You put up with them lecturing you. For three days, Levi. *Three days.* Then you can go back to whatever you think you have in Miami that's more important than your own father."

"Shit!" He put his head down on the table, wishing this wasn't his life. "Shit, shit, shit!"

His sister recognized his outburst for what it was—he was giving in. "Three days, Levi," she said again, her voice softer now. "That's all I'm asking."

He sighed. Three days. Three days of being the sinner in a family of *saints.* "Fine," he relented. "I'll be there."

He only had a few minutes before he was due at Jaime's for a massage. Levi called the club and requested Labor Day weekend off as soon as he hung up the phone so he wouldn't have time to change his mind. Then he had to race to get Jaime's on time.

Jaime had him start facedown, but even as the massage began, Levi couldn't stop worrying about his upcoming trip. The idea of seeing his family again filled him with equal parts happiness and dread. He hoped things would be different this time, but deep down, he knew it was a groundless hope that would only leave him angry and disappointed. Again. He regretted giving in to Ruth. And Ruth had undoubtedly already called to inform his mother. Was there any way to get out of it now?

"You're quiet today," Jaime said. "Is something wrong?"

"No." *Yes.*

Were all family relations this hard? If he were straight, would they just find something else to fight over? Did Jaime have this kind of trouble with his family? Of course, Jaime never talked about his family at all.

It seemed strange. Over the weeks, Jaime had learned a great deal about Levi, but Levi still knew next to nothing about Jaime. The only thing Levi remembered had occurred during Levi's second massage. Levi had said his relationship with his family was complicated, and Jaime had said, "It always is when it comes to family."

"Where are you from?" Levi asked. He was still on his stomach, so he couldn't see Jaime's face.

"Cleveland."

"Yuck," Levi said. "No wonder you left."

There was a tense pause, then Jaime said, "Yeah."

"When did you move here?"

That same awkward pause, which meant Jaime wasn't comfortable with the question. "Right after high school."

"You came here to go to school?"

"Take a deep breath, Levi. Let's work out some of this tension in your lumbar."

He suspected Jaime was simply evading his question, so instead of doing what Jaime said, he asked another question. "Do you have any family here?"

"No. Take a deep breath."

"Brothers or sisters?"

Jaime sighed in frustration. "I'm an only child. Take a deep breath!"

"Are you close to your parents? Do you—"

Jaime suddenly pushed hard on his lower back, and as so often happened, Levi hadn't realized how sore it was until Jaime's strong hands started kneading on it.

"Ow! You don't have to hurt me."

"Would you like to cooperate now?"

"Jesus Christ," Levi grumbled. "Fucking sadist." But he took a deep breath, and they spent the next several minutes working through a series of movements that hurt like hell, but left his back feeling an inch longer on the left side than it had before.

Afterward, Jaime had him turn onto his back. He began massaging Levi's arm.

"Are you out with your family?" Levi asked. He'd asked Jaime once before, but Jaime had evaded the question. He wondered if he'd do the same now.

"Why are you suddenly asking about my family?"

"Because you never talk about them."

"What makes you think I want to start now?"

"I'm just making conversation, that's all. Forget I asked." He knew he sounded bitter as he said it, but he couldn't help it. In truth, he was smarting a bit from Jaime's unwillingness to share anything of himself. He thought they were becoming friends, but now he felt as if their friendship was terribly one-sided.

Jaime eyed him, and Levi could sense him weighing his reluctance to discuss his past against his desire to make peace. "I don't have a father," he said at last, not meeting Levi's eyes. "And I haven't spoken to my mother, or anybody else in my family, since I left Cleveland. You asked if I'm out with them and the truth is, I don't know. I never attempted to hide anything from them, but I never really shared anything with them either. So whatever they know or whatever they may have guessed..." He shrugged, but the obvious pain in his eyes belied the casual gesture. "It doesn't matter."

The confession had obviously cost him a great deal, and Levi said, "I'm sorry. I didn't mean to be an asshole."

Jaime smiled at him, a perfect Boy Scout smile. "I know."

"Your mother hasn't tried to contact you?"

"Not for several years, no."

"Sometimes I wish my family would forget about me, too. Sometimes I think it'd be easier than fighting the same battle over and over again."

"Is that what this is about? Did something happen with your family?"

"My dad's birthday is Labor Day weekend, and they're having a big party for him."

"And you're going?" Jaime asked in surprise.

"I guess."

"I bet you'll have fun."

"Not likely."

"Remind me before you leave so I can take you off my schedule for the days you're gone." He shook his head. "I'm not going to have many clients that week. It seems like everybody's leaving town."

"That's it," Levi said, sitting up on the table. His movement was so sudden, Jaime backed away from him in alarm. "You should come with me!"

Jaime blinked at him in surprise. "Are you serious?"

Was he? He hadn't actually thought it through before blurting out his invitation, but as he thought about it, he realized he really did want Jaime to come. It was nearly a twelve-hour drive from Miami to Georgetown, and it'd be nice to have company and to have somebody to split the driving time with. And at his parents' house, it'd be comforting knowing there was *somebody* there who was on his side. Not that the inevitable argument would take place in front of Jaime, or that he would expect Jaime to jump in, but knowing he had an ally *somewhere* nearby would help somehow.

Jaime was still looking at him expectantly. "I *am* serious," Levi said. "Would you like to come?"

"Will they approve?"

"If we were lovers, no, they wouldn't approve. But we're friends, so yeah, I think they'll be fine with it. They'll be happy to have you."

"And Dolly, too?"

Levi laughed. He wasn't sure how his parents would feel about a dog, but his nieces and nephews would probably love it. "Sure," he said. "Dolly, too."

It took him several days to scrape together enough courage to call his mom. Although he still felt awkward about the way their previous conversation had ended, his mother acted as if nothing had ever happened.

"Hi, honey! I'm so happy you called. Did you have a good weekend?"

"I did." And it was the truth. Teaching Jaime to surf had been the most fun he'd had in a long time.

"Ruth says you decided to come for your father's birthday. Honey, I'm so happy you changed your mind."

"That's what I'm calling to talk to you about, Mom."

"You're *not* coming." It wasn't even a question, and it was a testament to their relationship over the last few years that she would assume he was calling to cancel.

"I am coming, but not alone. I'd like to bring a friend."

"Who?"

"His name is Jaime."

There was a tense pause, then his mother said cautiously, "What kind of friend is this, Levi?"

"He's not my boyfriend. He's my massage therapist, actually. And he's *just* a friend, I promise."

"You want to bring your massage therapist to your father's birthday?" She was teasing now. Whatever reservations she'd had were gone now she knew Jaime wasn't his lover.

"He doesn't have any family, and I feel bad leaving him to spend the holiday alone."

"Of course he's welcome here. We have plenty of room."

"Plenty of room" was a bit relative when you were dealing with six kids, their spouses, and nineteen of their children, but it was certainly true one more wasn't going to make much difference. "We have to bring his dog, too. I hope that's okay."

"As long as it's friendly."

"Dolly's sweet. And Jaime's a total Boy Scout. You'll love him. But don't try to hug him or anything, okay? He's got kind of a phobia about being touched."

"Is he afraid of germs?"

"No, it's not that." He wondered how much he should say to his mother. In the end, he decided to simply tell her the truth. "All I know is, he left home when he turned eighteen and he hasn't spoken to his family since. He will *not* talk about his past. And he freaks out a bit if people get too close. Anything else I could say would be pure speculation."

His mother absorbed that for a second before saying, "I understand, Levi." And she did. He could tell by the gentle compassion in her voice. "We'd be happy to have him."

CHAPTER 11

Jaime felt as if he was living somebody else's life. Getting drunk with Levi, then learning to surf, and now heading away for a weekend with Levi's family. It seemed a bit surreal.

It didn't take much discussion to conclude they should take Jaime's car to South Carolina. Levi had only his motorcycle and the beat-up old truck he used for surfing. Jaime's Escort would be far more comfortable.

Most of Levi's family would be arriving on Thursday. Although none of his siblings lived in Georgetown, they were all relatively close. The drive from Miami would take close to twelve hours. They debated leaving on Wednesday evening and stopping in Jacksonville for the night, but in the end they decided to leave early Thursday morning and drive straight through. At five A.M., they packed their bags in the trunk, settled Dolly into the back seat and left Miami. Jaime drove, and Levi promptly reclined his seat and went back to sleep.

Jaime had been thinking all morning about Levi's invitation, and once Levi was awake again, he said to him, "It occurred to me that you're bringing me along as some kind of buffer between you and your family."

Levi thought for a minute before he answered. "When you say it that way, it makes me feel like an asshole."

Jaime laughed. "Don't worry about it. I understand."

"Good," Levi said, "because I'm not sure I do. Putting you between me and my perfect fucking family seems kind of selfish."

"Levi, I wasn't trying to make you feel guilty. I'm glad you invited me."

Levi gave him a killer smile, the kind he normally reserved for surfing. Or maybe for the men at the club. "I'm glad you said yes."

"Are they going to try to convert me?"

Levi laughed. "Not unless you ask them to. They're pretty good about the whole 'live and let live' thing, at least when it comes to non-family members."

"Should I lie about being gay?"

"You don't need to. They won't lecture *you*."

"Why not? It's a sin, right?"

"It is. But you have the right to make your own choices."

"So they think being gay is a choice?"

"No, that's not what I meant. They believe there may or may not be genetic or environmental factors that make us gay. But according to them, that's not the point."

"So maybe God made us gay, but it's still a sin?"

"Right. Just because it's 'natural' doesn't mean it's not a sin. Almost the opposite. 'For the natural man is an enemy to God, and has been from the fall of Adam, and will be, forever and ever, unless he yields to the enticings of the Holy Spirit, and putteth off the natural man and becometh a saint through the atonement of Christ the Lord.'" He smiled over at Jaime. "Still remember that shit from seminary."

"I don't understand."

"It means it's in man's nature to sin. I think it's similar to the Catholic idea of original sin, although I've never been Catholic, so I could be wrong. But basically, almost everybody has a natural inclination to sin one way or another at some point in their life. The trick is to overcome. My dad's favorite saying is, 'Self-mastery is the spiritual goal of the faithful.'"

"Okay, but I still don't understand why they'd lecture you and not me."

"Because you're your own person, and although they may see your choices as wrong, they'll accept your right to make them. I, on the other hand, am family, and they have a stake in where I end up spending my afterlife."

"So you're saying, they don't want *you* to burn in hell, but they don't care if I do."

Levi didn't answer, and when Jaime looked over at him, he found Levi was smiling at him, looking highly amused. "You really want to get into Mormon doctrine?"

"Not too deep."

"Okay then. Simple version: Mormons don't believe in the strict dichotomy of heaven and hell. There's perdition, for the really bad people, but for everybody else, there's the three kingdoms of heaven: the celestial, the terrestrial, and the telestial. The simple way to look at it is that the celestial kingdom is for Mormons. And by that, I don't just mean you call yourself Mormon. I mean, you have to be a *good* Mormon."

"Not like you."

"Not like me," Levi agreed. "You"—he pointed at Jaime—"can't ever achieve the highest kingdom because you're not Mormon. But it doesn't mean you burn in hell. It just means you go to one of the others kingdoms of heaven. Probably the terrestrial since you're such a Boy Scout."

"I love the way you make that sound like an insult."

"Mormons also believe families can be 'sealed,' which means they can stay together for all eternity and not be separated by death."

"So if you're not 'sealed' with them, you won't see them in heaven?"

"Right. And in order for us to be sealed, all family members must live righteously and must attain the celestial kingdom."

"Aha," Jaime said with dawning understanding. "So they need you to resist your 'natural man' so you can all live happily together in the celestial kingdom after you die?"

"Exactly."

"And you don't want to do that?"

Levi laughed. "Let's just say I find 'natural man' a lot more spiritually fulfilling."

They stopped for lunch, and Levi took over driving. Several hours later, they arrived in Georgetown. Jaime was doing his best to not be nervous about meeting Levi's family. Once they'd left the highway and were making their way through town, Levi gave him the rundown.

"Isaac's the oldest, and he and his wife are perfect Mormons. He's nice enough, but just once I wish he'd not be so fucking perfect. Jacob's next and he puts up a pretty good front, but mostly he just hates to let Isaac beat him at anything." He looked over at Levi with a smile. "They're only a year apart," he said, as if that explained everything.

"Ruth and Jackson toe the line, but they're cool. Caleb's wife isn't LDS and she disagrees with the church on most things. He'd be the black sheep of the family if it weren't for me. And Rachel"—at her name, his voice turned disdainful—"is the baby of the family and would never dream of doing anything to upset Mom and Dad."

"Is that bad?"

Levi shrugged. "Isaac, Jacob and Rachel give me the hardest time," he said. "The difference is, Isaac and Jacob have brains. They've actually thought about the church's position. Unfortunately, they agree with it. But at least they have some basis for their belief, you know? I think they actually feel a bit bad about it. I mean, they pray I'll see the 'error of my ways' and turn away from the 'homosexual lifestyle,' which about drives me fucking nuts, and it will still piss me off when they get too self-righteous. But their hearts are in the right place."

"But not Rachel's?"

"Rachel spouts the party line like it's the goddamn pledge of allegiance. If somebody told her President Monson had declared the sky was green, she'd never even stop to question it."

Jaime had grown up with only the bare bones of a family and with no solid idea of religion at all. He imagined Levi's family as some kind of club, with shared beliefs and goals, and himself as an outsider, who was bound to get something wrong. "Is there anything I should know?" Jaime asked.

Levi looked at him in surprise. "Like what?"

"I don't know. Anything that might offend them, or—"

He stopped, cut short by Levi's laughter. "Are you planning to do something crazy?"

"Well, no. But—"

"We're just like any other family," Levi said. "And frankly, you're such a Boy Scout, you'll fit right in."

Jaime flipped him off in response, which made Levi laugh hysterically. Apparently Boy Scouts weren't supposed to use crude finger gestures.

"Seriously," Levi told him, once he'd stopped laughing, "don't worry. They may piss *me* off, but they'll be perfectly civil to *you*." He grinned over at Jaime. "If it'll make you feel better, I'll give you the house rules."

"Okay," Jaime said, although based on Levi's shit-eating grin, Jaime suspected he was only going to tease him.

"Don't come down with a sudden case of Tourette's and call my dad a filthy cock-sucker."

Jaime smiled. "Got it."

"Don't do a striptease on the dinner table."

"I'll keep it in mind."

"And don't grab my sister's ass."

"Can I grab your brother's ass?"

Levi winked over at him. "You can grab my ass, if you get desperate."

Despite Levi's reassurance, by the time they arrived at the house, Jaime was terrified. He had no idea why he'd agreed to come.

"There's nothing to worry about," Levi told him as they got out of the car.

Jaime might have believed him more if Levi himself didn't look like he was walking into his own execution. He and Dolly followed Levi up the sidewalk to the front door. Levi stopped with his hand on the knob.

"My family can be a bit overwhelming."

Jaime discovered over the next few hours that "a bit overwhelming" was an enormous understatement.

Ruth met them at the door, hugging Levi and calling him "Leviticus." Then she turned to him. "Hi, Jaime! It's so great to meet you." The friendly smile she gave him seemed completely genuine.

"I'm happy to meet you, too." He was surprised she didn't try to shake his hand. Handshakes were something he'd grown accustomed to, but he was still relieved.

"Come on," she said. "Everybody's out in the back yard."

Jaime followed Ruth and Levi through the entryway and past the family room, weaving through a maze of abandoned toys on the floor. They went through the dining room to a sliding glass door.

She turned to Levi with a smile. "You warned him, right?"

"I tried," Levi said.

Ruth laughed and opened the door. And they led Jaime into the circus.

For some reason he couldn't quite explain, Jaime had pictured Levi's family in muted shades of grey. He figured the children would be hushed and oppressed. He'd imagined the women being quiet and submissive, wearing housedresses and headscarves. He'd pictured the men dressed like

Quakers. In his mind, they'd all sat together in a quiet room, glaring with silent disapproval at the rest of the world.

He could not have been more wrong.

There were kids everywhere, and the noise to prove it. There was a swing set crawling with them, and another group that seemed to be running around screaming with no purpose at all. Several of them swarmed to Dolly like she was some kind of magnet, and Dolly soaked it up.

Adults were scattered amongst the mayhem. One was at an industrial-sized grill, cooking enough hamburgers and hot dogs to feed an army. Two more stood in the middle of the yard tossing a football with a couple of the older kids. Another was sorting out a tearful argument between two young boys. There were women sitting around a picnic table, drinking lemonade and eating tortilla chips and guacamole. One was pregnant. One was nursing a baby. And it seemed nobody held still for more than thirty seconds at a time.

This swarm of people—bright and friendly, smiling and yelling, teasing and laughing—stood in stark contrast to the dour family in his mind. And except for there being three times too many of them, they were, as Levi had tried to tell him, just like any other family. Jaime felt like a bit of a fool for having ever thought otherwise.

Levi took his arm, and Jaime was too overwhelmed to protest. In all the chaos, it gave him something to hang on to, figuratively as well as literally. Levi led him into the fray, introducing him to people as they passed.

Ruth and Rachel were easy to tell apart, partly because Rachel was pregnant. She was also bubblier and generally more annoying than her older sister.

"She's like a goddamn cheerleader on speed," Levi said under his breath.

Ruth seemed solid and no-nonsense. Levi's dad, Abraham, was quiet and imposing, yet not overly stern. Then again, maybe it was impossible to be stern while three grandchildren hung from you like a jungle gym. Levi's mother Nancy looked like an aging hippy. She wore an ankle-length flowing dress and had grey hair hanging in a long ponytail down her back. After that, it became unbelievably confusing. Levi's brothers all looked alike. Only Levi's deep tan and his overgrown hair kept him from looking like Isaac, Jacob and Caleb. To make matters more confusing, they were married to women named Kristine, Kristin, and Kirsten.

"You're pulling my leg," Jaime said, when Levi told him.

"I swear I'm not," Levi said, laughing.

"We told Levi if he married a girl with a K name, he was in big trouble," Nancy said. She seemed to regret it as soon as she said it. She glanced nervously at Levi.

"Well, Mom," he said with a strained smile, "no chance of that, so I guess we're safe."

After asking again which brother was which, Jaime was able to distinguish them by the shirts they wore. Of course, he'd be lost again tomorrow, assuming they didn't all opt to wear dirty clothes the rest of the weekend for his sake.

Ruth's husband Jackson was a big man, like a football player gone soft. Rachel's husband was quiet and shy. And he was also named Isaac.

"Did you all do this on purpose?" Jaime asked.

"Just wait," Levi said. And then he started naming kids. Isaac and Kristine had six, Jacob and Kristin had four, as did Ruth and Jackson. Caleb and Kirsten had two, and Rachel and the non-Binder Isaac had three, with a fourth on the way. Boys outnumbered girls roughly two to one. The oldest was sixteen, and the youngest was still nursing. The task of pointing out who was who was made even more difficult by the fact they were kids and, with the exception of the nursing babies, none of them stayed in one place for more than three seconds. It was like trying to name leaves in a whirlwind.

"I'll never keep them all straight," Jaime said when Levi was done.

"Call the boys 'Champ' or 'Ace' and the girls 'Princess,' and you'll be safe." It seemed like good advice.

Jackson, Jacob and Caleb were still tossing the football among them in the middle of the yard.

"Come on, Levi," Caleb called.

"What are we playing?" Levi asked as Caleb tossed the ball toward him.

"Smear the Queer," Caleb said, just as Levi caught it.

Jaime was shocked, and he could tell Jacob was as well by the look on his face. But Caleb, Jackson and Levi all laughed. In one quick movement, Levi flicked the ball to Jacob and tackled Caleb. Jackson, still laughing, grabbed Levi around the waist and attempted to pull him off Caleb, but before he could, he was bowled over by Isaac, who had abandoned his post at the grill to join the pile.

"Is this normal?" Jaime asked Ruth, who was standing next to him watching her husband and her brothers with a bemused look on her face. Jacob and Isaac's sixteen-year-old son had joined the "game" now, too. There was still some scrambling for the ball, but it seemed to be more about having an excuse to tackle each other.

"Pretty much," she said, glancing at him. "Aren't you going to join them?"

For somebody who relied on personal space to keep him sane, the idea of being in a pile of bodies was terrifying. "No!"

The kids had noticed the men on the ground and were piling on, too. The entire group devolved into smaller groups of squealing, giggling kids being tickled by their dads and uncles, brothers and cousins. When that wore off, there were just grown men lying on the ground, grinning like fools as they caught their breath.

"He seemed so worried about coming," Jaime said to Ruth. "I don't understand."

Her smile faded as she watched the men on the lawn slowly helping each other up, groaning and complaining together as they did that they were too old for this crap.

"It always starts out friendly," she said. "They're brothers. They love each other." Jaime could hear the "but" in her voice, and he waited for her to go on. "One way or another, by Sunday it'll all go wrong."

CHAPTER 12

Sleeping arrangements were always a bit of a chore. Levi's parents' house had eight bedrooms. Each of the married couples had a bed to share. The last two bedrooms held only one twin bed each. These were given to Levi and Jaime. The kids were all in sleeping bags. The older kids slept in the study. The babies and toddlers were with their parents. The rest were on the floor of Jaime and Levi's rooms.

Friday morning was chaos, as mornings often were when Levi's entire family was involved. With nineteen hungry kids and nearly as many tired adults, it was a bit of a circus. Levi was surprised at how happy and comfortable he felt being back with his family. Isaac and Jacob sometimes looked at him askance, and he saw them eyeing Jaime appraisingly. He sensed them watching his and Jaime's interactions, trying to determine if there was more to their relationship than Levi claimed. He knew Jaime had been nervous the night before, but by the time lunch ended on Friday, he seemed at ease. For the most part, everybody was still on their best behavior.

After lunch, the family went several ways. Some of the kids went outside to play and some went downstairs to watch a movie in the family room. The last few went with Levi's mother to the store. After his shower, Levi found Jaime playing Uno at the dining room table with his brothers and Rachel. Jackson, Ruth, and Caleb's wife Kirsten were sitting around the table with them, chatting happily while they ate Crunch 'n' Munch and pretzels.

"But I'd never done anything to them!" Rachel said as Levi sat down next to Jaime. He could tell by the nervous glances his other siblings tossed in his and Jaime's direction that the conversation was making many of them uncomfortable. "They had no right to be so mean to me."

"What's going on?" he asked Jaime quietly.

"Apparently your sister ran afoul of some angry lesbians," Jaime said with obvious amusement.

"We live in Tennessee," Rachel said. "Why should they care what happens in California?"

"*Riiight*," Caleb's wife Kirsten said sarcastically. "Why should any of us care about the rights of our fellow American citizens?"

Rachel stared at her blankly, obviously missing her point.

"Don't start," Caleb said over his shoulder to his wife. She rolled her eyes, and Levi knew she wasn't about to listen. She disliked Rachel to begin with and she wasn't one to back down from an argument.

"The church didn't make any friends by backing Proposition 8," Jackson said. "Churches are supposed to stay out of politics. A lot of people would like to see their tax-exempt status revoked for what they did."

"For standing up for what they believe in?" Rachel challenged.

"No," Kirsten said. "For pushing their beliefs on others. And for failing to recognize the division of church and state."

"Gay marriage is against church doctrine—"

"Church doctrine has no place in secular law. You can't take away people's rights to meet your own religious criteria."

"What about *my* rights?"

"Rachel," Jackson said, "just because it offends you doesn't mean it violates your rights. You don't have a *right* to not be offended."

Rachel looked to Isaac for support, but Isaac shrugged. "I agree with them, actually," he said.

"You do?" Levi asked in surprise.

"Don't get me wrong," Isaac said. "I don't agree with gay marriage, and I'll vote against it every chance I get. But I think the church should've stayed out of it."

"Why?" Rachel asked.

"Nobody takes us seriously as it is," he said. "What's the first thing people say when they find out you're LDS?"

"Polygamy," Jaime said.

"Exactly. Either they ask how many wives or mothers you have, or they start telling you how *Big Love* is their favorite show. We've been fighting for years to be taken seriously, and any progress we made has been wiped out in one fell swoop. The only thing the church accomplished was to give more ammo to people who want to marginalize us."

"It is rather ironic," Jackson said, "that a church ostracized for its beliefs about marriage would seek to ostracize another group for the same reason."

"It's not the same thing at all," Rachel snapped.

"I think Mormons are just pissed because they didn't have the balls to stand up for polygamy back when it mattered," Kirsten said.

"Stop," Caleb said to his wife over his shoulder.

Kirsten ignored him. "Has it ever occurred to you," she asked Rachel, "that the constitutional amendment protecting *your* right to follow Mormon doctrine is the same amendment that's supposed to protect everybody else from being forced to live according to *your* religious beliefs?"

"Stop," Caleb said again.

Rachel ignored him, too. "So you think the church should be forced to accept it, even if God has told us is a sin?"

"No. They don't have to accept it. They don't have to like it. But they can't force their beliefs on other—"

"Enough," Caleb said, louder this time. "We should change the subject. Your turn, Isaac."

"I agree," Jacob said shakily. "We'll never agree on this issue and we'll probably offend our guest in the process."

"Don't mind me," Jaime said.

"Caleb and Jacob are right," Isaac said. "We should drop it." He laid a card on the table. "I'm skipping Jacob. Your turn, Rachel."

"That's how it always goes," Rachel said as she set a card down. "We're supposed to be quiet. We're supposed to ignore it. And then we wonder how the gays manage to push their agenda all the way to the Supreme Court."

"Don't be ridiculous, Rachel," Caleb said. "There is no 'gay agenda.'"

"No, she's right," Jaime said, without cracking a smile. He tossed down a card and turned to Caleb. "Your turn. Draw two."

But Caleb didn't even look at his cards. "There *is* a gay agenda?" he asked.

"Naturally. Although marriage is the second item. Draw two."

"So what's the first?" Jackson asked, grinning. He seemed to be the only person at the table besides Levi who realized Jaime was kidding. Everybody else was staring at Jaime with open-mouthed shock.

"Recruitment. Especially of children. That's why I'm here, in fact. We're having a membership drive this month, and whoever recruits the most minors wins two free tickets to see Kathy Griffin live."

Jackson and Ruth were trying not to laugh, as was Caleb's wife. The best thing was, Jaime wasn't even smiling. "It's still your turn, Caleb. Draw two."

Caleb sat there looking confused until Kirsten elbowed him in the ribs, making him jump. "Sucker," she said.

Caleb turned back to Jaime with obvious relief. "You're joking," he said, although Levi couldn't tell whether it was a statement or a question.

"Am I? By the way, if you join in the month of September, they'll send you a nice little lapel pin, *and* you'll be entered in a drawing to win a free juicer. It's a sweet deal."

Ruth was laughing now, and Caleb smiled. The others were finally catching on. They were starting to smile, looking a bit unsure, but relaxing a little. All except for Rachel, who sat stiff and silent, fuming in her anger.

"I do like lapel pins," Jackson said.

"You'll love this one, Jack. Levi, show Jackson your lapel pin."

Levi patted the collar of his T-shirt, then shrugged. "I don't seem to have it on me."

"You see?" Jaime said to Jack and Ruth, shaking his head in exasperation. "Levi barely even tries. If he's not careful, they'll revoke his membership."

Levi was about to say his family would probably be thrilled to see his membership revoked, but Rachel spoke up before he could open his mouth. "Very funny," she snapped, although it was clear she thought no such thing. "Go ahead and make fun of those of us who still believe in old-fashioned values!"

Isaac and Jacob suddenly looked confused as to whether or not they should be amused at Jaime's joke. Jaime just shrugged. "Your turn, Caleb," he said. He seemed to be the only one at the table who cared they were still in the middle of a card game. "Draw two."

"You think it's funny to come into our home and mock us?" Rachel asked.

"It's not *your* house," Ruth said. "And anyway, he wasn't mocking 'us.' He was mocking *you*."

"And you started it," Caleb added.

Rachel looked at Isaac and Jacob for assistance, but they stared back at her, obviously unsure what to do. They probably agreed with her in principle, but they didn't seem to want to get involved in the argument and her inability to take a joke had always been a bit beyond them.

"Fine," she said, slamming her cards down on the table and standing up. "I don't want to play anymore!"

She stormed off, and her siblings all shared knowing smiles.

"Typical," Jacob said. "She always quits when she starts to lose. It's still your turn, Caleb. Draw two."

Chapter 13

The rest of the day passed without incident. After dinner, Nancy brought out a giant birthday cake and they sang "Happy Birthday" to Abraham. Afterward, they all crowded into the family room to watch *Shrek*. Saturday was the day it all fell apart because that was the day his dad called the confab.

"The *what?*" Jaime asked, when Levi told him.

"It's a family meeting. We always have one when we're all together."

"Is this a Mormon thing?"

"No. It's a Binder thing."

For as long as he could remember, his family had met this way. As a kid, it was once a week. They settled arguments or discussed conflicts at confabs. They also prayed together if somebody was having a problem, like when his grandmother had been diagnosed with cancer, or when Jacob's wife had suffered from repeated miscarriages.

But for approximately the last twelve years, every Binder confab Levi had been part of had ended up being about one issue—him. Specifically, his sexuality. He'd been a senior in high school when he confessed his same-sex attraction to his parents. At the time, he'd believed they'd be able to help him change. They'd believed it, too. He hadn't gone on a mission after high school as so many Mormon boys did because his parents felt he wasn't spiritually ready. Instead, he'd gone straight to BYU.

Back then, the confabs always came down to praying for him or giving him blessings in an effort to help him overcome his yearnings. And for a few years, he'd tried. He really had. He'd read books and met with LDS counselors. He'd sworn to lead a "normal" life. No matter how hard he prayed, though, and no matter how many same-sex attraction support groups he attended, he couldn't change his desires.

The more he tried, the angrier he became. And the more frustrated he became, the more his family assured him that he simply wasn't trying hard enough. Their blindness, more than anything, was what made him start to lose hope. They were his family. They said they loved him, and he believed them, but why couldn't they see how hard he was trying? Why couldn't they see how depressed and lonely he was? All the effort he put into denying his sexuality felt like nothing less than trying to cut out his very soul. Couldn't they see it was tearing him apart?

Then, halfway through his junior year at BYU, he'd had his first real sexual encounter. It was a nervous, frightening, bumbling experience, groping and kissing and grinding together in a pitch-black dorm room. But the sheer joy of it—not the sexual pleasure, although that had been nice, too, of course—but the feeling of release, of finally letting his heart out of the box he'd been trying desperately to nail shut, was overwhelming. It was a revelation. The boy he'd fooled around with left BYU a few days later. Levi never saw him again. He didn't even remember his name. But that boy had changed his life.

After that, he quit trying to redirect his sexuality. He'd come home for spring break and told his parents he was done pretending. He'd asked them to accept him as he was. He'd begged them to support him in his decision.

Their response was to go completely apeshit.

What followed was a week of tears, arguments, prayers and threats, until his father announced with red-faced finality that he wouldn't pay for another credit at BYU until Levi had renounced his same-sex attraction.

Levi could have finished out the semester. It was, after all, half-over and already paid for. Instead, he'd bought a bus ticket for Miami. And now, ten years later, his parents were still trying to change his mind.

His family began filing into his father's study, where the meetings were always held. Levi felt like he was going on trial, and he already knew the verdict wouldn't be in his favor.

"I can tell you don't want to do this," Jaime said. "Can't we just go out for pizza and you can accidentally miss it?"

Levi winced. It would have been nice. But no. His parents had specifically picked a time when they would all be present. If he left, they'd only wait and ambush him later. "Not really."

"Do I wait out here?"

The meeting was for his parents and his siblings only. Spouses were allowed to sit in and listen, but they weren't allowed to participate. Most of the spouses chose not to attend, primarily because most of them were needed to watch the children while the Binders met, but Jackson always came.

"I wouldn't go in if I didn't have to," Levi said. "Trust me. You'll have more fun out here."

Once inside, they all sat in a circle as they always did.

"I'm going to say the opening prayer," his father said.

Everybody crossed their arms over their chests and bowed their heads.

"Heavenly Father, we thank thee for this day. We thank thee for bringing our family together, and for the joy we have found in each other's company these last few days. We gather now as a family to discuss any issues we may have, and we ask for guidance. We ask thee to bless us with thy spirit, that we may listen to each other with love and understanding. We say these things in the name of Jesus Christ. Amen."

"Amen," the rest of the family mumbled.

"Okay," Abraham said, smiling around the circle. "Any new business?"

"One thing," Jacob said. "I'm sure you're all aware, but I wanted to remind you little Samantha will be blessed tomorrow at church, so I hope everybody's willing to get up early since Mom and Dad's ward meets at eight."

His siblings all chuckled and assured him they'd be there. Levi kept his mouth shut. He and Jaime would have to leave by eight anyway to make the twelve-hour drive back to Miami.

"Anything else?" his dad asked.

Rachel raised her hand. "My sister-in-law recently took a job at a homeless shelter in Salt Lake City," she said. "It's in a rough neighborhood, and I'm worried. I'd like to ask you all to keep her in your prayers, that she'll be safe."

"We will," his mother said, and the rest of them nodded.

"Anything else?" his father asked. The circle was silent. "Okay," he said with obvious reluctance. "Any *old* business?"

And without fail, all eyes turned to Levi.

Levi sighed in exasperation. "Do we have to do this?" he asked. "*Again?* Can't we finish the weekend in peace?"

A couple of them had the decency to look embarrassed, but the rest of them simply looked confused that he didn't want to discuss his homosexuality for the thousandth time.

"Levi," his mother said, "we just want what's best for you."

Levi sighed and leaned back in his chair with his arms crossed. All that remained was for the inquisition to begin.

"Levi," Isaac said, "Jacob and I have been doing some research and we think we've come up with what might be a good compromise for our family with regard to your issue."

Levi tried not to groan. Anything Isaac and Jacob thought was good, especially when it came to his so-called "issue," was bound to piss him off.

Jacob produced a stack of printed sheets, sorted into packets and stapled, and he stood up and started handing them around the circle as he talked. "I printed these off the Internet from the website of a group called Evergreen International." He offered a packet to Levi. Levi refused to take it, so Jacob placed it in his lap and continued around the circle. "They're not technically affiliated with the church, but they support church doctrine. They help people who suffer from same-sex attraction."

"I don't *suffer* from anything, except you trying to shove a straight camp down my throat."

"These places don't work," Caleb said as Jacob reached his seat and sat back down. "Their success rate for 'turning' people straight is negligible."

"This isn't a 'straight camp,'" Isaac said. "And they don't claim to be able to 'turn' anyone."

That intrigued Levi a bit. He picked the paper up from his lap and started to read it, not because he was considering going to whatever bullshit thing his brothers had come up with, but simply to see what it said. Next to him, Caleb did the same.

"The language is interesting," Caleb said as he read. "They say they can help you 'diminish' same-sex attraction and avoid homosexual behavior." He looked over at Levi in surprise. "Isaac and Jacob are right. They don't say they can 'cure' you. They just say they can help you control it."

"I don't want to 'control' it. Call it what you want. I'm not going to any camp where they make me talk about my childhood and we sit around singing "Kumbaya.""

"Levi," Isaac said, calm as always. Exceedingly rational. Always perfect. "It's not a camp. You don't *go* anywhere. It's a series of support groups. There are several in Miami. Look on the last page I gave you." Paper rustled as the entire family did as he directed. "There's a summary of same-sex attraction issues. See the third one, What Causes It? Look what it says." He read aloud from his sheet. "'No one chooses to have same-sex attraction feelings. It is not a sin to have these feelings. It only becomes a sin when the individual acts upon those feelings with homosexual behavior.'" He looked over at Levi, as if he expected some kind of response.

"So what?" Levi asked.

"Don't you see, Levi?" Rachel spoke for the first time, her eyes full of excitement. "They're saying you're right. All these years we've said you could change if you wanted to, but they understand it's not so simple!"

Levi could only stare at her in shock. She thought this was a compromise. His entire family, with the possible exceptions of Ruth and Caleb, thought this was something he might appreciate. They were finally accepting his attraction to men couldn't be changed. It couldn't be taken away, not by prayer or fasting or denying himself. And by finding a group that acknowledged this fact, his brother and sister actually thought they were moving closer to his own position.

"I think you're missing a key point here, Rachel," he said, fighting to keep his voice level and not start yelling. "You'll notice in the next section, it says, 'People must desire to move away' from their homosexuality. I don't—"

"Levi," his father said, cutting him off before he could say more, "I really don't see how you can object to this. In the past, maybe we've had unrealistic expectations. We believed you could change if you applied yourself. If this group is correct, and you're correct, then your attraction to men can't be changed. But it can be diminished. Isn't that a good thing? They claim if you're dedicated, they can help you reduce your homosexual behavior and find peace in a heterosexual marriage."

"And do they explain how the hell I'm supposed to ever have sex with my heterosexual spouse? Or am I supposed to be celibate for the rest of my life?"

"Sex is a gift God gives us to share with our spouse. If you were truly committed to living righteously with a wife, I'm sure you would find yourself attracted—"

"No, I wouldn't! You have no idea what you're talking about! Could you suddenly be attracted to a man?"

"Levi, you're completely missing the point."

"No, *you're* missing the point!"

"This is a compromise," Isaac said, his calm demeanor starting to crack for the first time. "Don't you see?"

"I'll tell you where you can shove your compro—"

"Levi!" his mother snapped, and Levi sat back in his chair, fuming.

Jacob sat up, leaning into the circle. "Levi, the family only wants what's best for you."

"No. You want what's best for you. And you refuse to accept that maybe it isn't the same as what's best for me."

Isaac opened his mouth to say something else, but was cut off by Rachel.

"I call the vote," she said.

This was the other factor involved in the Binder Confabs: the vote. Any family member could call a vote, but whoever called it didn't get to contribute. In a family of eight, that was supposed to keep the vote from splitting evenly, although that still happened occasionally when one or more of the family members passed on an issue. It wasn't a secret ballot. They went around the circle and each person was given a chance to cast his or her vote, and an opportunity to explain the reasons for choosing the way he or she did. Nobody was allowed to discuss or argue during the vote, and when it was over, nobody was allowed to debate the decision. The entire family was expected to abide by the result. Now that everybody but Levi was married, the extended family was expected to abide by the vote as well.

"You can't call a vote on this," Levi said. It was true the vote had been used many, many times in his life, but always for things related to the entire family. They voted to settle arguments when they were kids, like when they had to decide between buying a pool table or trampoline, or whether they'd get a guinea pig or a bunny. They voted on where they'd go for vacation, or whether they'd have turkey or ham for Easter dinner. But to vote on the personal life of one particular family member was far more personal than they'd ever made it. "This is my life. You can't vote on whether or not I want to go to support groups."

Rachel looked confused, but Levi's father came to her rescue. "You're correct, Levi," he said. "We can't vote on whether or not you go. What we *can* vote on is whether or not we as a family think you should *try*. We'll simply have to hope your conscience does the rest."

Levi crossed his arms and sat back angrily in his chair. There was nothing else he could do.

"Rachel has called the vote," Abraham went on. "I agree with her that this is a good compromise. We've had unrealistic expectations in the past, but this group seems to be very compassionate. I think it's a wonderful idea. So I vote with your siblings."

He turned to the next person in the circle, Isaac. "I'm the one who brought the info," he said. "I think it's pretty obvious what my vote is." He turned to Jacob.

Jacob simply shrugged. "I helped Isaac do the research. My vote is with him." He turned to their mother.

Nancy smiled over at Levi, trying to be supportive. "Levi, we love you so much. We only want you to be happy. I vote for Evergreen, too."

Rachel was next in the circle, and since it was her vote, she remained silent. And then it was Levi's turn.

"Whether this group talks about 'turning' me straight or 'diminishing' my 'same sex attraction,' it's the same thing. Either way, it means trying to be happy with a wife I don't love and never having sex again." He couldn't keep the bitterness out of his voice as he said it. "Maybe that sounds acceptable to the rest of you, but I'd rather slit my own wrists. I vote no."

Caleb was next and he looked incredibly uncomfortable. He was leaning forward on his knees, staring down at his shoes. Finally he said, "I think I vote with Levi on this."

Levi sighed with relief. He couldn't win the vote now, but it was nice to have the support of somebody. "Thank you," he said.

Caleb turned on him, and Levi was surprised by the obvious anger in his eyes. "Don't thank me. I don't believe homosexuality is a sin, but the way you're living just might be. And it pisses me off. You're so determined to show us all just how bad you can be. Your lifestyle is selfish, self-destructive, and frankly, downright dangerous. And the worst part is, you don't seem to give a rat's ass about destroying our family."

"Caleb!" Nancy snapped. "That language is not allowed in my house."

Caleb sighed in resignation and sat back in his chair. "Sorry, Mom." He glanced sideways at Levi. "I vote with you only because I think these support groups would be a complete waste of time if it's not what you want."

He turned next to Ruth. Hers was the final vote. It couldn't change anything now, but Levi expected her support. She had always stood by him more than any of the rest of them. She picked nervously at her cuticles, and glanced warily at Levi before saying, "I vote for Evergreen."

"What?" Levi asked. "Are you serious?"

"I agree with Caleb. In my mind, the problem isn't being gay. The problem is the way you're living. Maybe you don't want what this group offers, Levi, but I don't see what harm there would be in trying."

"How about that it's a complete waste of time?" Levi snapped, unable to keep his voice from getting louder. "How about that it's not what I want? How about the fact I don't *want* to commit to life where I never get to have sex again?"

"Levi," his mother said, "nobody is saying you have to be celibate—"

Levi jumped to his feet, cutting her off. "It's *exactly* what you're saying! Why can't you see that? Why can't you understand I can no more have sex with a woman than you could?"

"Celibacy is at least a righteous way to live," Isaac said.

"Oh, yeah?" Levi asked him. "You want to try it? 'Cause if it appeals to you so much, go for it! But I'm not interested."

"This is a compromise," Rachel said.

"No, it's not! Why the hell do you keep saying that? It's still all of you telling *me* how to live! How in hell can *you* call it a compromise?"

"Levi, the yelling won't help anything—" his dad started to say.

"What the hell else am I supposed to do?" Levi yelled, louder than before. "Nothing else works. No matter what I say, no matter how many times we have this ridiculous argument, you just keep spouting the same goddamn bullshit you've been spouting for years."

"Levi!" said his mom. She was upset about the language, but he didn't really care.

"It's always *me* who's supposed to change, and *you* who's so perfect and righteous. And no matter how many times I tell you this is it, this is *me*, I'm *gay*, get the fuck over it, you keep throwing the same shit back at me. I'm tired of it!"

"Enough, Levi," his mother said, standing up. Her usual compassionate smile was gone. She was downright angry. "I will *not* listen to foul language in my house. If you can't respect my rules, you're going to have to leave."

"Don't worry, Mom," he said, kicking his chair out of his way on the way to the door. "I'm way ahead of you."

CHAPTER 14

Jaime hadn't thought anything of it when Levi followed his family down the hall and into the study. He sat down in the den where two of the wives were watching *The Wizard of Oz* with a bunch of the kids. He couldn't keep any of the wives straight and had dubbed them the K-wives in his mind. The wives were glancing at him nervously. One of them finally asked, "Have you packed yet?"

"No," Jaime said, surprised at the question. "We're not leaving until tomorrow."

The other wife laughed without much humor. "That's what you think." Her tone wasn't cruel or snide. She sounded resigned.

The other wife nodded. "You might want to be ready."

The first wife pointed down the hall toward the study where Levi's family was. "These never go well for him," she said. "I can pretty much guarantee he's going to storm out of there in a rage."

The other wife nodded in agreement. "If he's not ready to leave when their meeting's over, it'll be a miracle."

Jaime's first instinct was to laugh it off, but then he remembered Ruth's words from the first day. *One way or another, by Sunday it will all go wrong.* He went upstairs and packed his things, which turned out to be a good thing. The K-wives hadn't been wrong.

Not long after he'd zipped his bag closed, Levi stuck his head in Jaime's room. Jaime could tell just by looking at him that he was fuming mad.

"We're leaving," he said.

Nancy cried. Abraham was stoic. Levi's siblings ran the gamut from angry to complacent. Jaime barely had time to thank Levi's parents before Levi was shoving him and Dolly into the car.

The drive was uncomfortable, to say the least.

"Do you want to talk about it?" Jaime asked after the first forty-five minutes of awkward silence.

"No."

Just as well, since Jaime had no idea what to say. It was six o'clock, and his stomach was starting to remind him that they should have been sitting down to eat dinner about now. "Are you planning to drive straight through?" he asked Levi. It would mean driving all night.

It took Levi a second to answer, and he was afraid he'd somehow pissed him off more, but when Levi spoke, he sounded a bit closer to normal. "We'll stop in Jacksonville for the night."

That gave Jaime enough courage to say, "Can we get something to eat before then?"

Levi almost smiled. Almost. "I'll stop at the next Subway I see."

And he did, although it quickly became clear he still didn't feel like chatting, so after eating, Jaime put his headphones on and leaned his forehead against the cool glass of the side window and watched the landscape fly past.

It was ten o'clock when they arrived in Jacksonville. Levi seemed to know just where he was going and pulled into an old motel. It was two stories, all of the doors opening either into the parking lot or onto the narrow second-story balcony clinging to its face. Jaime waited while Levi checked them in, then they took their bags out of the car, and Jaime and Dolly followed Levi halfway down the length of the building.

Whatever friendliness had returned on the road was gone again now. Levi was edgy and surly. Jaime could hardly stand to meet his eyes. He was afraid the whole evening was going to be awkward.

That was when Levi turned and handed him a key. "This is my room," he said. "Yours is next door."

Jaime felt his heart sink. He looked down at the old-fashioned key hanging on the plastic key ring with the room number on it. No fancy key cards here. "We're staying in separate rooms?" He realized as soon as he said it how pathetic he sounded, but the idea of sleeping alone in a strange motel room frightened him. There would never be enough locks on the flimsy door to keep the terror at bay.

Levi smiled, but it wasn't the smile Jaime was used to seeing. It wasn't happy or carefree, or even teasing. It was cruel. Levi took a step toward him, and Jaime instinctively backed away.

"What's the matter, Jaime?" he asked, his voice low and threatening. "Did you want to watch?"

Watch what? He almost said it out loud before it dawned on him what Levi was saying. He felt the color rise in his cheeks. "Oh," he said weakly. "You're going—"

Out. That was what Jaime planned to say. *You're going out.*

But Levi interrupted him with a leer. "I'm going to get laid. Why?" He stepped closer, and Jaime backed up again, bumping into the wall behind him. "Do you want to come?"

There seemed to be a couple of ways to interpret Levi's question, and Jaime blushed more. Either way, the answer was the same. "No." He shook his head, turning away from Levi's gaze. He hated what he saw there—something that was part pity and part loathing and a whole lot of raw anger. "I'll stay here."

Levi opened his door, tossed his bag on the bed, and left without a backward glance. Jaime went like a martyr to his room, Dolly trailing at his heels.

The room was dark and dingy. Turning on every lamp did little to chase the shadows away. Dolly immediately set out to explore the entirety of the small space with her nose. Jaime closed the door, feeling as if he was sealing himself into a jail cell. There was a deadbolt and an old-fashioned chain, and he told himself over and over they would be enough. There was really nothing to fear.

The monsters were already in the room with him anyway.

He got ready for bed and settled under the sheets with Dolly at his side. He turned on the TV. There was no satellite or cable service. There were a dozen channels to choose from, half of them clouded with static, and none of them Syfy.

He was watching a *M*A*S*H* rerun when he heard Levi return. He recognized Levi's voice outside his door, and another voice answering, although he couldn't make out their words. He heard the door to Levi's room close, then shared laughter through the thin walls. He turned up the TV. Could he still make out the muffled sound of their voices or was it only his imagination? He turned the TV up a bit more. That did it. He couldn't hear them talking anymore.

Of course, they probably weren't talking.

Even though he had the TV ridiculously loud, he found himself listening, straining to hear more. Underneath the sound of Winchester and Hawkeye bickering and canned TV laughter, could he hear muffled moans or the rhythmic pounding of the bed against the wall? Would he hear Levi cry out?

"Shit!" he cursed, and Dolly jumped up, looking at him in alarm.

"It's nothing, girl." His voice shook as he said it. "I'm being an idiot."

She threw herself down on the bed with a huff that sounded for all the world like an exasperated sigh. Jaime grabbed his iPod off the bedside table and put in his earbuds. Once the music blared in his ears, he turned off the TV. He lay there, determined to hear only the music. He tried not to think about what was going on in the room next door.

He failed.

He thought about Levi kissing somebody. He thought of Levi undressing some nameless, faceless man. Was Levi a top or a bottom? Was he using a condom? Jaime wondered if Levi was on his knees right now in front of the other man, and the thought made Jaime's cock grow hard.

He fought his arousal. He flipped through songs on his iPod, trying to force his mind to think of something else. He almost succeeded. But then, in the silent moment between songs, he heard the sound he'd both longed for and dreaded—a low moan from the room next door.

He had no way of knowing which man had made the sound, but the images instantly flared to life in his head: Levi on the bed with his head thrown back, his eyes closed, his cock lying erect against his flat stomach, and another man there, between his legs. Was he going to fuck Levi or straddle him and be fucked? He imagined Levi's long, tan fingers wrapped around the man's shaft. He imagined the strokes. He heard the moans and the panting breaths. He saw Levi's mocking eyes, and he heard Levi ask again, "Do you want to come?"

And suddenly there was no other man there. There was only Jaime and Levi. He imagined touching Levi's thighs, running his hands up his hips and over his stomach. He thought of the way Levi smelled, like the ocean and sunlight. He imagined Levi's hand stroking him. This time, the low moan he heard was his own.

He gave up fighting it. He gave up pretending he didn't hear it or didn't care. He rolled onto his stomach, pulling his earbuds out as he did. It was faint, but he *could* hear them. Not constantly, but every once in a while, he caught a moan, a low laugh, or a thump as something hit the wall. What he couldn't hear, his imagination filled in.

He thrust himself against the bed as he imagined Levi underneath him. He imagined Levi's moans were for him. He imagined Levi going down on him, his hands on Jaime's hips. He imagined pushing his erection deep into Levi's waiting mouth, and seeing Levi's soft, full lips sliding down his shaft. He imagined letting himself go as he thrust harder, panting, reaching for something he couldn't quite see.

And then he heard a noise—a sound from next door—a wrenching cry of release and relief. It went from his ears straight to his groin, triggering the tightness deep in his balls, and he came hard, burying his face in his pillow to muffle his own cries, lest Levi hear him, too. He came like he hadn't come in a very long time, for once feeling more pleasure than guilt at his own orgasm, and he thrust against the bed one last time, sliding in the sticky warmth of his own seed against the fabric of his boxers. And God, it felt it good. It felt *so goddamn good.*

It wasn't that the guilt was gone. It was still there, in the back of his brain, trying to find some purchase to crawl into the light. But right now, it was kept at bay by the sheer pleasure of what he'd done. What he'd *allowed* himself to do.

He lay there in his own mess, smiling, no longer listening for anything next door. He felt tired and relaxed and sated and not a bit scared. For one of the first times in his life, he felt normal. Or close to it. He felt at peace.

Once he'd caught his breath, he squirmed out of his wet shorts, using the dry part to wipe himself off. He rolled away from the wet spot he'd made to the other side of the bed, and he fell sound asleep.

That night, the nightmares found him.

CHAPTER 15

The man Levi'd picked up at the bar was young and blond and a bit overconfident, but they'd had a good enough time. Levi never even asked his name. He'd fallen asleep next to Levi in bed, but when Levi woke the next morning, the blond was already gone. Levi was relieved. He hated making small talk with strangers over breakfast.

Jaime barely looked at him when he answered Levi's knock on his door. "You ready to go?"

"Sure," Jaime said, "but I'm hungry. Can we get breakfast first?"

"There's a restaurant a couple of blocks away."

They loaded their bags in the car and headed out, and still Jaime wouldn't look at him.

At first, Levi was annoyed. It wasn't enough for his family to treat him the way they did, now Jaime was going to pass judgment on him, too? Then he remembered his words from the night before. He remembered the cruel pleasure he'd taken in asking Jaime if he wanted to come.

"I'm sorry," he said, and Jaime turned to him in surprise.

"What for?"

"For what I said last night."

"It's no big deal."

"Then I'm sorry for whatever it is you're pissed at me for."

"I'm not pissed." Now that he could see Jaime's face, he realized Jaime didn't look mad at all. He looked exhausted. And, for some reason, a bit embarrassed. But not angry. "I didn't sleep well."

"Why not?"

In typical Jaime fashion, he avoided the question altogether and asked a new one. "Does this happen often?"

"What do you mean?"

"I get the impression you've stopped here before. Not just Jacksonville. I mean, at that motel."

"Fairly often on the way home, yeah. It's kind of a routine. My family pisses me off. I leave early. Can't drive straight through." *And always feel the need to go out and blow off some steam afterward.*

"What happened with your family?"

Levi sighed. "You really want to hear about it?"

"Only if you want to tell me."

"I will," Levi said as he pulled into the parking lot of the restaurant. "But not on an empty stomach."

He told Jaime over scrambled eggs, bacon, and pumpkin pancakes about the confab, Evergreen International, and the vote.

"They actually thought that was a compromise?" Jaime asked.

Levi was relieved to find Jaime at least felt as he did. "Apparently."

"And I assume you won't be looking up the nearest support group once we're back in Miami?"

"You assume right."

"Natural man, one. Righteous living, zero. Not that I blame you." He eyed Levi appraisingly. "So Isaac, Jacob and Rachel believe everything your church tells them. And your parents, too, it seems. Ruth seems to half-ass it. Caleb doesn't seem to buy it at all. Am I right?"

"I'd say that's an accurate summary."

"So what about you? What do you believe?"

Levi groaned. "I don't know any more."

"That's a cop-out answer. Do you believe in God?"

"Absolutely."

"Are you Christian?"

"Define 'Christian.'"

"Are there different definitions?"

"Most people think Mormons aren't Christian, but Mormons say they are."

"Fair enough. Do you believe Jesus was the Son of God and he died on the cross for your sins?"

"My church believes that, yes."

Jaime smiled. "Nice try, but not what I asked."

Levi pushed his plate out of the way and leaned back in the booth. "I think Jesus probably existed, but I don't necessarily think he was divine. I'm not even sure he was one man. I think maybe he was a conglomerate of different men. Different stories all meshed together."

"The original urban legend?"

"Something like that, yeah."

"So what about Joseph Smith?"

"Do I believe he was a prophet? No, not really." He pointed a finger at Jaime. "But don't you dare tell my parents I said that."

"I won't." Jaime laughed. "So you think Joseph Smith was lying?"

"I don't know. I don't want to think he made it up, but I don't quite buy it either."

"It's one or the other, Levi."

"Is it?" Levi shrugged. "Maybe he ate some bad rye and had one hell of a dream."

"He was tripping his balls off and a religion was born?"

"Hell, I don't know." Levi threw down his napkin in annoyance. "Are you finished? We should get going."

"I'm *not* finished, actually," Jaime said with obvious amusement. "So if you don't believe Joseph Smith was a prophet, then what about the rest of church doctrine?"

"Some of it, I get. Some of it makes sense. I may not follow it all, like the no drinking thing, but I get it. Even then, though, I don't believe it's the will of God. I think it's just common sense."

"And is their stance on same-sex attraction common sense, too?"

"Yes and no. Look, back in 1969 the First Presidency issued a statement saying blacks weren't yet ready to receive the priesthood."

"So they couldn't be priests?"

"Mormons don't have priests."

"Then what does 'the priesthood' mean?"

Levi groaned. He hated trying to explain Mormon practices. "Basically, it's the power to act with divine authority."

"That sounds like a priest to me."

"I suppose so," Levi relented. "But in the Mormon Church, any worthy male can receive the priesthood."

"Ahh. Unless he's black."

"They can now. In 1978, God 'revealed' to President Kimball that blacks were ready to receive the priesthood. Now, did God really pick a specific day to make this revelation? Did the entire black population suddenly become worthy in His eyes? Or was it only that church leadership was finally in the hands of somebody who was a progressive thinker?"

"So you think it was more a matter of the church finally caving to political pressure?"

"Probably. Or maybe President Kimball was open-minded enough to be able to overcome the prejudice of his predecessors. I don't know. I don't think any of them were *lying*. I don't think they were trying to make it a political issue. I think they probably prayed, and whatever felt right to them, they called it a revelation."

"So you're hoping the church will eventually have a revelation on this issue as well?"

"It'd be nice, but I'm not holding my breath."

Jaime pushed his plate away.

"Are you satisfied now?" Levi asked. "Can we go, oh, sadistic one?"

Jaime smiled at him, looking like a perfect Boy Scout once again. "We can go."

Levi offered to drive. It wasn't until they were in the car and back on the interstate that Levi thought again about the night before. "Jaime, listen. I really am sorry. I didn't have to be such an ass to you last night."

Jaime shrugged and, for some reason, he started to blush, turning away to look out the window. "I told you: it's no big deal."

"I think you're still mad."

"I'm really not."

"Then how come every time I bring it up, you turn beet-red and can't look me in the eyes?"

"Oh God." Jaime covered his face with his hand and scrunched down low in his seat. "Am I doing that?"

"Yes," Levi said, laughing. It wasn't often he saw Jaime become so flustered.

Jaime sighed, his eyes still hidden behind his hand. "I could hear you."

It took Levi a second to realize what Jaime meant, but when he did, he laughed. "Having sex, you mean?"

"Maybe next time, you should ask for rooms that aren't side by side."

Levi couldn't help but laugh again. Maybe he should have been embarrassed, but Jaime's discomfiture amused him. "I didn't realize we made so much noise."

"Apparently the walls were thin."

Levi thought about it—his time with the blond, what they'd done, the sounds they'd undoubtedly made—and Jaime on the other side of the wall, listening. He found the idea intriguing. Had Jaime liked it? Had he gotten off? It turned Levi on a bit just thinking about it, and his voice was a thicker than it should have been when he said, "You should've come over."

Jaime seemed to be over his embarrassment now. He rolled his eyes at Levi's suggestion. "I'm sure that would've been incredibly awkward."

"Maybe," Levi said, even as his mind continued to explore the possibilities. Maybe Jaime was right. Maybe it would have been awkward. Then again, maybe not. "Is that why you didn't sleep well?" he asked. "We weren't up *that* late."

"No." Jaime reached into the center console and pulled out his iPod and earbuds. "It's not your fault I couldn't sleep."

"Are you an insomniac or something?"

Jaime put his earbuds in and leaned against the window. "Wake me up when you're tired of driving."

"How come you can force me to answer your questions, but I can't force you to answer mine?"

Jaime smiled, but didn't open his eyes. "You have a lot to learn about being evasive."

CHAPTER 16

The next few weeks were hard for Jaime. The night in Jacksonville had wakened the monsters in his mind. No matter what he did, the nightmares seemed to find him more often than not.

Night after night, he woke in a cold sweat, his heart pounding in his chest. The dreams started out erotic, only to turn terrible and frightening before he reached his climax. Sometimes the horror of it overrode the sexual component, but other times when he woke, his cock was so hard it was almost painful. He'd feel like he was only one stroke away from the orgasm of his life. Then he'd remember his dream, and it was all he could do to make it to the bathroom before losing what was left of his dinner.

He knew his nightmares were related to his growing attraction to Levi, but he had no idea what to do about it. The only logical answer was to stop seeing Levi, but that was the last thing in the world he wanted. He wasn't sure it would help anyway.

At two-thirty Wednesday morning, he woke from yet another disturbingly erotic dream. He couldn't stand to stay in his bed, replaying the terrifying visions in his head. He knew he wouldn't be able to fall back to sleep. He got out of bed, and Dolly followed him downstairs. She sat on the couch next to him with her head in his lap, and he petted her absentmindedly while watching bad late-night television. This had become routine. On good nights, he'd fall asleep on the couch around four or five, but not this time. He felt like he'd hardly slept in days, but he was still awake at six-thirty when Dolly started nuzzling him and whining to go out.

He took her for her morning walk and fed her before starting his own breakfast. He only had three clients scheduled for the day, with the third one being the very object of his turmoil—Levi.

He was exhausted. On top of that, every passing minute brought him a minute closer to seeing Levi. The thought filled him with something that was half excitement and half dread. He knew both feelings were completely ridiculous, but chastising himself changed nothing. He worked through his first two clients in a bit of a daze. He had an extra half-hour after his second appointment before Levi was scheduled to show up. He was supposed to use that time for lunch, but he couldn't eat anything. His stomach was full of butterflies.

Levi arrived for his massage, cheerful as always. He'd obviously been surfing. His hair was still damp, and the smell of the ocean and sunlight followed Levi into the small, dark room. Jaime couldn't even make eye contact as he told Levi to get undressed and lie down on the table, face up.

"I'm sorry I didn't shower first," Levi said, when Jaime came back in the room. "Seems rude not to, but you're only going to get me all greasy anyway."

"It's fine." Jaime tried not to think about pouring massage oil all over Levi's naked body. He straightened the sheet over Levi, pulling it up higher on him than he usually did on men, in an attempt to keep from being distracted by Levi's bare stomach and chest.

"Are you okay?" Levi asked as Jaime sat down on the little stool behind Levi's head. Levi was straining his neck backward, trying to meet his eyes.

"Of course." Jaime pulled on Levi's head to stretch the neck muscles, then put his fingers up into Levi's sub occipitals. "Let's start with three deep breaths."

Jaime tried to concentrate on his job, but he was losing his ability to be professional with Levi. He didn't just want to massage him. He wanted to look at him and really touch him.

He spent too long on Levi's hands, simply because he knew how much Levi liked it. He needed to spend more time on Levi's psoas and lumbar and less on his thigh. Yes, Levi had pain in his leg, but Jaime knew his psoas was the real problem, and the thigh just a symptom. Still, he loved how it felt to rub Levi's leg. He liked that when he did it, he could see most of Levi's stomach. Of course, there was also the tantalizing bulge between Levi's legs, covered by the thin sheet. Levi no longer became aroused during his massages. On one hand, that was good. But sometimes, Jaime couldn't help but wish his touch still turned Levi on. He sometimes wondered what would happen if he pushed the thin sheet aside.

"Are you sure you're okay?" Levi asked, startling Jaime out of his thoughts.

"Yeah. Why?"

"You don't look so good. And you're a little spacey."

Jaime felt the heat of his blush. He hoped Levi couldn't guess what he'd been thinking. "I haven't been sleeping well."

"Why not?"

The answer to that question was more than he wanted Levi to know, so he changed the subject. "Do you feel like the therapy is helping?"

"I do, but…" Levi hesitated.

"But what?"

"But can you tell me how much longer this is going to take?"

"It's hard to say for sure. It took several years to get your body to this point of imbalance. You've made a lot of progress, but it's common to reach a bit of a plateau. It might feel like it's not getting any better, but the massage keeps it from reverting to how it was before."

"It keeps it from getting worse again?"

"Right. Think of it as maintenance."

"Well, the thing is,"—and Jaime was surprised to see that for once, it was Levi who was embarrassed—"I can't really afford maintenance. I could afford to come once a month, I think. Twice maybe. But this twice a week thing is going to break me."

Many clients had to quit treatment or come less often due to the cost, but never before had Jaime experienced such a sense of loss over one. Levi had become a bright spot in his life—a bright spot that sometimes blinded him and made everything a bit more complicated than he liked—but a bright spot nonetheless. He didn't want to let Levi drift away.

"Keep coming. You shouldn't quit now. I'll do the massages for free."

"You shouldn't have to do that."

"I want to." He didn't look at Levi's face. He was afraid Levi would look at him and see how desperate he was to keep him around. He didn't want Levi to think he was pathetic. Even if he was. Jaime went back to rubbing his arm, then moved to his hand.

"Not many people want to come to a male therapist," he said, and it was the truth. "Women are too self-conscious, I guess, and men get freaked out about having another man touch them this way. They worry they'll be turned on." He couldn't help but smile as he thought about it. "Not all of them, of course, but enough. The women don't mind if they know I'm gay, but it's not like I'm going to list my sexual orientation in my Yellow Pages ad."

"You could put a little rainbow penis," Levi said.

It surprised Jaime enough he burst out laughing. "What?"

"People put those little Christian fish in their ads. It's the same idea. It's like a code. You could start a new trend."

"No, thanks," Jaime said, still laughing. "Full color ads cost extra. Anyway, my point is, my schedule's fairly full, but it's not like I have anyone clamoring for your spot. So if you want to keep coming, you should."

"I can pay you twenty-five dollars per treatment," Levi said, and Jaime could hear the embarrassment in his voice. Twenty-five dollars was a third what he normally charged.

"That'll be fine."

"Twenty-five dollars, and you go surfing with me."

Jaime smiled. "Okay. Maybe next week—"

"Tonight."

"*Tonight?*"

"This afternoon. When we're done here."

"Are you serious?"

"Why wouldn't I be?"

"You've already been surfing today."

Levi gave him a killer smile. "No rule says I can't go twice. Besides, some exercise might help you sleep, and you could use the practice. What do you say? Do we have a deal?"

Yes, Levi was his bright spot. And Jaime swore he could feel Levi's light filling him up. He couldn't help but smile. "Deal."

Jaime was surprised when he followed Levi outside to find Levi's motorcycle parked by the curb. He knew Levi had come straight from the beach, so it was odd he wasn't in his truck.

Like he was reading his mind, Levi said, "My apartment was on the way, and the truck's too fucking hot. Didn't figure we'd be going straight back out." He climbed on and looked at Jaime expectantly. "You coming?"

The motorcycle was shiny chrome and bright red speed, and just looking at it made Jaime break out in a cold sweat. "No way am I getting on that thing."

"It's perfectly safe," Levi assured him.

That may or may not have been true, but as was so often the case with his fear, logic did little to abate it. "I'll take my car and meet you at your place," he told Levi, and although Levi rolled his eyes in good-natured exasperation, he agreed.

The surfing turned out to be a good idea. Levi surfed a little, but mostly he floated on his board in the surf while he helped Jaime. The sun and the water and the Levi's cheerful company burned away some of Jaime's lethargy and the depression that had been building over the past weeks. When they were done, he was tired, but it was a weariness that made him feel strong and healthy. He climbed back into Levi's truck sunburned and hungry, but feeling better than he had in days.

"You want to go out?" Levi asked him as he started his truck.

Jaime shook his head. "I don't have the energy."

"You want to come over?"

"Why?" Jaime asked in surprise.

Levi shrugged. "Why not?"

"Can we stop and get Dolly first?"

Levi practically rolled his eyes at him, but he smiled, too. "I suppose it's on the way."

It wasn't. Not really. But Levi took him back by his house and barely blinked an eye when Jaime put Dolly in the cab with them instead of in the back.

"She's never been in the back of a truck before," Jaime told him. "I'm afraid she'll jump out."

Levi just shook his head. Once they were at his place, Jaime sat down on the couch. Dolly hopped up next to him and lay with her head in his lap. Levi raised his eyebrows at her, but only said, "What do you like on your pizza?"

"Mushrooms."

"That's it?"

"No. Anything else is fine. Just as long as there're mushrooms, too. Not those rubbery canned kind, though." He leaned back on the couch, closed his eyes, and finally relaxed. His week without sleep was catching up to him fast. "*Real* mushrooms. Lots and lots of mushrooms."

He drifted for a while, Dolly's head a comfortable weight on his thigh, and Levi's sultry voice in the background. His mind couldn't quite make sense of Levi's words, but knowing he was close was reassuring.

The next thing he knew, the doorbell was ringing. He hadn't meant to nod off, and part of him hated to wake up, but the smell of pizza made his stomach grumble, and he remembered he hadn't eaten since breakfast.

"You want a beer?" Levi asked as he set the pizza down on the coffee table.

"No."

"I have Pepsi."

"Do you have milk?"

"Are you serious?"

"Yeah. Why not?"

"Why not? Because it's weird."

"I like milk with tomato-based things," Jaime said defensively. "Pizza. Spaghetti. Chili. You know."

Levi shook his head, but he went in the kitchen and came back out with a beer and a glass of milk and a roll of paper towels.

Jaime'd ordered pizza before, of course. He'd asked for extra mushrooms. What he found was it didn't matter how many times he said it, he was still lucky to get a couple per slice. But Levi apparently knew what to say because the pizza was loaded with them.

"That was the best pizza ever," Jaime said afterward.

"I'm glad," Levi said, smiling at him. "Now, do you want to tell me why you're not sleeping?"

The question surprised Jaime. He closed his eyes and leaned back on the couch and thought about how to answer. He didn't want to lie to Levi, but he was embarrassed to admit that, at the age of twenty-six, he was still afraid of the dark. Or, more accurately, afraid of the nightmares the darkness brought with it. "I have horrible dreams."

"You want to talk about them?"

He felt his cheeks turning red. "No."

"Okay. Have you tried taking something?"

Years ago, a therapist had given him sleeping pills, but they only made it harder to wake from the dreams. It was better to go without. "I hate that stuff," he said.

Levi didn't say anything, and Jaime opened his eyes and looked over at him. Levi was fidgeting with a hole in the knee of his jeans. He actually looked nervous. Jaime had never seen him look so uncomfortable before.

"Don't take this wrong, Jaime," Levi asked with obvious hesitation, "but maybe I could spend the night? Maybe you'd feel better having someone else in the house. I bet you have a spare bedroom, right?"

He did, although there wasn't a bed in it. Jaime had it set up as an office. But he knew in his heart it wouldn't matter. The thought of going back to his house and his own bed made his gut heavy with dread, and the thought of having Levi across the hall did little to alleviate it.

Levi was still watching him, and Jaime shook his head. "I don't think it would help."

"What would?"

"I don't know."

"There must be something."

"There's not," Jaime said, but even as he spoke, he knew it was a lie. There *was* something. He wanted to stay at Levi's. He wanted to climb into Levi's big, soft bed, bury himself down in Levi's sweet scent, and lose himself forever. But it seemed like a ridiculous thing to ask. He leaned his head back again and closed his eyes. "You can't help me."

"Jaime?"

Jaime didn't lift his head, but he cracked his eyes open and turned toward Levi. Levi waited until he was watching and then slowly, *slowly* reached across the couch. Jaime found he didn't even have the strength to object when Levi touched him. It wasn't much. Only his fingers on the back of Jaime's hand.

"You need to sleep," Levi said softly. "Tell me what I need to do."

This was his chance—it was now or never. He took a deep breath and asked, "Can I stay with you?"

For some reason, he expected Levi to balk or maybe even to laugh, but he didn't. He smiled with obvious relief. "Of course you can."

"And Dolly?"

Now, Levi did laugh. "Dolly can stay, too."

"I'll sleep on the couch—" It wasn't what he wanted, but he had to say it.

Levi shook his head. "No, you won't."

The tightness in his chest eased. The relief of knowing he'd be able to get a decent night's sleep was overwhelming. Levi's fingers were still on the back of his hand, and Jaime turned his hand over. He saw Levi's surprise and his hesitation, but then Levi's palm met his. Jaime gripped Levi's hand tight and didn't bother to fight the tears that filled his eyes. "Thank you."

All Levi said was, "You're welcome."

CHAPTER 17

Levi wasn't sure why he was doing any of it. He didn't know why he'd asked Jaime to go surfing or to come to his house. He didn't know why he let Jaime's big, hairy dog in his truck or on his couch. He didn't know why, when he called to order the pizza, he specifically asked if they used canned mushrooms, and, when they said yes, he hung up and called a different place altogether. He didn't know why he wanted more than anything to take care of Jaime. All he knew was that he did. Jaime was obviously lost. He was obviously exhausted. He obviously needed something. And Levi was determined to give it to him.

It wasn't until Jaime turned his hand over and his strong fingers grabbed onto Levi's hand that he realized why he'd done all of it: he cared about Jaime. It was such a simplistic explanation, but it was true. Looking back on his years in Miami, he realized he hadn't bothered to care about anyone in a very long time. He looked over at Jaime, who still had tears on his cheeks, but was already falling back to sleep.

Jaime needed him. He knew it with every fiber of his being. And the truth was, it felt good to be needed. It made him feel lighter, knowing maybe he could do something good.

Something important.

"Come on," he said to Jaime as he stood up and tugged on his hand. "Let's put you to bed."

"It's only eight o'clock," Jaime grumbled, but he let Levi push him down the hall to the bedroom. Once there, Jaime started pulling off his clothes, leaving them in a trail from the door to the bed. Levi knew Jaime would have wanted him to turn away, if he'd been awake enough to think about it, but Levi couldn't help but watch him undress. He'd discovered the first day he took Jaime surfing how beautiful his body was. He wasn't huge or muscular, but he wasn't too soft either. He was thin, but not overly so. His skin was the golden-pink shade that only true redheads had, and it was almost flawless. No freckles marred his shoulders or his arms. He had sparse red hair across his chest. His legs were muscular.

And his ass? Levi eyed it appreciatively as Jaime stepped out of his shorts. He wished he could see more of it because the shape was absolutely perfect.

Wearing only his boxers, Jaime burrowed under the comforter and onto the bed. His head surfaced again on the other side, a spot of reddish-blonde curls above Levi's blue comforter, and he settled down with a sigh. Dolly jumped up on the bed, and Levi bit back his urge to tell her no. She turned in several circles before throwing herself down, practically on top of Jaime.

"I really love your bed."

Levi smiled. "Get some sleep."

"Levi?"

"Yes?"

"You can sleep here, too. I'll stay on my side."

"Don't worry about me."

He wasn't sure Jaime heard him. He had a feeling he was already asleep.

It was eleven-thirty when Levi turned off the TV and headed for his bedroom. Dolly, who was curled up by Jaime's legs, didn't raise her head, but greeted him with a wagging tail as he climbed into bed. Jaime was sound asleep, buried deep under the covers. Only one arm stuck out from under the comforter, lying across the bed, almost as if he was reaching out to Levi in his sleep.

Levi hadn't anticipated how hard it would be to share a bed with Jaime. Jaime had said he'd stay on his side, but Levi quickly realized he was going to have a very hard time doing the same. For a long time, he lay looking at the smooth, pale skin of Jaime's arm. He remembered how scared he'd been on the couch as he'd reached for Jaime's hand, and how pleased he'd been when Jaime didn't pull away. He wondered what would happen if he touched Jaime now. Could he touch the hand that was only inches away? What about Jaime's thin wrist? Maybe he could slide his fingers up Jaime's arm. Was it possible Jaime would give in to his touch? Or would Levi only destroy the trust he'd managed to build so far?

He reached toward Jaime. He didn't dare touch him, but he moved the comforter out of the way, so he could see Jaime's face. When Jaime was awake, Levi always thought he looked younger than his twenty-six years, but when he was asleep, he actually looked his age, and Levi realized it was Jaime's eyes that made him look so young. No matter how good a front Jaime sometimes put up, the hint of fear and vulnerability lingering there always betrayed him.

Levi longed to touch him. His fingers itched to trace Jaime's cheekbone or his jaw. He imagined brushing his thumb over his lips. He imagined kissing him and felt every part of his body react. It wasn't just that his cock stirred, although that happened, too. He felt it everywhere—a lightness in his chest, his heart beginning to race, butterflies in his stomach, and he had to close his eyes and breathe deeply. He imagined Jaime's mouth opening underneath his. He wondered how he would taste and had to fight the urge to slide across the bed and find out.

He felt as if he was wound tight, tense and aching, his entire body practically humming with the need to touch Jaime. To kiss him and hold him and—

Levi sprang out of bed so fast, he made Dolly jump up in alarm. He grabbed his pillow and headed for the living room. The couch was old and lumpy and a little too short, but anything was better than lying in his own bed, seeing and wanting what he couldn't ever have.

Jaime knew, before he even surfaced from his dream, that he was in Levi's bed. It felt good. It smelled good. It was as if somehow, something about Levi had rubbed off on his sheets, and now Jaime was wrapped in it, cocooned and comfortable, and feeling better than he had in a week.

He hoped Levi would still be there when he opened his eyes. He hoped he'd have a moment to watch him sleep. But when he finally turned to look, he found the other side of the bed empty. Dolly rose from her spot by his feet and came to greet him, bumping his face with her nose and wagging her tail.

Jaime checked his watch. It was nearly six. "Time for your walk, isn't it, girl?"

She whined pitifully, although her tail continued to wag.

"Okay, okay. I'm coming."

He barely remembered climbing into Levi's bed the night before. His clothes were strewn across the floor, an indicator of how exhausted he'd been. He was never so sloppy. He wondered with some embarrassment if he'd at least managed to wait for Levi to leave before performing his little striptease.

He was surprised to find Levi asleep on the couch. He was on his side with one leg and one arm hanging off at awkward angles. It made Jaime's back hurt just looking at him.

He sat down on the floor next to him. He wasn't sure how to wake him. He wasn't sure if it was fair to touch him or not. In the end, he fell back on what he knew. He took Levi's hand and started to massage it, working the channels between his fingers as he knew Levi liked. Levi's eyes didn't open, but his breathing changed, and he sighed.

"I bet your neck hurts," Jaime said.

"It does."

"You shouldn't sleep like that."

Levi smiled. "It's okay. I know this great massage therapist. He'll fix me right up."

"I told you you could sleep in the bed."

Levi was silent for a second, but finally he said, "I snore."

"You weren't snoring just now."

Levi's eyes opened, and Jaime found it easier to look back down at Levi's hand rather than to face him. "I didn't want to wake you," Levi said. "You needed the sleep."

"I'm going to take Dolly for a walk and then I need to get home. You should go sleep in your bed."

"I will," Levi said. But he didn't move. "Did you sleep well?"

"Yes."

"No bad dreams?"

"No. I know it sounds crazy, but your bed…" Jaime kept his head down, hoping Levi wouldn't see his embarrassment, but knowing his cheeks were probably so red Levi would have to be blind not to. "It makes me feel safe," he said, as he continued to massage Levi's hand. "Thank you."

"You're welcome." Levi turned his hand, catching Jaime's fingers in his own.

Jaime's instinct was to pull away, but before he could, Levi stood up, pulling Jaime to his feet at the same time. He let go of Jaime, then went to the table by the door and dug around in the drawer. He was wearing only a pair of shorts, and Jaime did his best to keep his eyes on Levi's face when he turned and walked back over to him. Levi's eyes were dark and sexy, seeming to ask him a question as he slowly reached for Jaime's hand.

Jaime resisted the urge to pull away and Levi rewarded him with a smile as he took his hand. He placed something in Jaime's palm, curling his fingers over it with his other hand. But he didn't let go. They stood there, Levi holding Jaime's hand in both of his. It could only have been a second or two, but they felt to Jaime like the longest seconds he'd ever experienced. Levi seemed to be staring at his lips, and Jaime felt himself blush again.

Levi hesitated, as if he didn't know what to do next, and then he took a tiny step forward. Without even thinking, Jaime backed away. Levi stopped short, his smile faltering and becoming a bit sad, as if Jaime's reaction was exactly what he had expected, and yet still not what he'd hoped. He dropped Jaime's hand, stepping backward as he did.

Jaime opened his hand and looked down at what Levi had given him. It was a key.

"Is this to your apartment?" he asked in surprise.

"I have to work tonight," Levi said, "but my bed will still be here."

Levi felt good about giving Jaime a key to his place. Each night that weekend, Jaime and Dolly arrived at his apartment as Levi was leaving for work, and when Levi came home shortly after five in the morning, he'd find them both sound asleep in his bed. Jaime always seemed to wake up when Levi came in, even when Levi tried to be quiet. And even if Levi told him to keep sleeping, he wouldn't. He'd get up and take Dolly for a walk before heading home, and Levi would climb into a bed still warm from Jaime's body heat and fall sound asleep before Jaime was even dressed.

Levi had assumed Jaime would come over again on Sunday, just as he'd done on the nights Levi was working. He was disappointed when the evening passed with no sign of him, but Monday afternoon was his regular massage appointment. He could tell Jaime hadn't slept well just by looking into his blue eyes.

"Where were you last night?" he asked as Jaime moved around and started to massage his arm.

Jaime seemed surprised by the question. "I was home."

"I thought you'd come over."

Jaime kept his gaze on his work, as he often did, rather than making eye contact. "It's one thing for me to use your apartment while you're working, but you don't want to put up with me on your nights off, too."

"You know that for a fact, do you?" Levi asked. Jaime smiled, but didn't answer. "So you plan on not sleeping again until Thursday night when I go back to work?"

Jaime's cheeks began to turn red. "I'll be okay."

"I'm your last client, right?"

Jaime seemed reluctant to answer, but finally nodded. "That's right."

"Let me take you out, then you can come over."

"Out where?" Jaime asked with a distinct lack of enthusiasm.

"Anywhere."

Jaime had finished with his upper body, and Levi could see him debating as he performed his magic trick with the sheet, leaving one of Levi's legs exposed. Finally he asked, "Do you like *Torchwood?*"

"Is that a restaurant?"

Jaime laughed. "No. It's a TV show."

"Never seen it."

"One of my clients loaned me the box set of season two. I could go by KFC on my way to your place."

It took Levi a second to figure out what Jaime was saying. He didn't want to go out. But he *did* want to come over. He was deliberately not making eye contact again and he was blushing. *Again.* Levi couldn't help but think how damn cute he was when he did that.

"It's just a suggestion," Jaime said nervously, and Levi realized he still hadn't answered.

"It sounds great," he said.

Torchwood turned out to be a bit too cheesy for Levi's tastes, but then again, he was quickly realizing just about everything Jaime enjoyed was. He remembered the first night they'd gone out, when he'd mentioned going to a movie. Jaime had said, "Nothing heavy. Nothing sappy or sad." It seemed Jaime had dealt with enough drama already. He didn't want to be subjected to more. But melodrama seemed to suit him just fine.

They had fun together. It was a mellow, friendly, Boy Scout kind of fun. It was very much the kind of fun Levi might have had with his brothers once upon a time, and being with Jaime made him realize how much he missed it. He'd spent so many years telling himself he didn't need it, but Levi couldn't deny how much he enjoyed it. At some point during episode five—or maybe episode six; Levi had lost count—he looked over to find Jaime asleep on the other end of the couch.

"Come on, kid," he said, gently tapping the back of Jaime's hand with his finger. He didn't think Jaime would appreciate being touched any more than that. "Wake up."

Jaime's eyes drifted open. "I should go home."

"No," Levi said, "but you should go to bed. Come on." He took Jaime's hand and pulled him off the couch. He started to lead him down the hall, but Jaime stopped suddenly, bringing him up short.

"Why are you doing this?" he asked when Levi turned to look at him. "I won't sleep with you."

Jaime's assumption he had an agenda annoyed him. And yet, it wasn't as if his suspicions were unjustified. "I'm not looking to get laid. I just want you to be able to rest. That's all. I won't touch you."

Jaime's eyes were tired, but wary. "Why?"

"Because we're friends." The words seemed to confuse Jaime, but Levi could also see him wavering. "It's okay, Jaime," Levi said. "Let me take care of you."

And when Levi tugged his hand again, Jaime followed. Levi made a point of looking through his closet for nothing in particular while Jaime undressed, then he heard Jaime sigh as he settled down into the bed.

"Don't sleep on the couch, Levi," he mumbled. "It's bad for your back."

That was true, of course. "I won't." And he meant it. Sleeping on the couch didn't sound a bit appealing. Then again, sleeping next to Jaime was bound to prove trying in other ways.

Jaime was asleep by the time Levi finished brushing his teeth, and Levi climbed into the empty side of the bed.

It was a restless night. No matter how hard he tried, he couldn't stop thinking about the soft warm body on the other side of the bed. He ended up jacking off in his bathroom, then sleeping on the couch until three in the morning, when he finally managed to return to his own bed.

Tuesday night was better. He stayed up late, and by the time he climbed into bed, he was exhausted. He wasn't awake long enough to obsess about Jaime. But Wednesday was the worst.

He managed to fall asleep next to Jaime without much trouble, but he woke a few hours later. Jaime had kicked the covers off them both, but had drifted in his sleep toward the warmth of Levi's body. Levi could feel Jaime against his back. Jaime wasn't tight up against him, not spooning, but he seemed to be curled in a ball against Levi's back. Levi could feel his breath on the back of his neck, and it felt unbelievably good.

He debated rolling over and trying to make something happen, but knew right away it was a bad idea. He had promised not to hit on Jaime, and Jaime trusted him. He couldn't violate that trust now. But the longer he lay there, feeling Jaime behind him, the more aroused he became.

He sat up quickly, thinking maybe he'd sleep on the couch after all, but his sudden movement cause Jaime to stir. Jaime's eyes opened a crack and he seemed to realize he wasn't on his own side. He mumbled something that might have been an apology, although it sounded suspiciously like "Captain Jack," then rolled over, back to his own side of the bed, and went back to sleep. If he'd ever really been awake to begin with.

Levi lay back down. But he knew he wasn't going to sleep. He couldn't take his eyes off Jaime.

Jaime's back was to him. He wore only boxers. He'd rolled forward from his side so he was mostly on his stomach, and his position accentuated the arc of his back. His boxers had ridden up one leg, revealing the curve at the top of his thigh. Levi couldn't help but think of the things he couldn't see: Jaime's ass, which had always appealed to him, a little rounder than some, and probably soft and pale. Levi pictured it with very little hair. Maybe a bit on the lower part of his cheeks, where they rounded into his perineum. The hair would be faint and sparse and red, just as it was on his chest.

Levi's hand drifted down to his own engorged cock. It was wrong to want Jaime this much. Or was it? He didn't want to hurt him. He didn't want to take advantage of him. But he very much wanted to be intimate with him.

He eyed Jaime's smooth back and the tempting swell of his ass inside his shorts, and he knew he needed to do something about the sweet ache in his groin. He debated going to the bathroom to do it, but he couldn't quite make himself do it. He couldn't seem to pull his eyes away from Jaime.

He reached down and pushed his briefs out of the way. Simply freeing his erection from his shorts gave him a bit of relief, but not enough. He didn't want to sleep in a wet spot, though, so he reached behind himself, off the side of the bed, and found his discarded T-shirt on the floor. He wrapped it around his cock and started to stroke.

He went slowly, in part because he didn't want to shake the bed and risk waking Jaime. But it was also because his fantasy of Jaime felt slow and erotic. When he'd thought of seducing Jaime back when they'd first met, he'd thought of bending Jaime over his massage table and fucking him hard. He'd thought of driving into him, quick and raw and as impersonal as his encounters at the club.

But this time was different.

He imagined feeling Jaime's skin, waking him with gentle caresses. He imagined kissing him, first the back of his neck, then his chest, and finally his soft, pink lips. He imagined running his hands up Jaime's pale thighs. He imagined the tender flesh on the inside of those thighs, high up, between Jaime's legs. He imagined himself on his knees in front of Jaime, sucking his cock. He imaged Jaime's hands tangled in his hair. He imagined the sounds Jaime might make. Through it all, he stroked himself, stifling his moans, trying to still his quickened breathing.

He imagined pushing into Jaime. Not thrusting hard. Not driving home. But looking down into his gorgeous blue eyes as he slowly worked his way inside. He imagined Jaime's legs wrapped around his waist, and seeing Jaime's face flushed with desire, his eyes closed, his head thrown back.

He worked himself, stroking toward his climax. He didn't examine what his fantasies meant, if they meant anything at all. He only knew it felt *unbelievably* good. He couldn't remember when he'd found so much satisfaction masturbating. When he finally came, pumping into his soiled shirt, his face buried in his pillow to keep from making a noise, it felt like a dam bursting, and it took him a long time to catch his breath.

On the other side of the bed, Jaime slept on.

CHAPTER 18

Levi was relieved to go back to work on Thursday. He felt a bit guilty for what he'd done the night before. It was harmless, he knew, but it had been incredibly satisfying, and he knew if he'd had to sleep next to Jaime another night, he would have wanted to do it again. And doing it a second time somehow felt wrong.

Both Friday and Saturday morning, he returned from work to find Jaime asleep in his bed. Both mornings he'd locked himself in the bathroom for a quick wank, and by the time he'd emerged, Jaime was awake and halfway dressed, urging Levi to go to bed.

On Saturday, Jaime actually came over earlier than normal, and they ordered pizza and watched a bad movie on Syfy before Levi left for work. Levi faced his shift at the club with more dread than he normally did.

"What ever happened with the guy?" Max asked him midway through the night.

"What guy?" Levi asked as he mixed a drink for a skinny twink wearing pink, feathered wings and glittery eyeliner.

"The *guy*. The one you couldn't nail."

It took Levi a minute to realize Max was talking about Jaime, and Levi's cheeks flushed. Now that he knew Jaime, he felt bad for ever having had that particular conversation with Max at all. "Nothing. It's over."

"It's over, as in you fucked him?"

"No. 'It's over' as in we're friends. That's all."

"Friends? Like, with or without benefits?"

"Without." Decidedly without the particular benefits Max was alluding to. Unfortunately.

"So you got a boyfriend now or what?" Max asked.

"When have you ever known me to have a boyfriend?" Because the one time Levi had tried had been before Max had worked at The Zone. And even then, the effort he'd put into his "relationship" had been pathetically weak. He'd liked fucking guys at the club a hell of a lot more than he'd liked playing house with Lance.

Max shook his head. "You must have something on the side, man. You haven't been with anybody all weekend."

The statement shocked Levi. Was it true? No, that couldn't be right. Certainly he'd been with somebody on Thursday, right? He must have been, although he couldn't recall any specifics. And Friday? Well, they'd been awfully busy at the bar. Still, surely he'd made time to visit the storage room. Or had he?

"Levi! What the fuck, man?" Max's outburst startled Levi out of his thoughts. He'd poured about five shots worth of vodka into the rocks glass in front of him. It was about to run over the edge. He put the bottle down. He stared at the glass.

A voice in the back of his brain told him he needed to do something about it. The man on the other side of the bar watched him with obvious confusion. But Levi was still thinking. He hadn't been with anyone the last two nights? The thought seemed to short-circuit his thinking completely. He couldn't remember the last time that had happened.

Maybe because it never had.

"Dude," the guy waiting for his drink said, "is that my drink or what? You didn't leave room for the orange juice."

"Sorry." Levi shook himself out of his daze. He quickly mixed a new drink in a new glass, and when the guy was gone, Levi picked up the too-full glass of vodka and drained half of it in one swallow.

What the hell was wrong with him?

He scanned the men around the bar. The night was still young, after all. But as the hours of his shift drifted by, Levi had to admit there was nobody he wanted to fuck at the club tonight. Lots of twinks and fairies, most of whom he assumed were college students, and a few bears. Quite a few of the guys Levi thought of as standard gay men—the ones who didn't fall into any specific stereotype, wearing khakis or jeans, polos and Ts. There was Jon or Josh or Joe—Levi still didn't know his name. There were men, yes. Some of them cute. Many of them willing. But none he felt compelled to fuck, or even to let suck his cock, and so for the first time in his ten years at the club, Levi went an entire weekend at work without once visiting the back room.

If Levi thought the week before had been bad, the next week was torture. It was his own fault. He didn't just invite Jaime over each night. He *insisted* Jaime come over. He practically coerced Jaime into spending the night. And then he'd lie there, watching Jaime sleep, cursing his own arousal and his inability to do anything about it.

Sunday night he told himself to grow up. He needed to get his hormones under control. He had promised himself, for some reason he couldn't quite accept, that he was going to take care of Jaime, which apparently meant he needed to get used to having Jaime in his bed. He told himself he wasn't going to resort to jacking off each and every night before going to bed to do it.

His resolution lasted until early Monday morning, when he woke so painfully erect and aroused, he was surprised he hadn't come in his sleep. He thought with some reservation about how embarrassing that would have been. He went in the bathroom and did what needed to be done. Monday night he found himself in the bathroom again, frantically trying to alleviate his arousal. Tuesday he stayed in the bed, opting instead to gratify himself while watching Jaime sleep, but it wasn't the same the second time. Nor was it as good on Wednesday night. He couldn't seem to reach the same level of satisfaction he'd felt the first time he'd done it.

He was extremely relieved to return to work on Thursday. Jacking off definitely wasn't cutting it. He needed to get laid, and he made up his mind before he even clocked in that he was visiting the back room at least once that night.

But as the night wore on, he found himself becoming frustrated. The men who were willing to bend over or open their mouths for him seemed unsatisfactory. They were too big or too rough, too young or too old. And by the time he rode his bike home, he was as frustrated as he'd been at the beginning of his shift.

Friday arrived along with a fall thunderstorm. Lightning crackled outside. The air felt charged. The crowd was thin. Levi watched the customers, looking for…

Looking for red curls and creamy white skin. Looking for a Boy Scout face that hid Freddy Krueger's sense of humor. Looking for a person he would never, *ever* see at The Zone.

He cursed himself. He told himself he was a fool. He told himself sex was sex, and whatever he may feel for Jaime had nothing to do with it. But the truth was, it did. And for the second weekend in a row, he abstained.

He felt it was the right thing to do, but he couldn't say why. He wished it were easier. He worried it couldn't last.

And he was right.

The third week of Jaime staying with him took him to the edge. He couldn't blame Jaime. The truth was, he loved being with him, even if all they did most nights was watch TV. He loved his dry humor and his shy blushes. Every night, he convinced Jaime to stay. And every night, he felt his patience running out.

He gave up any self-delusion this was about being a friend. He wanted Jaime. He wanted him in a way he never would have believed possible. He wanted him in a way that eclipsed all reason and scrambled his mind. He longed for him each and every night. And Jaime seemed oblivious.

By Monday night, Levi was back to sleeping on the couch, and when Jaime asked why, Levi claimed insomnia. Jaime bought it that night, but when Levi gave the same flimsy excuse the next two nights, he could see Jaime didn't believe him. Levi hated lying to him, but he couldn't tell him that, even though he was the one who had convinced him to stay, he really, really needed him to go.

By the time Saturday rolled around, Levi was a mess. There was simply no other way to put it. If he'd been on edge earlier in the week, he was now tipping perilously over the side. That, by some cruel twist of fate, was when he got the call.

"Hey, Leviticus, how's life?"

He hadn't spoken to anybody in his family, even Ruth, since Labor Day weekend. He found time hadn't eased his anger. Not one bit. "Fine," was all he said.

"Levi, please don't tell me you're still mad."

"Of course not. You convince me to go home for the weekend and the entire family attacks me. *Again*. Why in the world would I be mad?"

"Don't be melodramatic. We did not *attack* you."

"Call it what you want. Doesn't change the facts."

"You know, Levi, you bring this on yourself. Did you even hear what Caleb said to you? For some of us, it's not about you being gay. It's about—"

"My goddamn 'lifestyle.' *I know!* Christ, Ruth, I've only heard you say it a million times!"

She was silent for a moment, and he knew she was waiting for him to calm down before she tried again. "Are you still working at the club?"

"Yes."

"Still having sex with different guys every night?"

"*Yes.*"

"And you think that's a valid way to live? You think we have no right to be worried?"

"I think I have to go, Ruth. But I'll tell you what. Go ahead and pretend like I feel enlightened, if it'll make you feel better."

"Levi—"

"'Bye!"

He slammed his phone shut and resisted the urge to throw it across the room. It never ended. The expectations and the judgment would always be there.

He'd lied to Ruth, of course. The truth was, he hadn't sex with anyone in nearly three weeks. He'd never gone so long without some kind of sexual contact in all of his years in Miami. But he hadn't wanted to tell her that. He hadn't wanted to hear the triumph in her voice. He didn't want her to think she'd won some kind of victory. Because she hadn't. He was still the same guy he'd always been. The guy who wasn't good enough for his perfect goddamn family of saints.

He was midway through what could arguably have been called the most frustrating shift of his life when Max elbowed him in the ribs.

"What the fuck's your problem?" Levi snapped.

Max nodded his head toward the end of the bar. A man stood there, his eyes issuing Levi a blatant invitation. He wore black leather pants and biker boots. A leather harness made an X across his broad, bare chest.

"His name's Jory," Max said.

"I don't care."

"I know. He's a hell of a bottom."

"I don't care about that either."

Max looked at him in surprise. "Since when?"

Levi slammed the register shut so hard it shook the bar, knocking the tip jar over.

"Damn, Levi," Max said as he righted it. "You're wound up so fucking tight right now, you're making *me* nervous. You need to get laid."

"You're full of shit." But he knew as he said it that he didn't sound very convincing. The truth was, he couldn't remember being so sexually frustrated since his days at BYU trying to be straight. "I'm fine." His words were little more than a growl.

"Yeah, so fine you bite the head off anyone who comes within three feet of you."

Levi sighed in frustration, but couldn't think of what he should say. He looked again at the guy in the harness. Jory leaned against the wall. His eyes were dark and sultry. He rubbed his hand over the bulge in his leather pants, and Levi almost moaned aloud. He turned away.

"What the hell you waiting for, Levi?" Max asked.

"I just don't want to. That's all."

"What do you mean, you don't want to? Since when do *you* not want to get your wick wet? You sick or something?"

Levi bit back his annoyance. "He's not my type."

"Your *type*? Let's see. He's male. Between the ages of legal and fifty. Has a pulse. He's a bottom." Max ticked his points off on his fingers. "Oh, yeah—and he's practically beggin' you to fuck him. How the hell is he *not* your type?"

"Jesus, why the fuck do you care?"

"'Cause you're being a surly fucking asshole, man! You're driving me nuts. You need to come so bad, I can practically smell it."

Just the thought of being able to come with somebody else again made Levi's knees weak and his hands shake. He felt his resolve slipping. Max was right—he needed it. The ache in his balls had reached an all-new level of discomfort. He didn't know why he was trying to deny it.

Max seemed to sense he was waffling because he said, "I've been with him before. He's flexible. Put him on his back, you can push his legs up by his ears if you want."

That mental image, and the accompanying flush of arousal, were undeniable. The man in question *was* hot. He crooked his finger at Levi.

"I don't know what the fuck you're trying to prove," Max said. "You seriously trying to tell me you don't want to nail that?"

In the blink of an eye, Levi knew he was right. He fell away from whatever he'd been trying to be, and there in front of him was who he *was*: the Levi who fucked a different guy in the back room every week. Every *night* if he could. The Levi who never looked back. This was what he did. Despite everything his sister and his mother and his father wanted of him. Or maybe *because* of what they wanted.

Like Max was reading his mind, he said suddenly, "It's who you are, man. It's who you've been as long as I've known you. Quit fighting it. Go bend that bitch in half and fuck him 'til he can't stand anymore." He elbowed Levi in the ribs. "He'll thank you for it when you're done, I promise."

Levi *did* want it. Everything from the last few weeks hit him—lying on the couch night after night wanting Jaime but not having him, jacking off in his bathroom like a goddamn teenager again. His sister and his mother and his father and his brothers all telling him what he should do with his life. And what he *shouldn't*. And now Max, egging him on. He was filled with a frightening dark hostility that was equal parts frustration and rage and lust. He'd been trying to hold it down, trying to keep it in check. It was a blackness—not evil, but something dark and erotic and purely primal. It welled up in him. It made his skin tingle and his pulse race. It made his cock hard. His vision narrowed to a single point: a man in a leather harness with a wicked glint in his eye.

A slow grin spread across Jory's face. He turned and headed for the back room.

And Levi followed.

The guy was prepared. His leather pants had snaps down the side, and once the door to the storage room was locked, he pulled them off, leaving only the leather harness, leather boots, and a very erect cock. Levi felt the blackness filling him, practically blocking his vision as the blood roared in his veins and his cock strained against his pants. Jory could see the blackness, too. Levi could tell. Not only that, but he liked it. His eyes drifted halfway closed and he fell to his knees.

"Do anything you want," he said, his voice thick with arousal. "I'm ready for you."

Levi didn't hesitate. He undid his pants as he stepped closer. Jory opened his mouth, and Levi shoved his aching cock into that wet, warm abyss. He went slowly, pushing in deep, savoring the feel of Jory's mouth as it slid up his length, until Jory's nose was buried deep in his pubic hair.

It was so good to finally feel it. After denying himself for so long without even knowing why, the pleasure of pushing himself deep into Jory's mouth was unbelievably gratifying. He pulled out and thrust in again, faster. Why had he ever tried to say no? He wanted to fuck Jory. He wanted to fuck him hard. He *needed* to fuck him. He needed to make him beg and cry and squirm. The blackness filled him, pouring out of him, saturating him and Jory and the whole fucking room. And it wanted *more.*

He grabbed Jory's hair with both hands and fucked his mouth as hard as he could, but it wasn't enough. He leaned the back of Jory's head against the edge of the table so he couldn't pull away and he thrust as far as he could, wanting to fill Jory and choke him and make him swallow the blackness. Jory took it all, moaning in pleasure, his face flushed with desire. He beat his own cock with one hand and gripped Levi's ass with the other, guiding him in faster. His fingernails dug into the cheek of Levi's ass, scratching, and Levi heard himself cry out. It was a sudden, sweet pain, and it made him frantic.

He pulled away. He grabbed Jory's harness and yanked him to his feet, and he did as Max had suggested. He pushed him back on the table. He pushed Jory's knees toward his ears and drove into him, with only Jory's saliva on his cock to ease the way. Jory was tight and hot and the lack of lubricant made it even better, and God, he didn't know when an ass had ever felt so fucking good. And yet it still wasn't enough. The blackness in him wanted more. He couldn't fuck hard enough or fast enough to satisfy the rage that filled him. Jory held his own knees up, and Levi grabbed onto his leather harness and slammed into him harder.

"Oh fuck, yes. More, more, *more!*" Jory yelled out.

And for the first time ever, Levi wished he *had* more. He wanted to beat Jory and hurt him and come on him and come in him. He wanted to pour all of his blackness into him and have him take it all and more. He wanted to fuck every part of him at once, drive into his tight ass, and deep into his throat, and come on his face. He wanted to push him down and use him. He wanted to abuse him. And then he wanted to do it again.

"Oh God, *yes!*" Jory cried, and he started to come without even a hand on his cock. His channel tightened around Levi's cock as he shot his load onto his stomach, and the blackness in Levi exploded. He came hard, slamming into Jory, trying to push deeper. Trying to find the satisfaction he longed for.

But it wasn't there.

"Holy shit, that was awesome," Jory said, collapsing back onto the table. "You're way better than Max."

Levi closed his eyes, fighting the rage and the disappointment and the self-loathing that threatened to choke him. He hadn't even used a condom, something he'd never done before. He pulled away from Jory, covering his face, trying to find his center. Trying to remember this was *okay*. There was no reason to think it was wrong.

Except it *was*.

He put his hands on his knees and bent over, fighting the sudden urge to be sick.

"You okay, man?" Jory asked, and Levi opened his eyes. He took a deep breath to steady himself. He made himself stand up. He forced himself to smile.

"Fine. Thanks." He started to do up his pants, although his shaking hands made it difficult. He had to get out—out of the back room and out of The Zone and out of his own damn head. "I have to go."

"I'll give you my number if you want it. No strings. You can call anytime you want to fuck me again—"

"Maybe later." Levi knew as he said the words how weak they sounded, but he didn't care. "I have to get back."

He didn't remember walking back to the bar. There was a roaring in his head, and the world spun around him like some kind of crazy carnival ride. The kind of ride that had always made him sick.

"Good, isn't he?" Max asked, but Levi barely heard him.

He worked the rest of his shift in a daze, oscillating between blinding rage and near crippling self-disgust. Max kept glancing at him out of the corner of his eye, but he didn't try to talk to him the rest of the night. Levi was glad.

He left an hour before his shift was over. He didn't care if he got in trouble. He didn't care if he got fired.

He rode his bike home, driving like a mad man, taking the turns as fast as he could, pushing the bike to its limit. He knew he was driving too fast, taking too many risks, but he didn't care. He could only think about one thing: getting his board and losing himself in the ocean.

He almost hoped it would be for good.

CHAPTER 19

Jaime woke to cursing and the sound of drawers slamming shut. That meant Levi was home, which meant it was time for Jaime to get up so Levi could have his bed. Otherwise, he'd sleep on the couch, and Jaime hated to make him do that.

Another drawer slammed, and Jaime opened his eyes. Levi was standing in front of his dresser wearing nothing but a towel wrapped around his hips. He was digging in a drawer for something. He'd obviously showered, which was a bit unusual—usually sleeping was his first priority after his shift at the bar.

Jaime checked his watch and was surprised to see it wasn't even five o'clock yet. "You're home early," he said.

Levi froze, but didn't turn around. "I know."

"You can have the bed," Jaime said. "I'm getting up."

"Don't bother," Levi said, sounding annoyed. "I'm going surfing."

"In the dark?"

"Yes."

"Don't you want to sleep first?"

"Obviously not," Levi said.

Jaime sat up on the edge of the bed and rubbed his hands through his hair, trying to wake up. Dolly wiggled against his side, sniffing at his ear and wagging her tail. Levi was still digging through drawers.

"Are you looking for your swim trunks?"

Levi froze again, but didn't answer.

"They're on the floor under the chair."

Levi turned without looking at him and crossed over to the chair. He picked up his trunks and, keeping his back to Jaime, dropped his towel to put them on. Jaime started to turn away, but then stopped. There were scratches across one side of Levi's ass. It took Jaime a second to figure out what they were, but then he felt himself blush. He was glad Levi had his back to him and couldn't see it.

"Looks like you had a good time last night," he said.

"What the hell's that supposed to mean?" Levi snapped.

The anger in Levi's voice surprised him. "I mean whoever you were with left a mark."

"So what?"

"So, nothing. I was just—"

"You got a problem with it, Jaime?"

"No, I…" Jaime stumbled. He had no idea what was going on. He obviously wasn't awake enough for this conversation quite yet. "Is something wrong?"

Levi turned on him, and Jaime was taken aback by the fury he saw in Levi's eyes. "No, Jaime, nothing's wrong. I fucked some guy's face so hard he left handprints on my ass. Is that okay with you?"

Jaime felt his cheeks turning bright red. His heart started to race. He hated Levi to be mad at him. "No. I mean, of course. Yes. I mean—"

"I still have sex, all right? I still fuck other guys every chance I get. I know you think maybe I don't, but I do. And it's none of your goddamn business anyway, is it?"

"I never said it was—"

"You want to tell me how I'm not supposed to or how it's a sin?"

"No, Levi. I only meant—"

"I have a life, too, you know. And when I have a chance to get laid, I take it. That's how I am, Jaime. That's how I've always been, and you don't get to say anything about it."

Jaime felt like he'd been slapped. Or punched in the gut. He was trying to keep up, trying to figure out what Levi was saying, trying to figure what he'd done to make Levi so mad. Of course Levi still had sex. Jaime had never thought otherwise. What he couldn't figure out was why Levi was suddenly yelling at him about it.

Levi glared at him, waiting for an answer. Jaime didn't have one, but it was clear he'd worn out his welcome here at Levi's house.

In Levi's bed.

That was when he realized what was going on. How could he have been such a fool?

"Shit, Levi, I'm sorry," he said, getting up. His clothes were folded and stacked on the chair by the side of the bed. He picked up his pants and started putting them on. His face burned, and he couldn't even look at Levi. "I guess I thought you were only with guys at the club. I didn't realize…"

He buttoned his pants, and picked up his shirt. "Well, I mean, I guess it was stupid of me to think you didn't ever bring guys home, and I should've realized. I should have figured it out. I didn't mean to cramp your style or anything. I really didn't. I just, uh…"

He knew he was babbling like an idiot, stuttering over words. He was so embarrassed to have not realized Levi might want to bring somebody back to his apartment. Back to his bed. And here Jaime was, sleeping in that bed and not even making it worth Levi's time. His reading glasses were on the bedside table. He picked them up and put them in his shirt pocket. He pulled his shoes on, then picked up his keys and found the one to Levi's apartment. He started to take it off the ring.

"Jaime, wait," Levi said. He didn't sound angry anymore. He sounded beaten.

Jaime was still too embarrassed to face him, though. He didn't want to guilt Levi into taking it back.

"It's okay. I get it. I mean, I should've realized, right?" He put the key down on the bedside table and made himself look at Levi.

Levi looked completely deflated. All the anger that had been directed at Jaime only moments before was gone, and Jaime was relieved. It meant he was right. Levi had wanted to bring somebody home, and couldn't because of Jaime. And he had snapped, understandably. After all, how long could a grown man expect to share his bed with somebody like Jaime? Levi had obviously expected him to fight back, but how could he? Levi was right. The fact that Levi didn't seem to be mad anymore meant Jaime's apology had worked. It meant everything would be okay between them again. Yes, he'd have to learn to sleep at home in his own bed again. But for crying out loud, he was twenty-six years old. It was about time he did that anyway, right? Levi had already done more than he ever expected.

"Thank you for letting me stay so long. I really appreciate it."

"Jaime—"

"It's okay, really. I'll see you for your appointment tomorrow, okay?"

He turned to Dolly and patted his leg, and she followed obediently behind him, out of the bedroom, down the hall, and out the door.

Jaime hoped things wouldn't be awkward between them the next day at Levi's appointment, but he could tell as soon as he let Levi in his door his hope had been in vain. Levi was red-cheeked with embarrassment and could barely meet his eyes.

"Jaime, I'm so sorry."

"It's okay. You don't need to be sorry. I'm the one who should apologize for taking advantage of your hospitality."

"You don't understand—"

"I *do*, Levi." He forced a smile. "It's *okay*."

Levi slumped a bit, whether in defeat or in relief Jaime didn't know.

"I'll go out while you get undressed." That made him think of watching Levi, and of the marks that would most certainly still be visible on his ass cheek, and he felt his face turning red. He hated the way he blushed so easily, especially in front of Levi. "Let's start face up today."

When he came back, Levi wouldn't look at him. He kept his gaze on the ceiling, and Jaime sighed. He had no idea how to make things right. He only knew how to do one thing. Luckily for him, that was the thing Levi was there for.

He put his hands under Levi's neck and pushed his fingers up into Levi's sub occipitals. "Start with three deep breaths."

"Jaime, I can't. Can I talk to you? Please?"

"You don't owe me anything, Levi. You certainly don't owe me an explanation or an apology." If anything, Jaime thought Levi had been incredibly patient with him, putting up with his childish terrors. "Just relax. Let your head hang heavy." He pushed on Levi's neck, kneading with his fingers until he felt Levi relax a bit. "Good. Now take three deep breaths."

Levi obeyed, and Jaime started to work, massaging his sternocleidomastoids and his scalenes. Levi was rarely so tense, and Jaime spent a long time on his neck, wanting to feel the muscles give way beneath his hands. He knew it was time to move on to Levi's arms, but something told him Levi needed this more. He started to rub Levi's scalp, working his fingers through Levi's dark hair, then rubbing his temples. He slid his fingers down Levi's sideburns to rub his jaw. He could tell Levi's teeth were clenched.

"Relax," he said quietly. "Quit fighting me."

Levi closed his eyes, sighing in frustration. "I can't." He put one hand up and gripped the fingers of Jaime's left hand.

Jaime instinctively tried to pull away, but Levi held him until he stilled. "Jaime, please, I need you to understand—"

"I *do*," Jaime assured him. "I'm not mad at you. I don't blame you at all." He stroked Levi's cheek with his free hand while looking down into Levi's troubled eyes. He wanted to soothe him. He wanted to take away all of his doubts. Without quite knowing he'd decided to do it, he leaned forward. He put his lips on Levi's forehead. He felt Levi's grip on his fingers tighten as he kissed him, first in the center of his forehead, then one eyebrow, then the other. He heard Levi's breath catch. Part of him wanted to go on kissing Levi forever—his eyes and his cheeks and maybe even his gorgeous full lips. But he stopped. He looked down into Levi's hazel eyes, and said, "You're the best friend I have in the world. I don't want that to change."

Levi sighed and let go of his hand. Jaime finished his massage. But Levi never did relax.

Levi barely made it through his massage without crying. It was a horrible feeling. He'd seen Jaime cry and he hadn't thought any less of him for it. But for himself? He didn't cry. Certainly not in front of other men.

He couldn't stop thinking about Jaime's gentle touch on his cheeks and how it had felt when Jaime kissed him. His heart had hammered in his chest, and he'd had to fight to keep from reaching for him. He'd wanted to beg him for more. And then Jaime had said those words: "You're the best friend I have in the world. I don't want that to change." Levi knew then that Jaime wasn't ready for whatever it was Levi longed for. And although Jaime nagged him through the entire massage about how tense he was and how he needed to relax, Levi couldn't let go for fear he'd lose himself completely. He'd either burst into tears or he'd open his heart up to Jaime and never get it back. Or both. So instead, he fought and he managed to keep his emotions in check until he made it home.

He knew he'd been a fool on Saturday night. He'd been given a chance with Jaime to do something right and good, and he'd fucked it up. The worst part was, he didn't even know why.

It wasn't about sex. He hadn't gone back to the storage room because he was horny or because he really wanted to get laid. Those things had been part of it, but they weren't the parts that led to the blackness. He'd gone with Jory because he felt he had something to prove. The question was, to whom? To Max or to his parents? To himself? Or was it to God?

They all had expectations. Max had said, "It's who you are," and for some reason, Levi had believed him. After all, wasn't that what he'd been trying to prove to his family all these years—that even God could not take away what he was? So he'd gone into the back room and fucked Jory hard, putting all his frustration, his anger, and his rage into it. He let the blackness rule him, and when he was done, he hadn't felt better. He hadn't felt vindicated. He'd only felt angry and ashamed.

He'd wanted to prove something to the family who had hurt him—the family whose expectations he could never meet—but what about his own expectations? Jaime needed him, and Levi had sworn to himself, if not to anybody else, that he would take care of him. And he had failed. Why? Because it was who he was. He hated who he'd let himself become.

Of course, what had happened with Jory wasn't the worst part. The worst part had come later. He'd gone home full of shame, anger, and pain, and he'd taken it all out on the one person who'd never asked him for anything. Everybody else had expectations he hated, but Jaime had only one—that Levi be his friend. And Levi had failed at that, too.

He opened his cell phone. He scrolled through the names with no idea of who he was going to call. He hit the call button without even realizing he was going to do it.

"Hello?" Ruth said.

He was so surprised when he heard her voice he almost hung up the phone. It took a second to make himself say, "It's me."

"Hey, Leviticus." And despite their unfriendly conversation less than forty-eight hours before, her voice was warm. "What's up? You're not in jail or anything are you?"

"Why would you ask that?"

"Because you've never called me before. I figure it must be an emergency."

Was she right? He'd never called his own sister? Out of his entire family, she was the one who made a little bit of an effort for him, and this was how he repaid her? "I wouldn't quite call it an emergency, but I do need your help."

"What's going on?" she asked, suddenly serious.

He couldn't believe, now that he was on the phone with her, how hard it was to keep himself together. However, unlike with Jaime, he didn't have to fight it. It wasn't as if Ruth had never seen her little brother cry before. He put his head down in his hands and he let the tears come. "Ruth, if God tests you and you fail, do you think you can get a second chance?"

"I suppose it depends on the test and the reason you failed. What's this about?"

"I had a chance to do something right, and I screwed it up. Part of me wants to make it right, but it might be too late. And I'm not sure if trying to fix things now, after I've already done it wrong, I don't know if that's good, or if it's cheating. Like I'm doing it for the wrong reasons. I don't know if changing my life now will make a difference. And if I do change things, how do I know that's right if I still failed to begin with?"

He had to stop and wipe and eyes, and he knew he wasn't making any sense at all. "I don't know what to do, Ruth. I don't know what He wants me to do. And if it's what you all think, then I don't want to do it anyway. But if it's what I think, then… Well then, I think maybe I do. But is it wrong for me to want to place conditions on it? What if it is what you all think, and doing what I think only make things worse? What if—"

"Levi, stop," she said with a gentleness that reminded him of his childhood and of a ten-year-old Ruth putting a Band-Aid on his skinned knee. "Listen. I don't know what you're talking about, but I don't need to know. You obviously have a question for God. You feel like He's put you at a crossroads, and you don't know which way to go. You have us telling you to go one way, and you've always insisted on going the other. But now it sounds like there's a third path before you, and you don't know if He wants you to take it or not. Is that it?"

"Yes," he said, feeling relieved she understood. "Tell me what to do."

"Let me ask you this, Levi: if you need to know what God wants you to do, why on Earth are you wasting your time talking to me?"

"Because…" *Because God won't listen to me. Because I'm a sinner. Because I'm an abomination. Because I've done everything I can to turn my back on Him.*

"All I can tell you is, if you talk to Him, He *will* listen. I can't say He'll answer you instantly, but He'll hear. And if you have repentance in your heart Levi, He'll know. And you have nothing to lose by trying."

Levi hung up the phone with a heavy heart. He'd wanted Ruth to give him an answer, but he wasn't sure he liked the one he'd received. Yet, what she'd said at the end was true—he had nothing to lose by trying. So Levi did what he hadn't done in nearly ten years: he prayed.

It wasn't a good prayer. Not in the way he'd been taught. Certainly his parents wouldn't have approved. But his church taught that it was okay to talk to God any time. He only needed to open his heart. So that's what Levi did.

"Dear Heavenly Father, I know you may not approve of me or of the way I've lived these past several years. And I'm not asking you to forgive me for that because I'm not sure I'm sorry. But I *am* sorry for what happened on Saturday. I think you led me to Jaime for a reason, and I've screwed it up. I don't like what I've let myself become. I don't mean being gay, and if that's something you don't like, I can't change it. But there are other things I can change. And I think maybe I should. So I'm going to do what I can, and if you really did send me to Jaime for a reason, then I'm asking you please to let me try it again. Because I know I've failed at a lot of things, but I don't want to fail with him. Amen."

He climbed into bed and fell asleep. When he woke in the morning, he had a plan. He couldn't have said if it was God answering his prayer, or if it was only a matter of having finally admitted what he knew was right. But he knew what he needed to do.

CHAPTER 20

Jaime worried all morning things would be awkward again during Levi's massage. He hated how he'd messed things up between them so much. Levi was the closest thing he had to a friend and somehow Jaime had managed to ruin it.

He was relieved when Levi arrived to see that he seemed considerably more at ease than he had on Monday. On the other hand, he looked completely exhausted. He was pale and had ugly dark circles under his eyes.

"How are you?" Jaime asked as he let him in.

Levi shrugged, his eyes intent on Jaime. "How are *you?*" he challenged.

"Fine." He wasn't exactly lying. It was mostly the truth.

Levi sat down on the massage table in front of him. "Are you sleeping?"

"I'm doing okay." That, however, was an outright lie. He was only getting a few hours a night, and that mostly on his couch, but he didn't want Levi to know. He didn't want to make him feel guilty for wanting his life back. Besides, looking at Levi, he could tell he wasn't the only one having trouble with insomnia. he reached up and brushed Levi's hair out of his eyes. Levi's eyes drifted closed, but he didn't move.

"How about you?" Jaime asked. "Are *you* sleeping?"

Levi opened his eyes again, and Jaime was surprised by how sad they looked. "About as well as you, I'd guess."

Jaime smiled. He ran his finger down Levi's cheek. He wanted to touch him so much. He knew it was unprofessional. On the other hand, that was why Levi was here—for a massage.

"I'll go out so you can get undressed—"

"No," Levi said. Jaime's hand was still touching Levi's cheek, and Levi reached up and pulled it away. He held Jaime's hand in his.

Jaime trusted him more than he'd trusted anybody in a long time – maybe ever – but it still took some effort to not pull away.

"I'm not getting a massage today," Levi said.

"You're not?"

Levi shook his head. "I can't…" He let the sentence die away, looking down at where he held Jaime's hand in his. He took a deep breath, and Jaime was surprised to see Levi seemed to be having a hard time keeping himself together.

"Are you okay?" he asked.

Levi nodded. "I came to tell you I quit my job at The Zone."

"Why?" He'd always thought Levi loved his job, and not only because of the sexual perks.

"It was time. That's all. I told them I'd work this weekend, so I don't leave them in a jam. But after Saturday, I won't be going back."

"What are you going to do?"

"I don't know." Levi finally met Jaime's eyes again. "I have no idea, and it scares the hell out of me, but I know this is the right thing to do."

"That's why you're not getting a massage—because you might be unemployed for a while and you need to save money? Because I'll do it for free."

Levi shook his head. "That's not it, Jaime."

"Then what?"

"Think of it as penance."

"Penance? Don't you just say some Hail Marys or something?"

"Not in my church."

"So it's like Lent?"

Levi laughed. "No. Forgiveness comes from works, not grace." The words confused Jaime, and Levi must have seen it on his face because he smiled, waving his hand as if he were shooing the idea away. "Forget I even said it." He didn't let go of Jaime's hand, but used his other hand to pull something out of his pocket. He held it up for Jaime to see. It was the key to his apartment. "This wasn't a short-term loan." He tucked the key into Jaime's hand and closed his fingers over it. "It's yours. You can use it any time."

It was exactly what Jaime had been afraid of. Despite making every effort to put him at ease, Levi still apparently felt guilty. "Levi, you don't have to do this. You shouldn't have to put your life on hold—"

"I'm not—"

"I was in the way."

"You weren't."

"What if you want to bring somebody home?"

"I won't."

"But—"

"Jaime," Levi said, smiling and shaking his head in bewilderment. "Will you *stop?*"

"Stop what?"

"Stop making this harder than it needs to be."

Jaime wasn't really sure how to answer, so he kept silent.

"I have to work tonight," Levi told him. "It's ridiculous for you to be here, fighting nightmares, when you could be there, sleeping fine."

Jaime felt the heat of his blush at how childish it made him feel. But Levi's eyes weren't laughing at him. They were kind.

Jaime didn't know what to do. He worried going back to Levi's would eventually lead to Levi being mad at him again.

On the other hand, the thought of settling down into Levi's fabulous bed and sleeping through the night again was unbelievably tempting.

"You can think about it," Levi said as he let go of Jaime's hand and stood to leave.

Jaime resisted the urge to call him back.

Levi stopped before walking out the door. He turned back with his sexy smile. It didn't quite fit with the obvious strain and exhaustion on his face. "When I get home," he said, "I hope you're there."

Although he'd slept well on Monday night, Levi'd hardly slept at all since then. He kept second-guessing himself, even though he knew what he was doing was right.

Part of him had wanted to tell Jaime everything—to fall to his knees and tell him how much he meant to him and beg him to come back—but he knew it would be a mistake. It would either scare Jaime away or it would put pressure on him, and Levi didn't want either of those things. He needed to make amends first, if not to Jaime, then to God and to himself. And in the meantime, he'd wait and nothing more. He knew in his heart it was the only thing he could do, and he resolved he would be happy with their relationship, whether they were only friends or whether they managed to become more.

Of course, that didn't mean he didn't have a definite preference in regard to that particular issue.

He worked his shift at The Zone. He tried not to think about whether Jaime would be there when he got home or not. He ignored Max's sideways glances and the advances of a ridiculous number of customers, including Jory. He'd never had trouble finding partners, but he was sure he'd never had quite this selection before either. It didn't matter. He was never going back to the storage room again.

Finally, his shift ended and he drove his bike home, forcing himself to keep his speed somewhere close to legal.

He turned into his building's parking lot with a mixed sense of dread and anticipation. He scanned the spots, looking for Jaime's car, and when he finally spotted it, the tightness in his chest eased. It almost brought tears to his eyes.

He snuck into the house and into his room. Dolly's tail thumped against the bed in greeting. Levi was ridiculously happy to see her. He was so relieved to find Jaime sleeping in his bed, it was all he could do to keep from grabbing him and holding him close. But he knew Jaime would never allow it. He quickly stripped down to his briefs. He debated between trying to sleep next to Jaime, or waking him, which Jaime would expect, but it would mean he would leave. Levi could go to the couch. But first, he wanted to look at him.

Jaime was lying on his right side, with Dolly at his back and his right arm stretched out across the bed. Levi moved as quietly as he could, scooting onto the bed so he could look down at Jaime. The last thing Levi wanted was to wake him, but he couldn't stand not to touch him. He wanted to run his fingers down his neck or along his jaw, but he didn't dare. Jaime's outstretched hand was right in front of Levi, palm up, his fingers slightly curled. Levi reached down and took Jaime's hand in his. Jaime didn't stir. Levi stroked Jaime's fingers and the palm of his hand, keeping his touch as light as he could. There were strange shadows on Jaime's wrist, and Levi moved his fingertip over them.

They weren't shadows.

There were three of them. They ran diagonally across Jaime's wrist. They were faint, but definitely there. They couldn't be veins. Levi leaned closer, his finger tracing the faint ridges.

They were scars.

Levi felt as if his heart had stopped beating inside his chest as he realized what those scars meant. He couldn't even breathe.

"I was fifteen," Jaime said quietly, surprising Levi. He hadn't realized Jaime was awake. "I wanted to do it right. I tried to buy a gun, but the man at the pawnshop wouldn't sell me one without my mom's permission."

If Levi thought the scars were bad, they were nothing compared to the thought of a gun. He thought of Jaime with the barrel against his head, or even worse, in his mouth, and he had to force himself to breathe, choked up by the threat of tears.

"Oh God, Jaime. No." Levi gripped Jaime's hand tight, as if by holding on to him now, he could stop the Jaime back then from ever having tried.

"I used my mom's best knife, but I didn't do it right. I apparently don't have much of a threshold for pain because I passed out. I didn't go deep enough."

It was strange how Jaime could talk about it now as if it didn't matter a bit. And it was strange how an event that had happened so long ago, before they'd ever met, could inspire such terror in Levi's heart. He felt as if he'd almost lost Jaime all over again. He leaned over and kissed those lines on Jaime's wrist, as if he could take away the pain of whatever had caused Jaime to make them, and he felt Jaime's hand cup his cheek. What if the pawnshop owner hadn't been so honest? What if the knife had been sharper? What if Jaime had been able to stay conscious and keep cutting? The thought that he might never have had a chance to know him at all was surprisingly painful.

Jaime's fingers were in his hair, and Levi realized his lips were still touching Jaime's wrist, and Jaime wasn't pulling away. This was right. He was sure of it now, more than ever. Not only had God saved Jaime all those years ago, but He had brought him to Levi.

"Don't ever try again," Levi begged. "Please." His vision was blurry with tears, and he turned his head to look into Jaime's clear blue eyes. "Promise me."

"It was a long time ago."

"*Promise me.*"

"I promise."

At those words, the dam inside Levi broke and the next thing he knew, he was sobbing into Jaime's hand. "I'm sorry, Jaime. I'm so, so sorry."

"Levi," Jaime said, his voice gentle and warm, "you're exhausted. You need to sleep."

He was aware of Jaime pulling his hand away and sitting up next to him. Jaime pushed him down so he was lying on his stomach on the bed, then sat across his ass. Jaime was only wearing boxers, and Levi only briefs. He could feel Jaime's package wedged into the crack of his ass. At any other time, he would have found it arousing, but here and now, he was too overwhelmed by everything else that had happened.

Jaime's soft hands moved on him, rubbing gently, massaging and kneading, doing what he did best. His touch was magic, his strong fingers finding exactly the right spots. He moved slowly up Levi's body. First his back and then his shoulders and then his neck, and Levi felt the world fall away. Here and now, there was only him and Jaime, and Jaime's beautiful touch. It wasn't long at all before his eyes closed. His breathing slowed. He felt himself drifting away.

"I'm so sorry," he tried to say.

He didn't know if he'd really spoken. And when the answer came, he didn't know if it was Jaime's voice or not. "Whatever you think you did, Levi, I forgive you."

CHAPTER 21

Levi's mother called on Saturday to ask if he would come for Thanksgiving. After the Labor Day incident, he told her he thought it was a bad idea. The phone call ended with him angry, and her in tears. It was another hour before he realized he'd never even told her about quitting the club.

His last night at The Zone was uneventful. Max had given up asking why he was leaving, and nobody else cared.

He was happy when Jaime came over on Sunday. Things had quickly returned to normal between them, but Jaime still asked three different times if it was really okay for him to stay. Of course, Levi said yes each and every time. Still, it was with some trepidation he decided to try sharing his bed with Jaime again. He was afraid of the frustration it had caused him before, but he knew he couldn't sleep on the couch every night either.

He was surprised to discover sleeping next to Jaime no longer felt like the self-torment it had before. He wanted Jaime, yes, but he had to wait. It was that simple. He still longed to touch him and he foresaw more time spent jacking off in his bathroom than he might have liked, but it didn't seem as daunting. Lying next to Jaime listening to his quiet breathing was a bit like torture, but it was a pleasant kind of torture. Levi thought of it as penance. He was serving his time now, but he hoped eventually his patience would pay off.

Jaime and Dolly were gone long before he crawled out of bed on Monday morning. The first thing he did was make an appointment with his doctor to be tested. The night with Jory had been the one and only time he'd ever had sex without a condom, but there were always risks. When he thought about Jaime, who he was fairly certain was still a virgin, he knew he didn't want to take any chances.

Next, he had to face the bleak prospect of finding a new job. He had enough savings to get by for a few weeks, but he knew he couldn't delay too long. It pained him to admit he was unqualified for almost everything. He vowed to not be too picky, but he hoped he could find something better than waiting tables. He confessed his doubts to Jaime that night over pizza and beer—except Jaime was drinking milk—while they watched a ridiculous movie called *Mansquito.*

"You shouldn't worry," Jaime said. "You went to college."

"I dropped out of college."

"What was your major?"

"Landscape Management."

For some reason the answer had made Jaime smile.

"What?" Levi asked.

"It seems so perfect for you, that's all. Being outside in the sun. Playing in the dirt." Being outside in the sun was exactly what had first appealed to Levi, although he realized he hadn't thought about it in years. "There are plenty of landscapers and nurseries around. I think you should look into them first."

Levi spent the next couple of weeks watching the wanted ads and filling out applications for anything that sounded even remotely promising. The week before Thanksgiving, one of the nurseries called to schedule an interview. It was only a part-time position, but Levi figured he didn't have the luxury of being picky. They asked to meet with him the week after Thanksgiving.

Levi was just hanging up the phone when the door opened behind him. He didn't have to turn his head to know it was Jaime. And Dolly, of course.

"What have we got tonight?" Jaime asked as he came in.

"*Sharktopus*." Levi said it with the same dramatic relish they'd used in the commercial.

"You're making that up."

Levi tipped his head back to look up at Jaime. "I'm really not. Pretty sure you're going to love it, too."

Jaime smiled and put his hand on Levi's head, brushing his hair back off his forehead. Levi loved how Jaime seemed to touch him more now, but he tried not to get his hopes up it meant Jaime was ready for a relationship. It was more like Jaime was finally settling into being friends without second guessing himself at every turn. "The nursery over on Collins Avenue called. I have an interview in two weeks."

Jaime smiled at him. "Told you it would be fine."

"I don't have the job yet."

"You will."

Jaime went into the kitchen and came back out with a Sprite, and they sat on the couch with Dolly between them watching the movie. Although Levi still didn't quite see the appeal of the crappy monster flicks, he had to admit they weren't any worse than most of the sitcoms the networks showed, and anything was better than reality TV.

"You know," Levi joked during a commercial, "it's pretty obvious the best way to avoid being eaten by Sharktopus is to not be wearing a bikini." He expected Jaime to laugh, but when he turned to look, he found Jaime wasn't smiling. He was looking at him nervously, as if he wanted to ask a question but didn't know how. "What is it?" Levi asked.

Jaime blushed, of course, as he so often did. He reached across Dolly's napping form and took Levi's hand. But he didn't hold it. He started to massage it, the way he knew Levi liked. "Thanksgiving is next week." He didn't look up when he said it. He concentrated on massaging Levi's hand, and Levi realized the massage gave Jaime a sense of security—he was relying on what he knew to get him through something that made him nervous. What Levi couldn't figure out was what it was about Thanksgiving that would make Jaime nervous in the first place.

"I know," Levi said. "Do you want to have dinner? I'm sure the deli at the grocery store will have turkey and stuffing."

Jaime still didn't meet his eyes. He continued to massage Levi's hand, wringing his fingers. "Won't you be going home for Thanksgiving?"

"Not after what happened last time. Why? You trying to get rid of me so you can have the bed to yourself?"

Levi was joking, but Jaime's head jerked up in alarm. "No! Of course not."

"We could do Boston Market instead. Their gravy is better."

Jaime let go of Levi's hand, turning back to the TV. "Sure. That'll be great."

But Levi could tell by his voice he was only saying the words. He didn't mean them. Jaime was pointedly not looking at him, although his cheeks were reddening. It puzzled Levi. What could Jaime have been getting at? He'd made a point of bringing up Thanksgiving, but didn't seem to want to spend it together. He thought Levi would be going home.

Home. That's what this was about.

"Jaime?" He waited until Jaime turned to meet his eyes. "Do you want me to take you to my parents' house for Thanksgiving?"

Jaime didn't even need to answer. Levi could see it all in his eyes. He practically lit up. But then he seemed to beat his enthusiasm back down. "Not if you don't want to go back."

"I'm surprised *you* want to go back. There's so many people there, and you're so—"

"Anti-social?" Jaime asked, smiling.

"I was going to say 'introverted,' but yeah."

"It's not like a party, where you have to mingle or stand against the wall. Or a bar where everyone has an agenda. Your family is more like…" He thought for a second and when the answer came to him, he smiled. "Like a carnival. They're all running their own little booths. And I can try to win the stuffed bear or I can just walk by, and either way, it's kind of fun."

"You're saying my family reminds you of carnies?"

Jaime laughed. "Well, your family members have more teeth and fewer tattoos."

Levi was still surprised. He watched Jaime, and slowly Jaime's smile faded from laughter to something shy and embarrassed.

"I haven't had a real Thanksgiving dinner in almost ten years," he said quietly. "I bet your family does it right."

And if there had been any doubt in Levi's mind he was going to do what Jaime asked, it all disappeared in a heartbeat. He couldn't possibly face Jaime on Thanksgiving Day over plastic plates full of pressed turkey slices and instant mashed potatoes now. Whatever Jaime wanted, Levi wanted to give him. This time, Jaime wanted real turkey and ham, mashed potatoes that still had lumps and gravy that was thick and salty, green bean casserole and candied sweet potatoes. And homemade pumpkin pie.

"I'll call my mom right now."

He was more apprehensive than he should have been about calling his own mother, but when she answered, her voice was warm and cheery as always. "Hi, honey! I'm so glad you called. Is everything okay?"

Exactly like when he'd called Ruth. It made him sad that he'd been so negligent about calling his family they would immediately assume he would only call if he was in trouble. He'd complained for years about how his family had forgotten him, but he suddenly realized the lines went both ways. "Hi, Mom. Everything's fine."

"Are you sure you won't change your mind about Thanksgiving? You know everybody will be here this year."

"That's actually what I'm calling about. Jaime and I would like to come, if the invitation still stands."

"Oh honey, that's wonderful. What changed your mind?"

"Jaime batted his big puppy-dog eyes at me. Apparently, you all made an impression."

She laughed. "He's a nice boy, isn't he?"

"You have no idea."

This was met with a moment of silence, then she asked hesitantly, "Levi, has something changed between you and Jaime?"

Yes. As far as Levi was concerned, everything had changed between them since their last visit. But not in the way his mom was worried about. "No. We're friends." But that was something he hoped would change with time, and he couldn't help but wonder how his mom would handle it if and when it did.

They left at a disgustingly early hour on Wednesday, only because Jaime offered to drive the morning shift again. Levi slept as well as he could in Jaime's passenger seat until ten, then took over driving so Jaime could sleep if he wanted to. Jaime claimed he didn't need to sleep, but was happy to take a break from driving.

Levi couldn't get over how happy Jaime was to be going to the Binder house. His enthusiasm was contagious, and Levi found himself dreading the visit far less than usual. Whatever happened, Jaime would be there, smiling his Boy Scout smile, making his dry jokes, making Levi happy simply by being there.

"Tell me something about you," Levi said to him as he turned on the cruise control.

"Like what?" Jaime asked in surprise.

"Anything. You know all about me and my family, and I don't know anything about you at all, except you're from Cleveland."

He glanced over at Jaime and saw the haunted look that always appeared in his eyes when the conversation veered anywhere near his past. "Let's stop for lunch at the next town."

"Okay," Levi said, trying not to smile at Jaime's evasiveness.

"Not Wendy's."

"I know."

"Not McDonald's, either. Find a Subway."

"I *know*."

"If you're tired of Subway, we could look for one of those burrito places, like Qdoba."

"Subway's fine."

"But not Taco Bell."

"Jaime, I *know*. Now quit dodging the question."

Jaime sighed. "I don't like to talk about my past."

"No!" Levi said with exaggerated surprise. "Really?"

Jaime shot him a withering glare. "Smart ass."

"Come on. I'm not asking you to reveal your deepest, darkest secrets." Although he had a suspicion what that was already. "Isn't there *something* you can share?"

Jaime was silent for a long time, thinking. Levi started to wonder if he'd upset Jaime so much he wasn't going to answer at all, not even to be evasive. But finally, he took a deep breath and jumped in. "I was on the tennis team in high school."

"Really?"

"I was terrible."

"But did you like it?"

Jaime shrugged. "It was okay. Kind of boring."

"Then why did you play?"

"There aren't many sports that don't involve physical contact. It was either tennis or swimming." The tone of his voice indicated swimming hadn't really been an option.

"Ah," Levi said, with sudden understanding. "All those boys in their Speedos."

"Exactly." Levi's eyes were focused on the road, he could hear the smile in Jaime's voice.

"What else?"

"I was in the choir."

"I've never heard you sing."

"I didn't say I could sing. I said I was in the choir."

Levi laughed. "Fair enough. So why did you move to Miami? No massage schools in Cleveland?"

It took Jaime a moment to answer that question, too. "I left Cleveland the day I graduated," he finally said, not looking at Levi. "Loaded everything up the night before and, as soon as the ceremony ended, I got in my car, and I didn't stop until I was in Charleston."

"South Carolina?"

He laughed. "No. West Virginia."

"So you drove all the way to Miami by *yourself?*" He knew enough about Jaime's anxieties to be surprised.

Jaime shrugged. "I didn't really know where I was going. I only knew I had to leave. So I got on the road and I drove."

"Weren't you scared?"

"Terrified. I'd stop at hotels, then be awake half the night. But I felt like if I kept going, it'd be okay. There was some place just down the road that was *safe*, and I wouldn't have to be afraid anymore."

"And that place was Miami?"

"No." His voice was sad. "Miami's where I ran out of road. If I'd had a passport and more than twenty dollars to spare, I probably would have kept going."

"So you never found your safe place?" Levi asked.

Jaime didn't answer, and when Levi turned away from the road long enough to glance over at him, he saw Jaime's cheeks were bright red. He couldn't seem to look anywhere but down at his hands, clenched in his lap, and Levi realized he already knew the answer. Jaime had found his safe place. But for some strange reason, that place was with Levi.

Levi held his hand out to Jaime. Jaime hesitated, as Levi had known he would, but he eventually reached over and took Levi's hand.

"I'm glad you ran out of road."

CHAPTER 22

Only Ruth's portion of the family had arrived ahead of them. It seemed strange to Jaime to be in the house without it being crammed to the gills with kids. After saying hello to everyone and putting his bag in the room he'd stayed in last time, Jaime wandered downstairs to find Ruth, Nancy, and Ruth's son Carter sitting at the kitchen table snacking on pretzels. Carter was engrossed in some kind of hand-held electronic game. The room was warm and the smell of whatever was in the oven made Jaime's mouth water.

"Get yourself something to drink," Nancy said, "then help us finish these pretzels."

Jaime found a ginger ale in the fridge and sat down with Ruth, Nancy, and Carter just as Levi returned from putting his own bag away.

"What's for dinner, Mom? It smells great."

"Lasagna. But I forgot the garlic bread, and I'm out of ranch dressing. I have to go to the store in a few minutes here and get some."

"No, Mom. You stay here. I'll go."

"Are you sure, honey? You don't have to do that."

"Jaime will want Sprite anyway."

"Will you get dog food while you're there, too?" Jaime asked. "I gave Dolly her last can this morning."

"Of course."

"Don't get the kind with the peas in it."

"I know."

"It makes her throw up."

"I know. I've had the pleasure of stepping in it more than once."

"And don't buy the store-brand Sprite knock-off either."

"I know."

"And not 7-Up."

"Jaime," Levi said, laughing, "I know."

"Okay." Jaime suddenly became aware of Nancy and Ruth sitting on the other side of the table, looking back and forth between he and Levi. Ruth looked highly amused. Nancy looked surprised. Jaime felt his cheeks heat up when he thought of how their conversation probably sounded.

Levi seemed oblivious to the awkwardness in the room. "I have my cell phone when you guys think of something else you need," he said as he walked out the door.

Once he was gone, Nancy and Ruth both turned to Jaime at once. Their expressions were so intensely inquisitive Jaime found himself backing his chair up a bit.

"What is *up* with him?" Ruth asked.

"What do you mean?"

"He's so…" She looked to her mom for help.

"Different," Nancy said.

"Cheery," Ruth said.

"Happy," Nancy added.

"I don't know." The question confused Jaime. Levi was always happy. There was nothing different about him.

"And I still can't believe he's here," Ruth said. "After what happened last time, I didn't think we'd see him again for at least a year."

"I thought the same thing," Nancy said, never taking her eyes off Jaime. "Levi says I have you to thank for bringing him home."

Jaime was alarmed. What had Levi told them? "No, not really."

"What did you do?" Ruth asked. "Bribe him?"

"I just told him it'd been a while since I had a real Thanksgiving dinner. That's all."

Nancy frowned and nodded in apparent sympathy. Ruth seemed intrigued. "Still," she said, "I'm surprised. Especially since it meant taking so much time off from *that club*." She said the last two words with obvious disdain.

He was surprised Levi hadn't told them about leaving The Zone. "He doesn't work there anymore."

He regretted it immediately. Nancy actually dropped the pretzel she was holding, and Ruth leaned halfway across the table toward him. "Really? Since when?"

"Since…" Their questions made him uncomfortable. He felt like he was gossiping about his best friend. "A couple of weeks ago, I guess."

"Where does he work now?" Nancy asked.

"Nowhere, but—"

"He quit his job without having another one lined up?" Ruth asked. "In this economy?"

"Well," Jaime said, feeling even more like he should shut up, but not knowing how to extricate himself from the conversation, "I don't think he thought it through much. It seemed like it happened kind of fast."

"What made him quit?" Ruth asked.

"I don't know."

"When was this exactly?" she asked. She had the look and feel of a bloodhound on the trail. She'd found the scent. She just hadn't followed it to the end yet.

"Two or three weeks ago."

Ruth nodded, looking pleased. But all she said was, "Very interesting."

"Is he looking for a new job?" Nancy asked.

"He has an interview next week at a nursery."

Nancy and Ruth were obviously pleased to hear it. Carter, who until then had shown the lack of interest typical of kids when it came to adult conversation, looked confused. "He's taking care of babies?"

"No," Ruth said, without looking away from Jaime. "A plant nursery."

Carter went back to his game, obviously unimpressed.

"Tell me, Jaime," Ruth said, "is Levi still…" She waved her hands in a circle in front of her, as if she didn't know quite how to say what she wanted to ask. She seemed to think Jaime would catch her meaning, but he had no idea what she was getting at. She blushed when she realized she was going to have to spell it out. "Is he still"—she lowered her voice to a whisper—"seeing lots of people?"

He was still confused by her meaning, and she sighed in frustration. She glanced at Carter, apparently to make sure he wasn't listening, before leaning closer to Jaime. "S-E-X," she spelled quietly. "Is he still seeing lots of people?"

Jaime felt his cheeks heating and knew they were turning bright red. He felt like an idiot for not having caught on to what she was asking sooner. "I don't know," he said. It wasn't something he'd thought about before. The idea that Levi was suddenly celibate seemed odd, and highly unlikely. And yet, when would he see another man? He'd quit the club, which meant his primary means of finding partners was gone. He certainly never brought anyone home in the evenings, even though Jaime did his best to assure him he wouldn't be offended if Levi asked him not to come over once in a while. Of course, Jaime didn't know everything Levi did during the day while Jaime was home working, but he went to Levi's house every single night, and not once had he seen anything there to indicate another man had been there before him.

Nancy and Ruth were both watching him with unabashed curiosity in their eyes, and Jaime could only shrug. "I don't know," he said again.

Ruth nodded, a knowing smile on her face. "Yep," she said, nodding smugly, "that's very interesting indeed."

The rest of Levi's family arrived after dinner, and the kids argued over who'd sleep where. Jaime wished he had the option of trading with one of them. When they'd visited Levi's family back in September, he hadn't had any nightmares, but that was before Levi had awakened them. Looking back, Jaime couldn't help but marvel how Levi was simultaneously the cause of his terror and the remedy for it.

He was used to falling asleep in Levi's bed, cocooned in soft sheets and Levi's comforting smell. He'd grown accustomed to listening to Levi's quiet breathing on the other side of the bed. He would have been happy to sleep on the floor in a sleeping bag like one of the kids if he could have done it in Levi's room. Instead, he found himself in a twin bed with rough, starchy sheets smelling of laundry detergent. There were three boys in the room with him, sleeping on the floor, but their presence did nothing to keep the nightmares at bay.

He woke shortly after one o'clock, sitting bolt upright in bed, gasping for breath, his heart pounding and his sheets damp and tangled around his legs. For one horrifying moment, he thought he'd wet the bed again, just as he had when he was a child. But no, it was only sweat causing his sheets to stick to his body.

"You okay?" one of the boys asked from the floor.

Jaime fought to regulate his ragged breathing. "Yeah."

"You scared me." Jaime thought it was Carter talking.

"Sorry." Jaime thought about lying back down and trying to sleep more, but the ugliness lurked in his brain, crouched in dark corners and crannies, waiting for him to sleep again. It was like being in one of those Halloween haunted houses and knowing there was a man in a mask right around the corner, waiting to scare the piss out of you. No way did he want to face that.

He climbed out of bed and made his way through the sleeping bags on the floor to the door, with Dolly behind him.

"Where you going?" Carter whispered.

"To the bathroom," Jaime lied. "Go back to sleep."

He went down to the family room, which was dark and empty. Dolly sat on the couch next to him as he turned on the TV. He turned the volume down low and flicked through the unfamiliar channels until he found Syfy. He could always count on them in the middle of the night. He fell asleep again sometime before five and was awakened at six by Ruth. She was still in her pajamas.

"Did you sleep down here all night?" she asked.

He knew she'd ask questions if he told her the truth, so he lied. "I came down a few minutes ago."

She yawned as she flopped down on the couch. "Oh man," she moaned, "don't tell my mom, but I'd kill for a cup of coffee right now. How about you?"

"I don't drink it."

"Really? No coffee?"

He shook his head.

"Tea?"

"Nope."

"Pepsi? Mountain Dew?"

"Sprite."

"Do you drink alcohol?"

He laughed, thinking about piña coladas. "Once with Levi, but no, not normally."

She shook her head in amusement. "You're a better Mormon than any of us real Mormons."

Dolly had apparently decided they'd been chatting long enough. She had more urgent matters on her doggy mind. She stood up, nudging his ear with her nose and whining.

"Okay, girl," he said, pushing her off the couch and standing. "Let me get my shoes and we'll go."

Dolly turned in frantic circles, panting, as if she couldn't even wait that long, and he laughed.

"Care for some company?" Ruth asked, surprising him. "Maybe a bit of exercise will help wake me up."

And so, five minutes later, the three of them set off on foot in the fresh morning air. It was chilly, but not quite cold. There were few cars out, and the only other people they saw were lone joggers.

"There's a park around the block," Ruth told him, and he followed her around a couple of corners, then across the street into a small grassy area with an empty playground in the middle. She kept up a constant stream of chatter as they walked around it. It wasn't until they were leaving the park that she said, "Levi seems happier now than he's been in a long time."

She and Nancy had said the same thing the day before, but Jaime couldn't see any significant difference. "He always seemed happy to me."

"Hmm." They walked in silence for a bit. "You guys really aren't…" She glanced at him sideways.

Jaime laughed. "No."

"But you live together, right?" she asked, sounding suspicious. "It sounded like it."

Jaime kept his eyes on Dolly, who was sniffing along the sidewalk ahead of them. "It's not like that."

"Then like what?"

Her questions strayed dangerously close to his secrets. He certainly didn't want to tell her he spent the night at Levi's more often than not because he couldn't bear to sleep alone in his own house. "We're friends," he said.

"Why not more?" she asked.

"Because." It was the only thing he could say. The rest was too hard to put into words, but it boiled down to two simple things: because Levi could have anybody he wanted, and because Jaime was damaged. Levi may not have known the details, but Jaime suspected he had an idea, and nobody could be expected to deal with that. Even Jaime himself couldn't quite handle it.

"What is it, Jaime?" she teased, when she realized he wasn't going to say more. "Is my brother not cute enough for you?"

He laughed. "Yeah, right." He shook his head at the idea Levi would be not good-looking enough for anybody.

"Don't you like him?"

"Of course I like him," he said. "He's my best friend." He ducked his head in embarrassment when he realized how childish he sounded. He turned to find her watching him, her eyebrows up, bangs hanging in her laughing hazel eyes. He'd never noticed before how much she looked like Levi, and it struck him that this woman was Levi's sister. Of course he'd known, in theory, but it suddenly dawned on him what it really meant—shared genes and shared memories. Years of eating breakfast and dinner together, watching cartoons on Saturday mornings, teasing each other and fighting over toys as kids, and probably over CDs and bathroom time as teenagers. Sharing tears and frustrations, joys and sorrows. Having no secrets. As an only child, he couldn't imagine having someone be such an integral part of your everyday life whether you wanted them or not.

She was looking at him now as if she couldn't quite believe what he was saying. It made him uncomfortable.

"Why do you think he quit the club?" she asked.

Jaime shrugged. She'd already asked him the day before, and his answer hadn't changed. "I don't know."

"Did you ask him to quit?"

"What?" he asked, startled. "Of course not. Why would I?"

She looked like she was tempted to laugh at him, but instead she shrugged. "No reason." Thankfully, she seemed to have run out of questions, and they walked back to the house in silence.

Most of the family was up when they got back. Nancy, Rachel, and one of the K-Wives bustled around the kitchen. The turkey was in the oven. Levi sat at the kitchen table with a slew of his nieces and nephews, vying for space between clean bowls, jugs of milk, and at least eight boxes of cereal. Ruth moved two of the kids to the breakfast bar so she and Jaime could sit down across from Levi, who was pouring what appeared to be neon confetti into a bowl.

"What the hell are you eating?" Jaime asked.

"Fruity Pebbles." Levi offered the box to him. "Want some? They're good."

"No, thanks," Jaime laughed as he reached for the Corn Flakes.

"Jaime?" Levi said, his voice suddenly low and serious.

"What?" Jaime looked across the table and found Levi regarding him with troubled eyes.

"You okay?"

"Of course."

Levi didn't look convinced. "Did you sleep last night?"

Jaime tried not to squirm in his seat under Levi's scrutiny. "Sure." He hated sometimes how easily Levi could read him. He glanced around the table. It wasn't just Levi watching him. Ruth and a couple of the older kids were staring at him, too. "I slept fine," he said weakly.

"He woke up around one and left to go to the bathroom and never came back to bed," Carter said.

Ratted out by a ten-year-old. Jaime found he couldn't meet Levi's eyes. "I'm fine," he said, and was glad when Levi didn't argue.

Thanksgiving dinner was fantastic. As a kid, Jaime had always envied children from large families. His own family meals had been lonely and pathetic. It was only he and his mother, if she wasn't working, and her mother, until she died when Jaime was fourteen. And, of course, his aunt and his uncle, who Jaime did his best to avoid. Holidays had never been very comfortable.

But in Jaime's mind, Levi's family was perfect. It wasn't that each individual person was perfect. Far from it. They were human, after all. Rachel's husband rarely spoke, but when he did, it was only to complain. Caleb's wife did her best to avoid Rachel, and Rachel was for some reason being overly friendly to Jaime and Levi. Levi was obviously suspicious of her motives. Jackson and Isaac seemed to circle each other warily. They were always civil to one another, but sometimes their politeness was too stiff to feel genuine.

Jaime also knew the Binders had upset Levi on their last visit. Despite it all, though, or maybe because of it, to Jaime they were beautiful. They were bright and animated and happy, and even when there was a disagreement, like when two of the K-Wives argued over whether or not to put giblets in the gravy, it felt normal. It felt the way he'd always imagined a family would. They loved each other. That was the simple underlying truth behind it all.

In the end, they had two pans of gravy, one made by each wife, and Jaime tried them both. The turkey was dry, and the cranberry sauce came out of a can, but the ham was good and the stuffing was so delicious it made Jaime's eyes roll back in his head. They drank Sprite and lemonade and ginger ale and chocolate milk, and even though he heard Levi, Jackson and Caleb wishing they had a beer, Jaime thought it was better this way. There were no bitter arguments. No Jerry Springer drama. No jabs thrown after somebody'd had a few too many. And even with nineteen kids talking and laughing and crying and arguing, Jaime felt at peace.

That night, some of the family spread around the table to play Trivial Pursuit and the rest of them packed into the family room to watch a movie. Levi pushed Jaime down in the corner of the couch and sat next to him, almost on top of him. It confused Jaime until he realized the adults were cramming themselves onto the couch. Jaime would have preferred to not be touched at all, but if he had to be crammed up against somebody, he was glad it was Levi, and he was glad Levi had foreseen the problem and nipped it in the bud.

"What are we watching?" Levi asked.

"*My Little Pony*," one of the little girls yelled, and the parents issued a collective moan.

"No, baby," Rachel said. "We have to pick something everyone will like."

"*The Notebook*," one of the K-Wives said, and the men all groaned.

"No chick flicks," Caleb said, and Jaime silently echoed the sentiment.

"*The Breakfast Club*," another K-wife said.

Isaac turned to her with a smile so much like Levi's teasing expression Jaime was taken aback. "Something that doesn't suck," he told her, and she laughed.

"*Transformers*," one of the older kids said.

"Yeah, *Transformers*," several of the others chorused, but Nancy shook her head.

"Too many little kids in the room," she said. "Something not so violent."

There were more moans, but no real protest, and they went back to arguing.

Levi turned to Jaime with a grin. "It's all your fault we're here, you know."

Jaime smiled. "Thanks for bringing me."

"You're welcome." Levi's hand nudged his leg, and Jaime thought he might have been reaching for his hand. Jaime might have let him take it, but then he glanced over and found Ruth watching them. He pulled away instead, feeling his cheeks burning for no reason he could name.

They finally settled on *The Watcher in the Woods*. Jaime'd never seen it, but it had obviously been a favorite of Levi and his siblings when they were young. The little kids were scared, and the big kids pretended not to be. Jaime found the movie amusing, but he hoped it didn't give the younger ones nightmares. He knew firsthand how awful they could be.

a lot of tall trees in the back yard, but he knew there was a spot near the back of the yard that would afford them a clear view through the branches.

He stopped when he got there and spread out his bag, and Jaime followed suit, and they climbed into them. It reminded Levi of a hundred different times he'd done this as a kid, with one of his brothers or sisters. Sometimes with all of them. Dolly lay down on Jaime's other side, and Levi looked up past the trees at a tiny patch of sky. They couldn't see many stars, but a silver sliver of moon floated above them.

Jaime sighed, sounding content. "This was a good idea."

Levi smiled. "I thought so, too."

"I haven't slept outside since…" His words trailed away as he thought about it. "Since the summer before my senior year of high school." The way he said it was odd. Sad, and yet with a hint of fondness.

Levi turned toward him, propping his head up so he could look at him, although it was too dark to read his expression. He could see just enough to know Jaime was staring up at the moon. It was so rare for Jaime to volunteer information about his past. He waited, wondering if he would have to prod him to get him to say more, but after a minute, Jaime started talking again.

"It was a lot like this, actually," he said. "My friend Craig knew I had nightmares. Sometimes he'd invite me over, and we'd sleep in his back yard." Jaime stayed on his back, but turned his face toward Levi, and Levi resisted the urge to lean closer in an attempt to read his expression. "Did you ever read *Christine?*"

The apparent change of subject surprised him. "By Stephen King? No."

"I read it when I was sixteen, and I always felt like I was Arnie and he was Dennis. I was the loser, and he was the popular kid who somehow ended up being my friend." He looked back up at the night sky. "He lived around the block from me, so I'd see him a lot in the summer. He had a lot of friends, though, and girlfriends. Once school started, I'd kind of fade away."

"That's shitty," Levi said.

In the low light, Levi could barely see Jaime's shrug. "Not really. It wasn't like he was an asshole or anything. He had a life, and I didn't. But he was the best friend I had back then." He stopped for a minute, then said, even more quietly, "Especially that year. Sleeping in his back yard is the only thing about Cleveland I've ever missed."

The way he said it sparked a twinge of jealousy in Levi. "You were in love with him."

"I guess I was. I didn't really think of it in those terms at the time, but yeah. I used to live for those nights."

"So what happened?"

"Same thing that happens to everybody at that age. We graduated; he went to OSU, and I came down here."

"And that's it?" Levi asked.

"That's it." He turned toward Levi again. "I haven't seen him since."

"I'm so sorry, Jaime." He knew as soon as the words were out if his mouth he shouldn't have said them.

"For what?" Jaime asked in surprise.

For not being there. For not meeting you sooner. For not protecting you all those years ago. But of course, he couldn't say any of those things.

Jaime watched him silently. Now his eyes had adjusted to the dark, Levi could barely make out the features of his pale face—his strong jaw and soft lips. His eyes were lost in shadows. And suddenly, Levi wanted him so much, it took his breath away. He'd grown used to being close to Jaime, even sleeping in the same bed without letting his feelings get the best of him. But now, lying in the moonlight in his parents' back yard, he felt he couldn't stand to wait another minute. He ached for him.

They were in separate bags, with less than a foot of space between them. He imagined leaning across the gap. He imagined kissing Jaime, claiming the softness of his lips, stealing his breath. He imagined feeling Jaime's arms around his neck, and he felt his body respond.

He wanted to kiss Jaime's neck, to whisper in his ear. The bags would be between them. Was it possible that would give Jaime the barrier he needed to feel safe? Even as he thought it, Levi knew he wanted more. He wanted to unzip Jaime's bag and slip his hands inside. He wanted to feel Jaime's skin against his fingertips. He wanted to slide his hand under his waistband, to cup his soft, round ass in his hands, to pull his slim body tight against him. He wanted to hear Jaime gasp, to make him squirm, to hear him moan. He wanted to slide down his body, to suck him deep into his mouth, to feel Jaime's fingers clench in his hair. He wanted to make him come undone.

He had to try. He had to risk it. He reached out, moving his hand slowly across the grass toward Jaime. He wanted to touch Jaime's hair and run his fingertip down his cheek. If that didn't scare him away, it would be easy to lean closer. His heart pounded in his chest as he anticipated feeling Jaime's lips against his.

But before he made contact, Jaime sighed sleepily. "Goodnight, Levi," he said, turning away. He rolled onto his side and snuggled against Dolly, who slept on his other side. "Thanks for bringing me out here."

Levi bit back a sigh of frustration. "Goodnight," he said. He flopped onto his back, his heart in his throat, his cock hard and aching inside his bag.

And he resolved once again to wait.

He woke to the sound of birds singing, and the distant drone of a leaf blower. Curled inside his sleeping bag, his body was warm, but the morning air was cold against his face. His lower back and his left hip hurt. It had been a long time since he'd slept on the ground. He was definitely getting older.

He heard a snuffling sound, then Dolly's cold nose butted against his ear.

"Dolly," Jaime whispered. "Leave Levi alone."

Levi chuckled. "I'm awake." He opened his eyes to find Jaime watching him. "How did you sleep?"

"No bad dreams." Jaime propped himself up on his hand so he could look down at Levi with his clear blue eyes. "How about you?"

"Good," Levi said, "but my back hurts."

Jaime smiled. He reached over and took Levi's hand. "I guess I'll owe you a massage."

Levi was surprised at the contact. He held perfectly still, fighting the urge to pull Jaime closer. It was hard to breathe, let alone speak, but he managed to say, "I guess you will."

"Thanks, Levi."

"You're welcome."

And just like that, the moment was over. Jaime let go of his hand and rolled onto his back to stretch, just as Ruth called from the back door, "What are you boys doing out here?"

"Camping out," Levi called back. "No girls allowed!"

"Whatever." She laughed as she crossed the lawn in her bare feet. She was already dressed and carrying two small paper Starbucks cups. She sat down in the grass next to Levi and held one out to him. "Here," she said in a mock whisper. "Contraband."

"Oh, Ruth," Levi moaned as he sat up and took the cup from her. "God, I love you."

"You should," she said, as Levi took a drink.

It burned his tongue, but it was worth it. He felt like his eyes were about to roll back in his head.

"Would your parents really be upset?" Jaime asked.

Levi shrugged, and when he looked at Ruth, he saw her mirror the gesture. "Not really," she said. "They'd be a bit disappointed, but they wouldn't be angry or anything."

"Then why all the sneaking around?"

Ruth looked at Levi, and he smiled and answered for her. "Because being sneaky is what makes it fun."

Jaime shook his head. "I think you're supposed to leave your teenage rebellion behind once you reach the age of thirty."

"What fun would that be?"

"I hope you two enjoyed your little two-man campout," Ruth said, "because I have a feeling you'll have most of the kids out here with you tonight."

Levi was less than thrilled at the prospect, but to his surprise, Jaime smiled. "That'd be great." And he was pretty sure Jaime meant it, too. Jaime started to climb out of his bag, and Dolly spun excitedly in a circle.

"Are you leaving us?" Ruth asked.

"Dolly needs her walk," he said as he gathered up his sleeping bag. "We'll be back in a bit."

Levi watched Jaime cross the lawn, headed for the house, with Dolly at his heels. He was amazed at how at-home Jaime seemed to be with his huge, crazy family.

"He has no idea, does he?" Ruth asked, interrupting his thoughts.

"About what?"

"About you."

He looked over at her in confusion and was a bit annoyed at the laughter he saw in her eyes. "What in the world are you talking about?"

She smiled smugly. "You're in love with him."

Such simple words, but it felt like being punched in the gut. Levi put his head down, closed his eyes, and tried to catch his breath. He tried to find the words to tell his sister she had no idea what she was talking about. Of course, they would have been a lie. He did love Jaime, more than he ever could have believed was possible. Although he'd never thought of it in just those words before—being *in love*—he certainly couldn't deny they were true. "How did you know?"

She laughed. "It's pretty obvious. I don't know how he can't see it, but he doesn't. Why haven't you told him?"

"I can't."

"That's not an answer."

Levi sipped his coffee while he thought about what to say. "I think something happened to him. I don't really know what or when. I only know it happened before he was fifteen."

"What kind of 'something' are we talking about?"

He hesitated. He didn't want to reveal Jaime's secrets, especially since he really only had guesses at this point anyway, but he trusted Ruth. "I think maybe…" It was still hard to say the words out loud. "Sexual abuse."

"Oh, Levi, how awful!"

"I don't know for sure, but I know he's…" He debated what word to use. He knew Jaime would have said "damaged," but that wasn't the way he saw it. "Scarred."

"And you being in love with him would make it worse?" she asked with obvious doubt.

"It's not the 'love' part that's the problem. It's what goes with it he couldn't handle." He felt awkward saying it. Sex was something he'd never really discussed with his sister.

"You can't have one without the other?"

"If I told him how I felt, he'd feel pressured about the rest."

"So what are you going to do? Keep it a secret forever?"

The thought of never being able to express his feelings for Jaime made his heart ache. "All I can do is wait," he told Ruth quietly. "And pray."

"What do you pray for?" He could hear the hint of disapproval in her voice at the thought he might ask God to grant him a lover. But it wasn't like that.

"I pray I'll do the right thing."

"The right thing for who?"

"For Jaime."

The relief on her face was obvious. She tousled his hair like she hadn't done for years. "You're a good man, Levi," she said. "You gave us reason to doubt for a few years there, but I knew you'd come around."

"Is that supposed to be a compliment?"

She shrugged. "Call it whatever you want." She drained her coffee cup and handed him the empty.

"What am I supposed to do with this?"

"I bought them," she said as she stood up and headed for the house. "You get to hide the evidence."

CHAPTER 24

Friday passed in a mellow way, with holiday specials on TV, turkey sandwiches, and plenty of naps in between. That night, Jaime and Levi had eight kids sleeping in the back yard with them. It seemed to annoy Levi a bit, but Jaime thought it was a blast. Levi often teased him about being a Boy Scout, but the truth was, with the exception of those nights in Craig's back yard, Jaime'd never had the opportunity to camp out before, and certainly not with a group of laughing, teasing kids. He loved being with Levi's family. They made him feel normal.

And then suddenly it was Saturday, and the confab. Jaime knew Levi was nervous about it, and he couldn't blame him. The weekend had been pleasant so far, and everybody was reluctant to have it all come crashing down.

Jaime's plan was to head to his room and pack his bags, in case they had to leave early again, but Ruth stopped him as the entire family was heading for the study.

"Come on, Jaime," she said. "You should join us."

"Yeah, right," Jaime laughed, thinking she was joking. Then he looked in her eyes and saw she was absolutely serious. "I don't think it's a good idea."

"Of course it is."

Jaime looked over at Levi, hoping for some kind of support. Levi looked as confused as Jaime felt. He was staring at Ruth suspiciously. "Why?" he asked.

"Why not?" She shrugged. She turned back to Jaime. "It's okay. Jack will be there, too."

"Yeah, but Jack's your husband. I'm only—"

"Are you really so interested in watching *Charlie and the Chocolate Factory?*" She pointed toward the family room where one of the K-Wives was putting a movie in for the kids.

"Well—"

Ruth didn't wait for him to answer. She turned and went down the hall, leaving behind a bemused Jackson and a confused Levi. Levi saw Jaime's questioning look and shrugged. "It's up to you."

"I don't think I'd be welcome," Jaime said.

"They won't care," Levi said. "You're not supposed to talk. Just listen."

"I think it'd be awkward."

"I think you should come and keep me company," Jackson said.

"How can I keep you company if we can't talk?"

Jackson sighed in exasperation. "Look, I was told by my wife to do everything in my power to convince you to come. Now, I know neither of you has ever had to deal with an angry wife, but I'm asking you to take pity on me."

Levi laughed, and Jaime found himself relenting. After all, Ruth was right about the movie, if nothing else. He'd never been a fan of *Charlie and the Chocolate Factory*, whether starring Gene Wilder or Johnny Depp. So instead of watching a movie or packing his bag, he followed Levi and Jackson into the study. The Binder family members were all taking their seats in a circle in the center of the room. Jackson led Jaime to two chairs against the wall.

"Why's Jaime here?" Jacob asked, and Jaime started to blush. This was exactly what he'd been afraid of. He stood up to leave, but Jackson put his hand on his shoulder, urging him back down.

"Please don't touch me." He shrugged Jack's hand away, but it had already served its purpose because Jaime heard Ruth's response.

"I invited him," she said, as if no other explanation was needed, and maybe she was right because nobody else seemed to care, and Jacob let the matter drop.

Jaime settled uncomfortably into his chair, wishing he could somehow make himself invisible.

Abraham began the meeting by saying a prayer, then asking if there was any new business. It took a minute for anybody to answer, but Isaac spoke first.

"As of next week, Kristine's mother will have been cancer-free for two years," he said simply, then stopped as if he wasn't sure what else to say.

"That's wonderful," Nancy said, and the rest of the family agreed.

Then Rachel spoke. "Some of you know this already, but we had the ultrasound a few weeks ago and we're having a boy." She looked around at her family, smiling. "Big surprise, right?" she asked, and they all laughed.

"Do you have a name yet?" Nancy asked.

"You know she won't tell us, even if she does," Caleb said. "She's superstitious."

Rachel blushed, and they all laughed and congratulated her before looking around the circle expectantly. Ruth surprised everybody by saying suddenly, "Levi has something to share."

Levi turned to her in surprise. "I do?"

"About your job?"

Levi's jaw clenched. He seemed hesitant to say anything.

Ruth seemed to have anticipated his reaction because she kept talking for him. "Levi left his old job a couple of weeks ago. He has an interview next week at a nursery." She turned to Levi, beaming, ignoring the fact he was beet-red and looked terribly uncomfortable. "I think it's so wonderful you're finally moving on from the club, and I want you to know I'll be praying for you to get the job."

"So will I," Nancy said.

"What made you quit?" Caleb asked. "After all these years."

"I don't know. I just…" Levi glanced nervously over at Jaime. Jaime wondered if Levi thought he knew the answer because he didn't.

"I think," Ruth said, "Levi has personal reasons for quitting the club, and I don't think we need to go into them here. I wanted him to know that I—well, that *we*, as his family, support the new direction he's taking."

Everybody seemed to agree with this, and his siblings congratulated him and wished him luck, even though Levi still looked like he wanted nothing more than to find a deep, dark hole to hide in. Jaime saw Caleb lean over and ask Ruth a question. She whispered something back and then, for some reason Jaime could not comprehend, they both turned to look at Jaime. Jaime sank a little lower in his chair.

"Okay," Abraham said finally, "anything else?" Nobody answered, so he asked, "Any old business?"

They all looked at Levi nervously, but it was Jacob who broke the silence. "Of course there's old business." He sighed. "The same 'old business' we've been discussing for the last ten years."

"I don't like it any better than you do," Levi said. "I'd be perfectly happy not to discuss it at all."

"Levi," Abraham said, "I know you don't want to hear this, but I've done more research into Evergreen International. And the more I learn, the more impressed I am. They're not a bunch of charlatans out to take people's money. They're a non-profit organization. They've helped a lot of other Mormons who suffer from same-sex attraction."

"I wish you wouldn't say it that way," Levi said. "You're the ones who seem to 'suffer' because of it. Not me."

"So you admit you're causing your family pain and grief?" Isaac asked.

Levi's laugh held more bitterness than humor. "That was sarcasm, Isaac."

"Did you even try?" Jacob asked. "After the last meeting, did you even look for a support group?"

"No."

"Why not?"

"Do you really need me to answer?"

"I'm not asking why you didn't change your whole life. I'm only asking why it's so hard for you to even consider it?"

Levi crossed his arms, scowling, but he seemed to decide it was best to not answer.

"I think Levi is making progress," Nancy said. "I'm not saying I wouldn't like to see more, but I think quitting the club is a wonderful start."

"I didn't do it for you," Levi said quietly.

"Daddy," Rachel said, sounding scared to death, "I'd like to say something."

Levi groaned, sinking lower in his chair, and Rachel's cheeks flushed red.

"Go ahead, sweetpea," Abraham said.

Now that everybody was looking at her, she looked even more unsure, but she didn't back down. She gripped her hands tight in her lap, in front of her very round, pregnant belly, and sat up straight. "You all know where I stood on this issue in the past."

"You mean mindlessly echoing whatever Isaac and Dad said?" Levi asked bitterly.

Rachel looked down at her lap. "That's probably true. But something happened recently to change my mind."

Her statement surprised everyone, including Levi. They all sat up a little straighter, attentive to what she had to say.

"You might remember me telling you about Cheryl taking a job at a homeless shelter in Salt Lake."

Jaime glanced over at Jackson, wondering who Cheryl was, and Jackson whispered, "Her husband's sister."

"She sent us this email the other day." She reached with a shaking hand into her back pocket and pulled out a piece of paper, which she proceeded to unfold. She glanced over at Levi. "It turns out a lot of homeless kids are gay, too." She looked around the circle again. "And I think there's something here we should think about.

"Listen to what she said: 'The most recent study I read said only five to eight percent of American youths identify as GLBT, but among the homeless, the numbers seem to be much higher. One recent nationwide study showed as many as twenty to forty percent of homeless youths are GLBT. An informal survey done at shelters in the Salt Lake area indicates the numbers here are even higher, close to fifty percent.'"

Rachel looked up from her paper, and Jaime was surprised to see there were tears in her eyes. "Every day, they get kids in the shelter who were kicked out of their homes for being gay. Last week in Salt Lake, two of these kids froze to death on the street. She says it happens every year. Usually it doesn't happen this early in the year, but a couple of weeks ago, they had a cold snap. They had record lows for November. And these kids *died.* Not only that, but they have several more who commit suicide. Every single year."

She stopped to wipe her eyes, and when she spoke again, her voice was firmer. "Homosexual behavior is a sin," she said, "but what about *this?* What about these parents who find out their kids are gay and throw them out and let them die on the street because of it?" She looked around the room, her eyes full of tears, but blazing with anger, too. "Isn't that a far worse sin? These were *children.* And instead of loving them, helping them and protecting them, as our Heavenly Father intended, their parents tossed them out like garbage. And now they're dead."

"Rachel," Isaac said, his voice calm and patient, and more than a bit condescending, "Levi's not homeless. And he's not going to freeze to death."

"That's not the point." But the wind seemed to have gone out of her sails. She slumped a bit in her seat, looking down at the crumpled paper in her lap. "I think we've all been behaving shamefully," she said in a soft voice. "Myself included."

Ruth and Caleb looked pleased. Jacob and Nancy looked confused. Rachel was still crying. Abraham and Isaac looked stunned. And Levi? He looked the most stunned of all. He slowly reached over to Rachel and took her hand. She looked up at him in teary surprise.

"I'm sorry, Levi," she said. "I always thought I was doing what was best. I know you don't believe that, but I really did think it was the right thing."

Isaac snorted in disgust. "How can you think it's *wrong* now?"

She looked over at him indignantly. "I still believe homosexual behavior is a sin. I still wish Levi would consider Evergreen. I don't think we're wrong for wishing he could find happiness in a righteous life. I still pray every night he'll change his mind. But what I've realized is, we're *family*. And I'd rather have a brother who's gay than one who decides never to come home again."

"You're exaggerating," Isaac snapped. "You're completely confusing the point!"

"I am not!"

"This isn't something we can turn a blind eye to. You're letting your emotions cloud your judgment."

"Why is it when I agree with you, I'm being logical, but when I agree with Levi, I'm being emotional?"

"Because your position before was supported by church doctrine."

"The church also teaches us that family is the most important gift we're given. It's an integral part of our Heavenly Father's plan. It should be cherished above all else."

"Even if one member of the family is a sinner?"

"We're *all* sinners. That's part of church doctrine, too, but you like to forget that part."

"And when Levi comes home with a husband, what then? Will you introduce your new baby to his two *uncles* and tell him that's part of God's plan?"

"Enough," Ruth said, loudly enough to override them both. She looked around the circle at them all. "I think we've all said enough," she said, quieter. "I propose we end the meeting."

"We haven't resolved anything," Isaac said.

Jacob sighed. "We never do."

"Exactly," Ruth said. "And screaming at each other isn't the solution."

Rachel looked relieved. Isaac actually looked ashamed. He hung his head, red-faced. "You're right," he said.

Abraham looked unsure, but most of the rest of them were nodding. Ruth wasn't finished. "I think for years we've been having the same old argument, but things have changed now." She glanced over at Levi, then, to Jaime's surprise, she glanced at him. She smiled at him and then looked over at Rachel. "We have new things to think about. I think instead of letting ourselves become emotional and start hurling insults at each other, we should close the meeting. We should take the next four weeks to pray on what's been said here today and we should discuss it again at Christmas."

"I agree with Ruth," Nancy said. "Just once, I'd like to end our weekend together on a happy note. I'd like for us to all walk out of this room feeling like family."

"We can't resolve this issue by ignoring it," Abraham said to his wife.

"We can't resolve it by fighting, either," she countered.

Abraham debated for a moment. He looked around at his children and sighed in resignation. "Fine. I think I'm outnumbered here, and it *is* getting late. Let's say the closing prayer—"

"I'd like to say it, Dad," Ruth said.

"That's fine."

Everybody crossed their arms and bowed their heads, even Jackson. Jaime crossed his arms, but kept his eyes on the family. Ruth took a minute, seemingly to compose her thoughts, before she started the prayer.

"Heavenly Father, we thank thee for bringing us together today. We thank thee for the many blessings you have seen fit to bestow upon us. We thank thee for the love we share here, as a family.

"We gather here together today in the spirit of contrition. In the past, we have asked thee to help turn Levi away from the path of sin he has chosen."

Jaime glanced at Levi, and saw that his jaw was clenched tight.

"Heavenly Father, we ask now for thy forgiveness for having presumed to know thy will. We offer a new prayer today. We ask instead that in thy wisdom and thy love, you help Levi find that which he seeks."

Levi's eyes snapped open, as did Abraham's, and they both looked at Ruth in surprise. But they said nothing, and nobody else moved at all.

"We ask thee to help Levi find the happiness he deserves. We ask thee to fill the empty place in his heart, and help him become whole, so our family can be whole again too. We ask for thy divine guidance Heavenly Father, in this as in all things.

"We say these things in the name of thy Son, Jesus Christ. Amen."

"Amen," the rest of the family mumbled.

Everybody stood up, and Jaime lingered in the back of the room, waiting for Levi. Jackson, Jacob and Nancy were already leaving. Abraham, Ruth and Isaac were having a quiet but intense conversation in the corner. Levi and Rachel were talking quietly together. Rachel was still crying, and as Jaime watched, Levi pulled her into his arms and hugged her. It was nice to see him making peace with her.

"What did you think?" asked a voice next to him.

Jaime turned to find Caleb beside him. "I'm glad it ended well," Jaime said.

Caleb smiled, looking at him appraisingly, and Jaime felt himself shrink under the obvious scrutiny. "He really quit the club?"

"Yes." Why did they keep asking him that? And, of course, he knew what was coming next. "No, I don't know why," he said, before Caleb could ask.

Caleb seemed to find his answer funny because he laughed. "I'm sure you'll figure it out."

He clapped Jaime on the shoulder, a gesture that was somehow kind and fraternal, and although Jaime didn't like to be touched, the contact was too brief to trigger his anxiety.

"I'm glad you're here, Jaime," Caleb said. "I hope you'll be back for Christmas."

CHAPTER 25

The Binder children and their families were all heading back to their respective homes on Sunday, and with everybody trying to track down scattered possessions as they packed and said goodbye, the morning chaos was worse than usual. As a result, Jaime and Levi left Georgetown several hours later than they'd originally planned, which meant they'd arrive home late. Jaime offered to drive the first half because he knew he'd be too tired to drive at night.

They were less than an hour out of Georgetown when he looked down at the gas gauge and frowned. "Didn't you fill it up in Charleston on the way up?"

"Yeah. Why?"

"It's almost empty."

"That's impossible."

There was no way they could have burned an entire tank of gas already, but the gauge was frighteningly low. "Shit," Jaime said. "How far is it to Charleston?"

"Ten more minutes. Will we make it?"

"Yeah, but we'll be staying the night. There must be a leak somewhere in the gas line. We'll have to take find a mechanic tomorrow and have it checked."

"It was gonna be a long-ass drive home anyway," Levi said with obvious relief.

They made it Charleston and filled the tank again. Even if it were leaking somewhere, they'd still need to be able to start it in the morning and get it to the service station.

"Now we need a hotel." Jaime glanced at Dolly sleeping in the back seat. "One that takes dogs."

"Something by the beach," Levi said.

They found a hotel and checked in. Jaime had to call all his Monday clients and change their appointments. "I've rescheduled everybody but you," he said to Levi half an hour later. "Can you switch to later in the week?"

"I don't know," Levi said, smiling. "You already owe me one from the other day."

"Now I guess I owe you two."

They went out for dinner and lingered over dessert, then went back to the room to get Dolly and headed for the beach. It was a bit chilly, and they zipped their jackets as they walked. They stopped a few yards from the water and stared out at the ocean. The light was fading, but they could still see the waves crashing several yards offshore.

"It's nice here," Jaime said.

"I've always liked Charleston. This is where I learned to surf."

"Too bad it's so cold. We could rent a couple of boards and go surf while they fix the car."

Levi smiled over at him. "I've converted you."

Jaime laughed. "I guess so. But by the time it's warm enough to go again, I'll probably have forgotten how."

Levi gazed at him, his eyes uncharacteristically intense, and Jaime found himself a bit disconcerted by what he saw in them. He couldn't tell if Levi was laughing at him, or proud of him, or—

"I'll just have to teach you again," Levi said.

Jaime laughed, feeling uncomfortable for no reason he could put his finger on. "I'm sure you have better things to do with your time."

Levi didn't laugh. He stood there, looking gorgeous as he always did, and he continued to give Jaime that look. "Why would you think that?" he asked.

Jaime felt like they weren't having the same conversation at all. He felt as if he was in a play, but only Levi had the script. His heart was suddenly hammering in his chest. "I was kidding," he said, and was surprised to find his voice shook.

Levi hesitated, his head cocked to the side as if he was debating something. Then he seemed to make a decision. He reached over, moving very slowly so Jaime could pull away if he wanted to. But Jaime didn't want to. He let Levi take his hand.

Levi stepped closer. Jaime's instinct was to back up, but Levi anticipated him and used his grip on Jaime's hand to keep him from stepping away.

Jaime tried to stop shaking. He tried to make himself breathe.

Levi reached up with his other hand and brushed his finger down Jaime's cheek. "I'll always have time for you." He put his hand on the back of Jaime's neck as he moved closer.

Was Levi going to kiss him? The very thought of it took Jaime's breath away. He closed his eyes and willed his heart to stop racing.

He was aware of everything. The surf pounded to his right. People laughed on his left. A cool breeze off the ocean ruffled his hair. He held Dolly's leash in his left hand, and Levi still had hold of his right. His knees felt weak. Levi's hand was warm and strong on the back of his neck. He had no idea what had come over Levi to prompt this moment, but he found he didn't care.

He tried to make sense of what he was feeling. It was a bit like panic. It was a bit like joy. It felt like flying—giddiness and sheer, heart-stopping terror all rolled in one. It was the curve at the top of the big hill where the roller coaster train stops climbing, but gravity hasn't quite pulled it down. It was the moment on top of the high board, knowing it was time to jump. It was a heartbeat of drawing breath, waiting to fall, waiting to scream. It was the most exhilarating moment of his life.

He wondered briefly how he'd manage to even go on living after this moment. He felt certain he'd never be able to think rationally again. He wondered how Levi would taste. He knew with sudden certainty he wanted to find out. He leaned a bit closer and heard Levi's breath catch. He felt Levi's breath against his lips.

"Jaime," Levi said, his voice shaky. "I—"

"Hey!" yelled somebody to Jaime's left, shattering their moment. "This is a public beach. People have families here you know!"

"Shit," Levi muttered, and Jaime sighed. He didn't open his eyes, but he felt Levi draw away from him. He felt the loss deep inside his chest. "Come on," Levi said. "We should get back."

Jaime didn't know if the feeling flooding through him was disappointment or relief. It took him a moment to pull himself together. He had to assess each piece of himself, one step at a time. His heart was still beating a bit too fast. Air moved in and out of his lungs as it always had. His hands shook, and his knees felt like rubber.

He wondered if he'd lost his one and only chance to ever be kissed.

By the time he opened his eyes, Levi was halfway up the beach.

The worst part of it was, things between them over the next half hour were unusually awkward. Jaime was suddenly self-conscious of everything he said and everything he did, and Levi seemed unwilling to look at him. Jaime wondered if Levi regretted what had happened. And if he did, which part did he regret—the fact he'd almost kissed Jaime, or the fact they'd been interrupted?

When they got back to the hotel, Levi went in the bathroom to shower. Jaime checked the TV and was pleased to see Syfy was available. By the time Levi came out of the bathroom with a towel around his hips, beaded with water and looking unbelievably gorgeous, two coeds had been swallowed whole and Jaime felt marginally better. He felt more like himself again.

"There's plenty of hot water left," Levi told him, and Jaime was happy to see Levi's normal smile again.

He took a ridiculously long shower. He wasn't sure what had happened – or *almost* happened – between them. He wasn't sure if he wanted to pursue it or if he wanted to maintain the status quo. In the end, the decision was moot. The only thing he could *really* do was get dressed and walk back out of the bathroom.

He put on his boxers and a T-shirt. When he emerged, Levi was wearing the shorts he usually wore to bed. His eyes were closed, but Jaime could tell he was awake by his breathing. He lay sideways across the bed, his feet hanging over the far edge. His head nearly hung off the near side. Dolly lay next to him, with her head across his stomach. Levi's hand rested on her golden fur.

Jaime wasn't sure what he wanted to happen, but he knew one thing—he wanted to touch Levi. There was a chair at the desk, and Jaime pulled it over next to the bed, so he could sit near Levi's head, the same way he'd sit on the stool if Levi were on his massage table. He put his hands under Levi's neck and pulled gently.

Levi didn't open his eyes, but he smiled. "Should I take three deep breaths?"

"You can if you like." He rubbed Levi's scalp first, running his fingers through his hair as he pulled it all up, away from his neck. He spent a long time doing it. He knew how much Levi liked this part of the massage. "How's your back?" he asked as he worked.

"It was doing great until we spent three nights sleeping on the ground."

Jaime laughed. "It'll be nice to sleep in a bed again, won't it?" He moved lower and began to work Levi's neck. "Thank you for taking me to your parents' house."

"I'm glad you talked me into it."

"It went well, didn't it?"

"Better than I expected." Levi sighed. "Better than it ever went before, that's for sure."

"You seemed reluctant to tell your family about quitting the club."

"My job's been a point of contention for a long time. I hate to let them think they won. It's probably childish, but I didn't want them to think I did it for them."

"Why did you do it?"

"You keep asking me that."

"You keep not answering."

"I'm learning to be evasive." Levi opened his eyes and tipped his head back to look up at him. "You taught me well."

Jaime had to laugh. "Fine."

They fell silent, and Jaime continued to work. He felt at peace. Massage allowed him to touch Levi and be close to him without feeling threatened. He rubbed Levi's neck until he thought he'd done some good, then moved down and worked as much of his chest as he could reach from his position on the chair. When he was done, he smacked Levi playfully on the cheek to wake him up. "Why don't you turn over now?"

Levi obediently rolled onto his stomach. Jaime hadn't brought any oils, but he went in the bathroom and found the complimentary bottle of lotion. It wasn't ideal, but it'd have to do. He climbed onto the bed and sat across Levi's ass. He took the lid off the bottle and shook it over Levi's back until a glop fell out and landed on Levi's spine. Levi jumped, which made Jaime laugh.

"Fucking sadist," Levi mumbled.

"Do you want a massage or not?"

"Does it involve you torturing me?"

"Do you think that's what I'm doing?" Jaime teased.

"You have no idea how much."

"So you want me to stop?" he asked, trying not to laugh.

"Definitely not."

"Okay then," he said as he dropped more lotion onto Levi's back, just to watch him jump. "Shut up and be good."

"Yes, master."

He started low on Levi's back, which was extremely tight on one side, as it often was. He couldn't make Levi do the movements that would help loosen it—not while sitting on him—so he settled for basic massage. Once the muscles had loosened a little, he moved up Levi's spine. He'd massaged Levi many times, but only one other time had it been like this, straddling Levi as he lay on a bed, and as Jaime worked his way higher on Levi's back, he began to realize how arousing it was. Levi's ass was soft underneath him, his crack cradling Jaime's balls. He leaned forward to rub Levi's neck and realized how good it felt to push against him. Levi's hair was everywhere, covering his face, and Jaime pushed it up, off his face and his neck. He wanted to lean over and put his lips on the nape of Levi's neck. He longed to lie on top of him, to see what it would feel like to be skin to skin with him.

He was becoming more and more aroused, his cock beginning to harden, and he wondered with embarrassment if Levi could tell. He'd certainly be able to tell if Jaime leaned too far forward, so he went back to Levi's lower back. He rubbed his sciatica some, too, although only through Levi's shorts. He worked and worked until Levi was limp and pliant beneath him, and until his own physical response was back under control.

"Better?" he asked.

It took Levi a moment to answer. He was so relaxed, Jaime thought he might have been half asleep. "Yes," he finally said with a sigh.

"Good." The movie was over, and Jaime started to reach for the remote, but Levi's voice stopped him.

"Jaime?"

"Yes?"

"God, I love you so much."

Jaime's heart jumped in his chest. For one fraction of a second he thought Levi meant it. But then he realized Levi was talking about the massage. Jaime smiled. He leaned over and kissed Levi's temple before rolling off him to grab the remote. "I know," he said to Levi. "That's what all my clients say."

CHAPTER 26

Their car was fixed by two o'clock on Monday afternoon, but even driving too fast and barely stopping on the way, it was after midnight by the time they got home. Levi was glad his interview with the nursery wasn't until Thursday. That meant he'd have two more days to study. He'd found some of his old textbooks at his parents' house and spent as much time as he could re-reading them during their stay in Georgetown and on the drive home. He'd forgotten far more than he liked to admit.

Jaime groaned as they climbed the stairs to Levi's apartment. "I have to be awake again in three hours."

"Your first appointment isn't until nine-thirty."

"I put one of the reschedules at eight."

"Sleep until seven at least," Levi urged, although he was sure Jaime wouldn't listen. Once inside, Jaime crawled straight into Levi's bed and fell fast asleep. Levi lay awake in bed, watching him sleep, as he seemed to do so often.

He thought about how close he'd come to kissing Jaime on the beach. He'd wanted to so much, but he'd been afraid of scaring Jaime away. He'd stood there, holding Jaime's hand, wondering if he should do it, wondering if he was about to ruin everything, wishing Jaime would give him some kind of sign. And then…he had! He'd leaned forward, as if he was reaching for Levi, as if he longed for the kiss as much as Levi did, and Levi had known a moment of pure joy.

Until the asshole next to them had ruined it.

Back at the hotel, lying underneath Jaime had been a wonderful form of torture, especially for those few minutes when he could have sworn Jaime was as aroused as he was.

It had been surprisingly easy to confess his feelings to Jaime. Then again, he'd known when he said the words that Jaime wouldn't take him seriously. It didn't matter. Whether Jaime believed him or not, Levi had meant what he'd said with all his heart. And by saying it aloud, he'd made his feelings real, to himself at least. He loved Jaime. He loved him so much he sometimes thought he might lose his mind. It was hard to believe his heart could go on beating minute after minute, day after day, when it felt so distorted and huge and fragile. But go on beating it did, and he could only hope each beat brought him a second closer to being with Jaime.

He was unbelievably nervous for his job interview on Thursday. He was sure he didn't remember enough to be of any benefit to the nursery, but it seemed they disagreed because he was offered the job. It was a part-time position and it paid very little. By some random stroke of luck, he received a second job offer the same day, this one for a bartender position at a golf course. He would have preferred the nursery, but the job at the golf course was full-time for better pay and it included tips. He swallowed his pride and accepted the fact that, for a little longer at least, he was to remain a bartender.

The position was for weekdays. Working Monday through Friday nine-thirty to six would be a big change from working weekend nights at the club, but he looked forward to it, especially since it left his evenings and weekends free to be with Jaime. However, it also meant giving up his massage appointments.

He had a massage scheduled for that afternoon, and Jaime smiled when Levi told him it would have to be his last one.

"Your last appointment during my regular business hours maybe," he said. "I'm sure we can make other arrangements."

"You're willing to torture me on the weekends?"

"Only because you're such a willing victim."

Levi sure couldn't deny that. "So I get more massages like the one in Charleston?"

He was pleased to see Jaime blush. "Maybe," Jaime said, smiling, but refusing to meet Levi's eyes. "The truth is you don't need to come as often as you do. We've had your psoas straightened out for a long time now. I should've moved you to every other week by now anyway."

"Really? So why didn't you?"

"Because I like taking your money."

It was an obvious lie. Jaime had quit charging him for massages weeks earlier, arguing it was the least he could do in return for staying at Levi's apartment every night. "I think it's because you really are a bit of a sadist and you like torturing me."

Jaime smiled. "How about on laundry day?" Laundry day was a new thing for them. Jaime had realized shortly before Thanksgiving that Levi still took his dirty clothes to a Laundromat. He offered to let him do his laundry at his house instead. Since Jaime was so seldom at his own house anymore, it had become a regular thing for them to spend Sunday afternoons together at Jaime's house while the washer and dryer ran.

"It's a deal," Levi told him.

He was embarrassed when his mother called a few days later and he had to confess he was once again working at a bar. He hadn't even wanted his family to know he'd left The Zone, but now they did know, he wanted to prove to them he could do better. And yet, maybe he couldn't.

"Don't worry about it a bit, honey," his mother told him. "You may not have found the place you want to be quite yet, but it's still better than where you were."

Working the golf course bar was a strange change of pace from The Zone. Some days the place was completely dead. Some days it was unbelievably busy. His fellow bartender was a woman in high heels and a mini-skirt who told him, with a straight face, that her name was Candy Rose. She was about his age with fake breasts the size of small watermelons. The male golfers ignored Levi in favor of Candy, and for the first time in his life, Levi found himself dealing almost entirely with women. Not just any women, either. Most of them were older than he was, and not a bit shy about coming on to him. Their sexual aggression made him surprisingly uncomfortable.

"Just flirt with them," Candy told him.

"I can't," Levi countered. At The Zone, there wasn't much casual flirtation. Either you weren't interested in the other guy, or you went in the back room and fucked. There wasn't much middle ground. "I don't want any of them to think I'll sleep with them."

Candy laughed so hard, she almost fell off of her chair. "Look, loverboy, they don't want to sleep with you. All they want is to flirt and feel sexy again. Then they can go home to their fat, inattentive husbands and their ungrateful kids, and they can think, 'At least somebody still sees me as a woman.' You're not leading them on. You're just reminding them they've still got it. That's all they want."

Levi still wasn't sure it was the right thing to do, but a little bit of flirting did wonders for his pay. His tips practically doubled, and he soon realized Candy was right. Most of the women he flirted with wanted nothing more to do with him.

The following Sunday, he and Jaime took their dirty clothes to Jaime's house as usual. Levi was supposed to get his massage that day, too, and he was definitely looking forward to it, not because his back was bothering him, but because he loved having Jaime touch him. But the massage wasn't meant to be.

Levi was digging in the fridge, thinking he needed to start bringing beer over on Sundays when Jaime came in from the front porch with his mail from the day before.

"Bills, bills, junk," he recited as he flipped through it. "What's this?" He stopped short, and when he spoke again, his voice was shaky. "Oh God."

"What's wrong?" Levi asked, turning to look at him.

What he saw stopped him dead in his tracks. Jaime was on the other side of the kitchen, leaning against the counter in the corner. He wore his reading glasses, which Levi saw so seldom he sometimes forgot they existed at all. Jaime stood staring down at an envelope in his hand, his face deathly white. His hand shook so hard the envelope seemed to vibrate.

"What is it?" Levi asked.

Jaime didn't answer him. He tore open the envelope, dropping everything else on the floor as he did. He pulled out a yellow sheet of stationary and began to read. His eyes flew across the page. When he finished, he bent over, putting his hands on his knees and breathing deep. "I think I'm going to be sick."

"Jaime, what the hell is going on?"

Jaime didn't answer. He shrank into himself, sliding down the cabinets until he was sitting on the floor. He put his head between his knees and his arms over his head.

"Jaime?" Levi said, stepping toward him. "Are you okay?"

He reached out to touch Jaime's shoulder, but Jaime flinched away from him. "Don't touch me!"

"Jaime, talk to me."

Jaime curled tighter in on himself. "Leave me alone," he begged. "Go away."

"Who's the letter from?"

Jaime offered no answer. Levi was quickly going from concerned to downright scared. He was afraid Jaime was going into shock.

"I won't touch you," he said, "but I want to help."

"You can't," Jaime whispered. "Just go away, please."

Levi debated what he should do. He thought about snatching the letter out of Jaime's hand and reading it himself, but that wouldn't be right. He had no idea how to comfort Jaime without touching him. He wished they'd never come to Jaime's house. He wished they'd stayed at his apartment.

And suddenly, he knew exactly what Jaime needed. "I'll be back," he told Jaime. "Will you be okay? I'll be gone fifteen minutes, max."

No response from Jaime at all. Visions of the scars on Jaime's wrist floated into Levi's mind. He hoped he was making the right choice.

"Jaime, promise me you won't do anything. Promise you'll wait for me to get back."

"Just go," Jaime said, not looking up.

Levi drove like a maniac. The farther he got from Jaime's house, the more his imagination ran away from him. He imagined going back to find Jaime lying in a pool of blood or with an empty bottle of pills in his hand. He worried he never should have left, but it seemed foolish to turn back now. He raced up the stairs to his apartment, where Dolly napped on the couch, and then drove even faster back to Jaime's house, praying the entire time he wouldn't get pulled over or be too late.

Jaime was still sitting on the kitchen floor when he got back. It looked as if he hadn't moved an inch, but when Dolly sniffed him, wagging her tail and nudging him with her nose, he looked up. She butted her head under his chin, sitting down almost on top of him.

Jaime laughed. It was a sad, hollow laugh, but it was a laugh nonetheless. He wrapped his arms around her. "Hi, Dolly," he said. "You're such a good dog."

And then he buried his face in her fur and burst into tears.

Levi waited in the living room. The silent withdrawal had scared him to death, but now Jaime was crying, Levi knew he'd be okay. He turned on the TV. Luck was with him, and Syfy was showing another horrible made-for-TV monster movie. Levi turned the volume up. Jaime needed his space right now, but Levi wanted him to know he was still there.

Sure enough, Jaime eventually wandered in. His eyes were red, but his cheeks were dry. He sat down next to Levi, although he couldn't meet his eyes. He seemed to be debating what to say. Levi turned off the TV and waited patiently.

"Something happened to me," Jaime said at last, his voice shaky and weak. "When I was young. Something…" He put his head down, squeezing his eyes tight against tears that wouldn't be stopped.

"You don't have to tell me," Levi said as gently as he could. He'd had his suspicions before and he didn't need the details to confirm them. "When was this?"

"I was just a kid."

"Who was it?"

"My uncle."

Levi fought back the horrible rage welling up in him—it wasn't that it was unwarranted, but it wouldn't do Jaime any good right now. "Is that who the letter's from?"

Jaime nodded, still unable to meet Levi's eyes. "He has emphysema. He only has a few weeks to live." Jaime wiped his eyes and sat up a little straighter. "He might even be dead already. Who knows?"

"What does he want?"

"My *forgiveness,*" Jaime said, his voice thick with tears and anger. "Now he's about to die, he thinks it's time we 'bury the hatchet.' He says he's confessed his sins and made his peace with God, but the priest told him he needed to apologize to me. He says God has forgiven him, but he needs me to forgive him as well."

"What are you going to do?" Levi asked.

"He can burn in hell," Jaime said with far more bitterness than Levi had ever heard from him. "I don't give a fuck."

"I don't think he can expect to be forgiven for what he did."

"I don't know, Levi." Jaime's voice broke on the words. "Will I go to hell, too?"

"Why would you?"

"Because," Jaime said, and now the tears were coming again, faster this time. "I'm supposed to forgive, but I can't. *I won't!*"

It broke Levi's heart to see Jaime tearing himself up over some selfish bastard who had already done so much damage. Levi reached for him slowly. Jaime didn't stop him, and when Levi took his hand and pulled, Jaime came to him willingly. He buried his face in Levi's chest and sobbed. Levi wrapped his arms around him, holding him tight. "It's okay," he told him. "Whatever you're feeling right now, it's okay. You can hate him. You can be angry. It's okay to have all those feelings."

"I don't want to forgive him!"

"I don't blame you."

"How can *God* forgive him?" Jaime asked through his tears. "How can *I* be the sinner? How can I be the one who's wrong?"

"You're not," Levi said, rocking him a little, rubbing his back. "You're not." He thought about what he could say to make Jaime feel better. The only thing he had was his own faith. "I don't know how it all works, Jaime, but I'll tell you what I was taught. In my church, salvation comes from work and repentance, not from grace. You can't lead a life of sin up until the end and then suddenly be forgiven just because you see your judgment bearing down on you. Having regret isn't enough. You need to have true repentance and sorrow in your heart. And I could be wrong, but I don't think your uncle does. He's sorry now, but only because he fears having to face God, and I think God will look into his heart and see he's still the same man he always was."

"And what about me?"

"I think right now God would look into your heart and he'd see you're still the same scared little boy you were back then." Jaime cried harder, and Levi stroked his hair. "You won't always be. Even now, you're usually not."

"You're saying I should forgive him, too," Jaime accused.

"No. I'm saying God knows your heart. And I think he understands."

"Are you sure?"

"I'm sure." Because he believed a God who would judge Jaime more harshly than the uncle who had abused him wouldn't be much of a God at all.

He held Jaime as he cried, until the tears wound down. He hated that Jaime's uncle had caused him so much pain, but he couldn't deny how good it felt to be close to him. Never before had Jaime's defenses been so low he'd allow Levi to hold him. Levi stroked his hair and his back, and sometimes kissed the red curls on top of his head. He felt Jaime's breathing start to slow.

"Levi"—he sighed—"I'm so tired. I really want to sleep now."

"Go ahead, baby," Levi said. "I'll be right here."

Jaime's arms snuck around Levi's waist, and Levi's heart seemed to skip a beat. "Thank you for getting Dolly for me."

"You're welcome," Levi told him. And for the first time, but Levi hoped not the last, Jaime fell sound asleep in his arms.

CHAPTER 27

Jaime woke slowly. Oddly enough, the first thing he became aware of was the emptiness behind him. He seemed to be right on the edge of the bed, and if he tried to roll onto his back, he'd fall off. The second thing he realized was that somebody was holding him tight to keep him from falling. And it took only a heartbeat for him to know that person was Levi, not only because he knew Levi's smell and the sound of his breathing, but because there was nobody else in the world it could possibly be.

He opened his eyes. He could see the hollow of Levi's throat, but by turning his head a bit, he was able to get his bearings. He wasn't on a bed at all. They were lying on his couch, stomach to stomach, with Levi's strong arms around him.

He waited for panic to flare in his chest as it often did at physical contact, but it didn't come. He felt good lying in Levi's arms. Levi was warm and he smelled amazing. Jaime's head was cushioned on Levi's arm. Their legs were tangled together, Levi's right leg lying over Jaime's left. Jaime could tell by his breathing he was asleep.

Although his right arm was pinned slightly under Levi and between them, his left arm was free, draped over Levi's waist. Levi's shirt had ridden up a bit in the back, and Jaime could feel Levi's smooth skin against his fingers. He could feel Levi breathing.

Jaime closed his eyes and tried to put a name to what he was feeling. He felt lazy, yet a bit restless. He felt content, but a tad on edge. He felt good, although somehow unsatisfied. He felt, he realized suddenly, unbelievably turned on. Levi's body was tight against him. His neck was only a hairsbreadth from his lips. Levi's leg was wedged tantalizingly against his groin. Without thinking, Jaime pushed. Not hard. Only the tiniest shift against Levi's firm thigh, but it felt amazing. Jaime's breath caught in his throat. His heart hammered in his chest. His extremely erect cock ached for more.

And Levi slept on.

Jaime moved his free hand slowly up Levi's back and then down his side, exploring smooth skin over firm muscles he already knew by heart from the massage table. He put his lips against Levi's throat. Part of him knew he should stop, but he couldn't make himself obey. In the past, he'd often felt ashamed of his desires, but there was no shame in wanting to touch Levi. After all, who in the world *wouldn't* want to touch Levi?

He tried not to push against Levi's thigh, but he wasn't sure he succeeded. He parted his lips against Levi's smooth throat, and he tasted Levi's skin. It was salty, of course, but somehow, the feel of flesh against the tip of his tongue was incredibly arousing. He wanted more. He tilted his head back an inch and felt Levi's Adam's apple against his lips.

He froze there, his groin aching, his tongue tasting, his head swimming. As simple as it was, it was without a doubt the most erotic moment of his life. With a little more pressure, a few gentle grinds, he could almost have come. Never before had he been so close to another man, so close he could feel Levi's breathing. He could smell him and touch him, and push himself against Levi's thigh. So close he could feel…

He could feel Levi push back.

It was subtle, and he suspected Levi hadn't meant it to happen any more than Jaime had the first time. But now he realized he wasn't the only one who was turned on. He wasn't the only one pushing. He wasn't the only one whose slow exhalations were almost moans. Levi's groin pushed against him, his erection obvious against Jaime's hip.

Fear blossomed in his chest. Somehow, with Levi asleep, he'd been able to get around it. Now, his heart began to pound with something other than arousal.

Levi's arms tightened around him. Levi kissed his temple. Jaime would only need to tip his head back to feel those lips kiss him for real.

"Baby, please don't stop," Levi whispered. "We can go as slow as you want, but please, *please,* don't stop."

The fear in Jaime's chest exploded into something almost like panic. "I can't," he choked out, hating how he was suddenly ready to cry. *Again.* "I can't do this."

"Shh," Levi soothed, stroking his hair and his back. "You're doing fine."

"I can't," Jaime said again.

"Why not?"

Why not? It was a good question. Because the truth was, underneath his crippling fear, Jaime didn't want to stop. He wanted to keep touching Levi. And there was nothing wrong with that. Rationally, he knew that was true. In fact, it would have been strange not to want Levi. Levi was gorgeous, confident, and unbelievably sexy. His gaze sometimes sent shivers up Jaime's spine, and his smile made Jaime weak in the knees. And here he was, holding Jaime tight, begging him to touch him more.

"I'm scared."

"Of me?"

"No!"

Levi was quiet for a moment before he asked gently, "Because of your uncle?"

It all came back in a flash—his uncle and the letter, and the reason he was here in Levi's arms at all—and before he could do anything to stop himself, he was crying again, ashamed and frightened and embarrassed and completely unable to stop.

Because of his uncle.

It was because of his uncle he was damaged, and it was because he was damaged that he could never have Levi. He could never have any of the things other men had. He couldn't expect anyone to deal with his fears and his neurosis, let alone Levi, who lived for sex and surfing and nothing else in the world. It was ridiculous. Levi had already given him so much. It was selfish to expect him to give more, when Jaime had absolutely nothing he could give in return. But how could he say it all to Levi?

"Baby, it's okay," Levi told him, holding him tight. "I'm sorry. I shouldn't have pressured you. I'm so sorry."

"I'm such a mess, Levi. I'm an emotional basket case. I'm afraid of everything. I can't even sleep in my own bed!"

"You're doing fine—"

"I'm not doing fine! I'm a wreck! I'm worse than a kid! Why do you put up with me at all?"

It was a ridiculous, childish question, born of frustration more than anything. But Levi didn't hesitate. He tightened his grip around Jaime and said, "Because I love you."

The gentle sincerity in his voice only made Jaime cry harder. "No, you don't. You're just trying to make me feel better."

"No," Levi said, almost chuckling. "I'm finally being honest. I know you can't believe me right now, but it's true. I love you so much, and I have for so long. I don't know how you can't know it." He laughed. "My whole family knows. Even my mom. I don't know how you can't have guessed."

"No, you don't," Jaime said. "You can't."

Levi laughed again. "I don't think that's a decision you get to make."

Levi's words made no sense, but they gave him something to hang onto. Something to concentrate on while he calmed himself down. Levi loved him? Since when? How could that be?

Jaime thought back over evenings spent together on Levi's couch, and nights spent in Levi's bed. He thought back to the morning Levi had come home so angry, and about how sorry Levi had been afterward. He'd quit his position at The Zone. Jaime hadn't understood. He thought of Ruth asking him if Levi still had sex with lots of men. He thought of Caleb laughing and saying, "I'm sure you'll figure it out."

"You quit your job for me?"

"I couldn't work there and be the person you deserve."

Which meant Levi really was celibate right now. Because of Jaime. "But I can't…" He fought hard to keep from crying again. "I can't have sex with you."

"Shh, Jaime. I don't care about that."

"*You* don't care about sex?" Jaime asked, torn between laughter and bitterness.

Levi sighed. "I'm not going to lie to you. I want you so much, sometimes it's all I can do to keep my hands to myself. But I swore I'd be patient. I swore I'd wait and wouldn't pressure you." He kissed Jaime's head again. "I've been trying to be good. I'm sorry I pressured you just now."

It was still hard to get his head around it. But he knew whatever had just happened, it wasn't Levi's fault. "You didn't," Jaime said. "I started it." Levi didn't answer, just continued to hold him and comfort him. "I wish I could finish it. But it scares me so much."

"I understand."

He meant it, too. That was what amazed Jaime the most. Levi really did understand, as much as anyone could who hadn't been through it himself.

Jaime lay there in Levi's arms for what felt like ages, trying to make sense of it. His right arm began to fall asleep and his bladder started to complain, but he was reluctant to move. He was reluctant to leave the warmth of Levi's embrace. He was scared to have to look him in the eyes again. He was afraid he might have ruined everything. He tried to imagine how things might be different or awkward between them now. "Levi?"

"What?"

"Can I still stay with you tonight?"

"You can stay with me every night. Nothing's changed. We'll finish the laundry when you're ready. We'll get Dolly and we'll go home. I'll order pizza with loads and loads of mushrooms for you, and we'll watch some god-awful movie on Syfy until you fall asleep, and then I'll put you to bed."

Jaime tightened his arms around Levi. He kissed his neck once, allowing his lips to linger there for only a second. "And what about this?"

"I'll wait, Jaime. Whenever you're ready."

"What if I never am?"

Levi shrugged. "It's a chance I'm willing to take."

CHAPTER 28

If things were awkward between them, it was only for a couple of hours. Levi treated him the same way he always had, and when they went to bed that night, Jaime locked the handle of the bedroom door and stood staring at it, wishing it had a deadbolt like his bedroom door at home. But it didn't. The safety of staying with Levi still outweighed any security he managed to find in his own bed, but it suddenly wasn't enough. He turned to find Levi watching him.

"Do you want me to push the dresser in front of the door?" With anybody else it might have sounded sarcastic, but Levi was sincere.

"No," Jaime told him, as he climbed into bed. It was tempting, but he knew it would only make him feel more ridiculous in the morning. He curled up on his side of the bed, wishing he were stronger, wishing he wasn't so afraid. He reached across the bed and found Levi's hand in the dark, holding it tight until he fell asleep. Even the safety of Levi's bed, though, couldn't keep the nightmares at bay, and Jaime woke, shaking, crying into his pillow to keep from waking Levi. It broke his heart to admit he was vulnerable, no matter where he slept.

The next few days were awful. He felt as if he was stumbling around in a daze. He knew he was dangerously close to sinking into a terrible depression, but he couldn't seem to pull himself out of it. He hated how much the letter had shaken him. Just when he'd started to feel normal, his uncle had re-insinuated himself back in his life, waking old doubts, old fears, and the familiar sense of shame. He tried to act normal, but many times over the next few days, he turned to find Levi watching him thoughtfully.

He worked an entire week on autopilot. Saturday morning he buried himself under a blanket on Levi's couch. The day passed in a slow, dreary blur. Levi tried to talk to him, but Jaime felt as if his head was full of cotton. He could barely hear him. Half of Sunday passed the same way. He only roused himself at all because he could see the concern in Levi's eyes turning to panic.

It was nearly three on Sunday when he finally showered and dressed, and it took a ridiculous amount of energy to put on real clothes instead of his sweats again. When he came out of the bedroom, he found Levi digging through the pile of jackets and gloves and hats and who knew what else covering the floor of his coat closet.

"What are you looking for?" Jaime asked.

"This." Levi emerged from the closet and triumphantly held his find up for Jaime to see. It was a motorcycle helmet. "Here," he said, holding it out to Jaime. "Let's go for a ride."

Normally, the thought of riding a motorcycle would have terrified him, but he could barely even muster up fear. He couldn't make himself care at all. "I don't want to."

"I know you don't, but I'm asking you to do it anyway. For me."

"I'm afraid," he said because even if he couldn't quite feel the fear through his depression, he knew it was there.

Levi smiled, stepping closer. "I know you are. But I won't let anything happen to you, I swear." He put his hand up, and Jaime held his breath as Levi's fingertip brushed over his cheekbone. "Please let me do this. Let me try to cheer you up."

Jaime wasn't sure having the wits scared out of him could count as being cheered up, but he couldn't muster much enthusiasm for doing anything else either. "If we wreck and I die, I'll haunt you from the grave. I'm not kidding."

Levi laughed. "I'd expect nothing less."

Now he'd apparently committed to it, his heart began to race. His stomach filled with dread. Levi gave him the leather jacket he usually wore when he rode. It was a bit big on Jaime, but it helped calm his nerves simply because it smelled so damn good. "What about you?" Jaime asked.

"I have an old one I can wear," Levi told him as he pulled it from the closet.

"What about a helmet?"

"I don't usually wear one."

"You should."

Levi rolled his eyes. "You can lecture me later. Let's go." Jaime tucked the helmet under his arm and followed Levi out the door. Although his knees shook so hard he wondered how he managed to walk at all, he made it down the stairs to the lot where Levi's bike was parked. Once when faced with actually climbing aboard, he froze.

"I'm scared," he told Levi again. "What if we get in a accident? What if I fall off?"

"Jaime, trust me. We'll go slow." He smiled reassuringly. "It'll be fine." Levi took the helmet from his hands and placed it on Jaime's head, then climbed on the bike. He turned to look back at Jaime and said again, more emphatically this time, "Trust me."

The bike seemed huge. Bigger than any motorcycle really had a right to be. Jaime tried to tell himself the size should be reassuring. After all, wouldn't that make it more stable? His feeble attempt at logic did little to calm his nerves. He tried to think of some other excuse he might use to get out of going with Levi, but the simple fact was, there was nothing else. He was scared. And he could either run away and go back to sitting on the couch staring blankly at the TV, trying not to think about his uncle, or he could get on the bike and hope for the best.

Jaime threw his leg over the back of the bike and settled on the seat behind Levi. Levi showed him where to put his feet. There was no seat back behind him to lean against. There was nothing for him to hang on to but Levi. He wrapped his arms around Levi's waist and leaned against his back. "Is this okay?"

Levi held Jaime's hands with one of his, while reaching back with the other to pull Jaime's thigh tighter against his own. "Perfect." He smiled at Jaime over his shoulder. "Now you know my ulterior motive."

Jaime smiled despite his fear. Levi let go of him and kicked the bike to life. It rumbled beneath them. Jaime's instincts told him to get off and run back into Levi's apartment, but he made himself stay put.

"I'll go slow," Levi assured him again. "We'll stay on the side streets for now."

Jaime could only nod, and when they started moving, he closed his eyes and hung on tight. He was too afraid to do anything else. He felt as if he couldn't even think, as if his thoughts had to wade through the molasses of his panic.

Levi had promised to go slow, but it didn't feel slow at all. Jaime was sure they were driving much too fast.

The bike leaned alarmingly as they turned to the right. Jaime's balance felt all wrong, as if they were going to tip over, and he tightened his grip on Levi. A minute later, they turned again. He hated it just as much the second time. When the bike tilted into the turn, Jaime wanted to lean the other way, but Levi's body, which he was holding on to, leaned into the curve, scaring him more.

"Relax, Jaime," Levi said. "You're fighting it, which only makes it worse."

"I can't relax!"

"I want you to try something. Whenever we go around a corner, I want you to turn your head and look in the direction we're turning. It'll feel more natural to you."

Of course, he couldn't do what Levi asked with his eyes clenched shut. He took a deep breath and forced himself to open them. He made himself look.

He was surprised to find they weren't going as fast as he thought. They were cruising through a residential neighborhood, and when Jaime glanced over Levi's shoulder, he found they were barely doing twenty-five. The knowledge made him feel a bit better.

"We're turning right," Levi told him.

It seemed ridiculous. Why did it matter which direction he looked? But he did as Levi said and turned his head to the right as they went around the corner. It really did make it easier. He was concentrating so much on doing what Levi said that they were halfway around the curve before Jaime realized they were leaning.

"Now left," Levi told him. This time, the turn felt smooth. It felt natural. It was still scary. He still didn't like the way the bike tilted fractionally closer to the street as they turned. He still had to fight the urge to lean the other way, but he had to admit Levi was right. His tension had made it worse.

"You ready to get on a real road?" Levi asked at a stop sign.

"No," Jaime told him. "But I may never be ready, so you may as well do it now."

The worst part of the "real" roads was the traffic. It felt strange to have cars zooming past so close to them, and Jaime realized Levi was driving slower than everybody else.

"You can go faster," he told him, although his voice shook as he said it.

Being up to speed actually felt better, but Jaime was still terrified. When they stopped at a red light, Levi said, "Let go of me for a minute."

"Why?"

"It'll do you good. You're too tense. You can't enjoy it when you're so tight." He smiled back at him. "You should know this stuff. You're the one who's always telling me to relax."

Levi was right. He'd had been hanging on so tight, he hadn't realized his arms were practically trembling from the strain. It took real effort to make his muscles respond, and he forced himself to release his grip on Levi. He shook his arms a bit, willing the muscles to relax. When it was time to move again, he put his arms back around Levi's waist, but he tried to concentrate on keeping himself loose.

Levi took them west and eventually the traffic of the city seemed to spit them out onto a two-lane county road. "You ready?" Levi asked over his shoulder.

Before Jaime could answer, Levi accelerated. Jaime's heart raced and he fought the urge to grip Levi tighter. He was becoming accustomed to the peculiar movements of the bike and the feeling of being so exposed on the road. He wouldn't have said he was calm or relaxed. It was more like walking a balance beam over a sea of panic. If he thought about what they were doing, flying down the road on two wheels, or if he thought about how horrifying it would be to wreck, he'd fall off and drown. So instead, he concentrated on mundane things. He made himself notice the massive trees on their right, being overrun by kudzu. He noticed the swampy pools on the left and watched idly for alligators, even though he knew he'd probably never see one. He noticed most of the cars passing them going the other direction into Miami had Dolphins signs and banners on them, and he realized there must be a game that night.

He noticed he felt good. Better than he'd felt in days. If he sat up straight and let the wind blow against him, he could almost imagine it was blowing his depression away, clearing the cobwebs from his mind. He felt free. He found himself smiling. The fear wasn't gone—he was still scared—but he realized concentrating on it was a choice, not a requirement. That was interesting.

"Go faster," he said to Levi.

Levi turned his head, his eyebrows up in surprise, but then he accelerated, increasing their speed by another five miles per hour. Instead of thinking about how frightening it was to go faster, Jaime concentrated on the way Levi's hands moved on the throttle, and the way his hair blew back into Jaime's face, stinging his cheeks. His fear remained. Steady. Not better. Not worse either. It was simply there, and the thought felt like a revelation. It felt like triumph. It felt so good Jaime laughed out loud. He'd tried so hard to fight his fear, but there was a something liberating about giving up the battle and recognizing his fear was part of him. It wasn't something to be exorcised. It wasn't something to be obeyed. It needed only to be acknowledged. It was the same as knowing his body was mostly comprised of water. The key was "mostly". And the question that followed was, What else?

So Jaime accepted his fear. Yes, it was there. So be it.

Suddenly his fear wasn't a sea waiting to drown him if he fell. It was more like the snow back in Cleveland when he was a kid. Sometimes it had been so hard and crusty on top he could walk along on its surface, two feet above the ground. Even if his foot broke through, what was the worst that could happen? He'd sink up to his ankle? He'd sink up to his knee? Possibly. But if he did, he'd simply pull his leg out and keep walking. The only way he'd sink all the way was if he allowed himself to fall down and burrow into it.

So Jaime tread carefully upon the surface of his fear and asked himself, What else is there?

He felt strangely complacent. In his mind, Levi and the bike were one being. One machine, big and strong and sure. All Jaime could do was hang on. The road was straight, with very little traffic. The bike rumbled beneath him. His ass was numb from the vibration. The sun was shining. The wind on the exposed part of his cheeks was cold. His hands were cold, too. The warmth of Levi's body might have kept them warm, if his thick leather jacket hadn't been in the way.

Jaime let go of his grip around Levi's waist and put his hands in Levi's jacket pockets instead. That was warmer, but he felt less secure, so he put his arms back around Levi's waist. This time, he slid them up under Levi's jacket, so he could put his hands closer to Levi's flesh. It felt good. Levi's T-shirt was between them, but the heat was still there. He could feel Levi's stomach moving as he breathed. He could feel the indent of Levi's navel against his finger. And he decided he wanted more. He lifted Levi's T-shirt and slid his hand underneath and up Levi's stomach.

The bike jerked as Levi jumped at the unexpected contact, but went quickly back to normal. It scared Jaime, but he found it exhilarating as well. He liked the way Levi responded to his touch.

He kept his right hand on Levi's stomach, but moved his left hand down, brushing his fingertips over Levi's groin before sliding his hand down his thigh. It felt good to touch him like this, when Levi was unable to touch him back. It was similar to the day on the couch when he'd thought Levi was asleep. It was arousing without being threatening. He ran his hand back up Levi's thigh, stopping just short of cupping his groin in his palm.

Levi turned his head enough for Jaime to see he was smiling. "You trying to make me wreck?" he yelled so Jaime could hear him over the wind.

"Do you want me to stop?"

"You know I don't."

Jaime found himself smiling. "Torturing you helps distract me."

Levi laughed. "Distract yourself all you want, baby. You'll never find a more willing victim."

Jaime laughed, but Levi's words struck home. He knew Levi had meant them as a joke, but they were absolutely true. He'd never find another man who would allow him such freedom without demanding anything in return. He wished he had something to offer Levi in return.

Of course, he *did* have something. Jaime knew what Levi wanted, and on some level, he wanted very much to give it to him. But he was still so afraid. He wondered if his fear would ever fade. He wondered if he'd ever be able to reach across the bed to Levi without panicking.

"Faster?" Levi called over his shoulder.

Despite the anxiety still very much alive in his mind, Jaime answered, "Yes."

Levi accelerated again, and Jaime distracted himself from the speed by exploring Levi's stomach with one hand. His left hand still rested high inside Levi's thigh, and he wondered if he had enough nerve to explore more there as well. He marveled at himself a bit that he could even consider something so bold.

And suddenly he realized his fear of sex was no different than his fear of the motorcycle. He could have let his panic keep him from getting on the bike with Levi. It was shocking to think he could have lived his whole life and never had this moment. It occurred to him what a loss it would have been. And wasn't sex the same? He'd always believed he could never have a normal sex life. After all, who would be willing to tiptoe their way through the wreckage of his past?

Now, he knew: Levi. Levi was willing. Jaime didn't understand it. Even now, he couldn't quite believe it, but it was true. Levi wanted him. Levi said he loved him. And although Jaime wasn't sure yet if he believed in Levi's love, there were other things he *did* believe with all his heart: Levi would go slow. He would be careful and gentle.

Levi was safe.

Jaime could wait for his fear to go away, and end up missing out on the chance he was being offered. Or he could do as he'd done with the bike and he could let Levi drive.

He knew then, with absolute certainty, what he wanted to do.

"You ready to go back?" Levi asked.

Jaime felt as if his heart was lodged in his throat, but he didn't hesitate. "Yes." Although Levi probably didn't know it, Jaime was talking about a great deal more than the ride home. "I'm ready."

CHAPTER 29

Levi had only suggested the motorcycle ride in hopes of jarring Jaime out of the depression he'd been mired in since the arrival of his uncle's letter. He'd *never* expected Jaime to become so aggressive.

Not that Levi was complaining.

The ride home was interesting, to say the least. When they first turned around and headed back into the city, Jaime's hands had been everywhere. It was terribly distracting and wonderfully torturous. But as they neared Levi's apartment building, Jaime went from adventurous to still, from laughing to strangely quiet. He didn't say a word as he climbed off the bike and followed Levi up the stairs to his front door.

"Did you have fun?" Levi asked him once they were inside.

Jaime's cheeks turned red, as they so often did, but he smiled nervously. "I'm glad you talked me into it."

"Not so scary after all, right?"

"It was terrifying," Jaime said. "But that's why I'm glad I went."

Levi wasn't sure if he understood, but he was glad Jaime was smiling again. "What do you want to do for dinner?" he asked, turning toward the kitchen, but Jaime stopped him by grabbing his hand.

"Levi, wait."

Levi turned to him in surprise. Jaime didn't let go of his hand. He was fidgety, obviously flustered, barely able to meet his eyes. "I realized something on the ride. I realized if I wait until I'm not scared to try new things, then I'll never get to try them at all. So maybe…" He took a deep breath and looked into Levi's eyes. "Maybe now's the time to try."

Jaime stared at him expectantly, and Levi tried to think of what he was supposed to say. "So you want to go for another ride?"

Jaime managed to blush even more, but he smiled, too. "Levi, I'm not talking about the motorcycle."

"You're not? Then what—" Sudden understanding made Levi's heart race. "Jaime, are you saying—"

"Will you have sex with me?" The direct question struck Levi speechless, which turned out to be okay, because Jaime was suddenly backpedaling. "I mean, not *real* sex. Not yet. I just mean—"

"You don't have to do this because of what happened on the ride. Or what happened the other day. If you're not ready—"

"Don't you see? That's my point. Because I'll *never* be ready. I'll always be scared, but I don't want to spend my life not knowing what it's like."

Levi's mind raced with thoughts of finally touching Jaime, kissing him, proving to him how amazing two people could make each other feel. But he forced himself to take a deep breath and, against every instinct he had, he asked again, "Are you sure?"

Jaime stepped closer to him, although except for the hand he still held, he didn't quite touch him. "Stop giving me time to change my mind," he said. "Tell me what to do."

It took real effort not to grab Jaime right then, not to push him to the floor and lose himself in Jaime's body, but Levi knew it would be too much, too soon. He had to take his time. And the truth was, he wanted to go slowly. This was new to him, too. He couldn't even remember the last time he'd kissed anyone. He'd had sex with a great many men over the years, but he didn't believe he'd ever really made love. Even in his one short-lived, half-hearted attempt at a relationship eight years earlier, he'd always thought more about what he wanted than what his partner wanted. Never before had he cared more about pleasing the man he was with than pleasing himself. And Jaime was so fragile, Levi wanted to do this right.

He eyed the soft white skin at Jaime's throat. Jaime wore a light blue polo shirt, the exact same color as his eyes. The top two buttons were undone, and Levi's eyes were drawn to the triangle of pink flesh and sparse red hair he could see there. "Let me undress you," he said, looking up into Jaime's scared eyes.

Jaime laughed nervously. "I'll do it," he said, but he didn't move. "You first."

Levi did as he was told, quickly stripping and dropping his clothes into a sloppy pile on the floor. The blanket he'd used back in his couch-sleeping days was still in the room. Although he'd folded it, he'd never put it away. It had migrated to the seldom-used chair by the door. He pulled it out from under the pile of jackets and spread it on the floor and sat down cross-legged on it. He looked up at Jaime with a grin. "Your turn."

"I don't suppose I can get you to not look?"

"I know you like to torture me, but that'd be downright cruel."

Jaime smiled, but he turned his back on Levi before he started to undress. He pulled his shirt off over his head, and Levi realized right away Jaime had been wise to undress himself because, had Levi done it, he wouldn't have been able to stop himself from touching as he went. Jaime took his time. He stopped after removing each piece of clothing to fold it neatly and place it on the couch. Jaime was always meticulous, but Levi wondered if he clung to the habit now because he was nervous or self-conscious, or if Jaime did it to tease him. Whatever his reason, Levi found he didn't mind. He'd seen most of Jaime's body before, of course, but that didn't diminish the pleasure of watching him undress now. Especially when he bent over to remove his boxers.

"My God, Jaime, you have the sexiest ass I've ever seen."

"I doubt it," Jaime said with obvious embarrassment. He turned around and let Levi see his cock, which was short but thick and half-engorged. Levi thought immediately of how it would feel in his mouth.

"Don't look at me like that," Jaime said.

"Like what?" Levi asked, forcing himself to look up at Jaime's face.

"Like I'm one of the men you're usually with, because I know I'm not."

He was right. Jaime wasn't the type Levi had always gone for: guys who wasted their time in the gym and or at the beach. Guys who knew what they had and used it to get what they wanted. Guys like Levi. Jaime was real—soft, fragile and beautiful in his purity.

"You're better," Levi said, and he meant it, but he wasn't surprised when he saw the skepticism in Jaime's eyes. "Come here." He held his hand up to Jaime.

Jaime took it and let himself be pulled down to the floor so they sat face to face, in the circle of each other's legs. He looked terrified, and although Levi wanted this more than he could say, it was important to him that he not hurt Jaime in any way. He didn't want to do more damage than good.

"Are you sure about this?" he asked.

Jaime didn't look sure at all, but he nodded. "It's like the bike, Levi. You're going to have to drive. All I can do is hang on."

Levi nodded. He understood what Jaime meant, on some level, but he was afraid to move. "Tell me where I can touch you. Is there somewhere that's safe?"

Jaime thought about it before he answered. "It's not like it reminds me of it," he said at last. "It's not like I have flashbacks or anything. Not when I'm awake. But it's the only boundary I know will stick. If I tell people not to touch me, they won't. Once I let them, how do I know they'll stop?" He looked into Levi's eyes, as if Levi would have an answer. "If I let them touch me, I'm afraid of what they'll do to me next."

Levi struggled with how to answer him. It made him furious somebody had taken an act that should have been about trust and turned it into something ugly. He silently wished Jaime's uncle the slowest, most painful death possible. "I won't hurt you."

Jaime nodded. "I know." He picked up Levi's right hand and placed it on his knee, then took a deep, shaking breath. He was close to tears again. "But I'm still scared."

Levi started to run his hand up Jaime's leg. He started to reach for him with his other hand, to lean in so he could kiss him, but Jaime instinctively flinched away, and Levi stopped.

"I'm sorry," Jaime said, and Levi could see the effort he was making in an attempt to relax.

"Don't apologize." But he didn't want Jaime to be tense and scared at each new touch. He considered for a moment what Jaime had said. *I'm afraid of what they'll do to me next.* It seemed maybe those words were the key. He kept his hand on Jaime's knee, resisting the urge to slide it higher. "Can I put my other arm around you?"

Jaime looked surprised, and a bit confused, but he nodded. "Yes."

Levi slid his left hand around Jaime's waist and used it to pull Jaime closer. Jaime's skin was unbelievably soft, and Levi couldn't wait to taste it. "Can I kiss your neck?"

A heartbeat of hesitation, then a hesitant nod. Levi put his lips on Jaime's pulse point, kissing softly, pulling Jaime tighter against him. "You can say no," he whispered as he kissed Jaime's pale skin. "You can tell me to stop. I don't care when. I don't care what we're doing. I won't be upset. I won't be angry." He continued to nibble at Jaime's neck. Jaime's entire body was trembling, his breath shaky. "I won't hurt you." He kissed higher on Jaime's neck, up to his jaw line, then his cheek, which was wet with tears, and it brought Levi up short again. "Tell me what's wrong."

Jaime shook his head. "Nothing. Everything. I don't know. I'm such a mess. I'm sorry—" He started to pull away, to try to wipe his cheeks, but Levi stopped him and started to kiss them away instead.

"Do you want me to stop?"

"No!" Jaime said, although his voice caught. He put his arms around Levi's neck. "I definitely don't want you to stop."

Levi obeyed. He continued to kiss Jaime's cheeks and jaw and neck, although the tears fell too fast for him to keep up with. "Jaime," he whispered, "can I kiss you?"

"Yes."

Jaime's lips were trembling and salty with tears. His kiss was hesitant. It was the sweetest thing Levi had ever experienced. Jaime tasted like youth and innocence and it made Levi's heart ache to be able to claim that sweetness for himself. He wanted to savor it. To somehow open Jaime up to everything that could be good between two men, without spoiling Jaime's sense of innocence and trust. "Can I touch your thigh?" he asked, moving his hand up only an inch to let Jaime know which hand he meant.

"Yes."

He wanted to feel every part of Jaime's perfect skin, but he knew he couldn't rush. He let his fingers trail up Jaime's leg. He felt the top of his thigh, where the muscle was firm and strong. He slid his hand underneath and felt the back of Jaime's thigh, which was softer and meatier. He slid his hand down and explored the silky soft spot behind Jaime's knee and he heard Jaime moan.

And as he explored, he kissed him. He kissed his lips and his cheek, his jaw and his neck. The tears hadn't stopped, and Jaime still shook in his arms. Levi didn't know if it was the force of his emotions making him tremble, or if it was the slow gentleness of Levi's touch. Maybe it was both.

"Can I touch your stomach?"

"Yes."

He still jumped a little when Levi's fingers brushed his abdomen, but his arms tightened around Levi's neck. Levi stroked Jaime's skin, from his hip to his navel, resisting the urge to move his hand lower. He confined his touch to the soft, smooth skin of Jaime's stomach. He caressed him until he could feel him vibrating with energy, with the need to be touched more. "Can I touch your chest?"

"Yes."

Levi's thumb brushed his nipple, and Jaime moaned, arching his back. "Yes," he said again, as if Levi had asked another question, and Levi gently pinched the sensitive flesh, squeezing.

"Oh God," Jaime moaned.

Levi took his time, teasing each of Jaime's nipples as he continued to kiss him, until both nubs of flesh were red and swollen. Jaime was still crying a bit, but he was also panting, whimpering, squirming in Levi's arms as he strained for some release.

Levi moved his hand slowly downward, sliding it toward Jaime's navel and his erect cock. "Can I touch your—"

"*Yes!*" And as Levi's hand closed around it and began moving up and down, Jaime said it again, and again. "Yes, yes, yes…" Turning the word into a mantra or a vow. Maybe it was a testament he would not let his past continue to win. Levi stroked him and kissed him, his hand moving faster as Jaime's cries grew louder. "Yes, yes, yes…"

Jaime's arms were tight around his neck. His head was back, his cheeks still wet with tears. Although Levi's own cock was throbbing and hard, although its tip was moist, although he'd never been so turned on in all his life, he didn't care that Jaime's hand never ventured there. He didn't care that, given their position, he couldn't even relieve himself by rubbing against him. He didn't care that he couldn't use his own hand on it. Jaime was holding him tight, yet leaning back in order to give Levi's hand more room to work. It forced Levi to support most of Jaime's weight with his other arm. The muscle of his biceps began to ache with the effort, but he didn't care about any of it. All he cared about was hearing Jaime's frantic words in his ear.

"Yes, yes, yes…"

Levi stroked faster, held him tighter. The kisses he dropped on Jaime's neck became urgent. He locked his mouth over Jaime's soft rosy flesh and sucked hard as he stroked, and Jaime cried out one last time, "Yes!" His back arched, his body tensed, and Levi milked his thick shaft, urging him on, pulling his climax out of him, until he collapsed, spent and panting in Levi's arms.

They were both sticky from Jaime's release, but Levi knew this wasn't the moment to let go of him. Jaime was shaking harder than ever, his breath ragged and uneven. He might have been laughing, or crying, or simply trying to catch his breath. Levi suspected it was a little of each.

He rubbed Jaime's back, even though it meant spreading some of his own seed on him. He kissed the side of his head. "You okay?"

Jaime laughed. "I am," he said, as if it was a revelation. "I really am."

"Honey, I can't tell if you're happy or sad."

Jaime laughed again. "Oh God, Levi, I'm definitely not sad! I'm not sure what I am, but I know it's not that." Jaime let go of him enough to pull back and wipe his eyes, and although his cheeks were wet with tears, he was smiling, and his eyes were bright and clear. "I'm a little freaked out, but it's nice."

Levi touched his fingertip to the growing hickey on the side of Jaime's neck and was pleased when Jaime didn't flinch away. "I left a mark." He hadn't meant to, but it wasn't surprising Jaime's pale skin bruised easily.

"I don't mind." Jaime closed his eyes, remembering. "I liked that part." When he opened his eyes again, they were shy, but almost flirtatious. "Maybe you can do it again?"

Levi couldn't help but smile. "I wish I'd put you on that bike weeks ago."

Jaime laughed. "I'm not sure it would have had quite the same effect." He hesitated for a moment, but then leaned close and kissed Levi, his lips soft and unsure. "Thank you."

"Dear God, Jaime, don't thank me for that."

Jaime blushed, but didn't look away. "I don't know what happens next."

"What do you *want* to happen next?"

Jaime thought about it for a minute before a slow smile spread across his face. "I want to go out for dinner."

"Really?" The request surprised him. Jaime rarely wanted to eat out. "Where do you want to go?"

Jaime put his arms around Levi's neck again and kissed him, a little surer this time. "Take me someplace I've never been before."

And Levi obeyed.

CHAPTER 30

Levi took him to an Indian restaurant with an all-you-can-eat buffet. Jaime tried not to let his dismay show as he eyed the unfamiliar selection.

"Do you want to go someplace else?" Levi asked him.

"No." Jaime forced himself to meet Levi's eyes, even though it made his cheeks burn to do it. "I'll try it."

Levi smiled at him, then leaned in close to whisper in his ear, "I kind of like how you blush every time you look at me." Which, of course, only made Jaime blush more. Levi turned away and began loading his own plate with food. "You'll like the curry," Levi assured him. "And the tandoori." He picked up a piece of flatbread and put it on Jaime's plate. "And everybody loves naan."

Levi also ordered a glass of plum wine for him. It was syrupy sweet and unbelievably good, and the first glass went down a bit too fast. "I don't want to be sick again," Jaime said when Levi ordered him another glass.

"Don't worry," Levi said, and the hungry look in his eyes made Jaime squirm in his seat. "I'm cutting you off at two."

He felt amazingly good by the time they got back home. He took Dolly for a long walk, then they sat on the couch watching TV as they usually did until he started to fall asleep, and Levi dragged him off to bed.

He didn't think about much of anything as he brushed his teeth and got ready for bed, but when he walked into the bedroom and found Levi undressing, he was suddenly nervous. He hadn't thought forward to what it would be like now, sleeping together in Levi's bed.

Levi smiled at him as if he could read his mind. "We don't have to do anything."

Jaime debated as he watched Levi finish undressing. He was afraid to give Levi full rein just yet, but his first taste of sexual freedom had him wanting more. He thought about the day on the couch, touching Levi as he slept. He thought about being on the bike, and how exhilarating it felt to touch Levi without the threat of Levi touching back.

"If I asked you to do something, would you?"

Levi grinned wickedly at him. "Is this some new form of torture?"

Jaime laughed. "It might be."

Levi took Jaime's right hand. He turned it over and kissed the old scars on the inside of Jaime's wrist. "Your wish is my command, my sadistic Boy Scout master."

"Get undressed and lie down on the bed."

Levi stripped out of his briefs as Jaime had instructed, but he didn't lie down on the bed. Instead, he looked up at Jaime with hopeful eyes. "Let me undress you."

The simple request made Jaime blush, as it had earlier in the day, and he laughed nervously. "I'll do it."

Levi obediently sat on the bed and leaned back on his elbows. Jaime tried not to be self-conscious as he slowly removed his clothing, folding each piece as he went. He kept his back to Levi as he bent to remove his boxers, and he heard Levi groan.

"You're embarrassing me," Jaime said.

"Come over here then. I'll make you forget all about being embarrassed."

Jaime turned to face him, and the look in Levi's eyes took his breath away. There was so much heat there, so much longing, so much naked desire, and suddenly Jaime didn't feel embarrassed anymore. Self-conscious, maybe, yes. But he also felt…

Attractive. He actually felt sexy for the first time in his life.

"Turn over."

Levi obeyed, rolling onto his stomach. Jaime sat across his ass, and without even thinking, he started to massage Levi's shoulders and neck, until he felt Levi relax. Levi's hair was spread everywhere, and Jaime pushed it up and back, off his neck and off his face. He leaned down against Levi's back and kissed the back of his neck.

"I wanted to do this to you in the motel room in Charleston."

Levi laughed. "I won't tell you what I wanted to do to *you* in that motel room. You'd turn ten shades of red."

Which, of course, was enough in itself to make Jaime blush. He was glad Levi couldn't see his face. He continued to kiss Levi's neck, letting his hand wander down Levi's side. He came to Levi's ass. It was like the rest of Levi's body—not large, but firm and muscular—and he gripped it in his hand.

"I can't wait to do that to you," Levi said, and Jaime smiled with his lips pressed against Levi's shoulder. His cock was lying against Levi's ass, wedged against his crack, and he thrust against him. His erection slid against Levi with a tantalizing friction, making him moan, and Levi moaned in response, his hands white-knuckled in the comforter on either side of his head. Jaime did it again, reveling in the feel of Levi's ass under him. The next time he thrust, Levi's hips rose up to meet him. He gripped Levi's hip and thrust against him again.

Levi let go of the comforter with his right hand and it slid down the bed. "Let me show you…"

His hand slid between them. Jaime lifted his hips to accommodate him. Levi didn't grab his cock exactly, but he nudged it down, shifted his own body in relation to Jaime's, lifting his own hips up, and then he let go, and Jaime sank down into a warm softness unlike anything he'd felt before. He still wasn't *in* Levi, of course. Just as before, he was wedged into his crack, but now his cock was angled down, pointing toward the bed, sliding between Levi's cheeks and the tops of his thighs, rubbing against his perineum. Now Jaime could feel the wonderful friction of Levi's skin all around his glans, and God, it felt good. He rode that spot for a while, until Levi moaned.

"Jaime," he said, "please let me turn over."

"I don't want you to touch me."

Levi sighed in frustration. "Fucking sadist," he grumbled. The words themselves might have seemed like a jab, but there was laughter in his voice, and Jaime found himself smiling.

"I think I'm going to make you pay for that comment," Jaime teased as he moved enough to allow Levi to roll onto his back.

"I can't wait." And there was no mistaking the husky arousal in Levi's voice.

Jaime sat again, straddling Levi's hips. Their groins pressed together, their erections side by side. Jaime wasn't sure exactly where this would end but, for the moment, he was happy just to look at Levi. He'd seen Levi's body before, but looking down at it now, with Levi lying between his legs, was incredibly arousing. Levi's skin was smooth and tan. He gripped the comforter tight in an effort not to reach for Jaime, and it made the muscles of his chest and arms taut and firm.

Jaime put a finger on Levi's clavicle and ran it slowly down his chest. Levi's skin seemed to jump at his touch. He continued down to Levi's navel. He slowed then, but didn't stop. He continued downward, and Levi moaned, arching up against him. A drop clung to Levi's tip, and Jaime touched it, spread it around, circling his finger over the head of Levi's cock, and Levi moaned again.

Jaime leaned down, letting his chest rest against Levi's. Levi tensed, clearly fighting his impulse to touch Jaime or embrace him. Levi's eyes were closed, his breathing ragged, and Jaime looked down at him, amazed he could be this close to somebody as beautiful as Levi and not be paralyzed with self-doubt. Jaime let his hands wander over Levi. These were muscles he knew, by name and by touch. The psoas and the obliques. Pectorals and deltoids. But nothing had prepared him for how good it felt to explore them like this, with Levi tense and trembling beneath him.

He kissed Levi's shoulder and his neck, letting his lips and his tongue wander. He kissed Levi's jaw, which was prickly with stubble. Once, he tried to kiss Levi's soft, full lips. He loved the way Levi's open mouth seemed to invite him in, but the moment their tongues made contact, Levi lost some of his self-control. He reached for Jaime, and Jaime pulled back. He grabbed Levi's arms and pushed them away from him, back against the bed.

Levi groaned in frustration, but didn't fight him. "I'm sorry," he whispered.

Jaime couldn't be mad at him, though. It was true he wasn't ready to let Levi touch him, but the fact Levi *wanted* to touch him was an incredible aphrodisiac. "Eventually, I promise. Not yet, though."

"I know. I'm trying to be good."

Jaime laughed and bent to kiss him again, although not on the lips this time. He kissed his neck again and his clavicle. He moved down to his chest. He came to Levi's nipple, dark pink against Levi's tan chest. He'd been when Levi had touched him there earlier. He hadn't expected it to feel so good. He brushed his thumb over it and was thrilled at Levi's response. His breath hissed out between his teeth, and his arms and chest tightened in a way Jaime knew was an attempt to keep his grip on the comforter. Jaime looked up at Levi's face. Levi stared down at him, his eyes burning, and when Jaime rubbed his thumb over Levi's nipple, he saw the pleasure of it wash over Levi's face.

"Jaime," he whispered, "you're killing me, here."

Jaime bent his head to Levi's chest, touching his lips to the small bud of flesh, and Levi moaned. Jaime licked it, teased it with his tongue, exhilarated by the way Levi writhed underneath him, moaning and begging. "Oh God, Jaime, more, more, more."

He locked his mouth around Levi's nipple, almost biting, sucking hard. Levi's cries went right to Jaime's groin, and he moaned, too. He'd never known anything like this feeling of providing pleasure and gaining pleasure simply from his partner's labored breath and frantic moans. It had never occurred to him giving might be as gratifying as receiving. He moved to the other side, and Levi responded the same way, pushing toward him, groaning, panting his name. Jaime took the bud of flesh between his lips, flicking it with his tongue. Levi arched against him again, his cock thrusting against Jaime's stomach.

Jaime knew exactly what he wanted to do next.

He released Levi's nipple, moving back to the center of his chest, and Levi moaned in frustration. But as Jaime moved down, his lips and tongue brushing over Levi's stomach, he could sense Levi's growing anticipation. He could feel him shaking beneath him, lifting up, pushing his hard cock up toward Jaime's face, even as he fought to maintain his grip on the comforter. Then Jaime was there, staring down at drops of moisture on Levi's tip. He breathed in Levi's scent. It was at once the same smell he'd always associated with Levi—sunlight and the sea—but something else, too. Something thick and musky, like the smell of Levi's bed, but so much stronger, and Jaime couldn't believe how much it turned him on. He couldn't believe how something as simple as scent could make his head spin and his groin ache.

He put his head down, his nose in Levi's hair, and breathed deep. His own cock was against the bed and he ground himself against it as he drank in that beautiful smell. He thought he could work himself to climax simply rubbing on the bed while he reveled in the scent of Levi's sex, but he knew he wanted to do more.

He looked up again at Levi, who was watching him again with heavy-lidded eyes. Levi's cock butted against Jaime's chin. He wanted so much to taste it, to feel what it was like to give this to Levi, but he was afraid of doing it wrong. "I don't know how."

Levi smiled at him. "There's not much to it. Just watch the teeth."

Jaime put his tongue on the base of Levi's shaft and slowly moved up. Levi fell back against the bed again. Jaime's tongue reached his frenulum, and Levi moaned, a deep, low sound Jaime had never heard before. His tongue reached Levi's tip, tasting the drop clinging there. The saltiness surprised him. Levi didn't just smell like the ocean. He tasted like it, too.

Jaime closed his mouth over the head of Levi's cock, letting his tongue explore Levi's flesh. If he'd thought Levi's reaction when he'd teased his nipples was arousing, it was nothing compared to this. Levi cried out. He didn't let go of the bed, but his hips rose up. His cock pushed farther into Jaime's mouth. He pulled back, then thrust up again, and Jaime gripped his hips as he sucked Levi in deeper. He shoved his own erection against the bed as he did, moaning, and Levi thrust upward again, crying his name.

It felt amazing. Levi's cries, his smell, and the way his cock felt against Jaime's tongue. The way his hips arched up as he pushed deeper into Jaime's mouth, the way he tasted, the way he panted Jaime's name. The way it felt to grind his own aching erection against the bed as Levi lifted and pressed against him. It was more than arousing. It was intoxicating. Before Jaime knew it, he was lost, caught up in something strong and unbelievably primal, swept away in a flood of pleasure and longing. Then there was no thought at all, only the sensation of rubbing against the bed, gripping

Levi's ass, trying to suck him in and taste him and smell him, while Levi arched into him again and again.

Suddenly, Levi gripped his arm, calling out, "Jaime, stop," and Jaime pulled away, panting. Levi released his arm and collapsed back on the bed. "I'm sorry," he said, between panted breaths. "Didn't know if you'd want me to come."

Jaime'd been so caught up he'd been in the sensations of what he'd been doing, he foolishly hadn't thought ahead to what the end result would be. He was glad Levi had stopped him. He moved back up, sliding his body along Levi's until he could look down at his face. "I liked that."

Levi laughed. "I like that you liked it." His smile faded, replaced by something sexy and suggestive. "Let me do it to you. You'll like that even more."

The only thing Jaime could picture was being pinned beneath Levi, as Levi had been pinned under him, and it scared him. "Not yet." He glanced down their bodies, pressed together. "I could do it again. Just tell me before—"

Levi was shaking his head. "If you do it again, you'll have to tie my hands down. I was having a hell of a time following your rule."

"Then I guess we're at an impasse."

"I guess we are." Levi's smile was the sexiest thing Jaime had ever seen. "Looks like we might have to compromise."

"What do you suggest?"

"Kiss me again, and I'll show you."

As Jaime kissed him, he felt Levi's hand brush his hip. He jumped at the contact, but Levi didn't grab him. Instead, he worked his hand between them. Jaime lifted his hips to give him access, and Levi wrapped his hand around both of their shafts at once and started to stroke.

Levi's hand on him earlier in the day had felt good, but this was even better. There was something incredibly erotic about feeling Levi's cock against his, feeling their heads rub together at the top of each stroke, and knowing Levi was enjoying it, too. There was something beautiful about the way their bodies fit together, the way their cries merged and their moans overlapped. There was something amazing about the way their hips pushed together at the same time, as they both thrust in tandem through Levi's fist.

For the second time that night, Jaime lost himself in sensation. He lost track of everything else—every rational thought, every irrational fear. There was only Levi underneath him, his lips soft and his mouth sweet, and Levi's hand touching him, stroking him, teasing him, making him feel better than he'd ever felt. And even when he felt Levi's other hand brush over his cheek, even when that hand moved to the back of his neck and pulled him in for a deeper kiss, Jaime didn't mind. He gave every piece of himself into Levi's gentle hands until the world exploded around him, and all he could do was cry.

CHAPTER 31

Levi wasn't surprised when Jaime started to cry, and he didn't mind. It wasn't because Jaime was upset or scared. It was much like his orgasm: a simple matter of release. A lot had changed for him in one day. A lifetime of fears and sexual hang-ups were crashing down around him and Levi understood why he was so overwhelmed.

He wasn't sure if Jaime would be comforted by his touch or not, but when he hesitantly wrapped his arms around him, Jaime melted against him, clinging to him. Levi held him close, stroking his back, his arms, and his soft red curls, until Jaime sighed. "I'm sorry."

"Don't be sorry for anything, Jaime. You're doing fine."

Jaime laughed, his face still buried in Levi's neck. "I don't think this qualifies as 'doing fine.' I don't know much about sex, but I know crying after every time isn't exactly normal."

"Honey, there is no 'normal.' And 'every time' has only been twice. Give yourself some time."

"I'm not sure it will help."

Levi couldn't help but laugh. "It will. I think today, for the first time ever, you let your body lead instead of your brain. That's something most guys do frequently. Some of us even make a habit of it. But it's new for you."

"I don't know what you mean."

"It means once your brain catches up with the rest of you, you'll figure it out. I promise." He smacked Jaime's flank playfully. "Come on. We better clean up before this mess dries. I don't think you want to be stuck this way all night."

He was relieved to hear Jaime laugh. They got up and washed off, then he followed Jaime back into bed. Jaime curled up on his side of the bed, like he always did, with Dolly on his other side. Levi watched him, wondering if Jaime would allow him to hold him as they fell asleep.

Jaime must have seen it in his eyes because before Levi could formulate the question, Jaime smiled sleepily and said, "Yes."

Levi pulled him close, nudging him over onto his other side, so he was facing away. He wrapped his arms around him, pulling him tight against him—

"No," Jaime said, sitting up and pushing him away.

Had he misunderstood? Levi tried not to be heartbroken. He tried to hide his disappointment. "I'm sorry," he said, moving away again. "I didn't mean—"

"I know." Jaime put his hand on Levi's arm to stop him from moving farther away. He lay back down next to him. He turned and did to Levi what Levi had done to him: he pushed him onto his other side, then Jaime cuddled against his back. Jaime's arms wrapped around him and his lips brushed the back of Levi's neck, making him shiver. "Not behind me. Anything else, I think I can handle. But not from behind me quite yet."

Levi felt both relieved and ashamed—relieved he wouldn't have to continue to keep his distance, but ashamed he hadn't thought to ask Jaime first. He took Jaime's hand and kissed his fingers. "You have to tell me when I screw up, because I will. I won't mean to. But I will. Like just now."

"It's okay." Jaime's voice heavy with exhaustion. "I can't expect you to know what will set me off. I don't know myself half the time."

"It's not just that." He had to stop and think about how to make it clear. "I've wanted this for so long, Jaime. I've wanted *you* for so long. I'll try to be patient. I'll try not to rush you. But you may need to slap me from time to time."

"Do you want me to slap you now?" Jaime mumbled.

"No."

"Then shut up and let me sleep."

Levi woke to pitiful whimpering. He opened his eyes and jumped about a foot. Dolly's doggy face was less than an inch away.

"What the *fuck*, girl?" he whispered.

She whimpered again in response.

Levi pushed her head out of the way and checked the clock. It was seven-thirty. Behind him, he could hear Jaime's soft breathing. With the exception of the morning after Jaime's one and only drinking binge, Levi had never known him to sleep past seven. He rarely slept past six. It was no wonder Dolly was whimpering. Her little doggy bladder was probably about to burst.

"Come on," he said as he climbed out of bed. "I'll take you."

Jaime was still asleep when he got back. Levi kicked his shoes off and climbed back under the covers. He knew he couldn't let Jaime sleep any longer, but it didn't mean he couldn't make the most of waking him up. Jaime didn't stir when Levi kissed his forehead or his eyes. Levi slid his hand down Jaime's side as he kissed his cheek. His lips moved to Jaime's neck. He wanted to reach down and cup Jaime's soft ass in his hand, but he was afraid of pushing too far while Jaime slept, so he stroked his side and his back, kissing his neck, until Jaime stirred.

"Shh," Levi soothed, as Jaime went tense against him. "I won't hurt you." He continued to kiss Jaime's neck until Jaime sighed and relaxed against him. "How are you?"

Jaime sighed again. "I feel good."

Levi pulled him tighter against him, kissing his neck more, and felt Jaime's arms steal around his neck. "I feel really, *really* good."

"Yes, you do," Levi agreed, reaching down to grip Jaime's ass, and Jaime laughed. "Dolly's had her walk already."

"Really? What time is it?"

"Almost eight."

Jaime moaned. "I have to go."

"Are you *sure* you don't want to call in sick? Because I'd love to keep you here in this bed all day."

Jaime laughed nervously. "I'm sure."

"Can I shower with you before you go?"

"No."

Levi moved his hand from Jaime's ass to the tempting package in front. "Can I do anything else for you before you go?"

"No," Jaime said, but he was laughing.

"You're coming over tonight, right?"

Despite Jaime's words to the contrary, he was responding readily to Levi's touch. "Yes." He sighed, pushing against Levi's hand.

Levi moved down to tease Jaime's nipple with his tongue. "You positive about the shower?" he asked as he stroked Jaime's growing erection through his boxers.

"Mmmm," was all Jaime managed to say.

"Okay." Levi released him and stood up, struggling not to smile. "Guess you better get going."

Jaime moaned. His face was flushed, his eyes pleading. His erection made a tantalizing bulge in the front of his shorts. "Now who's being sadistic?"

It was tempting to give in, but he knew Jaime would regret it afterward. He hated running late.

"I'll make it up to you tonight," Levi promised. He was looking forward to it already.

Jaime left ten minutes later, which left Levi with more than an hour before he had to be at work. Christmas was less than two weeks away. They'd planned to spend it with Levi's family, but now he and Jaime were apparently past the "just friends" stage, he was worried about how his relatives would respond. He debated not telling them, but not for long. He didn't want to lie to them, so he took a deep breath and called his mom.

"Hi, honey," she said, sounding happy to hear from his as she always did. "I hope you're not calling to cancel Christmas, too."

"Who's canceling Christmas?"

She exhaled. "I shouldn't say it that way. It's a terrible thing, actually. You know this year was supposed to be our family's turn." Several of his siblings did every other year with their parents and opposite years with their in-laws. They always made sure their years home coincided. "Well, Kristine's mother's cancer is back and the prognosis isn't good, so she and Isaac decided to spend Christmas with her family this year since…" Since it might be her last, but she didn't say that part.

"And I don't blame them one bit, of course. It's the right decision. But then Caleb and Rachel started talking, and they decided it would be easier to switch years for everybody, rather than being a year off from Isaac. Plus Rachel's so close to her due date, she isn't sure she wants to be away from home, so they won't be here either."

The nice thing was, without the entire family present, there would be no Binder confab. It was possible he'd be able to go the entire visit without having to debate the sins of his "lifestyle." "What about Ruth and Jacob?"

"They're still coming as far as I know. You're coming, right? You and Jaime?"

"Well, Mom, I need to talk to you about that."

"You're not coming!"

"I didn't say we weren't coming. Jaime and I were planning on it—"

"I'm so glad!"

"Mom, stop interrupting me. I need to tell you something."

"What is it, honey? Is everything okay?"

"It is." He found himself smiling from ear to ear. "It's great, actually, but I thought I should tell you things are different now. With Jaime."

There was a stunned silence, then she said, "I see."

"I didn't want to lie to you, Mom."

"I appreciate that."

"Is this going to be a problem?"

"I don't know, honey. I honestly don't know how I feel about it. Part of me is so disappointed because now I know there's no hope of you turning away from this path. But Ruth told me this might happen. She said I should be happy for you."

He could hear the tears in her voice. She wasn't crying hard, but she was crying nonetheless.

"And I don't know how I feel about having it happen in my house. And in front of the children."

"We won't be doing anything in front of the kids, Mom. We're not perverts."

"I know. I didn't mean it that way. But kids are smart. They're bound to figure it out, and I don't know how everybody will feel about having to explain how Jaime fits in. And who knows what could happen by next year—"

"Mom, this isn't a fling. I love him. And if things go my way, this is going to be a permanent arrangement, so please don't assume you can ignore this problem and have it go away."

She sighed again. "Ruth told me that, too."

"I have to tell you," he said, half-joking but half not, "if we don't get to come, it's going to break Jaime's heart. He loves our family, and we all know he fits in better than I do."

He was happy to hear her laugh a little. "He's a nice boy, Levi. I don't want to say no, but I think I should talk to your father about it first."

"I figured you would."

Despite his conversation with his mom, he was in a ridiculously good mood all day. He knew he was grinning foolishly at everybody, and Candy rolled her eyes at him at least a dozen times, but he didn't care. Everything made him think of Jaime, and every reminder made him smile. He couldn't remember ever being so happy, and looking back on his time in Miami, he marveled he had ever thought he was happy at all. It wasn't as if things had been *bad.* He'd certainly had fun over the years. But it was a dim, empty kind of happiness compared to the sheer giddiness filling him now. He felt bright and buoyant and absolutely complete. And standing there at a golf course bar, pouring drinks for happy, flirty housewives, he vowed to God and to himself that he was never going back.

Jaime was already in his kitchen when he got home, making himself the same dinner he ate at least every other night—a salad and a chicken patty sandwich. Levi resisted the urge to push against him from behind and approached him from the side instead.

"How was your day?" he asked as he kissed Jaime's neck. He was stupidly happy when Jaime tilted his head away to give him better access.

Jaime laughed, the nervous laugh that meant he was embarrassed. "It was *tense.*"

It took Levi a second to connect those words to the state he'd left Jaime in that morning, but when he did, he laughed. He turned them so they were face to face, with

Jaime leaning against the counter. "I did say I'd make it up to you," he said, as he undid Jaime's pants.

"No, I didn't mean… Oh."

"You didn't mean what?" Levi teased as he pushed Jaime's pants out of the way and let his fingers explore bare flesh.

"Mmm…" was all Jaime managed.

Levi couldn't help but smile. He wrapped his other arm around Jaime's waist and kissed him as his right hand began to move, and Jaime practically melted in his arms. He didn't touch Levi back. He hung onto the counter behind him and let Levi drive. And Levi loved it. He liked to watch Jaime's face. His eyes were closed, and Levi found his pale eyelids beautiful. His head was back and his soft lips barely parted. As Levi kissed him, held him and stroked him, Jaime made the sweetest sounds, low moans and soft whimpers, and Levi thought he could go on hearing those sounds forever and never tire of them.

It wasn't long at all before Jaime spent himself all over Levi's hand and onto the kitchen floor, and the thing Levi loved the most was how Jaime looked down at the mess he'd made and blushed ten shades of red. He knew someday Jaime would stop being embarrassed by his own pleasure, but Levi found it endearing while it lasted.

"I'm sorry," Jaime said.

"I'm not," Levi assured him as he grabbed the paper towels and bent to wipe it up. "That's exactly what I intended to happen," he said with a wink, and was childishly pleased when Jaime blushed even more.

His phone rang as he finished. He wasn't surprised to see it was his mother calling. He left Jaime in the kitchen and took his phone into the living room to answer it.

"I talked to your father, and we made a decision."

He could tell by her voice she expected him not to like it. "Go on."

"Levi, I hope you understand we're trying to compromise here."

"Quit being defensive and tell me."

"We'd like you both to come, but only if you agree to sleep in separate rooms. And we expect you to be absolutely discreet in front of the children."

The latter part, of course, was easy. The first part, which he knew she expected to be the sticking point, was to be expected. And yet, he still felt himself bristle at it. "We have to sleep in separate rooms because we're gay? Or because we're not married?"

"Both. Caleb and Kirsten were together for more than a year before they got married, and your father didn't let them sleep together either." That part was true. Caleb was the only one of his siblings who'd openly been sexually active before his marriage, and their father hadn't approved of his and Kirsten's sexual relationship any more than he would approve of Levi's relationship with Jaime.

"And what happens if and when we get married? Are you going to make us sleep in separate rooms then, too?"

She sighed in exasperation. "I don't know, Levi. This isn't easy for us. It's especially not easy for your father. I'm doing my best to help you here. Is it too much to ask for us to take these things one step at a time?"

It annoyed him, and his first instinct was to dig in his heels and tell her their conditions were unacceptable, then he thought about Jaime. Jaime had been looking forward to Christmas ever since Thanksgiving. He'd be heartbroken if they had to miss it. He thought about how depressing Christmas morning would be, just the two of them and Dolly in his tiny apartment. He didn't even have a Christmas tree. Sure, he could get one, and they could decorate it together. But he could imagine all too clearly the false joy he'd see in Jaime's eyes as they did it, and the way he'd try to pretend it was all right. Levi knew seeing it would break his heart.

Would it really be so bad to grant his parents this one thing, for this visit at least? Because whether he liked it or not, Levi recognized his father was, in his own mind at least, making a huge concession by allowing Jaime to come at all.

And for the first time ever, his mother seemed to be on his side, instead of against him. He knew he had Ruth to thank for that. Maybe Caleb, too. His family was starting to come around. It was happening much more slowly than he would have liked, but he had to admit they'd come further in the past few months than he ever would have expected.

It was only one visit. They could tackle the rest later. He worried what would happen if Jaime's nightmares came back, but for now, it seemed there was nothing to be gained by arguing.

"I guess it's fine," he relented.

She sighed again, this time with obvious relief. "Thank you, honey."

"I still don't like it."

"I knew you wouldn't, but let's take baby step for now, okay?"

"For now," he agreed. "Thanks for letting me know, Mom. We'll see you on Saturday."

"Levi, wait."

"Yes?"

It took her a second to ask her question. "I'm only going to ask this once, Levi, but I want you to think about your answer: are you *sure* this is the right choice?"

There wasn't a doubt in his mind. "I'm positive, Mom," he told her. "I think it was meant to be."

CHAPTER 32

Jaime could tell Levi was talking quietly to whoever was on the phone so Jaime wouldn't overhear, but he didn't mind. In fact, he couldn't imagine anything he *would* mind at that particular moment. There didn't seem to be anything in the world that could mar his perfect mood. He felt good and surprisingly at ease. After an entire day of trying not to think about Levi lest an embarrassing tent form in his pants in front of one of his clients, the quick release all over the kitchen floor had been an enormous relief, even if he did feel a bit silly about it.

Levi finished his phone call, and they ate dinner, then settled on the couch together to watch a movie. Jaime started on the opposite end of the couch out of habit, but Levi moved closer, reaching for him, a question in his eyes.

"Yes," Jaime said, and Levi smiled before pulling him into his arms.

He was happy to relax against Levi, watching the movie. He might even have dozed off, if Levi had let him, but it soon became obvious Levi had other things in mind.

It started with Levi kissing his neck, stroking his thigh, whispering in his ear. Jaime was surprised at how quickly his body reacted. He would have thought after having spent himself only an hour before, he would be slow to rise now, but that didn't seem to be the case. After so many years of denying his sexual urges, it was an incredible relief to be able to let them go.

Levi's hand moved higher, stroking him through his pants, and Jaime arched his hips up without even thinking about it. Levi moaned and squeezed him again. Levi started to push him down on the couch, kissing his neck, stroking his erection, but Jaime felt a hint of panic at being pinned underneath his weight, so instead, he pushed Levi back and turned toward him, straddling his lap so they were face-to-face. He pulled off Levi's shirt, and Levi did the same to him, before pulling him down into a kiss.

Jaime quickly discovered how much he liked the position. Sitting across Levi's lap, he could feel Levi's cock straining against his own groin. Levi's hands gripped his ass as they kissed. Levi's kisses were hesitant at first, and Jaime knew he was trying to be gentle, but Jaime found he didn't want gentle.

Levi was already undoing Jaime's pants, and Jaime leaned back, pushing up onto his knees, giving Levi better access. Levi pulled his fly open and tugged his boxers out of the way, freeing his erection. His long fingers wrapped around Jaime's shaft, and Jaime arched his back, pushing his hips up toward Levi's hand. It brought his cock closer to Levi's face, and Levi moaned.

"Oh God, Jaime, you have to let me."

Levi grabbed him, turning them both at the same time, while pushing Jaime back on the couch. Levi's weight landed on top of him, and Jaime felt a moment of panic before Levi moved down and Jaime realized his intent. Jaime lifted his hips so Levi could slide off his pants, and Levi lay on his stomach on the couch between Jaime's legs. Levi didn't tease him. He didn't work his way there. He grabbed Jaime's ass with both hands, squeezing hard, lifting Jaime's hips a little, and before Jaime knew what was happening, his cock was enveloped in the warmest, wettest heaven he'd ever imagined.

He cried out, wrapping his fingers in Levi's long hair. Levi sucked him in deep, then pulled out long enough to tease Jaime's frenulum with his tongue before swallowing his length again, and if Jaime hadn't come an hour earlier, he thought he probably would have done it right then. Levi's fingers dug into his ass cheeks, kneading and squeezing as he repeated the motion, teasing Jaime's tip before sucking him in deep again and again. It was amazing and a bit overwhelming. Jaime used his hands in Levi's hair to slow him down, to keep him a moment longer at his glans so he could catch his breath, relishing the way it felt when Levi's tongue circled his head. Then he pushed Levi down his length. Levi moaned, and although his hands still held Jaime's ass, his grip loosened. His movements seemed to slow, and Jaime realized what he was doing—he was giving Jaime control.

Jaime thrust again into Levi's mouth and heard him moan in response. He felt the vibrations of it in his cock, and he did it again, harder this time, and Levi let him. Jaime could tell by the sounds Levi made and the way he moved that he liked it. He remembered how good it had felt the night before when he'd sucked Levi, how much he'd loved giving pleasure to Levi. He was surprised and thrilled to realize Levi felt the same way about doing it to him.

He stopped Levi at the end of his cock and held him there, letting his tongue circle around and around. When Levi stopped to tongue his slit, Jaime thrust into Levi's warm mouth, reveling in the sensation as Levi swallowed his length. Something inside of him tore free. Some animal living in his mind and his groin and wearing his body—some animal that wanted this very much—took over. He gripped Levi's head and gave himself over to it. It was better than anything he'd ever dreamed, being able to give in to his desire. There was no shame. There was no fear. There was nothing but pleasure, and Jaime lost himself to it as he drove again and again into Levi's mouth.

Suddenly, Levi released him, quickly pulling away. The air felt surprisingly cool against his wet cock. It shocked him a bit. It brought him back from wherever he'd been. He was worried he'd done something wrong. "I'm sorry—" he started to say, but the heat in Levi's eyes stopped him.

"Good God, Jaime, don't apologize," he said, his voice thick with arousal. He pushed his own pants down, wiggling out of them as he moved up to kiss Jaime. "You're so fucking hot when you let go like that." He kissed him harder, sliding his naked body against Jaime's as he did. Their cocks rubbed together, trapped between their bodies. Levi wrapped one arm around him, kissing his neck as he ground into him. His other hand slid down to grip Jaime's ass. "Do it again," he whispered. "I want you to lose control like that again."

But for Jaime, the eroticism of the moment was quickly being lost to panic. One of his arms was pinned between Levi and the back of the couch. Levi's body was on top of him, holding him down. Levi was heavy, and Jaime felt like he couldn't breathe.

Relax, he told himself. *You can breathe fine.* But even though his lungs were satisfied, his brain was not. He tried to concentrate on Levi's touch. Levi's lips were against his neck and his hands were gentle. *Roll with it*, Jaime told himself. *The panic will pass.* But as Levi kissed him and pushed against him, Jaime found himself hoping it was over soon.

It occurred to him that although he'd climaxed very recently, Levi had not, and judging from the intensity of Levi's thrusts against him, it wouldn't take much. Jaime worked his free hand between them. Levi pulled up enough to give him room, which was good. It took some of his weight off Jaime, making it easier to breathe.

See? Jaime thought. *It's going to be fine.*

Of course, wrapping his hand around Levi's hard cock made something in his mind revolt. The fear had already wormed its way through the pleasure, and now the shame surfaced as well. He didn't want to do this. He didn't want to hear the grunts and feel the warm stickiness on his hand. And yet at the same time, he did. He wanted to give Levi pleasure. He liked the way Levi moaned as he stroked him. He liked the way he arched against him. He wanted to erase those times with his uncle from his mind. He wanted to drown out the voice in his head saying he shouldn't be holding Levi's cock, he shouldn't be stroking him, he shouldn't be doing any of this. He *shouldn't.* But he wanted to.

Or did he?

Maybe his hand stopped. Maybe it didn't. Jaime never knew. All he knew was that suddenly, there was a hand on his. A hand *around* his, strong fingers gripping his fist tight, squeezing his hand as he stroked warm, hard flesh. In a heartbeat all of his defenses were gone. It was his uncle's hand, his uncle's cock, his uncle's weight pushing him down, and he *had* to get away. He had to run!

He didn't even remember breaking free. He had no idea how he'd done it, if he'd pushed Levi or hit him or hurt him. He only knew he could finally breathe. He was in the corner, gasping for air, his back against the smooth, cool wall of Levi's living room, and Levi was talking to him.

"Jaime, I'm sorry. God, I'm *so* sorry. Are you okay? Did I hurt you? Oh God, Jaime, talk to me. What did I do? I'm sorry. I'm so, *so* sorry."

Levi's voice was shaky and pleading, and Jaime had only to look at his face to see how much he meant what he said. Levi had never meant to hurt him. He'd never meant to scare him.

"Oh God." Jaime moaned, putting his head in his hands. The images in his brain roared into life: his uncle in front of him. His uncle's strong, fat hand squeezing his own. *It's our secret game.*

"Jaime?" Levi asked.

"I'm going to be sick," Jaime told him. And he was surprisingly calm as he went down the hallway, closed the bathroom door behind him, and lost all of his dinner.

Once his stomach was empty and his hands had quit shaking, Jaime sat back on the floor to think. It was no surprise they'd triggered this reaction. It was to be expected. It was exactly what Levi had meant when he'd said Jaime hadn't let his mind catch up to his body. They'd been rushing headlong through the wreckage of Jaime's past, and they'd finally tripped and fallen. It wasn't Levi's fault. It wasn't Jaime's either. It was simply a misstep.

There was a knock on the door. "Jaime, are you okay?"

"I'm fine," Jaime said, and he meant it. Somehow, the past had overtaken him for a moment there, but he was in control again now. Eventually he hoped he'd learn to keep it at bay, but until then, it looked like they'd have to deal with his occasional loss of composure. "I'm fine," he said again. "I'll be out in a minute."

"Do you need anything?"

"No." He had everything he needed at Levi's already, including a toothbrush. He washed his face and hands in achingly cold water, brushed his teeth, then decided it wasn't enough, so he stepped into Levi's shower. He let cool water run over him, washing away the dark things wanting to linger in his mind.

Levi would *not* hurt him. Logically, he knew that, but logic was a poor weapon against the panic. Using logic against his fear was like trying to keep a dragon in its cave by brandishing a butter knife. But now the dragon was back in the cave, and all Jaime could do was work to slowly block the door.

He turned off the shower and dried himself off before wrapping the towel around his waist and going to face Levi.

Levi had put his shorts back on. He was on the couch with his elbows on his knees and his head in his hands, undoubtedly beating himself up for what had happened. Jaime brushed his fingers through Levi's long hair, and Levi's head jerked up. He didn't stand, but looked up at Jaime with worried eyes.

"Are you okay?"

"I'm fine. I'm sorry I freaked out."

"Don't be sorry." Levi tugged his hand, and Jaime let himself be pulled onto the couch, straddling Levi's lap. "Tell me what I did."

"It wasn't your fault." Because it wasn't. It was his uncle's fault.

"Honey, this isn't about assigning blame. It's about me learning what I need to be careful of."

Jaime sighed, feeling frustrated. "I don't want to make rules. I don't want things to be off-limit. That's like letting him win." He was glad Levi didn't have to ask who he meant.

"That's your call to make," Levi said. "But I'd still like to know where the thin ice is."

His insistence made sense to some degree. It didn't mean Levi would avoid the ice altogether. It simply meant he'd tread lightly. "Having your weight on top of me scares me." He was embarrassed by the admission and he had to look at some point above Levi's head to say the rest. "I have a hard time with hand jobs. Even on myself. And that part I want to get over. But you really, *really* can't put your hand on top of mine."

"Ahh," Levi said with dawning understanding.

"Is that what set me off?"

"Yes. I'm sorry."

"Stop. I feel like we're both saying those two words way too much."

"I think you're right," Levi said. "What else?"

Now they'd come this far, he figured he may as well say it all. "I'm not sure right now how I feel about anal sex."

"Bottom or top or both?"

"Both." Bottom would remind him of what his uncle had done, but top would mean somehow becoming his uncle. Both frightened him. "I know you'll want to, though—"

"No. I don't want anything that scares you, or hurts you. There are plenty of couples who don't do it at all, and if we're one of those couples, it's fine with me."

That was good to know, but Jaime didn't want to make any decisions just yet. "I'm not ruling it out, but it may not happen for a while."

"I understand."

The best part was, Jaime believed him. He believed Levi wasn't in this for a quick thrill. Levi would abide by whatever rules Jaime needed to give him. And that knowledge by itself was a strong weapon against the dragon.

He leaned closer and kissed Levi. *This* he loved—being on top of Levi, feeling his strong, beautiful body underneath him, tasting him, feeling Levi's hands gripping his ass. Jaime kissed him again, deeper this time, wanting to lose himself again. He wanted to erase the whole terrible incident.

"Do you have a blanket?" he asked. "I brought some massage oils."

The eagerness he saw in Levi's eyes made him laugh. Levi brought a blanket from his hall closet and spread it on the floor. Jaime lost his towel, and Levi stripped out of his shorts before joining him on the blanket.

"How do you want me?" Levi asked in a teasing tone. "Face up or face down?"

"Face up."

He did as he'd done the night before, sitting across Levi's hips, their groins pressed together. He opened the bottle of massage oil he'd brought and drizzled some down Levi's chest and stomach. Levi's skin jumped as the oil hit, and Jaime laughed.

"Sadist," Levi said, and Jaime laughed more.

He took Levi's hand and poured a generous amount into his palm, then poured more into his own hand, before tossing the bottle aside.

"You're going to need another shower after this," Levi said.

"So will you." Jaime spread the oil over Levi's arms, chest and stomach. He leaned down to kiss Levi, savoring the way their chests slid together, the way their cocks felt trapped between their oiled bodies, the way it felt when

Levi's oily hands gripped his ass, the way it felt to ravage Levi's mouth with his tongue.

It was easy to lose himself this time. There was so much pleasure to be had, so many places to touch and taste. When he started to move down, Levi stopped him. Jaime was confused at first, but Levi nudged him off, and while Jaime lay on his side, Levi turned so their heads were at opposite ends. Jaime groaned with pleasure at the thought of what was to come. He'd never even thought of 69, but now he realized how unbelievably perfect it would be.

He knew from the night before how much he loved sucking Levi, but the pleasure of having Levi suck him at the same time was overwhelming. He felt as if their bodies were a circuit, and an electric charge circled through them, Levi's mouth to Jaime's cock, Jaime's mouth to Levi's cock. Around and around it went as they moved together, moaning and panting. Jaime's nose was deep between Levi's legs, and he couldn't believe how much he loved it. He loved the way Levi smelled. It fed the electricity racing through them both, faster and stronger with each passing moment until the circuit could no longer support the charge.

His orgasm tore out of him, and Levi sucked harder, pulling it free. Levi's hands gripped his ass as Jaime pushed himself in deeper. He felt Levi tense. He knew Levi was going to come half a second before the first shot filled his mouth. It was shocking—salty and slick—and as Levi pumped again, it became more than he could swallow, but he didn't pull away. He took what he could, knowing the rest was running down his cheek onto his neck, but he didn't care. He only knew he liked sucking Levi as much as he liked having it done to him. Maybe more.

When they were both spent, still except for the gentle shudders that followed, Levi let him go, and they collapsed side by side on the blanket, breathing hard. Jaime wiped his mouth as well as he could, but he could still feel Levi's cum on his cheek and neck. Levi suddenly loomed over him, smiling down at him.

"Goddamn, you're hot," he said.

Jaime started to laugh, but Levi cut him off with a kiss. For a fraction of a second, Levi's weight was on him, but then Levi grabbed him and rolled, so Jaime was on top, although Levi never stopped kissing him.

Jaime pulled away enough to look down at him. He knew he was grinning like an idiot and was glad to see Levi couldn't seem to stop smiling either.

"I like that," Jaime said.

Levi laughed. "I really, *really* like that you like it."

Jaime kissed him again, and when he pulled back, Levi's smile was different. It was somehow softer and incredibly sweet. He put his hand on the back of Jaime's neck and pulled him down for another kiss, this one gentle and slow. He held Jaime there and whispered against his lips, as if the words were too big to say out loud, "I love you, Jaime. God, I love you so much."

Jaime had heard Levi say the words before, but this time he felt them to the very depth of his soul. They fell into a peaceful place inside of him, where he'd known it all along.

He kissed Levi again and whispered back, "I love you, too."

CHAPTER 33

They packed the car the night before they left for Georgetown so they could leave early in the morning. Jaime didn't even bat an eye when Levi told him they'd be sleeping in separate rooms.

"Aren't you worried about the nightmares?" Levi asked him.

Jaime smiled at him. "Not so much anymore." He leaned in close and kissed Levi. "I'll miss this, though."

"You and me, both."

Ruth practically tackled them when they walked in the door. "I'm so happy for you," she said into Levi's ear as she hugged him. Before he could answer, she released him. She grabbed Jaime and hugged him before Levi could intervene. Jaime looked startled by her affection, but otherwise, he didn't seem to mind. She whispered something in his ear as he hugged her back. Jaime blinked in surprise, his eyes glancing Levi's way.

"What did she say?" Levi asked him, once Ruth had moved on.

"She said I was the best thing that ever happened to you."

Jaime's blue eyes were shy, begging the question, and Levi wished right then he could kiss him. He smiled instead and vowed to himself to make up for it later. "She was right."

Levi's mother and Jacob were a bit standoffish with Jaime at first, but it didn't take them long to warm back up to him. His father, however, was another matter. He managed not to speak to Jaime at all, and he pulled Levi aside the first chance he had. "I don't approve of this, son. You may think you love him—"

"I *do* love him."

"But this behavior is still a sin. And if it were up to me, you wouldn't be here together in my house."

Levi fought back the anger welling up inside of him. This was why he'd talked to his mother about it first—to avert awkward moments like this one. This was supposed to be a happy time. He hated his father for making it so uncomfortable. "Do you want us to leave?"

Abraham sighed. "Your mother would have my hide. And your sister would never forgive me."

"I'm not sure what you want me to say. Do you want me to apologize? Because I won't."

"I didn't expect you to." He glanced over at Jaime with barely-disguised hostility. "I do, however, expect the two of you to behave appropriately while you're in my house." He looked directly into Levi's eyes as he said it. "You know what I'm talking about."

"I promise," Levi said, in order to end the awkward moment.

He wasn't sure if he meant it or not.

The house wasn't nearly as crowded with only Jacob and Ruth's portions of the family there. There were, after all, six fewer adults and thirteen fewer children. Although Levi and Jaime were back in their usual rooms with their usual twin beds, there were no kids sleeping on their floors this time.

Christmas Eve day passed playing board games and watching holiday movies, and since they felt like their house was only half-full, his mother invited two missionaries for dinner. One was nineteen and one was twenty. As usual, one was shy and other never shut up.

"Why are they here?" Jaime asked quietly.

"They don't get to go home until their mission's over, so people from the church invite them for holiday meals."

"How long is their mission?"

"Usually about two years."

"They don't go home at all for two years?"

"Nope. They only even get to *call* home twice a year." How many of the missionaries followed the rule, he didn't know, but he knew it was the guideline. He wondered, as he studied the boys, if emails were allowed. The talkative one seemed fine, but he felt sure the younger one was terribly homesick. "They'll get to talk to their families tomorrow, for Christmas."

Jaime suddenly looked a little bit ill. "I don't think I'll ever be quite so rude to them again."

They watched another movie after dinner, then it was time to get the kids all into bed, promises of Santa herding them on their way. "Aren't they going to midnight mass?" Jaime asked in confusion.

"No midnight mass in my church," Levi told him. "Church on Sundays as usual. But nothing special for Christmas."

"That seems odd."

Levi shrugged. "Can't tell you why, but trust me, you don't want to sit through a Mormon service even if it *is* Christmas. Our hymns are all dirges. They'd put you right to sleep."

Christmas Day was much the same. There were presents, of course, and stockings full of candy, and an early ham dinner. And then there were more movies, and the adults took turns falling asleep on the couch while pretending to monitor the kids.

Despite having to constantly stop himself from touching Jaime, Levi had fun. But more importantly, Jaime seemed to be in heaven. He never stopped smiling. Levi thought he might be able to put up with his father's ire for the rest of his life if he had to, if that's what it took to see Jaime so happy.

That night, Levi was roused from a peaceful slumber by Jaime's voice. "Levi!"

Levi instinctively reached across the bed for him, but long before his hand would have encountered Jaime's soft, warm body, it ran instead into a cold hard wall.

Levi opened his eyes. His parents' house. He was in a twin-size bed, and Jaime was most definitely not there with him.

"Levi, wake up!"

Or maybe he was.

Levi turned over to find Jaime sitting on the edge of the bed. The room was dark, so he couldn't see his face, but after keeping their distance from each other for the last two days, Levi didn't care.

"God, I'm glad to see you," he said as he sat up and tried to pull Jaime into his arms. "Tried" being the operative word because Jaime resisted.

"We can't," Jaime said as he tried to head off Levi's wandering hands. "We promised not to do anything in your parents' house."

"We could go in the garage."

Jaime laughed. "We're not doing it in the garage."

"Good," Levi said, still trying to get his hands past Jaime's guard. "We'll be more comfortable here."

"Your parents will freak."

"They don't have to know." Levi kissed Jaime's neck. "Come on, baby." His hand managed to bypass Jaime's. It found Jaime's thigh and traveled north. Jaime was wearing a T-shirt and pajama pants, which he never wore to bed at home, but seemed to think were necessary here. Levi's fingers tugged at his drawstring waist.

"Levi!" Jaime squeaked, trying to squirm away. "What if they hear?"

"Honey, you're never loud. Let me show you." He stroked Jaime's growing erection through his thin pants, and Jaime gave a soft, low sigh. "See? They won't hear a thing. Just relax and let me get you off."

Jaime groaned and seemed to give in, relaxing into Levi's arms, leaning in to his touch.

"Lie back, baby. Let me pull down your pants."

Jaime groaned again, but this time it was a sound of frustration rather than arousal. He pushed Levi away, firm this time rather than playful. "No, Levi. I'll feel guilty."

Levi collapsed back onto the bed with an exasperated sigh. "I hate that you're such a Boy Scout."

"And I have the tent to prove it," Jaime said.

Levi burst out laughing.

"Shh!" Jaime hushed him urgently. "They'll hear."

"It's okay," Levi told him. "We're not doing anything wrong." *Not now, anyway.*

"I don't want to give them reason not to trust us. Your dad gives me enough dirty looks as it is."

"And yet, here you are, sneaking into my room in the middle of the night."

Jaime sighed and took his hand. "Come downstairs with me?"

"Are you having nightmares again?"

"No. I want to talk to you about something."

His words surprised Levi and he tried not to worry as he got up and put on shorts and a T-shirt before following Jaime downstairs to the family room. He sat down on the couch, and Jaime sat across his lap as he liked to do, although he blocked Levi's hands when Levi tried to grab his ass as *he* liked to do. Instead, he took one of Levi's hands and began to massage it in a familiar way. It meant he didn't have to look in Levi's eyes while he talked.

"It occurred to me we have kind of a ridiculous situation at home."

"What do you mean?"

"Well, we have a house big enough for both of us that we're never at because I'm afraid of it, and we have your apartment, where Dolly's technically not allowed, and I have no place to work."

"So you want to find a new place to live?"

In typical Jaime fashion, he didn't answer. Instead, he asked another question. "Why did you move to Miami?"

The question surprised him, but he knew the answer. "To piss off my family."

"Right. And I went there to escape mine. I was looking for a safe place, and…"

"And you ran out of road," Levi finished for him, and Jaime nodded. "I remember."

"What would you say if I told you I still want to find my safe place, but this time with you?"

It still took him a moment to think about what Jaime was saying. "You're asking me to move away with you?"

Jaime finally looked up at Levi, his eyes scared but hopeful. "Would you?"

Levi didn't even have to think about it. Jaime was the only thing in Miami worth staying for. "Where would we go?"

"I don't know," Jaime said, smiling with relief. "I hadn't really thought much beyond asking you."

"Come on." Levi nudged Jaime off him. He took his hand and led him to his father's study. He was happy to find things hadn't changed much over the years. In the third drawer of the file cabinet in the corner was a folder full of maps. He dug out the one he was looking for, then led Jaime to the dining room, where he turned on the light and spread the map out on the table. It was a giant map of the United States. His father'd had it for years. The creases were frayed and worn through in spots. Levi remembered many nights with members of his family, bent over the map as they worked on homework or planned their next vacation.

He pulled Jaime up to the table. "Close your eyes and pick a spot."

Jaime laughed, but he did as he was told. He closed his eyes and circled his hand over the map on the table before coming down with his finger on one spot. He opened his eyes and bent over the table to see where he'd landed. He didn't have his reading glasses, so he had to lean close to read it. "Columbus, Ohio." He glanced up at Levi with obvious distaste. "Too close to Cleveland."

"Do it again."

Jaime closed his eyes and picked again.

"What'd you get this time?" Levi asked.

"Coda, Colorado."

"Never heard of it."

"It's near Rocky Mountain National Park." Jaime sounded skeptical. "It looks really small. We'd probably be the only gay guys in town."

"Forget it. There's no surfing in Colorado anyway."

"Good point. Staying on the coast narrows it down considerably." He leaned over the map again, and Levi almost groaned aloud at the sight of Jaime's pajama-clad ass right in front of him. "How do you feel about California?"

"I don't know." Levi tore his eyes away from Jaime's backside to look down at the map. California was nice, but he found the idea of moving so far from his family upsetting. It was strange. He'd spent so long running from them, and yet he found comfort in having them close. The giant expanse of country between California and South Carolina depressed him. "I don't know," he said again, turning to Jaime, who had straightened up and was looking down at the map again.

Jaime wasn't looking at him, but Levi found himself enthralled with the curve of his neck, his pale cheeks, the soft shell of his ear. He stepped closer to Jaime and began to kiss behind his ear and down the side of his neck.

Jaime studiously ignored him. "Maybe we should stay in Florida. How about Palm Bay or Titusville?"

"Sure." He cupped Jaime's ass in one hand, pushing closer to his side as he kissed his neck.

"We could go to Nova Scotia," Jaime said. "Good surfing there, I hear."

"You're just trying to see if I'm paying attention."

"You're right. How about Tampa? Can you surf in the Gulf?"

"Not very well." And the truth was, Levi really was losing interest in talking. "God, this is killing me, Jaime. Please let me touch you."

"I think you already are."

"You know what I mean."

"Not in your parents' house."

"There's a tool shed out back. Would you feel better there?"

"No!" Jaime laughed.

Levi moaned as he thought about facing four more days without being able to make love to Jaime. "Let's leave a day early. We can go to Charleston—"

"Charleston!"

"Exactly," Levi said, holding Jaime tight. "We'll check into the hotel we stayed in before, and—"

"Levi!" Jaime said, pushing him away. He grabbed him, one hand on each side of his face, and made Levi look in his eyes. "That's the answer: Charleston!"

Levi forced himself to stop thinking about what he could do to Jaime once he managed to get him alone, away from his parents' house, and thought about what Jaime was saying.

He thought about Charleston, where he'd spent so many summer days at the beach with his family and where he'd learned to surf. They'd be close to his family, but not too close. Trips home would take an hour instead of twelve. He'd only had one visit there recently, after Thanksgiving with Jaime, but it was a warm, wonderful memory. He remembered Jaime leaning in for the kiss they were denied, and Jaime sitting across his ass dripping cold lotion onto his back. He remembered how they weren't supposed to have been in Charleston at all that day. It was only by some strange twist of fate they'd been stuck there for the night, and it had felt unlikely and providential and strangely perfect.

Jaime was still looking at him expectantly, waiting for an answer, and Levi smiled. "I think it's a great idea."

"Really?" Jaime asked, looking almost like a child in his excitement, his eyes huge and hopeful.

As if Levi could have said no.

"Really."

Jaime nearly knocked him over backwards as he threw his arms around Levi's neck. "Thank you."

"You're welcome," Levi said, hugging him back, although his motives were decidedly more carnal than Jaime's. He thought he was showing great restraint by only groping Jaime's ass with one hand instead of both. "My question is, can I take you there tomorrow and do naughty things to you? Because being here and not being able to touch you is driving me crazy."

Jaime laughed as he stepped away. "Well, if we're going to move there, we really should go there soon. You'll need to find a job. And we have to look for a house to rent or buy. We should at least *get a feel* for the area." He grinned wickedly at Levi, and it was made even more alluring by the fact Levi had rarely seen Jaime look so blatantly sexual before. "It's not like we'd be going there *only* for sex."

"Let's leave right now," Levi said, reaching for him.

Jaime pushed his hand away. "Stop!" He smiled at Levi, and his laughter mellowed to a warm smile. He stepped close. "Are you sure?"

"Absolutely."

The kiss Jaime gave him was exquisite torture. It was deep, teasingly erotic, promising so much more, and Levi thought maybe Jaime had changed his mind. But Jaime let him go, grinning.

"You're killing me here," Levi said.

"Um-hmm," Jaime said as he turned to walk back up the stairs. "Looks like you're the Boy Scout now."

Levi had the tent to prove it.

CHAPTER 34

Jaime had hoped Levi would be willing to consider his plan, but he'd never in his wildest dreams expected him to agree so readily. He woke the next morning wondering if it had all been a dream. One look at Levi at the breakfast table told him it wasn't, not because he could see anything on Levi's face alluding to their moving, but because he could see the hungriness in Levi's eyes that hinted at their parting kiss of the night before.

Jaime sat down across from him because he knew if he sat next to him, he'd be slapping Levi's hands away while he tried to eat. "Is it really a good idea," Jaime asked him, "or are we insane?"

Levi grinned at him. "I don't think those two options are mutually exclusive."

"So you still want to do it?"

"The sooner the better."

Of course, Ruth and Nancy were listening in, so their half-ass plan, concocted in the middle of the night around the dining room table, was presented for all to judge. The vote was unanimous. Levi's family, the portion present at least, loved the idea.

"We can look everything up online," Ruth said ten minutes later as she came back into the dining room with three different laptops. She handed one to Levi, one to Jaime, and kept one for herself. Levi's mom produced a Charleston phonebook from a drawer and ignored the good-natured ribbing from her children over hanging on to such a worthless relic. And the four of them went to work.

Levi's mother knew a woman from her church who had a sister whose daughter had married a man who was a Realtor in Charleston. Jaime felt the gears in his head start to jam as he tried to trace the string of connections.

"So, you know this guy how exactly?" he finally asked.

"Through the church," Levi said, laughing. "People sometimes think Mormons only want to work with other Mormons, but that's not really right. It's just, through the church, they always know *somebody* who can help them." He smiled over at his mom. "All the more reason you don't actually need a phonebook. All you really need is the ward directory."

"Except he's not *in* our ward, smart aleck."

They came up with a list of houses to look at, chosen specifically because they had some type of office or extra room for Jaime's massages, and before he knew it, they had an appointment to meet with somebody named Craig the very next day to look at them all.

Next, they looked up nurseries and landscape companies, and Levi was given a list and sent in the other room with the phone to call them all. Nancy and Ruth started on lunch, while Jaime looked into what it would take to get a license in South Carolina. Given his current licensure, experience, and certifications, it wasn't going to be difficult.

Levi came back in an hour later looking shell-shocked. "I have an interview, but I'm supposed to show them my résumé."

"You have an interview already?" Jaime asked stupidly. He couldn't quite believe it would happen so fast.

Levi didn't seem to register the question. "I don't have a résumé."

At which point Jackson was enlisted, and the two of them disappeared into Abraham's study. Eventually, Ruth and Nancy had to make dinner, and they all conceded they'd done enough for one day. Jaime watched them buzzing around the kitchen, making dinner, playfully scolding the kids who were trying to sneak cookies, even though they were eating some themselves, and he marveled at how comfortable he felt. He loved Levi's family. And he was amazed at how supportive they seemed to be of him and Levi.

Just then Abraham walked into the room, pointedly ignoring Jaime.

Not all of the family was supportive yet.

As usual, Jaime was the first one awake the next morning. It was freezing outside, and he opted to be lazy and let Dolly loose in the back yard rather than taking her for her usual walk. She only stayed out long enough to do what needed to be done. She didn't seem to like the cold any better than he did. He was letting her back in when Levi came down the stairs. He was wearing a pair of holey sweats and a T-shirt, and still somehow managed to look amazing. Sleeping apart didn't bother Jaime much, but he definitely missed the activities that went with it.

"Still no nightmares?" Levi asked him.

"No."

"Good thing. It's a bit too cold to sleep outside."

"I'm not worried about it. Things were different then." Levi looked confused by the answer, and Jaime thought about how to explain it. "I think last time, it had more to do with…" He faltered, and felt his face heating up. He couldn't help smiling. "Certain urges being suppressed."

Levi's face broke into a suggestive grin and he leaned against Jaime. He brushed his lips over Jaime's ear, and Jaime shivered. He was paranoid about somebody walking in, but it felt good to be close to Levi again. Levi's arm stole around his waist. "Are you telling me," Levi whispered in his ear, "those urges *aren't* being suppressed now? Because I feel terribly, *terribly* suppressed." Jaime laughed, and Levi leaned closer, kissing his neck. "I can't wait to get you alone and—"

"Good morning, boys!"

Levi jumped, and Jaime quickly pushed him away, feeling his entire face burn. Nancy smiled at them as she shuffled into the kitchen in a pink robe and matching slippers. Levi kept his back to her, pulling his T-shirt down low to cover the tent in his sweats. Jaime was glad his paranoia at being caught hadn't left him in a similar predicament.

"'Morning, Mom," Levi said, without turning her way.

Even without a tent in his pants, Jaime was too embarrassed to look at her. He kept his gaze on the wall over the fridge.

"Levi, honey, Ruth's leaving for her secret Starbucks run in about five minutes, and I bet she'll have her hands full today. Why don't you go with her?"

Levi was surprised, but also looked relieved to be handed an excuse to leave the room. "You bet. I'll go get dressed."

"Levi?" Nancy called before he reached the door. "Bring me back one of those caramel apple things, please. With whipped cream."

Levi looked even more surprised, but he turned and headed up the stairs to change. Nancy opened the dishwasher and pulled out the top rack.

"Have you tried the caramel cider?" she asked Jaime.

"No," Jaime managed to mumble, although he still couldn't meet her eyes.

"It doesn't have any coffee in it. You should have Levi get you one, too. You'll think you've died and gone to heaven."

He risked looking up at her. She was taking clean glasses out of the dishwasher and putting them away. She glanced at him and smiled.

"I can tell you're an only child. You blush at the drop of a hat." Which, of course, caused him to blush again, as if to prove her point. "I think having siblings inures you to embarrassment, to some extent at least."

"I'm sorry," Jaime said. "We promised to be discreet—"

"And you have been. You were alone. None of the kids are up yet. I can't say I was quite *ready* to see it." She shrugged, waving her hand at him dismissively. "But you didn't do anything wrong." She smiled at him. "Besides, if I was going to scold anybody it'd be Levi. It looked like he was guiltier than you."

If he blushed any more he was afraid he'd pass out. He hoped she'd change the subject, but Nancy had apparently decided she may as well go full speed ahead with her plan to embarrass him to death because the next thing she said was, "He loves you very much, doesn't he?" She stopped putting dishes away to wait for his answer.

What in the world was he supposed to say? He settled for, "I think maybe that's true."

"In the past, we'd try to talk to him about his life—about the choices he was making—and all he'd ever say was we should let him live his life the way he wanted. But he never looked happy." Her voice was strained and her eyes filled with tears. "He never *seemed* happy. But now, I don't know anymore." She stopped and wiped her eyes on her sleeve, sniffling. "When he looks at you, he lights up. It's the same look he'd get as a kid when we'd take him to the beach. Like he's been given his greatest wish."

Jaime wasn't sure what to say and he was relieved when Levi came back in, dressed in jeans and a sweatshirt. Nancy turned away quickly and continued putting dishes into the cabinet.

Levi took one look at Jaime and stopped. "Is everything okay?" he asked, glancing toward his mother, who was still sniffling.

Jaime was confused until he realized how it might look from Levi's point of view: first, his mother had caught them in an embrace in the kitchen, and now she was in tears and his lover was red-faced with embarrassment. He feared they'd been arguing. Jaime smiled at him. "Everything's fine."

Nancy smiled over at them. "I was just telling Jaime he shouldn't blush so easily."

Levi shook his head. "Don't you listen to her," he said to Jaime. And Jaime blushed again as, right there in front of Nancy, Levi kissed his cheek and whispered in his ear, "You're perfect exactly as you are."

The next few days were a blur, but without fail, every piece seemed to fall into place. They found a house in Charleston. They'd be renting for now, because it seemed easier than buying, especially since Jaime still had to sell his house in Miami. Levi was hired at the nursery in Charleston. They didn't get much business over the holidays and, of course, Levi still had to move, so they agreed he'd start on the first Monday after the New Year. He'd train for three days a week the first two weeks, after which he'd be a full-time employee.

Jaime was amazed at how easily things were coming together. Levi, on the other hand, seemed to take it all in stride once the "no résumé" hurdle was cleared. "I think it was meant to be," he told Jaime more than once. "It's proof this is the right choice."

"There's one more thing I want to ask you," Jaime said to him, the night before they were to head back home. They were downstairs in the Binder house, alone in the den except for Dolly, asleep on Levi's other side. The rest of the family was already in bed. Although he still worried it would get them in trouble if they were caught, Jaime had found enough courage to cuddle up to Levi as they sat watching TV.

"Yes, I still want to move," Levi said.

"That's not it."

"Yes, I still want to rip your clothes off and get you off right here in my parents' house, even though my entire family might hear."

"That's not it either," Jaime laughed. Of course, now Levi was trying to do exactly that, and Jaime had to push his wandering hands away. "Stop," he scolded, laughing. He was glad Levi was joking, though, because he was nervous about what he wanted to ask and the laughter helped relax him. He pulled away from Levi enough to take one of Levi's hands. He began to massage it almost out of habit as he considered what he wanted to say.

"It must be serious," Levi said. "You're breaking out the heavy artillery."

Jaime smiled. "You can say no. I know it's fast, so I won't mind if you think it's a bad idea."

"I'm trying to think of something you might want that I would say no to, and I'm not coming up with much. Unless it involves stretching this Boy Scout celibacy thing another damn day. I definitely vote no on celibacy."

"I'll basically be starting over in South Carolina. Applying for a new massage license, getting a new driver's license. Everything."

"Right."

He took a deep breath and made himself say it. "I was thinking, if I'm ever going to change my name, now would be the time to do it." He still couldn't look at Levi. He was afraid of what he might see in his eyes. He continued to massage his hand, waiting for an answer. His heart pounded, and his stomach was in knots. "I understand if you want to say no, because it's so fast. But I don't have any connection to Marshall, you know. My mother's last name is Miller. Marshall was my father's name, and I never even knew him."

He was talking faster now out of nervousness, his words running together. "It's something I've thought about before, changing my last name, just to start new, but I never knew what to change it to. But when I'm here, with you and your family, I want to be one of you. I know it sounds silly, but it's something I'd like to do. And I know it's really out of the blue, so it's okay if you want to say no if you think—"

Levi didn't say a word, but he grabbed Jaime's hand and pulled him into his arms, cutting off his breathless stream of words. He kissed the side of Jaime's head, and when he spoke, his voice was hoarser than normal. "I think it's a great idea."

"Really?" Maybe it was a stupid question, but he'd been so afraid to ask. In his heart he'd expected Levi to agree, but it hadn't stopped his imagination from showing him scenes where Levi laughed in his face instead. He was relieved to find out his heart had been right. "Are you sure it's okay?"

"It's perfect." Levi kissed the side of his head again. He was holding him too tight for Jaime to pull away and see his face, but he swore Levi was sniffling a bit. "What's your middle name?"

"Franklin." He'd always hated his middle name. "Maybe I'll keep Marshall and ditch that instead. What do you think of Jaime Marshall Binder?"

Levi laughed. "I think it's perfect," he said. "I love you so much, Jaime Marshall Binder."

A few days later they were back home, and the real chaos began. Levi had to break his lease and move right away, while Jaime stayed behind. He put his house on the market and started packing. He filed the paperwork to legally change his name and applied for a license in South Carolina. He trimmed his clients down to a few select people, all crammed into his schedule on Tuesday, Wednesday, and Thursday. Every Friday, he loaded his car with boxes and drove to Charleston. He'd spend the weekend with Levi, then make the lonely drive back to Miami on Monday.

He missed Levi so much it hurt, but he was relieved to find he could once again sleep in his own bed without facing nightmares every single night. As he'd told Levi in Georgetown, the horrible nightmares he'd faced for a while were the result of the sexual attraction he'd felt, yet tried so hard to deny. Now that they were exploring his sexual desires, the nightmares had become less frequent.

And exploring sexual desires was exactly how they spent a great deal of their weekends together. Jaime could barely get inside their new front door without Levi ripping his clothes off, and while he hated having only two days together, he had to admit they made the most of those two days. And it was unbelievably fun.

Not everything went well. Sometimes they had to stop. Sometimes his shame wiggled its way through his brain and he'd find himself freezing up, becoming depressed and unresponsive. Sometimes panic killed the mood. When it came, it hit fast and hard, and he'd be out of the bed and halfway across the room before he even realized what had happened, much as he had that day in Levi's living room. But no matter what, no matter how many times Jaime ended up saying no or freaking out, Levi took it in stride, always assuring him he understood. The best part was, Jaime believed him. And the fact he believed Levi made him more comfortable about pushing his boundaries.

They soon learned Jaime could not handle *anything* if he was flat on his stomach. The slightest touch when he was in such a vulnerable position would send him over the edge. But they also learned that as long as he was on his back, his side, or on top of Levi, he could usually keep his past at bay.

He liked oral sex. What wasn't to like? He *loved* 69. But what really surprised Jaime was how good it felt the first time Levi's tongue moved down, past his scrotum, past his perineum, to gently tease his entrance. It shocked him at first and he tensed up instinctively, so Levi moved away, directing his tongue back up Jaime's shaft instead. But the moment of contact woke something in Jaime—a curiosity, or a longing maybe. A desire to know for sure. He reached down and pushed Levi's head, directing him back where he'd been. Levi went willingly, his tongue making slow, soft circles around his rim.

Jaime couldn't believe how amazing it felt. It was a subtle pleasure, yet it seemed to make his cock ache for more. He'd always believed any contact with that part of him would revive horrible memories, but it didn't. Not even close. There was no panic. There was no shame. There was nothing even remotely like discomfort or pain. There was only sheer, untainted pleasure. Levi's tongue continued to move on him. His hand moved up Jaime's cock, but he didn't grip him or stroke him. Instead, the ball of his thumb made small, torturous circles over Jaime's frenulum. It was an amazing sensation, Levi's tongue circling his hole and his thumb gently teasing the most sensitive part of his cock. It made him want more, and yet, he had no idea what could be better than what Levi was doing. He let Levi tease him that way all the way to the end, and the result was exquisite.

"I want to do that again," Jaime said, as soon as he was able to breathe.

Levi laughed breathlessly. "You and me both."

Levi seemed to take the invitation as a personal challenge. Over their next few times together, his tongue seemed always to find its way there. Jaime especially loved when Levi suddenly released his cock and attacked him below instead. Feeling his tongue lapping at him, it was easy for Jaime to push down and feel Levi's tongue penetrate him. And that was all it took on that occasion to push him over the edge.

When Levi began to tease him there again the next day, Jaime reached over to the bedside table for the bottle of massage oil that seemed to always be there. But Levi hesitated when Jaime handed it to him.

"Just your finger," Jaime told him, hating the fact he blushed as he said it. "I want to try."

It was clear Levi wanted him to be ready before he attempted it. He teased him for a long time, his tongue licking, swirling, and eventually pushing in. But to Jaime's relief, when Levi slid his finger inside, there wasn't even an echo of the horror Jaime had suffered through all those years ago. This place where Levi's fingers gently entered and lovingly stroked wasn't the same part of him at all. Some other part of him had been beaten and used, violated and torn. But in his mind, that part of him was separate, blocked off from what he felt now. It wasn't the part of him Levi touched. It could not possibly be the part of him feeling such undeniable pleasure.

"More," he said to Levi, and when Levi slid a second finger inside, Jaime arched his back, gasping for air. Levi's warm, wet mouth closed around his cock. His fingers moved in and out, and Jaime grabbed Levi's hair, pushing deep, knowing he was about to come. Suddenly, Levi's fingers touched something inside of him, and the whole world seemed to light up like the sun. The entire universe ceased to exist. It was, without a doubt, the most amazing orgasm of his life, not least of all because of what it meant. He was whole. He was fine. He wasn't damaged after all. Scarred maybe, but nothing more. When it was over, Levi pulled him into his arms. Levi whispered in his ear that he loved him. He told him he was beautiful and strong, and Jaime finally believed it was true.

He hung on to Levi and he cried.

CHAPTER 35

Levi loved his new job. The nursery was owned by two women, Maggie and Serena Gomez. They were from Iowa and proudly announced to Levi during his interview they were married. He was fairly certain his easy acceptance of the fact was half of the reason they'd given him the job.

In some ways, working at the nursery wasn't much different from bartending. It was still helping people, selling them something, taking money. But even when he had dirt all over his hands from repotting, even when his back hurt from digging up saplings, he felt cleaner than he had at The Zone, and he looked forward to spring and summer, when he'd get to spend less of his time in the greenhouse and more of it outside in the sun.

It was mid-February when Jaime and Dolly finally moved in. Jaime's house in Miami was under contract, and he'd be licensed to practice massage in South Carolina early in March. Rather than an enclosed back porch, their new house had a study near the front door, which they'd outfitted as Jaime's massage room.

Levi loved that Jaime's business cards now said Jaime M. Binder, LMT, NMR, BMT. He kept one in his wallet so he could pull it out and look at it on occasion. It made him smile every time. And Dolly now had a fenced-in back yard. Levi was pretty sure she approved of the new arrangement.

Levi was happier than he'd ever been, but there was one thing making him nervous—sex. It was a strange predicament for him. It wasn't something he'd had to worry about in a very long time. At first, he'd been thrilled Jaime was so anxious to try new things. Now he worried he'd pushed Jaime too fast. The night he first introduced Jaime to anal play had changed things, and he wasn't sure it was for the better. He knew Jaime was moving toward intercourse and while Levi found the idea thrilling, it also scared him to death.

He'd offered more than once to bottom, but Jaime didn't seem to have any interest in that. On one hand, Levi was relieved. He'd only bottomed twice in his life, both times shortly after moving to Miami, and neither experience had been pleasant. The idea of trying again had scared him, but the idea of having Jaime bottom scared him even more. He feared if anything could bring his new life crashing down around him, it was that.

Not long after Jaime moved in, it became an issue. They were in bed, making out. Jaime was on his back with Levi on top. It was a position Jaime now seemed to like as long as Levi was careful not to pin his arms or put too much weight on him. There was no thought in Levi's head except for how good Jaime felt, and the sounds he made as they moved together, kissing, touching and tasting, straining against each other in a way that was becoming familiar, but was still new enough to make his heart soar. Then he felt Jaime's hand, slick with massage oil, slide down his length.

The contact made him shudder, and he held Jaime tighter, thrusting into his oiled hand. Jaime released his cock. He lifted his knees, locking his ankles behind Levi's back. "I want to try, Levi," he whispered.

Everything seemed to stop. Levi had to force himself to breathe. He looked down into Jaime's blue eyes, so trusting, and yet so scared.

This was something Levi had wanted from the first weeks they'd known each other. It was something he'd dreamed about months ago as he stroked himself to climax while watching Jaime sleep, but now it could truly happen, Levi was too scared to move. What if he hurt Jaime? What if he went too fast? What if the horrible panic that sometimes overtook Jaime during sex ruined everything? And it wasn't only this one encounter that might be lost. If it was something as inconsequential as one evening, Levi would have tried, but this was so much more. This could truly harm Jaime, not just physically, but mentally as well. It could hurt him in the same way he'd been hurt by his uncle. Levi imagined Jaime never being able to look at him with love or trust in his eyes again. He was afraid Jaime would end up fearing him, and he'd never be able to win him back.

"We don't have any condoms," Levi said, although he knew it was a weak excuse.

"You told me the tests were negative."

"They were, but we should still use one."

Jaime shook his head. "You said it was up to me, and I say we don't need them."

Levi *had* said that, but he hadn't ever dreamed it would become an issue so soon. The truth was, he wasn't nearly as worried about the tests being wrong as he was about the other problems that might arise. The thought of the pain he might cause Jaime paralyzed him.

"I can't," he whispered.

"You can," Jaime said, kissing him.

But Levi's words hadn't been rhetorical. The thought of what might happen had literally made him incapable. His erection was gone, and he could only pull Jaime close and hold him tight. "I don't want to hurt you, Jaime. I love you so much."

"Don't you see? That's why it'll be fine."

Levi could only shake his head. Jaime sighed, and if he was disappointed it was only for a moment. "Another time then." He rolled them over. He moved down on Levi and used his tongue and warm mouth to coax Levi's erection back to life. He turned around, offering himself to Levi as he continued his own attentions, and Levi happily obliged him, sucking him in deep. He felt Jaime's gratified moan vibrating in his own cock.

This was easy. This he could do. But even as he lost himself to the pleasure they shared, one thought remained in the back of Levi's mind: Jaime wouldn't be dissuaded forever.

Nancy's birthday was the last Saturday in March, and the entire family gathered at Levi's parents' house to celebrate. After the half-full house at Christmas, it was strange being together with all of them again. Jaime could sense the ones who hadn't been around at Christmas watching he and Levi, unsure how to act. Abraham was cold to both of them, and Isaac and Rachel especially seemed not to know how to handle it. Dinner was tense, to say the least.

When it was over, Abraham announced he wanted the family to meet in his study. Next to him, Jaime was surprised to hear Jacob groan.

"Don't go," his wife said to him. Nobody else heard, mostly because nobody else was listening.

"I have to," Jacob said.

"Maybe it won't be so bad this time."

"It'll be just like every other time," he said. "It never ends. It's the same old argument. I wish we didn't have to talk about it at all."

Jaime was distracted from his eavesdropping by Ruth. "Come on, Jaime," she said, pulling him out of his chair. "You should come, too."

Jaime didn't argue, but followed the rest of the family down the hall to the study. "Don't get upset when they start harping on our 'lifestyle,'" Levi told him quietly. "It won't do any good. Just bite your tongue and wait for it to be over."

The last thing Jaime wanted to do was draw attention to himself. "No problem."

The family members were all sitting in their seats around the circle.

"Here we go again." Levi sighed. "It never ends."

The words were so much like Jacob's, and Jaime debated if he should tell Levi. And then he realized, he had the answer.

Levi was turning away to take his seat, and Jaime grabbed his hand. "Call the vote," he said quietly to Levi.

"What vote? What do you mean?"

"Tell them you don't want to talk about this anymore. Tell them it's a dead issue, and you want to call the vote."

"Why?" Levi said, shaking his head. "It won't do any good."

"Levi?" Nancy called out. "We're waiting on you."

"Trust me," Jaime whispered. He let Levi go and took his seat near the door with Jackson.

The Binder confab started as it always did, with an opening prayer, asking God to guide them, and then Abraham clapped his hands and said, "Okay, people, any new business?"

Isaac spoke first. "You all know the prognosis for Kristine's mother is not good. The doctors say another three or four months. I'd like to ask you all to keep her in your prayers."

"We will, honey," Nancy said, and the rest of the family nodded.

"Anything else?" Abraham asked.

Everybody looked uncomfortably around the circle, but nobody spoke.

"Any old business?"

Nobody answered, although they all glanced nervously at Levi. Abraham was opening his mouth to speak, but Levi beat him to it.

"We all know what the old business is," he said drily. "It's me."

"Levi, it's a testament of our love that we continue to want what's right for you."

"I don't question your love for me," Levi said. "And I hope none of you question my love for you. But I'm tired of having this discussion over and over again. I know your side, and you know mine. And nothing is ever going to be resolved."

Ruth looked surprised, and pleased. Everybody else in the circle shifted nervously in their seats.

"I think it's time we accept there will never be a resolution to this issue and debating it every time we're together only causes heartache. I propose we put this issue to rest and never discuss it again."

"Levi—" Abraham started to say, but Levi spoke over him.

"I call the vote."

There was silence in the circle. Jaime's heart pounded so hard, he wondered that nobody could hear it. He hoped he was right to have suggested this course of action. Next to him, Jackson scrunched down in his seat and hid his smile behind his hand.

Ruth broke the silence. "In the past, I think we all had serious misgivings about the way Levi lived—and I think our concerns were warranted—but everything's changed now." She looked over at Jaime, and Jaime squirmed under her scrutiny. "Levi's quit working at the club. More importantly, he's forsaken the perks of working at that particular club." Levi blushed, but didn't look away. "He moved away from Miami. I think it's clear he's completely committed to Jaime, and I think Jaime's the best thing that's ever happened to him. I vote with Levi."

She sat back in her seat and looked past Levi, who was beside her, to the next person in the circle, Rachel.

Rachel didn't sound as sure of herself as Ruth had, but she didn't hesitate. "With regards to homosexuality, I think church doctrine is quite clear, but Ruth is right. Everything's changed now. It's still a sin, but I believe denying Levi and

Jaime the comfort and love of their family is a far worse sin." Jaime was touched and a bit amazed she had included him in her statement. "I vote with Levi."

She turned to Caleb, who was next in the circle. Caleb sat up straight, clearing his throat. "I disagree with the church on this issue. It's true in the past, I felt Levi's lifestyle was unhealthy and self-destructive. Now, though, I think he's on the right track. He obviously loves Jaime very much, and I don't believe love is ever a sin." He looked around the circle with a challenge in his eyes. "I'd also like to say my wife and I live outside the laws of the church as much as Levi, and I thank God every day you all have never passed judgment on us for it the way you have with Levi. I think it's time we afforded everybody in the family the same courtesy. I vote with Levi."

He turned to his father, sitting next to him. Abraham looked a bit shell-shocked. "I have to disagree with you all. Church doctrine is clear on this issue. I don't stand by that doctrine out of some blind devotion to the church elders. I stand by it because I love Levi, as I love all of my children, and I want him to live righteously. I want him to be able to meet his Heavenly Father someday and not have to hang his head in shame. My vote is no."

He turned to Isaac, who didn't hesitate to speak. "I agree with Dad. The fact Levi is apparently in a monogamous relationship now changes nothing. The fact they may love each other changes nothing. Choosing to continue homosexual behavior is still a sin. I vote no."

He turned to Jacob, who looked scared to death. His eyes darted around the circle. He looked over at Ruth, Rachel and Caleb, apparently realizing his vote could decide the issue if he took their side, which was what Jaime was counting on.

Jacob's voice, when he spoke, was shaky. "I have to agree with Isaac," he said. "The nature of Levi's relationship with Jaime doesn't make his lifestyle any less of a sin." He stopped, and Jaime felt his heart sink. "However, I have to agree with Levi, too. I'm sick and tired of talking about this every time we're together. Church doctrine isn't going to change any time soon, but I'm pretty sure Levi's feelings on the matter aren't going to change either. Especially now."

He stopped, staring at his feet, until Nancy said, "What is your vote?"

Jacob sighed. "I pass," he said, and put his head in his hands.

Everybody else in the circle now turned to Nancy. If she sided with Levi, it would be over, but if she voted against him, the vote would be tied. Jaime wasn't sure what would happen in the case of a tie.

"For years, we prayed for God to change our son. We prayed Levi would renounce his lifestyle and find his way back to the church and back home. And all those years we prayed, he drifted further and further away. After Ruth's prayer in November, I started thinking maybe she was right and I changed my prayer. Since then, I've prayed for two things with regard to Levi: I prayed he would find peace, and I prayed he would come home. And only *then* did our Heavenly Father see fit to answer me."

"Nancy!" Abraham said. "You cannot—"

"Dad," Ruth interrupted, "you can't argue during the vote!"

It took obvious effort on Abraham's part to abide by the rule. He crossed his arms and sat back in his chair, glaring at his wife.

Nancy took a deep, shaking breath, and met her husband's eyes. "I know God's law according to President Monson and his apostles. I know what the church says. But I know what's in my heart, too. Levi is my son, and I don't want to drive him away anymore. I love him. And he loves Jaime. Right or wrong, I don't think it's something I want to try to change. I think the best thing we can do, as a family, is to love them both, and let the rest be in God's hands. I vote with Levi."

Abraham bent over and put his head in his hands. "I cannot condone this," he said. His hands muffled his voice, but his words were still understandable. "I cannot abide by this vote."

"Yes, you can, Abe," Nancy said, her voice gentle, but firm. "This is how our family has always done things. You don't get to change the rules now just because things aren't going your way."

"Dad," Levi said in an obvious attempt to lighten the mood, "you certainly can't object to Jaime. He's a better Mormon than half the people in this room."

His joke caused a few of them to laugh, but Abraham wasn't one of them. He shook his head. "Levi, you know my feelings on the matter. I cannot in good faith condone this."

"I'm not asking you to condone my lifestyle or to change your mind about whether or not it's a sin. I don't expect you ever to approve. But debating this issue every time we see each other doesn't help."

"But to turn a blind eye to this sin, here in my own house? Levi, how can I?"

"The same way you pretend nobody in this room had coffee this morning. The same way you pretend Caleb and his wife don't drink. The same way you pretend Jackson's actually Mormon at all." Ruth ducked her head to hide her grin, and Jackson burst out laughing, although he quickly stifled it when everybody turned his way.

"Dad," Levi went on, "I know you hate this because it means we won't be together as a family in heaven. I'm sorry about that. But I want us to be a family here, in this life at least." He looked around at his siblings. "Isn't that better than nothing?"

"Yes," Ruth and Rachel said together. Caleb nodded as well.

"Abraham," Nancy said quietly, "God has brought my son back to me. Don't you dare try to take him away again."

"No," Abraham said, standing up. "This isn't right!"

"This isn't about right and wrong," Nancy said, her voice like ice as she stood to face her husband. "This is our family. The decision has been made."

"I won't accept it!"

"Yes, you will!"

"No," he said with finality, "I won't." He stalked out of the room, not quite slamming the door behind him. The rest of the family shuffled nervously in their chairs, looking around the room, but not meeting each other's eyes.

"Mom," Levi said, "I'm sorry—"

"Don't apologize," his mother said, leaving no room for argument. She took her seat again and smoothed her hair back, looking around the circle at her children. "The vote stands."

"What about Dad?" Isaac asked.

"That's not for you to worry about," Nancy said. She looked directly at him, and Jacob sitting next to him. "Will the two of you be able to abide by this vote?"

Jacob nodded, but Isaac looked uncomfortable. "Dad will never accept it."

"I'm not asking about your father. I'm asking about *you*. We've voted here today, and I'm asking if you can accept our decision?"

Isaac glanced around the circle at his siblings, then back at Jackson and Jaime. His cheeks flushed red, and he sighed. "Yes," he said to his mother. "I'll abide by the family's decision." He looked over at Levi. "I'll continue to pray you'll change your mind."

"Knock yourself out," Levi said with a forced smile. "Just don't expect me to pray with you."

They lapsed into silence, each of them apparently lost in their own thoughts. Levi looked back at Jaime, smiling, but with heartache in his eyes. Jaime wished he could go to him, but he stayed in his seat.

"Okay," Nancy said at last. "Let's bow our heads, and I'll say the closing prayer."

Everybody crossed their arms and ducked their heads, including Jackson. Jaime crossed his arms, but kept his eyes on the circle of Levi and his family.

"Heavenly Father, we gather before thee today with happy hearts, but with troubled souls. We are lost, as never before. Heavenly Father, when last we gathered together as a family in thy presence, we asked thee to guide my son Levi. We asked thee to help him find that which he sought. We asked thee to make him whole. This is something we have prayed for many times since. It would seem, Heavenly Father, that in thy divine wisdom, you have granted our prayer, and yet, not in the way any of us expected. We cannot help but question whether or not this is right. We cannot question your wisdom, Heavenly Father, and therefore we must question our own.

"We need your guidance, Heavenly Father. Our family is at a crossroads, and we do not know which way to go because it seems either way we turn, we will commit a grave sin in thy eyes. We have been told this love we see here before us is wrong. For us to embrace it and accept it in our homes must also be wrong. Yet, the other option we are presented with is to renounce our son and our brother. To pass judgment. To fracture our family. To cause pain and suffering to someone we love. And we know from thy teachings, Heavenly Father, that this is also a sin. We do not know which of these sins is greater.

"For ourselves, Heavenly Father, we feel we can no longer keep our family at odds. We do not know if this is thy will or not. We do not know if this choice will please thee. What we do know, Heavenly Father, is this: for the first time, we look at Levi and we see he is happy. We see he is strong. We see his heart is whole and full of love. Is that not according to thy will? He is as thou made him. Is it our place to question thee? Is it our place to pass judgment on that which thou hast seen fit to grant him?

"We do not understand, but we are grateful. We are thankful we can be here together, in the grace of thy love.

We ask thee, Heavenly Father, to open our hearts and our minds to thee. We ask thee to guide us. We ask thee to grant us a tiny piece of thy divine wisdom that we may choose the right path, and do what is right. We ask for thy guidance in this, as in all things.

"We humbly ask these blessings in the name of thy son, Jesus Christ. Amen."

It should have felt like a victory, but Jaime could see how heavily Abraham's disapproval weighed on Levi's heart. The rest of the family went out of the study, gathering in the kitchen, or in the family room to watch TV. Some were spending the night, and some, like Jaime and Levi, were driving back home.

Soon, too, the family room started to empty. Levi stalled, hoping to see his father before they left to make sure everything between them was okay. But he waited in vain.

CHAPTER 36

Levi tried not to be depressed about his father's unwillingness to speak to him. He called his mother several times over the next two weeks, but all she would say was, "He needs time." He told himself to be patient. After all, his family had already come further in the last few months than he'd ever expected. He felt he should be satisfied, but he wasn't. He was no longer ashamed to admit to himself how much he longed for his father's approval.

Two weeks later, Levi returned home from work to find Jaime sitting in the living room. Normally when he came home, Jaime was in the kitchen making dinner, or upstairs doing laundry, or in his massage room organizing the many bottles of scented oil he used. This time, he was simply sitting on the couch, still and silent. Dolly lay next to him, her head in his lap. He was staring at the TV, even though it wasn't on. In his hand was an envelope.

Levi knew right away something was wrong.

"Are you okay?" He got down on his knees in front of Jaime. Jaime's eyes had the haunted look in them Levi had come to associate with anything related to his past.

Jaime handed the envelope to Levi. It was addressed to his old house in Miami, but had been forwarded by the post office. The return address was Donna Miller, in Cleveland, Ohio.

"My uncle is dead," he said. "She wants to know if I'm okay." His voice was flat, completely detached. "She wants to know if I'll come home."

Levi hated that Jaime's family would intrude on them now. He felt a blinding hatred for every member of Jaime's family. He told himself it wasn't fair to be angry at Donna. She was Jaime's mother, after all. She had a right to worry, but he hoped it wouldn't cause Jaime to sink into another period of depression.

He pushed his anger aside. It wouldn't help Jaime now. He took Jaime's right hand and turned it over so he could kiss the horrible scars on the inside of his pale wrist. "Tell me what you want me to do."

"You once used me as a buffer between you and your family. Now I need you to be mine."

"I'll do whatever you need."

"Call her. Tell her I'm here. Tell her I'm okay. Tell her I'm..." For the first time, his voice broke a bit. "Tell her I'm with you. Tell her I'm doing better, but I'm not ready to talk to her quite yet."

"And what do you want me to say when she asks if you're coming home?"

"Tell her I already am."

The call went as expected. Jaime's mother went from relief at hearing he was okay, to confusion as to why Levi was calling in Jaime's stead, to anger because Levi wouldn't put Jaime on the phone, and finally ended in tearful resignation. "Will he ever let me see him again?" she asked in the end.

"I don't know," Levi said. "Maybe."

"Does he blame me?"

"I don't know that, either."

Jaime had never told him the details of what had happened to him, and he'd never said anything at all about his mother's part in it. Levi suspected his detachment from his mother was more a matter of cutting himself off from his past than a reflection of any harm she'd specifically done. But anything he told her would have been pure speculation.

"What can I do?" she asked.

And Levi said the first thing that came to his mind. "You can pray."

When the call was over, he found Jaime right where he'd left him, sitting on the couch in front of a blank TV. But Jaime didn't look haunted anymore. He looked relieved.

"Did it go okay?"

"I think so."

To his relief, Jaime smiled at him. He stood up and came over to put his arms around Levi's neck. "I need you to do something else for me now."

"Name it."

He wasn't sure what he expected, but it certainly wasn't what Jaime did. Jaime let go of him. He went to the coat closet and pulled out the motorcycle helmet. He turned to Levi with a smile. "Will you take me for a ride?"

It was much like their first ride. Jaime started out scared, but slowly relaxed. And as he did, his hands began to wander. He was much bolder now than he'd been before. When they got back home, they didn't make it more than three steps past the front door before Jaime was pulling Levi's clothes off. Jaime kissed him fiercely as Levi used his hand to stroke them both off together, and when they were done, Jaime smiled at him, his blue eyes clear and bright.

"I'm fine," he said in response to Levi's unasked question. "I really am fine."

Sunday afternoon, as he and Jaime were settling down to watch a movie with Dolly cuddled up next to them, their doorbell rang.

It surprised Levi. With the exception of his coworkers and Jaime's clients, they didn't know anybody in Charleston who might stop by unannounced. "Are you expecting somebody?" he asked Jaime.

"Yes, actually." Jaime didn't even look away from the TV. "I stopped by the local leather bar and invited everybody over for tea. I hope you're in the mood for whips and chains."

"Smart ass."

"That's what you get for asking stupid questions."

Of course, he had a point, and Levi laughed. He was halfway to the door when Jaime yelled after him, "If it's Girl Scouts, get Samoas!"

"What about Thin Mints?" Levi called back.

"No," Jaime said, and Levi laughed again. He should have known they wouldn't even be able to agree on something as simple as cookies. "I like Samoas! Get two boxes!"

"Yes, master."

But it wasn't Girl Scouts waiting on the other side. It was his father.

"What are you doing here?" Levi asked, torn between being pleasure at seeing him and apprehension at what his visit might indicate.

Abraham smiled at him, although it was a forced smile, and it ended up looking more like a grimace than anything. "Your mother sent me. She and I have been at odds for the past two weeks. We fought all the way home from church today."

"I'm sorry." It seemed like the thing to say, but it came out sounding more like a question than a statement.

"She locked me out of the house," his father said with some amusement. "She told me to come here and talk to you. She said to work things out, 'Or else.'" His smile became a touch more genuine. "I'm not sure what all 'or else' entails, but I'm pretty sure it involves me sleeping on the porch."

Levi couldn't help but laugh. His mother didn't put her foot down very often, but when she did, it was wise to do what she said. "I guess you better come in then."

Abraham followed him inside. The house they'd found was nice, and his father glanced around with grudging approval as they made their way into the living room. Jaime turned off the TV, and he and Abraham exchanged stilted pleasantries. Then they all stood there, looking awkwardly around the room. Abraham seemed unable to meet Levi or Jaime's eyes.

"Sit down," Levi said at last, indicating one of the empty chairs. "Do you want something to drink? We have Sprite." He wished he could slam a couple of shots of vodka before having this conversation. He wondered what new form this never-ending argument could possibly take this time.

"No, thank you," his father said as he sat down.

Levi and Jaime sat down next to each other on the couch, facing him. Levi could tell his father was trying to decide what to say, and he waited patiently. Finally, his dad sighed. He looked warily into Levi's eyes. Levi was surprised to see his father was close to tears.

"Help me understand, son," he said, his voice ragged. "You've somehow convinced the rest of the family. You've won over your mother. She keeps telling me I'm being a pigheaded fool." He stopped, and Levi waited, unsure what to say. "I need you to explain it to me. Help me come to terms with what's going on between the two of you."

It was the last thing Levi expected. His father wasn't here to argue. He was here to make peace. And yet, it didn't give Levi any sense of hope. "I'm not sure I can, Dad. I don't know what I can say now that hasn't been said before."

His father leaned forward with his elbows on his knees and looked directly into his eyes. "Try."

Levi didn't know what to say right away. He pondered it for what seemed to him like a very long time, and his father waited patiently. Levi thought back on all the years they'd been having this exact same argument. Except, he realized suddenly, it wasn't the same argument any more at all. Everything had changed. He thought about *why* the argument was different now. And he knew what he needed to say.

"I realize the way I was living before really was a sin." He saw his father's surprise, and he rushed on before Abraham could interrupt him. "I don't mean being gay or even because of the sex, but it was a sin because of *why* I was doing it." He'd never thought it through this way before, but he knew it was true. "I lived that way because I wanted to hurt you. I wanted to hurt the whole family, as much as I could."

"Why?" his father asked in surprise.

"Because once upon a time I asked you all to stand by me, and you wouldn't. You turned your backs on me when I needed you most, and it broke my heart, Dad. I wanted to hurt you for it. I wanted to cause you as much pain as you'd caused me."

"Levi, we never wanted you to feel that way. We did what we did out of love—"

"I believe you did, but it doesn't change how alone and betrayed it made me feel."

"I'm sorry," his father said, and he sounded sincere.

"I'm sorry, too. I'll happily apologize for wanting to hurt you, and Mom, and the rest of the family. I'll apologize for *then*, but don't ask me to apologize for the way I'm living now, Dad, because I won't. This is the first time in years I've felt like I'm doing the right thing."

"How can you say this is right? You're living here together in sin. You're not even married."

"Only because the state won't recognize it," Jaime said, speaking for the first time, and Levi looked over at him in surprise. Jaime's cheeks were red, but his gaze on Abraham didn't waver. "If it were legal for us, we'd have done it already." He glanced nervously at Levi for confirmation.

Levi smiled at him. They'd never actually talked about it before, but he was thrilled to hear Jaime's feelings on the matter were the same as his own. "That's true," he said, to

Jaime as much as to his father. He turned back to Abe. "We're not just playing house here, Dad. We're as serious about this relationship as any of your other kids are about their marriages. If the state legalizes it, we'll be the first in line. But until then, do you really expect us to live apart?"

"Is it so much to ask?" Abraham asked. "Is celibacy really out of the question?"

"How would you have responded when you were my age?" Levi asked, smiling. "Even now, Dad. Do you want to be celibate for the rest of your life?"

His dad winced, obviously sympathetic to his point, but unwilling to admit it.

"Besides, you're confusing the issue. You're assuming we're only in this for sex, which isn't the case. We love each other. Why should we have to deny it?"

"Because it's a sin."

"Why is it you can overlook Caleb's sins, or Ruth and Jackson's, but not mine?"

Abraham waved his hand dismissively, as if the question were moot. "They drink beer or use profanity. I have hope they'll repent of those sins someday. But this?" He shook his head. "I fear you'll never repent, Levi." He glanced accusingly at Jaime. "Especially now."

Levi fought back the anger blooming in his chest. It wouldn't help the situation. "You're right," he said as calmly as he could. "As far as I'm concerned, I have nothing *to* repent."

"Your lifestyle is a sin."

"You keep saying that, and I know you believe it, but I have to disagree."

"You know what church doctrine says—"

"Yes, I do, but I think it's wrong."

"What makes you think you know better than the church?"

"Because I think this is God's will. I think he sent me to Jaime for a reason." He saw the disbelief in his father's eyes, and he sighed. "I don't expect you to believe me, but it's the truth. A few months ago, I prayed for the first time in years. I asked God to give me a chance to do the right thing, and He answered my prayer." He glanced at Jaime and saw the confusion in his blue eyes. "That's how I know it's not a sin. Or at least, not a dire one. Because God knew Jaime needed help. And He sent me."

If Jaime looked confused, it was nothing compared to the complete shock on his father's face. "Jaime needed help? With what? How would a sin be the answer?"

Even as his father asked the questions, Levi realized he couldn't answer them. He couldn't tell his dad the truth without telling him Jaime's secrets. He looked again at Jaime, who was watching him, although Levi could read nothing in his clear blue eyes. His father waited expectantly. "I can't explain it any better than that," Levi finished weakly.

And to his surprise, Jaime took a deep breath and said, "I can."

"You don't have to," Levi said to him.

Jaime looked scared to death, but he met Levi's eyes. "I think I do." He turned to Abraham. "Mr. Binder, do you think some sins are worse than others?"

"Of course."

"And homosexuality? Where does it fall?"

"It's a very grave sin."

Jaime nodded, as if it was the answer he expected. Then he took a deep breath and dropped his bombshell. "Mr. Binder, when I was eight years old, my uncle raped me."

Abraham's eyes closed, and his face went white. And although Jaime's face was red, and Levi could see his hands shaking, he kept talking. "It happened more than once, I think, although I'm not quite sure how many times. The real events get all mixed up with the nightmares in my mind, so I can't say for sure.

"And I might not have been eight. I might have been nine. I'm not sure about that either. What I *am* sure about is that at least once, and probably more, my uncle held me down, pulled my pants down and raped me."

"Jaime," Abraham said gently, finally opening his eyes, "that's a terrible thing—"

"This is really hard for me," Jaime said. "Please let me say it all."

Abraham looked properly abashed. "I'm sorry," he said, ducking his head. "Go on."

It took another second or two for Jaime to compose himself enough to continue. "I've never really told anybody about this, except for a couple of therapists. Even Levi didn't know this much before now. I don't know if you've ever had anything like that happen to you—"

"I haven't," Abraham conceded.

"Trust me when I say it can really mess up your life. Until I met Levi, I'd had no relationships of any kind. And I don't just mean I was still a virgin." His blush deepened when he said that, but he didn't slow down. "I mean that ever since that day, I've felt like I was alone. I spent my teenage years struggling with depression. I tried to kill myself when I was fifteen. I thought about it several times afterward, too.

"As an adult, I went to counseling, which helped, but it didn't teach me how to trust people. I spent every holiday alone. I spent every weekend alone. I went weeks at a time with almost no sleep because I was afraid to go to bed at night. The only friend I had was Dolly."

At the sound of her name, Dolly's head came up, and she looked hopefully at Jaime, her tail wagging. Jaime smiled at her. "She's a good dog, Mr. Binder, but it was an awfully lonely way to live."

"I'm sure that's true," Abraham said.

"I'm not telling you this so you'll feel sorry for me. I'm telling you because I want you to understand what I mean when I say Levi gave me my life back. More than that, I guess, because that implies I actually had a life at some point before him, which I didn't. But I do now.

"Your church says our behavior is a sin and maybe it's true, but if it is, it's a sin along the lines of drinking beer or coveting your neighbor's wife but never acting on it. But you have to see it *can't* be anything more. Because I know what real sin is. I've seen it, and felt it. I've had to live with it."

He paused, his gaze on Abraham unwavering. "I have to tell you, Mr. Binder, when I hear you imply that what Levi and I share in our bedroom is somehow a dire sin, like what my uncle did to me, it makes me sick. And more than a little bit angry."

Abraham nodded. He ran a hand through his hair, and Levi was surprised to see his hands were shaking. "I think I can understand why," he said quietly.

Jaime looked down at his hands clenched in his lap. The red was finally fading from his cheeks. He took a deep breath, then another. He seemed to have to make a serious effort to pull his hands apart. Levi could see they were shaking. Jaime reached over to him, and Levi took his hand and held it tight.

Jaime looked up again, meeting Abraham's eyes. When he spoke again, he sounded surer of himself. "I know Levi loves me. He cares about me, and he wants what's best for me. He wants to take care of me, which is something I've never had before, Mr. Binder. Not since I was eight years old. How can that be a sin?"

Abraham ducked his head, but said nothing.

"Now, you might say eventually I'd have met a woman who'd have done the same thing for me Levi's done, but I can tell you with absolute certainty it would never have happened. Not in a million years. Whether you can accept that or not is out of my control. But if, by any chance, you can accept I could never have had this relationship with a woman, then you must see that, by your own definition, only a sinner could have helped me the way Levi has. And I don't see how helping someone can be a sin."

Abraham didn't say anything for several minutes. Levi was glad. If he wasn't arguing, it meant he was considering Jaime's words. "So," he said finally, "you're saying I need to accept my son is a sinner, but in sinning, he's also helping?"

"Yes," Jaime said with obvious relief. "That's what I'm trying to say."

Abraham continued to watch him, his eyes thoughtful.

Jaime took a deep breath and went on. "Mr. Binder—"

"Jaime," Abraham said, and Levi was surprised at the gentle humor he heard in his father's voice, "you can't call me that forever."

For a second, Jaime blinked at him in surprise. Then, his face broke into his sweetest Boy Scout smile. "Abraham," Jaime said.

Levi wondered if his father could tell how happy he'd made Jaime by granting him that simple thing. He loved his father for giving Jaime that much.

"Abraham," Jaime went on, "I think you want very much to make this black and white—to make us all out to be sinners or saints. But it's just not that simple. I think what you need to accept is that, just maybe, we're all something else. Maybe we're all something in between."

Abraham smiled, conceding with a reluctant nod. "You have a point there."

Jaime looked down into his lap, looking embarrassed, but also pleased. Levi wished he could kiss him right then and tell him how amazed he was and how proud, but his father was still watching them, so he decided it might be better to wait.

Abraham looked at Levi. "Is that what you meant about God sending you to Jaime?"

"Yes." The more they talked about it, the clearer it became in Levi's mind, and the clearer it became, the more he realized it was true. "Dad, you've spent all this time worrying about me, but this isn't about me at all. It's about Jaime. I want Jaime to be happy, and what makes him happy isn't just me. It's *us*. It's our family. He needs us all. *He's* who's truly important here."

His father smiled at him. "You're saying God knew Jaime needed a family and somehow your sin is the cost we all have to pay in order to do God's work?"

It all made sense in his head and in his heart, even if it sounded ridiculous when his father said it. "Yes. I think the good our family can do for him is more important than the sin I might commit in the process. It's certainly more important than the sin you might commit by accepting him."

His father nodded, looking at the floor again as he pondered what had been said. He wasn't arguing. He wasn't being defensive, and Levi suddenly realized how close they were to resolving the issue once and for all.

"Dad, I don't expect you to change your mind about church doctrine. That's too much to ask. But I hope you can accept that I'm happy. And, more importantly, I think Jaime's happy." He glanced over at Jaime, who smiled at him in confirmation. "I can't apologize for being happy, Dad. I won't. All I'm asking is for you to be happy for us, too. At the very least, be happy for Jaime, because his happiness is more important to me anyway."

His father leaned back in his chair, eyeing Levi appraisingly. Levi knew the look. He'd seen it many times. It meant just maybe his father was changing his mind. He seemed to ponder it for a very long time, and Levi tried not to fidget while he waited.

Finally, Abraham sat forward on his chair, scooting to the edge so he could reach over to Levi. He put his hand on his shoulder. "Your mom's right about one thing. Whatever you were doing before is in the past. And I believe you when you say what you have with Jaime isn't only about sex."

"Does that make a difference?"

"I don't know if it does to God, but I think maybe it does to me. The act itself is a sin, but I see what your mom means when she says your heart is whole again. You're putting Jaime's needs ahead of your own, and the only way a man can do that is out of love." His dad smiled. "Maybe that's not such a sin after all."

Relief flooded through him. He closed the distance between them, moving to his knees in front of his dad's chair and hugging him tight. "Thank you."

His dad hugged him back. "I love you, Levi. We all do. We always have."

"I know," Levi said, almost laughing. "But having you accept me means a lot more."

CHAPTER 37

"I can't believe it," Levi said to Jaime for at least the hundredth time as they climbed into bed that night. "I really can't believe it."

"Did you mean what you said?" Jaime asked as Levi pulled him across the bed and into his arms. "Do you think God put us together?"

"There's not a doubt in my mind."

Jaime smiled, relaxing against him, melting under his touch. Levi kissed him, letting his fingers explore soft, pale flesh. Jaime seemed to open up underneath him, inviting him in, kissing him hungrily, grinding against him as Levi's hands wandered. He loved the way Jaime sighed and whimpered. He loved the way he could still be shy, even when he was being aggressive.

He wasn't surprised when Jaime reached for the massage oil. Jaime's hand slid down Levi's shaft, covering him with oil.

"Don't say no," he said, looking up into Levi's eyes.

Although the thought of truly making love to Jaime was intoxicating, it still worried him a great deal. It felt like such a gamble, and it was a chance he wasn't sure he wanted to take. "I'm scared, Jaime."

"Of me?"

"Of losing you."

Jaime smiled at him, shaking his head. "I've learned over the last few months that being scared isn't a good reason to avoid something."

But Levi wasn't sure it was so simple. "I don't want to hurt you."

"I know." Jaime wrapped his arms around Levi and kissed him, and as he did, he rolled them over so he was on top, straddling Levi's hips. His kiss was insistent and sure. "You hang on," he said to Levi. "I think it's time I learned to drive."

MARIE SEXTON

Marie Sexton lives in Colorado. She's a fan of just about anything that involves muscular young men piling on top of each other. In particular, she loves the Denver Broncos and enjoys going to the games with her husband. Her imaginary friends often tag along. Marie has one daughter, two cats, and one dog, all of whom seem bent on destroying what remains of her sanity. She loves them anyway.

To learn more about Marie, please visit her website at:
https://www.mariesexton.net/

A Note from the Author

Dear reader,

Thank you so much for reading my book. I know your time is valuable, and I'm thrilled you've chosen to spend some of it with my imaginary friends. (I spend a lot of time with them too.)

I'm just a regular, sports-loving mom living in Colorado. I used to work as an administrative assistant at an OB/Gyn office until one day in 2009 when I woke up with a couple of those imaginary men in my head. I've been writing gay romance ever since. I have nearly forty published titles to date. I've written a bit of everything over the years—cozy, small-town romances, BDSM, kinky space pirates, twisted fairytales, and a few odd genre mash-ups in between. My books span the spectrum from sweet and fluffy to raw and dirty. If you like reading books about men who fall in love with other men, please consider checking out a few of my other titles. You can find a list of them on the next page.

You can also find me online at all the usual places—Twitter (where I mostly talk about football and hockey), Facebook, Instagram, and my website, www.MarieSexton.net. If you'd like to receive information on new and upcoming releases, please consider signing up for my (rather sporadic) newsletter. You can do that there.

Lastly, if you enjoyed the book you just read, please consider leaving a review. Or better yet, tell one of your friends about it! Nothing in the world helps independent authors like me more than a kind word from one reader to the next. And for those of you who stayed up past your bedtime because you just had to get to that happy ending before falling asleep, I sure hope it was worth it.

Thanks again,

Marie

Also by Marie Sexton

Coda Series

Promises

A to Z

The Letter Z

Strawberries for Dessert

Paris A to Z

Putting Out Fires

Fear, Hope, and Bread Pudding

Shotgun

The Heretic Doms Club

One Man's Trash

Terms of Service

Spare the Rod

No Good Deed

Tucker Springs

Second Hand

Never a Hero

Contemporary Stories

Trailer Trash

Between Sinners and Saints

Roped In

Family Man

Normal Enough

Making Waves

Flowers for Him

Chapter Five and the Axe-wielding Maniac

Apartment 14 and the Devil Next Door

Sci-Fi, Fantasy, and Genre Mashups

Song of Oestend

Saviours of Oestend

Lost Ship of the Tucker Rebellion

Blind Space

Cinder

Release

Return

Lost Along the Way

Winter Oranges

Damned if you Do

The Well

Other

One More Soldier

Twenty Thousand Leagues Under the Sea

www.ingramcontent.com/pod-product-compliance
Lightning Source LLC
Chambersburg PA
CBHW061323170626
46817CB00001B/293

* 9 7 8 0 9 9 6 1 7 4 1 3 8 *